KU-826-344

Chris Bunch was part of the first troop commitment into Vietnam. Both Ranger and airborne-qualified, he served as a patrol commander and a combat correspondent for *Stars and Stripes*. Later, he edited outlaw motorcycle magazines and wrote for everything from the undergound press to *Look* magazine, *Rolling Stone* and prime-time television. He is now a full-time novelist.

Allan Cole was raised as a CIA brat, travelling the world and visiting pretty much every global hot-spot before he was eighteen. Subsequently he has worked as a chef, a prize-winning newspaperman and a TV screenwriter. He has nineteen novels to his credit and has written more than a hundred episodes for television shows such as *Battlestar Galactica*, *The Rockford Files*, *The A-Team*, *Magnum, P.I.*, *Quincy*, *The Incredible Hulk*, *Walker, Texas Ranger*, and even *The Smurfs*. He currently lives in Boca Raton, Florida, with Kathryn, his strongest supporter, and 'Squeak' – the cat who rules all writer elves.

By Chris Bunch and Allan Cole
STEN
STEN 2: THE WOLF WORLDS
STEN 3: THE COURT OF A THOUSAND SUNS
STEN 4: FLEET OF THE DAMNED

By Chris Bunch
THE SEER KING
THE DEMON KING
THE WARRIOR KING

THE EMPIRE STONE

STEN 4

FLEET OF THE DAMNED

Chris Bunch
and Allan Cole

An *Orbit* Book

First published in Great Britain by Orbit 2000

Copyright © 1982 by Allan Cole and Christopher Bunch

The moral right of the authors has been asserted.

*All characters and events in this publication are fictitious
and any resemblance to real persons, living or dead,
is purely coincidental.*

All rights reserved.
No part of this publication may be reproduced,
stored in a retrieval system, or transmitted, in any
form or by any means, without the prior permission
in writing of the publisher, nor be otherwise
circulated in any form of binding or cover other
than that in which it is published and without
a similar condition including this condition
being imposed on the subsequent purchaser.

A CIP catalogue record for this book
is available from the British Library.

ISBN 1 84149 010 5

Printed in Great Britain by
Mackays of Chatham PLC, Chatham, Kent

Orbit
A Division of
Little, Brown and Company (UK)
Brettenham House
Lancaster Place
London, WC2E 7EN

*To
Owen Lock
Shelly Shapiro
and
Russ Galen*

Indictable Co-Conspirators

Note

The titles of Books 1, 2, 3, and 4 are derived from 17th-century A.D. Earth and were a series of commands used to bring oceanic warships of the British Navy into battle. Book 5's title was a semiformal command to ship's gunners.

—AC and CRB

BOOK ONE

LINE OF BATTLE

CHAPTER ONE

THE TAHN BATTLE cruiser arced past the dying sun. The final course was set, and in a few hours the ship would settle on the gray-white surface of Fundy—the major planetary body in the Erebus System.

Erebus would seem to be the last place that any being would want to go. Its sun was so near extinction that it cast only a feeble pale yellow light to its few heavily cratered satellites. The minerals left on those barren bodies would barely have supported a single miner. Erebus was a place to give one dreams of death.

Lady Atago listened impatiently to the radio chatter between her crew and the main port com center on Fundy. The voices on the other end seemed lazy, uncaring, without discipline—a marked contrast to the crisp string of words coming from her own crew. It grated her Tahn sensibilities.

The situation on Fundy had been neglected too long.

Lady Atago was a tall woman, towering over many of her officers. At casual glance some might think that she was exotically beautiful—long, flowing dark hair, wide black eyes, and sensuous lips. Her body was slender, but there was a hint of lushness to it. At the moment it was particularly well set off in her dress uniform: a dark green cloak, red tunic, and green form-fitting trousers.

At second glance all thoughts of beauty would vanish as a chill crept up the spine. This was Tahn royalty. A nod of her head could determine any one of many fates—all of them unpleasant.

As her ship punched into landing orbit, she glanced over at her captain, who was monitoring the actions of the crew.

"Soon, my lady."

3

"I'll require one squad," she said.

Her head turned away, dismissing the captain. Lady Atago was thinking of those undisciplined fools awaiting her on Fundy.

The big ship settled to the ice about half a kilometer from the port center. The engines cut off, and the ship was instantly enveloped in gray as sleet slanted in from a stiff wind.

Most of the surface of Fundy was ice and black rock. It was an unlikely place for any enterprise, much less the purpose it was being put to by its present occupants.

The Tahn were preparing for war against the Emperor, and the Erebus System was the cornerstone of their plan. In great secrecy, Erebus had been converted into a systemwide warship factory.

So distant and so undesirable was Erebus that there was little likelihood that the Eternal Emperor would discover their full-out effort to arm themselves until it was too late. Thousands of ships were being built, or converted, or refitted.

When Lady Atago's battle cruiser entered the system, she could partially see those efforts. Small, powerful tugs were towing hundreds of kilometer-long strings of the shells that would be turned into fighting ships and then transported to ground for final refitting. Huge factories had been hastily constructed on each of the planets, and the night skies had an eerie glow from the furnaces.

The Tahn had drafted every available laborer down to the barely skilled. The poor quality of their work force was one of the several reasons the Tahn had chosen to concentrate so much of their manufacturing on planets rather than in space. Deep space required highly trained workers, and that was something that the massive arming had stretched to the near impossible. Also, deep-space factories required an enormous investment, and the Tahn could already hear the coins clicking out of their treasury vaults.

They wanted as many ships as possible, as cheaply as possible. Any malfunctions, no matter how life-threatening, would be the problem of the individual crews.

The Tahn were a warrior race with stamped steel spears.

Lady Atago paused at the foot of the ramp, surrounded by a heavily armed squad of her best troops. This was her personal bodyguard, chosen not only for military skills and absolute loyalty but for size as well. Each member of the squad dwarfed even Lady Atago. The troops shuffled in the sudden, intense cold, but Atago just stood there, not even bothering to pull her thermo cloak about her.

She looked in disgust at the distant port center. Why had they landed her so far away? The incompetent fools. Still, it didn't surprise her.

Lady Atago began walking determinedly through the snow; the squad followed her, their harness creaking and their boots crunching through the icy surface. Big gravsleds groaned past, hauling parts and supplies. On some of them, men and women clung to the sides, catching tenuous rides back and forth from their shifts at the factories that ringed the port with smoke and towering flames.

The Lady Atago turned her head neither left nor right to observe the strange scene. She just stalked on until they reached the center.

A sentry barked from a guard booth just outside the main door. She ignored him, brushing past as her squad snapped up their weapons to end any further inquiry. Their boot-heels clicked loudly as they marched down the long hallway leading to the admin center.

As they turned a corner, a squat man came half running toward them, hastily arranging his tunic. Lady Atago stopped when she saw that he was wearing the uniform of an admiral. The man's face was sweating and flushed as he reached them.

"Lady Atago," he blurted. "I'm so sorry. I didn't realize you were arriving so soon, and—"

"Admiral Dien?" she said, stopping him in midgobble.

"Yes, my lady?"

"I will require your office," she said, and she walked on, Dien stumbling after her.

* * *

The Lady Atago sat in silence as she scanned the computer records. Two of her squad stood at the door, weapons ready. The others had placed themselves strategically about the overlush offices of the admiral.

When she had first entered the office she had given it one quick glance. A slight curl of a lip showed what she thought of it: very un-Tahn-like.

As she scrolled through records, Dien muttered on in an endless stream of half explanations.

"There . . . there . . . you can see. The storm. We lost production for a day.

"And that item! We had to blast new landing strips to handle the freighters. The pressure was enormous, my lady. The sky was black with them. And we had insufficient facil—"

He stopped abruptly as she palmed a switch and the computer screen went blank. She stared at it for a long, long time. Finally, she rose to her feet and turned to face the man.

"Admiral Dien," she intoned. "In the name of Lord Fehrle and the Tahn High Council, I relieve you of your command."

A painter or a physicist would have been in awe at the shade of white the man's face became. As she started out of the room, one of her squad members came forward.

"Wait, my lady. Please," Dien implored.

She half turned back, one perfect eyebrow lifting slightly. "Yes?"

"Would you at least allow me . . . Uh, may I keep my sidearm?"

She thought for a moment. "Honor?"

"Yes, my lady. Honor."

There was another long wait. Then, finally, she replied. "No. I think not."

The Lady Atago exited, the door closing quietly behind her.

CHAPTER TWO

STEN AND LISA HAINES squirmed through the mass confusion of the spaceport. As the main port for Prime World, Soward had always suffered from overcrowding. But this was clotting ridiculous—it was arm to tendril to antenna in beings.

The two became increasingly bewildered and unsettled as they pushed their way to the rented gravcar.

"What the hell is going on?" Sten asked, not really expecting a reply.

"I don't know," Lisa said, "but I think I'm already losing my tan, and if we don't get out of here, I'm gonna be sick."

"Give me a break," Sten said. "Homicide detectives don't get sick. It's part of the job requirement."

"Watch me," Lisa said.

Sten grabbed her by the arm and steered the police captain around a staggering hulk of a young soldier.

"I don't think I've seen so many uniforms," he said, "since basic training."

They slid into the gravcar, and Sten checked with local traffic control for clearance. They were told there would be a minimum forty-minute wait. An hour and a half later—after repeated delays blamed on military traffic—they were finally able to lift away.

Things weren't much better as they cut through the city en route to Lisa's place. Fowler was in nearly three-dimensional gridlock. The two hardly spoke at all until they finally cleared the outskirts and headed for the enormous forest where Lisa had her houseboat moored.

7

"Was it always like this?" Lisa asked. "Or did I just get used to it?"

Commander Sten, formerly of the Eternal Emperor's Household Guard, didn't bother answering. The uniforms plus the host of military vehicles and convoys they had spotted made it all pretty obvious.

It almost seemed as if Prime World were bracing for an invasion. That was an impossibility, Sten was sure. But the Emperor sure as clot was mobilizing for a major military undertaking. And, Sten knew, anything that involved shooting was almost certainly going to require that he once again risk his young ass.

"I don't think I even want to know—yet," he said. "Besides, we got a few days leave left. Let's enjoy them."

Lisa snuggled up to him and began softly stroking the inside of his thigh.

By the time they reached Lisa's houseboat, the almost heady peacefulness they'd found on their long leaves from their respective jobs had returned.

The "boat" swung lazily on its mooring lines high above the broad expanse of pristine forest. The forest was one of the many protected wilderness areas the Emperor had set aside on Prime World. However, since the headquarters planet of his enormous empire was overcrowded and rents and land prices were astronomical, people were forced to become fairly creative about finding living space.

Lisa's salary as a cop was hardly overwhelming. So she and a great many other people had taken advantage of a loophole in the Emperor's Wilderness Act. One couldn't build *in* the forest, but the law didn't say anything about *over* the forest.

So her landlord had leased the unsettleable land and then provided large McLean-powered houseboats to anyone would could pay the freight. It was a squeeze, but Lisa made sure she could afford it.

They tied up to the side and walked across the deck to the door. Lisa pressed her thumb against the fingerprint lock, and the door slid open. Before they entered she carefully checked the interior—a cop habit she would never lose. It was one of many things she shared in common with

Sten. After his years of Mantis service, it was impossible for him to enter a room without making sure that things were reasonably as they should be.

A few minutes later, they were sprawled on a couch, the windows opened wide to clear out the musty air.

Sten sipped at his beer, half hoping it would wash away the slight feeling of sadness growing in his belly. He had been in love before, had known his share of women. But he had never been alone with a lady for this long a time, with no other requirement than to enjoy.

Lisa squeezed his hand. "Too bad it's almost over," she said softly.

Sten turned to her.

"Well, it ain't over yet," he said. He pulled her into his arms.

Sten and Lisa had performed admirably, everyone agreed, in thwarting the high-level conspiracy against the Emperor. Things hadn't worked out even close to perfection, of course, but one can't have everything.

Regardless, they had both been promoted and awarded leaves of several months. Thanks to Sten's old Mantis chum, Ida, there was more than enough money to enjoy the leave in style.

So the two had bought tickets to a distant world that consisted mostly of vast ocean and thousands of idyllic islands. They had charted an amphib and had spent week after blissful week hopping from island to island or just mooring out in the gentle seas, soaking up the sun and each other.

During those months they had purposefully avoided all news of or contact with the outside. There were scorched nerves to soothe and futures to be vaguely considered.

Sten wasn't too sure how much he was looking forward to his own immediate future. The Emperor had not only promoted him but had heavily advised that he switch services from the army to the Imperial Navy. Advice from the Commander And Chief Of All He Surveys, Sten knew, was the same thing as an order.

So it was with a mixture of dread and some excitement

that Sten contemplated what would come next. Entering the navy, even as a commander, meant that he would have to start all over again. That meant flight school. Sten wondered if he could get his old job back if he washed out. Clot, he'd even be willing to go back to being a nice, dumb, not-a-care-in-the-world private.

Right. And if you believe that, my boy, there's some prime swamp land available at a dead bargain price on a Tahn prison planet.

Sten came slowly awake. He felt to one side and noted Lisa's absence. She was across the large main room of the houseboat, shuffling through her computer files for mail and phone calls.

"Bill," she muttered. "Bill, bill, bill, letter, bill, police union dues, letter . . . Clot! Knock it off, you guys. I've been on vacation."

"Anything for me?" Sten asked lazily. Since he had no home address—nor had he since he was seventeen—he had left word for everything to be forwarded to Lisa's place.

"Yeah. About fifty bleeping phone calls. All from the same guy."

Sten sat up, a nasty feeling growing slowly from his stomach to his throat.

"Who?"

"A Captain Hanks."

Sten walked over to her and bent over her shoulder, tapping the keys to bring up the file. There they were, all right: call after call from a Captain Hanks. And Lisa hadn't been exaggerating by much—there were nearly fifty of them.

Sten tapped the key that gave him Hanks's recorded message. He was a shrill, whiny man whose voice went from basic urgency to ten-alarm emergency. But the gist of it was that Sten was wanted immediately, if not sooner. As soon as he returned he was to consider any remainder of his leave canceled. He was to report to Imperial Flight Training.

"Drakh," Sten said.

He walked away from the computer and stared out the

open window at the green waving forest, his brain churning. He felt Lisa gentle up behind him, her arms coming softly around his waist.

"I feel like crying," she said. "Funny. I don't think I ever have."

"It's easy," Sten said. "You just squint up your eyes and think about almost anything at all."

Sten did not report immediately as ordered. He and Lisa had a lot of good-byes to say.

CHAPTER THREE

THE ETERNAL EMPEROR had definite ideas about a picnic.

A soft rain of five or ten minutes that ended just before the guests arrived added a sweetness to the air.

Said rain had been ordered and delivered.

He thought that a breeze with just a bit of an invigorating chill in it whetted appetites. As the day progressed, the breeze should become balmy, so the picnickers could loll under the shade trees to escape the warming sun.

Said gentle, shifting winds had also been ordered.

Last of all, the Eternal Emperor thought a barbecue the best form of all picnics, with each dish personally prepared by the host.

The Eternal Emperor scanned the vast picnic grounds of Arundel with growing disappointment as he added a final dash of this and splurt of that to his famous barbecue sauce. Meanwhile, all over the picnic grounds, fifty waldo cooks manning as many outdoor kitchen fires exactly copied his every dash and splurt.

Hundreds of years before, the Emperor's semi-annual barbecue had begun as a nonofficial event. He started it because he loved to cook, and to love to cook is to watch others enjoy what you have lovingly prepared. At first, only close friends were invited: perhaps 200 or so—a number he could easily handle with a few helpers. In fact, the Emperor believed there were many dishes that reached near perfection when prepared in quantities of this size: his barbecue sauce, for instance.

It was a simple event he could comfortably fit on a small shaded area of the fifty-five-kilometer grounds of his palace.

Then he had become aware of growing jealousy among the members of his court. Beings were irked because they felt they were not part of a nonexistent inner circle. His solution was to add to the guest list—which created a spreading circle of jealousy as far out as the most distant systems of his empire. The list grew to vast proportions.

Now, a minimum of 8,000 could be expected. There was no way the Emperor could personally prepare food in those proportions. The clotting thing was getting out of hand. It was in danger of becoming an official event—the likes of an Empire Day.

He had been tempted to end the whole thing. But the barbecue was one of the few social occasions he really enjoyed. The Eternal Emperor did not consider himself a good mixer.

The solution to the cooking was simple: He had a host of portable outdoor kitchens built and the waldo cooks to tend them. Every motion he made, they duplicated, down to the smallest molecule of spice dusted from his hands. The solution to the now-official social nature of the event, however, proved impossible. So the Eternal Emperor decided to take advantage of it.

He invited only the key people in his empire to Prime World, and he used any potential jealousy of the uninvited to his advantage. As he once told Mahoney, "It's a helluva way to flush 'em out of the bush."

The Emperor sniffed his simmering sauce: Mmmm... Perfect. It was a concoction whose beginnings were so foul-looking and smelling that Marr and Senn, his Imperial caterers, refused to attend. They took a holiday in some distant place every time he threw a barbecue.

The original creation was born in a ten-gallon pot. He always made it many days in advance. He said it was to give it time to breathe. Marr and Senn substituted "breed," but the Emperor ignored that. The ten gallons of base sauce was used sort of like soughdough starter—all he had to do was to keep adding as many ingredients as there were beings to eat it.

He dipped a crust of hard bread into the sauce and nibbled. It was getting better. He looked around the picnic area again. All the fires were ready. The meat was stacked in coolers, ready for the spits. The side dishes were bubbling or chilling, and the beer was standing in barrels, ready to be tapped.

Where were the guests? He was beginning to realize that either some of the beings he had invited were terribly late or they had no intention of coming at all. Already, retainers were putting tarps on tables that would obviously not be used.

Clot them! What's a picnic without a few ants? He refused to have his good time spoiled. The sauce, he told himself. Concentrate on the sauce.

The secret to the sauce was the scrap meat. It had taken the Emperor years to convince his butchers what he meant by scrap. He did not want slices off the finest fillet. He needed garbage beef, so close to spoiling that the fat was turning yellow and rancid. The fact that he rubbed it well with garlic, rosemary, and salt and pepper did not lessen the smell. "If you're feeling squeamish," he always told Mahoney, "sniff the garlic on your hands."

A few more gravcars slid in. Guests hurried out, blinking at the smoke rising from the fires. The Emperor noticed that they were gathering in tiny groups and talking quickly in low voices. There were many glances in his direction. The gossip was so thick, he could smell it over the sauce.

The sauce meat was placed in ugly piles on racks that had been stanchioned over smoky fires—at this stage the recipe wanted little heat, but a great deal of smoke from hardwood chips. The Emperor liked hickory when he could get it. He constantly flipped the piles of meat so that the smoke flavor would penetrate. In this case, the chemistry of the near-spoiled scraps aided him: They were drying and porous and sucking at the air.

Then he—and his echoing waldoes—dumped the meat into the pot, filled it with water, and set it simmering with cloves of garlic and the following spices: three or more bay leaves, a cupped palm and a half of oregano, and a cupped palm of savory to counteract the bitterness of the oregano.

Then the sauce had to simmer a minimum of two hours, sometimes three, depending upon the amount of fat in the meat—the more fat, the longer the simmer. The picnic grounds smelled like a planet with an atmosphere composed mostly of sulfur.

The Emperor saw Tanz Sullamora arrive with an enormous retinue that easily took over two or three tables. Sullamora would be a booster. The merchant prince was not a man whose company the Emperor particularly enjoyed. He didn't like the fawning clot, but he needed him. The man's industrial influence was huge, and he had also had close connections with the Tahn, prior to the current difficulties. The Emperor hoped that when the current difficulties were settled, those connections could be reestablished.

The Eternal Emperor had experienced many difficulties in his life—not to mention in his reign—but the Tahn had to be high up there on the lost sleep list.

They were an impossible people from a warrior culture that had been steadily encroaching on his empire. A thousand or two years ago he could have easily solved the problem by launching his fleets in one massive raid. But over time the politics of his commercial empire had made this an impossibility, unless he were provoked—and the provocation would have to be costly. The Eternal Emperor could not strike the first blow.

A few months earlier he'd had the opportunity to begin building a diplomatic solution to his difficulties. But the opportunity had been lost through betrayal and blood.

Who was that young clot who had saved the Emperor's royal ass? Stregg? No, Sten. Yeah. Sten. The Eternal Emperor prided himself on remembering names and faces. He kept them logged by the hundreds of thousands in his mind. Stregg, he remembered, was a vicious drink that Sten had introduced him to. It was a good thing to remember the young man by.

While he was waiting for the meat to simmer to completion, he could drink many shots of Stregg and prepare the next part of the sauce at his leisure.

There were many possibilities, but the Emperor liked using ten or more large onions, garlic cloves—always use too much garlic—chili peppers, green peppers, more oregano and savory, and Worcestershire sauce. He had once tried to explain to Mahoney how Worcestershire was made, but the big Irishman had gagged when told that the process started with well-rotted anchovies.

He sautéed all that in clarified butter. Then he dumped the mixture into another pot and set it to bubbling with a dozen quartered tomatoes, a cup of tomato paste, four green peppers, and a two-fingered pinch of dry mustard.

A healthy glug or three of very dry red wine went into the pot. Then he added the finishing touch. He stirred in the smoky starter sauce that he had prepared in advance, raised the heat, and simmered ten minutes. The sauce was done.

He drank some more Stregg.

Two of his cooks speared an enormous side of beef on a spit and set it rotating over the fire. Meanwhile, a pig's carcass was being quartered and set turning. It was time to start the barbecue.

By now, the Emperor realized that all the guests who were coming were there. A quick glance at the tables showed that a full two-thirds of his invitation list were busy elsewhere.

The Emperor decided to check the list later. He would remember the names.

He got out his brush and started sopping the roasting meat with sauce. The fire flared with the rich drippings. A smoky perfume filled the air all over the picnic grounds as the waldo cooks followed his motions. Usually, this was the time when the Emperor would settle back for a lazy basting: a beer for him, a brush of sauce for the meat.

It was also a time when he pretended great indifference to the rapturous faces of his guests. His mood blackened as he saw the sea of faces tight and worried.

What were the Tahn doing, anyway? Intelligence was zilch. Mercury Corps had never been the same since he had promoted Mahoney.

"Clotting Mahoney," he said aloud. "Where the hell is he when I need him?"

The voice came from just behind him. "Fetching you a beer, Your Highness."

It was Major General Ian Mahoney, commanding general, First Guards Division. He clutched two mugs overflowing with foam.

"What the clot are you doing here? You weren't invited."

"Arranged some leave, sir. Perks of being your own CG. Thought you wouldn't mind."

"Hell, no. If you're gonna sneak up on a man, I always say, do it with beer."

CHAPTER FOUR

MAHONEY WIPED THE last of the sauce off his plate with the thick stub of garlic bread, bit into the bread, and sighed. He took a deep honk of beer and then squeegeed the plate with the rest of the bread. He popped it down and settled back.

The Eternal Emperor, who'd barely touched his own plate, was watching him with great interest.

"Well?" he said.

"Heaven," Mahoney said. He took another sip of beer. "Excuse me. Heaven, sir."

The Emperor took a small bite from his own plate, frowning. "Maybe a bit too much cumin this time."

Mahoney gave a deep belch. He looked at the Emperor inquiringly, and the man passed his nearly full plate over to Mahoney, who shoveled in a mouthful of satisfying proportions.

"No. Not too much cumin," the Emperor said. He leaned his chair back to catch the last warm light of the sun. The Eternal Emperor appeared to be a man much younger than Mahoney. Midthirties, perhaps. Heavily muscled— like an ancient decathlon champion. He let the sun soak in, waiting to hear Mahoney's *real* purpose.

Finally, Mahoney took one more swig of beer, wiped his lips, straightened his tunic, and sat up in near attention in his seat.

"Your Majesty," he said, "I respectfully request permission to deploy the First Guards in the Fringe Worlds."

"Really," the Eternal Emperor said. "The Fringe Worlds? I suppose you're worrying about the Tahn."

Mahoney just looked at his boss. By now, he occasionally knew when he was being toyed with.

"Yes, sir. The Tahn."

The Eternal Emperor could not help sweeping the picnic grounds with his eyes. The few guests who had bothered to show had left early, and the waiter bots were already cleaning up. In half an hour the area would be pristine—all broad lawns and rare azaleas.

The Eternal Emperor pointed to one of the flowering bushes.

"You know how many years I worked on those, Mahoney?"

"No, sir."

"Too many. The things love dry climates. Aussie deserts, that kind of drakh."

"Aussie, Your Majesty?"

"Never mind. Point is, I hate clotting flowers. Can't eat the SOBs. What's the damned use of them? I say."

"Exactly, sir. What's the use of them?"

The Eternal Emperor plucked a flower from a nearby bush and began stripping it, petal by petal.

"What do you think they're up to? The Tahn, I mean."

"With all due respect, Your Majesty, I think they're getting ready to kick our rosy red behinds."

"No drakh. What the clot you think I've been doing?"

The Emperor pulled the handle of a keg and sudsed more beer into his glass. He started to drink, then set the glass down. He thought for a while, making endless concentric rings that cut in on each other again and again.

"The trouble, Mahoney," he finally said, "is that I got a clot more to move than the Tanh. Just to hold what I have, I have to double my fleet. For a counterattack, I need another third. For a full assault, twice more.

"A thousand years ago or so, I swore I'd never come to this. Silliness. Too big. Too much to protect.

"My, God, do you know how long it takes to bid out a simple ship contract nowadays?"

Mahoney, wisely, didn't answer.

"I tried to make up for it," the Emperor continued, "by creating the best intelligence corps that ever . . . well, that was ever.

"And what the hell do I get? I get drakh."

"Yes, sir," Mahoney said.

"Oh, do I hear a scent of admonishment in that, General? Criticism for your promotion?"

"And transfer, sir."

"And transfer," the Emperor said. "Under normal circumstances I would have said that I need a little disapproval in my life. Disapproval, properly put, keeps an Eternal Emperor on his toes.

"That's the theory, anyway. Can't really say. Don't have any other bosses of my type to rely on."

Mahoney had found the proper moment. "Who *can* you rely on, sir?"

There was silence. The Emperor watched the plates being swabbed, the forks being scrubbed, and the tables being put away. Besides the workers, the Emperor and Mahoney were the only two left. Mahoney finally tired of waiting on the Emperor's next move.

"About my request, sir. First Guards, Fringe Worlds?"

"I need to know more," the Emperor said. "I need to know enough to buy a great deal of time."

"Then it's the First Guards, sir?"

The Emperor pushed his glass aside.

"No. Request refused, General."

Mahoney almost bit his tongue through, trying to keep

back his logical response. Silence, again, was the wiser course.

"Find out for me, Mahoney, before you tell me I've missed a bet," the Eternal Emperor said.

Mahoney did not ask how.

The Emperor rose, leaving his nearly full glass.

"I guess the barbecue's over," he said.

"I suppose so, sir."

"Funny. All those no-shows. I imagine most of my alleged allies are thinking deeply about what kind of a deal to make with the Tahn. In case I lose."

The Eternal Emperor was wrong about that. The time for *thinking* was long past.

CHAPTER FIVE

PHASE ONE OF Imperial Flight Training was on the vacation world of Salishan. Sten and his fellow pilots-to-be motlied together at a reception center, broken down into thirty-being companies, and were told to stand by for shipment to the base itself.

The trainees ranged from fresh-out-of-basic men and women, to graduates of one or another of the civilian-run preparatory schools that fed into the navy, to a scattering of already serving officers and enlisted people. Mostly they were military virgins, Sten noted by the absence of decorations, the untailored newly issued semidress uniforms, and the overly stiff bearing that the conditioning process had ground into them.

But Sten could have been blind and known that his classmates were fresh meat.

As they waited for the gravsled, there was excited speculation—because they were on a rec-world, this should be easy duty. They should be able to get passes into paradise on a regular basis. Even the base itself would be palatial.

Sten kept a straight face and looked away.

He caught an amused flash from another trainee on the other side of the throng. That man, too, knew better.

Sten eyed the man. He looked like every commando officer's image of the perfect soldier: tall, rangy, battle-scarred. His uniform was the splotched brown of a Guards unit, and he wore three rows of decorations and a Planetary Assault Badge. He was a hard man who had seen his war. But he sure as hell was not the idea most people had of a pilot. Sten wondered what strings the man had pulled to get into training.

A gravsled grounded, and a dignified-looking chief got out, holding a clipboard.

"All right," the chief said. "If you people will form a line, we'll check you off and take you out to join the rest of the class."

Five minutes later, after the sled had lifted and cleared the beautiful city, the chief's next command was phrased differently. "You candidates knock off the chatter! This isn't a sewing circle!"

A basic rule of the military: Your superior's politeness is directly proportional to the proximity and number of potentially shocked civilians.

Sten, who had been through, he sometimes thought, almost all of the Empire's military schools from basic, Mantis, environmental, medical, weapons, et cetera ad ennui, also wasn't surprised that the landscape below them had become pine barrens.

In Eden, the military will build its base next to the sewage dump.

He was slightly surprised that the base, at least from the air, didn't look that bad. Most of it looked to be a standard naval base, with hangars, repair facilities, and various landing fields and hardstands.

To one side of the base was an array of three-story red brick buildings surrounded by gardens: base headquarters.

His second surprise came as the gravsled grounded in front of those buildings.

Sten, at that moment, remembered another basic law of military schooling and swore at himself. All military courses start by grinding the student into the muck and then reforming that being into the desired mold.

The instructors would illustrate this by instantly zapping some poor standout slob on arrival.

And Sten was a potential standout.

Hastily, he unbuttoned his tunic and unpinned his ribbon bar. The decorations were all real, even though a good percentage of them had been awarded for some highly classified Mantis operations, and the citation itself was a tissue. But there were too many of them for any young commander to deserve.

The ribbon bar was jammed into a pocket just as the canopy of the gravsled banged open and a rage-faced master's mate started howling orders.

"Out, out, out! What are you slime doing just sitting there! I want to see nothing but asses and elbows!"

New blood grabbed duffel bags and dived over the sides of the sled, and the mate kept screaming.

"You! Yes, you! You, too, come to think! Hit that ground! Do push-ups! Do many, many push-ups!"

Oh, Lord, Sten thought as he scrambled out. I'm back in basic training. Even the clottin' words are the same. This master's mate could be, except for sex, the duplicate of . . . what was her name? Yes. Carruthers.

"I want three ranks yesterday, people! Tall donks on my left, midgets over there."

Not for the first time, Sten was grateful that he was slight, but not so small as to qualify for the feather merchant squad.

Eventually the master's mate got tired of screaming and physical training. Sten thought he was doing all right—in the chaos, he had only had to turn out some fifty knee bends. There were too many other and more obvious victims for the mate to pick on.

"Class . . . ten-hup! Right hace! For'd harch."

Sten was grateful that at least all of them had been subjected to the barracks-bashing conditioning. He decided that he would not like to see what happened if one of the trainees went out of step.

They were marched into the central quadrangle, brought to a halt in front of a reviewing stand, and turned to face it.

On cue, a tall, thin man came out of one building and paced briskly to the stand. He looked typecast for what he was: a one-star admiral and the school commandant. No doubt a longtime pilot who'd flown every ship the Empire fielded in every circumstance known. Unfortunately, his voice didn't match the part. It would have been more suited to an operatic tenor.

Sten waited until the commandant introduced himself— Admiral Navarre—and then put most of his mind on other topics.

This was The Speech, given to every student at every military course by every commandant, and said the same things:

Welcome. This will be an intense period of training. You may not like how we do things, but we have learned what works. Those of you who learn to adjust to the system will have no troubles, the others . . . We have strict discipline here, but if any of you feels treated unfairly, my office is always open.

Ratcheta, ratcheta, ratcheta.

Phase One of flight training was Selection. The object of this phase was to determine absolutely that every candidate was *in fact* qualified to fly.

It was already famous throughout the Imperial military as a washout special.

Admiral Navarre informed them that, due to the unfortunate political situation, Phase One would be accelerated. Clotting wonderful, Sten thought.

Each student was told to remove his or her rank tabs. From that moment on, they would be referred to only as "candidate."

Ho, ho. Sten had a fairly good idea of some of the other titles: clot, drakh, bastard, and many, many other terms expressly forbidden under Imperial regulations.

That was about all that was worthy of note.

The main part of Sten's mind was reminding him that he was now a candidate. Not a hot-rod commander, not the ex-head of the Emperor's Gurkha bodyguards, not a Mantis covert specialist.

In fact, not even an officer.

Think recruit, young Sten. Maybe you can make it that way.

Sten was sort of neutral about becoming a pilot. He was here only because of personal and private suggestions from the Emperor himself. The Emperor had told him that the next stage in Sten's career should be a transfer to the navy —accomplished—and flight school.

Wash out of flight school, however, and Sten would probably be ordered into the logistics section of the navy.

He wondered for the hundredth time how hard it would be, if he *did* fail, to get back to the army and Mantis Section.

Somewhere during Sten's ponderings Navarre had finished, walked off, and the mate had the trainees doubling around the buildings, their duffels left stacked in front of the reviewing stand.

Now we meet the killers, Sten thought, or whatever flight school calls their drill sergeants, and they shall illustrate to us how worthless we are and how they're going to destroy us for even breathing hard.

That was, more or less, how the scenario went—with some considerable surprises.

The class was stopped in the middle of a huge square that was ankle-deep sand. The mate dropped them once more into push-up position, then disappeared. Minutes passed. A couple of the candidates collapsed into the sand. They would pay.

For Sten, the front-leaning rest position was no more than an annoyance.

A man ambled toward them, not at all the kind of sadist that Sten was expecting. Drill instructors always looked to be better soldiers than any of their student swine could dream of becoming. This man was heavily overweight and wore a rank-tabless, somewhat soiled flight coverall. One of the pockets was torn. The man walked up and down the line of prone candidates. He *tsk*ed once when another student went flat, wheezing.

"Good day, beings." The man's voice was a husky drawl. "My name is Ferrari. You will call me Mr. Ferrari or sir, or you shall surely perish.

"I am your chief instructor pilot.

"During this period, I shall do my best to convince you that becoming a pilot is the least desirable, most miserable manner a being could spend its existence.

"Like our honorable commandant, my door, too, is always open.

"But only for one purpose.

"For you to resign.

"During the long reaches of the days and nights that will follow, I sincerely want each and every one of you to consider just how easy it would be for this torment to stop.

"One visit to my office, or even a word to any of the other IPs, and you can be on your way to what I am sure would be a far superior assignment.

"By the way. We instructors here in Phase One personally feel that Sheol itself would be more favorable.

"Those of you from different cultures who don't know what Sheol is can ask a fellow student. But I am quite sure our program will also explain.

"Those of you who are still on your hands may stand. Those of you who collapsed should begin crawling. I would like you, while still on your stomachs, to crawl on line to the edge of this exercise yard.

"Crawl twice around it, please.

"This is not an exercise in sadism, by the way. I seem to have dropped a quarter-credit piece sometime today, and would be infinitely grateful if one of you would recover it."

Sten, seeing the weak-armed slither past him, hoped that none of them would get cute, take a coin from his or her own pocket, and give it to Ferrari in hopes that the long crawl would be ended. Ferrari would certainly examine the coin, declare with sorrow that there must be some mistake since the date proved the coin not his, and pull that candidate's toenails.

Ferrari stepped to one side.

Now comes the hands-on thug.

This man also wore a blank flight suit, but one that was tailored and razor-creased. A long scar seamed his face, and the man limped slightly. His voice had the attractive rasp of a wood file on metal.

"My name is Mason.

"I can't use words like Mr. Ferrari does, so I'll keep it short.

"I've looked at all of your files.

"Drakh. All of you.

"There is not one of you qualified to fly a combat car.

"If we screw up, and let any one of you onto a flight deck, you will end up killing someone."

He tapped the scar.

"That's how I got this. They let somebody—somebody just like one of you clowns—into my tacflight.

"Midair collision.

"Eighteen dead.

"My job now is easy. All I have to do is keep one of you from killing anyone but himself.

"Maybe you've heard something like this from another instructor, and think I'm just talking.

"Wrong, clots.

"I personally hate each and every one of you."

He looked up and down the formation. Sten chilled a little. He had, indeed, heard variations on that speech from DIs.

But Sten had the feeling that Mason really *meant* it.

"I've got one peculiarity," Mason added. "I'm going to make sure that every one of you washes out, like I said.

"But every selection course, there's one person that, for some reason, I hate more than most of you trash.

"And I pick him out early.

"And he never makes it."

Again, Mason looked up and down the class.

Sten knew, moments before the snake's head stopped, whom he would be looking at.

Clot, clot, clot, Sten thought, while remaining as petrified as any chicken caught by the glare of the snake.

CHAPTER SIX

BY THE TIME Ferrari and Mason had finished the torment they called "muscle toning," it was late afternoon. The master's mate—and Sten would never learn his name—took over the formation, doubled the trainees back to the barracks they were assigned to, and dismissed them.

The exhausted candidates timidly entered the brick building through double glass doors, knowing that inside would be another werewolf masquerading as an IP.

They also expected that the barracks, no matter how good-looking on the outside, would be polished plas floors, echoing squad bays, and clanging elderly lockers, just like in basic training.

They were very wrong.

Drawn up inside the foyer, which resembled the lobby of an exclusive small hotel, were about fifty middle-aged beings. They looked and were dressed like the retainers Sten had known at the Imperial palace.

One of them stepped forward.

"I would imagine you young people might like a chance to relax in the recreation room before we show you to your quarters. We hope you find the facilities adequate."

He waved them through sliding doors into a large wood-paneled room twenty-five meters on a side. At one end was a large stone fireplace. Along the walls were drink and food dispensers and, between them, computer terminals and game machines. Above them hung abstract paintings.

In the room were games tables and luxurious easy chairs and sofas.

Sten's alertness went to condition red! He saw one candidate gape an expression accentuated by the double rings of white fur around his eyes. The candidate scrubbed a small black hand over his gray-furred chest in excitement.

"Beer! They have a beer machine!" He started forward.

"Maybe you don't want to be doing that."

Sten, also about to say something, saw that the caution came from that scarred infantry sergeant.

"Why not?"

"Oh, maybe because they told us they were gonna be testing us for physical dexterity and like that, and a hangover doesn't speed up your reaction time.

"Or maybe they're watching that machine, and anybody who uses it gets down-carded for lack of moral fiber."

"That doesn't make sense." That came from a very small, very exquisite woman. "Every pilot *I've* ever known swills alk like it was mother's milk."

"No drakh," the sergeant agreed. "But that's *after* they get their wings. And maybe Selection is what makes 'em drink that way."

Maybe the sergeant was right, or maybe he was just paranoiac. But regardless, the beer machine sat unused throughout Selection.

Sten's quarters were also quite interesting. They consisted of two rooms—a combined bedroom/study decorated in soothing colors, and a 'fresher that included not only the usual facilities, but an elaborate Jacuzzi.

Sten had the idea that Ferrari's muscle toning would continue throughout Selection.

Unpacking took only moments—Sten, as a professional, had learned to travel light. The only extraneous gear he had in his duffel was the fiches he'd collected over the years, now micro/microfiched, and his miniholoprocessor that, in off-duty hours, he used to recreate working miniatures of industrial plants.

Sten had gotten the idea that he would have little time to play with the holoprocessor, but decided to hook it up regardless.

The manufacturers were lying, he decided after a few moments. Their universal power connection wasn't that universal, at least not universal enough to include the powerplate hookups that his room had.

Sten went out into the corridor, intending to see if his cross-hall neighbor had a diploid plug that would work, and also to check the terrain.

He tapped at the door, a tentative tap meant to tell whoever was inside that this was not an IP, so he/she didn't have to conceal whatever he/she might have been doing.

A sultry voice came through the annunciator, a voice as soothing as any emergency surgery nurse could have.

Sten told the box what he wanted.

"Orbit a beat, brother, and I'll be with you."

Then the door opened, and Sten dropped into horror.

Sten was not a lot of things:

He certainly wasn't ethnocentric. The factory hellworld he'd been raised in had given him no sense of innate culture.

He was not xenophobic. Mantis training and combat missions on a thousand worlds with a thousand different life forms had kept that from happening.

He also was not what his contemporaries called a shapist. He did not care what a fellow being looked or smelled like.

He thought.

However, when a door is opened and someone is confronted by a two-meter-tall hairy spider, all bets are off.

Sten was—later—a little proud that his only reaction was his jaw elevatoring down past his belt line.

"Oh dear," the spider observed. "I'm most sorry to have surprised you."

Sten really felt like drakh.

The situation called for some sort of apology. But even his century had not yet developed a satisfactory social grace for a terminal embarrassment. Sten was very pleased that the spider understood.

"Can I help you with something?"

"Uh . . . yeah," Sten improvised. "Wanted to see if you knew what time we mess."

"About one hour," the spider said after curling up one leg that, incongruously, had an expensive wrist-timer on it.

"Oh, hell. I'm sorry. My name's Sten."

And he stuck out a hand.

The spider eyed Sten's hand, then his face, then extended a second leg, a pedipalp, laying its slightly clawed tip in Sten's palm.

The leg was warm, and the hair was like silk. Sten felt the horror seep away.

"I am Sh'aarl't. Would you care to come in?"

Sten entered—not only for politeness but because he was curious as to what sort of quarters the Empire provided for arachnids.

There was no bed, but instead, near the high ceiling, a barred rack. The desk took up that unoccupied space, since the desk chair was actually a large round settee.

"What do you think—so far?"

"I think," the lovely voice said, "that I should have my carapace examined for cracks for ever wanting to be a pilot."

"If you figure out why, let me know."

The social lubricant was starting to flow, although Sten still had to repress a shudder as Sh'aarl't waved a leg toward the settee. He sat.

"I involved myself in this madness because my family has a history of spinning the highest webs our world has. If you don't mind a personal question, why are you here?"

Sten knew that if he told Sh'aarl't that the Eternal Emperor himself had punted him into this mess, he'd be ascribed either a total liar or someone with too much clout to be friendly with.

"It seemed like a good idea at the time."

"Perhaps I might ask—what is your real rank?"

"Commander."

Sh'aarl't exuded air from her lungs. Of course she was female—even huge Araneida seem to follow the biological traditions. "Should I stand at attention? I am but a lowly spaceman second."

Sten found himself able to laugh. "Actually, I'd like to see it. How does somebody with eight legs stand at attention?"

Sh'aarl't side-jumped to the center of the room, and Sten tried not to jump vertically. Attention, for a spider, was with the lower leg segments vertical, the upper ones at a perfect forty-five-degree angle toward the body.

"At full attention," Sh'aarl't went on, "I also extend my fangs in a most martial attitude. Would you like to see them?"

"Uh . . . not right now."

Sh'aarl't relaxed and clapped a pedipalp against her carapace. Sten surmised, correctly, that this signified amusement.

"I guess you had no trouble with the push-ups today."

Again the clap.

"How serious do you think these beings are?" Sh'aarl't asked, changing the subject.

"I dunno about Ferrari," Sten said. "But that Mason scares the clot out of me."

"I also. But perhaps if some of us hang on and survive until others are washed out . . . Certainly they *can't* throw everyone away—given what the Tahn are preparing. Am I right?"

Sten realized that she was desperately looking for reassurance, and so modified his answer from "I think these people can do anything they want" to, "Nope. There's got to be a couple of survivors. Speaking of which—why don't we go downstairs. See if this—" Sten almost said spiderweb "—tender trap they've put us in also feeds the fatted lamb."

"Excellent idea, Commander."

"Wrong. Candidate. Or Sten. Or you clot."

Again the clap.

"Then shall we descend for dining, Sten? Arm in arm in arm in arm . . ."

Laughing, the two went out of the room, looking for food.

Later that night, there was a finger tap at Sten's door.

Outside was one of the barracks staffers. If the staff members all looked, to Sten, like palace retainers, this man would be the perfect butler.

After apologies for disturbing Sten, the man introduced himself as Pelham. He would be Sten's valet until Sten completed Phase One.

"Complete or get flunked, you mean."

"Oh, no, sir." Pelham appeared shocked. "I took the liberty, sir, of looking at your file. And I must say . . . perhaps this is speaking out of school . . . my fellow staff members and myself have a pool on which of the candidates is most likely to graduate. I assure you, sir, that I am not being sycophantic when I say that I put my credits down on you with complete confidence."

Sten stepped back from the doorway and allowed the man to enter.

"Sycophantic, huh?" Sten vaguely knew what the word meant. He went back to his desk, sat, and put his feet up, watching Pelham sort through the hanging uniforms.

"Mr. Sten, I notice your decorations aren't on your uniform."

"Yeah. They're in the pocket."

"Oh. I assume you'll want—"

"I will want them put in the bottom of the drawer and ignored, Pelham."

Pelham looked at him most curiously. "As you desire. But these uniforms are desperately in need of a spot of refurbishment."

"Yeah. They've been at the bottom of a duffel bag for a couple of months."

Pelham collected an armload of uniforms and started for the door. "Will there be anything else required? You know that I'm on call twenty-four hours."

"Not right now, Pelham. Wait a moment. I have a question."

"If I may help?"

"If I asked you who Rykor was, what'd be your reaction?"

Pelham was very damned good—the only response to Sten's mention of the walruslike being who happened to be the Empire's most talented psychologist was a rapidly hidden eye flicker.

"None, sir. Would you explain?"

"I'll try it another way. What would you say if I suggested that you, and all the other people in this barracks, all of you who're so helpful and such great servants, were actually part of Selection?"

"Of course we are, sir. We realize that the candidates desperately need study time and relaxation time, and we try to help by taking care of the minor—"

"Not what I meant, Pelham. One more time. What would be your reaction if I said I thought that all of you are trained psychs, and this whole barracks, relaxed and gentle, is a good way to get us off guard and find out what we're really like?"

"You are joking, sir."

"Am I?"

"If you are not, I must say I am very honored. To think that *I* have the talents to be a doctor." Pelham chuckled. "No, sir. I am just what I appear."

"You did answer my question. Thank you, Pelham. Good night."

"Good night, sir."

Dr. W. Grenville Pelham, holder of seven degrees in various areas of psychology, applied psychology, human stress analysis, and military psychology, closed the door and padded down the hall. Some meters away from Sten's room, he allowed himself the luxury of low laughter.

CHAPTER SEVEN

THE FIRST WEEKS of Selection were quite simple—the IPs bashed the trainees' brains out in the morning, at noon, and in the evening. There were also unexpected alerts in the middle of the night, although the callouts were always handled by the staff. The IPs never entered the barracks.

In between the physical and mental harassment, the tests went on. To a large extent, they duplicated the basic exams —reflex testing, intelligence quotient testing, and so forth. The testing standards, however, were far higher than when a being entered the military. Also, the tests were readministered severally and at unexpected times.

Sten was not impressed.

He had the idea that this duplication wouldn't have happened before the Emergency began. There must have been better, if slower, ways to test for the same abilities.

Sten was starting to develop an active hatred for the Tahn.

Sten's belief that the testing was catch-as-catch-can turned from theory into certainty the day he was shuttled into a tiny room that had nothing more in it than a large chair and a livie helmet. His instructions were to seat himself, put the helmet on, and wait for further developments.

Sten had been through this, way back before basic training.

The idea was that, through the livie helmet, he would experience certain events. His reactions would be monitored by psychologists, and from this reexperiencing and reacting, his personality could be profiled.

When Sten had gone through the experience before, the livie tape had been that of some not very bright but very

heroic guardsman who got himself slaughtered trying to kill
a tank. It had made Sten nearly throw up and had, by his
reaction, disqualified him for normal infantry, but made him
an ideal candidate for the essentially lone-wolf Mantis Section.

Before he sat down, he went behind the chair and
checked the tape in the feed. Various codes appeared, then
the title: SHAVALA, GUARDSMAN JAIME, COMBAT/DEATH, AS-
SAULT ON DEMETER.

Possibly there could be some kind of validity for that
choice—for prospective infantry types. But for pilots?

Sten examined the helmet and found the input line. A
little subversion was called for.

He curled his right fingers, and the surgically sheathed
knife in his arm dropped into his hand. The double-edged
dagger was one of Sten's best-kept secrets. He had constructed it himself from an impossibly rare crystal. It had a
skeleton grip, and its blade was only 2.5 mm thick, tapering
to less than fifteen molecules wide. In other words, it could
cut through practically anything. But in this case cutting
wasn't what Sten was interested in.

He used the knife's needle point to rearrange a few tiny
wires inside the sheath of the helmet input line. Then he
replaced the knife and, as ordered, sat down and put the
helmet on.

*Let's see. The tape has just begun. I should express be-
wilderment. Fear. Excitement. Doubt as to my ability.
Shock on landing. Determination to accomplish the mission.*

Sten's Mantis schooling had included indoctrination on
the various ways to fool *any* sort of mental testing machine,
from the completely unreliable polygraph through the most
sophisticated brainchecks of Imperial Intelligence. The key,
of course, was to truly believe that what you were thinking
or saying was the truth.

This training worked. Coupled with a conditioned, near-
eidetic memory, it made Sten mental test–proof.

*Let's see now . . . Shavala should have seen that clotting
tank show up . . . Horror . . . seen his combat teammates
slaughtered . . . Anger . . . seen the tank rumble on . . . More*

determination...doodle around the tank getting various pieces shot off...Pain and still more determination...hell, the clot should be dead by now. Shock and such.

Sten pulled a corner of the helmet away from his ear and heard the tape behind him click to a halt.

More shock. Pride at being part of this Imperial stupidity.

Sten decided that was enough input, took the helmet off, and stood. He set an expression of sickness and firmness on his face and went out of the room, artistically stumbling just beyond the door.

Sten gasped to the hilltop, then checked his compass and watch. He decided he could take four minutes to recover.

The exercise was a modified version of that military favorite, the Long Run or March. But, typical of Selection, it had a twist.

Candidates were given a map, a compass, and a rendezvous point that they were supposed to reach at a certain time. Once that point was reached, however, there was no guarantee that the exercise was over. Generally the candidate was merely given, by an IP, another RP and sent on his or her way.

The exercise didn't have much to do with pilot training, but it had a lot to do with tenacity and determination. Plus, Sten grudged, it probably showed which beings had learned that their brains were fools, telling the body to quit when the body's resources had barely begun to work.

Again, it was simple for Sten—Mantis teams ran these exercises as recreation.

But it did trim the candidates. Already ten of the thirty-plus candidates in Sten's group had withered and vanished.

Sten, flat on the ground, feet elevated, and in no-mind, heard footsteps.

He returned to reality to see the small woman who on their first day had made the cogent observation about pilots trot smoothly toward him.

Instead of going flat and shutting the systems down, she dropped her pack, went flat, and began doing exercises.

Sten was curious—this was an interesting way to con

the mind into going one step farther. He waited until she finished, which added an extra minute to his time.

The downhill side of this part of the course was rocky. Sten and the female candidate—Victoria—were able to talk as they went.

Data exchange: She was a lieutenant in the navy. She was trained as a dancer and gymnast. Successful, Sten guessed, since she'd performed on Prime World. Sten even thought he'd heard of a couple of the companies she'd been with.

So why the service?

A military family. But also, dancing was work. She said being a professional dancer was like being a fish in sand.

Sten found the breath to laugh at the line.

Plus, Victoria went on, she had always been interested in mathematics.

Sten shuddered. While he was competent at mathematics—any officer had to be—equations were hardly something he joyously spent off-duty time splashing around in.

Sten's internal timer went off—it was a break for him. Victoria kept on moving at her inexorable pace.

Sten watched her disappear in the distance and felt very good.

If there was anyone who was guaranteed to get through this guano called Selection and become a pilot, it had to be Victoria.

Sten ducked as the wall of water came green over the boat's bows and smashed against the bridge windows.

The boat swayed, and Sten's stomach did handstands. Shut up, body. This is an illusion. Shut up, head, the answer came back. I am going to be sick. The hell with you.

Sten, puking to the side, had to fight to follow the instructions whispered at him.

"This is a twenty-meter boat. It is used to procure fish commercially. You are the captain.

"This boat has been returning to harbor, running just ahead of a storm.

"The storm has caught your boat.

"Somewhere ahead of you is the harbor. You must enter that harbor safely to complete the exercise.

"Your radar will show you the harbor mouth. But it is a failure-prone installation.

"You also know that the entrance to this harbor crosses what is called a bar—a shallowing of depth. During storm times, this bar can prevent any ship entering the harbor.

"Good luck."

Sten had become experienced enough with the testing to instantly look at his radar screen. Ah-hah. There . . . somewhat to the right . . . so I must direct this craft . . . and, just as implicitly promised, the radar set hazed green.

Sten evaluated the situation—the illusion he was experiencing through the helmet. Unlike the Shavala-experience, in these tests any action Sten took would be "real." If, for instance, he steered the ship onto the rocks, he would experience a wreck and, probably, since Selection people were sadistic, slow drowning.

Simple solution. Easy, Sten thought.

All I have to do is hit the antigrav, and this boat will—

Wrong. There were only three controls in front of Sten: a large, spoked steering wheel and two handles.

This was a two-dimensional boat.

There were gauges, which Sten ignored. They were probably intended to show engine performance, and Sten, having no idea what kind of power train he was using, figured they were, at least at the moment, irrelevant.

Another wave came in, and the ship pitched sideways. Sten, looking at his choices, threw the right handle all the way forward, the left handle all the way back, and turned the wheel hard to the right.

The pitching subsided.

Sten equalized the two handles—I must have two engines, I guess—and held the wheel at midpoint.

Ahead of him the storm cleared, and Sten could see high rocks with surf booming over them. There was a slight break to the left—the harbor entrance.

Sten steered for it.

The rocks grew closer, and crosscurrents tried to spin Sten's boat.

Sten sawed at throttles and wheel.

Very good. He was lined up.

The rain stopped, and Sten saw, bare meters in front of him, the glisten of earth as a wave washed back. Clotting bastards—that's what a bar was!

He reversed engines.

A series of waves swept his boat over the stern. Sten ignored them.

He got the idea.

When a wave hits the bar, the water gets deep. All I need to do is wait for a big wave, checking through the rear bridge windows, and then go to full power. Use the wave's force to get into the harbor.

It worked like a shot. The huge wave Sten chose heaved the boat clear, into the harbor mouth.

Sten, triumphant, forgot to allow for side currents, and his boat smashed into the causeway rocks.

Just as anticipated, not only did his boat sink, Sten had the personal experience of drowning.

Slowly.

GRADE: PASSING.

By now, Sten had learned the names of his fellow candidates.

The hard sergeant, who Sten had figured would be thrown out immediately, had managed to survive. Survive, hell—so far he and Victoria had interchanged positions as Number One and Number Two in the class standings. A specialist in ancient history would not have been surprised, knowing the man's name—William Bishop the Forty-third.

Sten, not knowing, was astonished, as were the other candidates, who had dubbed the sergeant "Grunt," a nickname he accepted cheerfully.

The furry would-be beer aficionado, whose name was Lotor, was a valued asset. He was the class clown.

Since normal military relief valves such as drunkenness, passes, and such were forbidden, the candidates tended to get very crazy in the barracks. Lotor had started the water-sack war.

Sten had been the first victim.

There had been an innocent knock on his door at midnight. He'd opened the door to get a plas container of water in the face.

Sten, once he'd figured out who the culprit was, had retaliated by sealing Lotor in his shower with the drain plugged. He'd relented before the water level hit the ceiling.

Lotor, after drying his fur, had escalated. He had decided that Sten had allies, Sh'aarl't being one. So he'd tucked the floor fire hose under Sh'aarl't's door and turned it on.

Sh'aarl't, awakened when her room got half-full, had sensibly opened the door and gone back to sleep.

Lotor had not considered that making a spider an enemy was a bad thing to do.

The next night, Sh'aarl't had spun her web out from her window up a floor to Lotor's room and gently replaced his pillow with a water bag.

Lotor, again looking for a new target, went after Grunt. He tied an explosive charge to a huge water bag, rolled it down the corridor, knocked on Bishop's door, and then scurried.

Grunt opened his door just as the water bag blew.

His revenge required filling Lotor's room with a huge weather balloon filled with water. Bishop, being the combat type he was, didn't bother to figure out whether Lotor was present when he set the trap.

It took most of the barracks staff to free Lotor.

At that point, through mutual exhaustion and because no one could come up with a more clever escalation, the watersack war ended.

The only good effect it produced was the linking of Lotor, Bishop, Sten, and Sh'aarl't into a vague team.

The team adopted Victoria as their mascot. She wasn't sure why but was grateful for the company. The four never explained, but it was just what Sten had felt on the map exercise: One of them had to make it. And Victoria was the most likely candidate.

The five had discussed their options—which all agreed

were slim—and also what those IPs really would turn out to be if they were required to wear uniforms instead of the blank coveralls.

Victoria had the best slander on Ferrari. She said the sloppy man must have been a Warrant-1, who probably blackmailed his commanding officer while stealing every piece of Imperial property that wasn't bonded in place.

They had laughed, shared a cup of the guaranteed-no-side-effects herbal tea, and headed for their rooms and the omnipresent studying.

At least most of them did.

Possibly the herbal tea had no *reported* effects.

Sten and Victoria bade Sh'aarl't good night at her door. Sten meant to walk Victoria to her room but found himself asking her into his own room.

Victoria accepted.

Inside, Sten gloried and dismayed. Victoria pressured the bed and plumped the pillows. She touched a finger to her flight suit zip, and the coverall dropped away from her tiny, absolutely perfect body.

Sten had fantasized about making love to a ballerina—specifically Victoria. He hadn't suggested it because he had the rough idea that if he suggested and she accepted, his capabilities would be exactly as impotent as Mason daily suggested.

Tension and all that.

Sten may have been accurate about his own potential. But he had no idea how creative an ex-professional dancer could be.

The next day both Victoria and Sten tested very, very low on the various challenges.

They'd had less than an hour's sleep.

CHAPTER EIGHT

SELECTION MOVED ON from written or livie tests to live problems, giving Ferrari and Mason a chance for real hands-on harassment.

Sten had the idea that the particular situation he was facing would be a real piece, since Ferrari was beaming and even Mason had allowed his slash of a mouth to creep up on one side.

"This is what we call a Groupstacle," Ferrari explained genially.

Group. Obstacle.

The group was Bishop, Victoria, Lotor, Sten, and six others.

The obstacle was:

"We're standing here," Ferrari said, "in the control room of a destroyer. Flower class, in case you're curious. It looks terrible, does it not?"

He waited for the chorus of agreement from the candidates.

"The reason it looks so bad is because it has crash-landed on a certain planetoid. This planetoid has acceptable atmosphere and water. But there is nothing to eat and very little which can be made into shelter."

Ferrari smiled.

"Any of you who are eco-trained, do not bother to explain how illogical this planetoid must be. I do not set up these problems, I merely administer them.

"At any rate, you see this control room we are standing in? Yes. Terribly ruined by the crash. You see this open

41

hatchway, exiting onto the planetoid, which is quite color-fully provided.

"Personally, I must say that I do not believe that trees can ever be purple. But I wander. Mr. Mason, would you care to continue?"

"Thank you, sir.

"I'll cut it short. You losers have crashed. The only way you're gonna live is by getting your survival kits out. The kits are down this passageway. You got two problems—the passageway is blocked."

No kidding, Sten thought, staring down the corridor. He admired how carefully the problem had been set up. As they entered the huge chamber, it did look as if half of a ship was crashed into a jungle, crumpled and battered.

The inside of the ship was, with some exceptions—and Sten was noting those exceptions carefully—exactly like the flight deck and nearby passageways of a destroyer.

Sten wondered why, before the IPs had led the group into the chamber, Mason had taken Bishop aside and told him something—something very important from the way that Grunt had reacted.

Mason continued. "Second problem is that the power plant is in a self-destruct mode. You've got twenty minutes until this ship blows higher'n Haman.

"If you don't get to your supplies, you fail the problem. All of you.

"If you're still working on the problem when the twenty minutes run out, you fail the problem. All of you."

"Thank you, Mr. Mason."

"Yessir."

"The problem begins . . . now!"

There was a stammer of ideas.

Victoria had cut in—clot everything. What did they have to take out?

Grunt had said that was stupid—first they needed some kind of plan.

Lotor said that if they didn't know how deep the drakh was, how could any plan be possible?

The situation was simple. The corridor to the survival kits was blocked by assorted ship rubble that could be easily cleared. But x-ed across the corridor were two enormous steel beams, impossible to move without assistance.

Two candidates proved that, straining their backs trying to wedge the beams free.

Lotor was standing beside a much smaller beam in the corridor ahead of the blockage.

"This," he said, "might make a lever. If we had a fulcrum."

"Come on, Lotor," Grunt put in. "We don't have any clottin' fulcrum."

"Hell we don't," Victoria said. "Couple of you clowns grab that big chart chest up on the flight deck."

"Never work," Bishop said.

Sten eyed him. What the hell was the matter with Grunt? Normally he was the first to go for new ideas. While two men shoved the map chest down toward the block, Sten did his own recon around the "ship."

By the time he came back to the corridor, the map chest sat close to the blocking beams. The small beam went under one, and everybody leaned.

The first beam lifted, swiveled, and crashed sideways. The team gave a minor cheer and moved their lever forward.

"This is not going to work," Bishop said.

Another candidate stepped back. "You're probably right."

He spotted a red-painted panel in the metal corridor, clearly marked ENVIRONMENT CONTROL INSPECTION POINT. *Do not enter without Class 11 Clearance. Do not enter unless ship is deactivated.*

The candidate shoved the panel open. A ductway led along the corridor's path.

"Okay. This is it," the candidate announced.

"Didn't you read the panel?" Sten asked.

"So? This ship's about as deactivated as possible."

"You're right," Bishop agreed.

Again, Sten wondered.

The candidate forced himself into the ductway. The panel clicked closed behind him. After five seconds, they heard a howl of pain.

The demons who set up the Selection tests had provided for that. In that ductway should have been superheated steam. But this was a dummy, so all the candidate got was a mild blast of hot water—enough for first-degree burns—and then the ductway opened and dumped him out on the other side of the set, where Ferrari told him he was dead and disqualified from the test.

After the "death" of the candidate, the team redoubled efforts to lever the second beam free.

Sten did his basic physics, said "no way," and looked for another solution. He went through the ship and then outside, looking for anything that could become a tool.

He found it.

By the time he'd dragged the forty meters of control cable that must have exploded from the ship's skin into the jungle back into the corridor, the others were panting in defeat.

There was seven minutes remaining.

Sten did not bother explaining. He ran the 2-cm cable down to the beam, looped it, and wrapped a series of half hitches around it. Then he dragged the cable back up to a solid port frame that had pulled away from the ship's walls, and back toward the beam.

Bishop stopped him. "What the clot are you doing?"

"I'm sending kisses to the clotting Emperor," Sten grunted. "Gimme a hand."

"Come on, Sten! You're wasting time."

"One time. Listen up, Grunt. We're gonna block and tackle this cable and yank that beam out."

"Sten, I'm not sure that is going to work. Why don't we talk about it?"

"Because we got five minutes."

"Right! We don't want to do anything wrong, do we?"

And Sten got it.

"Nope."

His hand knifed out, palm up. Sten's hands could kill, maim, or coldcock any being known to the Imperial martial arts.

The knife hand sliced against Bishop's neck, just below his ear. Bishop dropped like a sack of sand.

"Shaddup," Sten commanded against the shout of surprise. "Get this clottin' cable back around and then we have to pull like hell. Bishop was a sabotage factor. I saw Mason give him orders. Come on, people. We got to get out of this place!"

The block-and-tackled pulley yanked the beam free, and the team had its supplies out of the storage room and were clear of the "ship" a good minute before time ran out.

Bishop, after recovering consciousness, told Sten he was right—Mason had told him to be a saboteur.

Ferrari grudged that they were one of the few teams to successfully complete the test in five years.

GRADE: OUTSTANDING.

CHAPTER NINE

STEN WAS HAVING PROBLEMS.

It wasn't that he was quite a mathematical idiot—no one in the Imperial Forces above spear-carrier second class was—but he did not have the instinctive understanding of numbers that he did, for example, of objects. Nor could he, in the navigational basic courses Phase One shoved at them, translate numbers into the reality of ships or planets.

And so he got coaching.

From Victoria, there was no problem, since everyone knew that she was the only guaranteed graduate. But Bishop?

Math geniuses are supposed to be short and skinny, talk in high voices, and have surgically corrected optics.

So much for stereotypes, Sten thought glumly as Bishop's thick fingers tabbed at computer keys, touched numbers on the screen, and, with the precision and patience of a pedant, tried to help Sten realize that pure numbers more exactly described a universe than even a picture or words, no matter how poetically or OEDly chosen.

Sten looked at the screen again and found no translation.

"Clottin' hell," Bishop grunted to Victoria. "Get the fire ax. *Something's* got to get through to him."

Victoria found the solution.

It took less than one evening to crosspatch Sten's mini-holoprocessor into the computer. When he input numbers, the holoprocessor produced a tiny three-dimensional star-map.

Eventually, after many many problems, Sten glimmered toward an understanding.

His grade:

MATHEMATICAL PERCEPTIONS: NEED IMPROVEMENT.

For some unknown reason, almost every school Sten had been punted into tested for gravitation sensitivity.

Sten could understand why it would be necessary to know how many gees someone could withstand or how many times one could alter the direction of a field before the subject threw up—but once that was found out, why was retesting necessary?

Sten knew that he personally could function as a soldier, without benefit of a gravsuit, at up to 3.6 E-gravs. He could work, seated, under a continuous 11.6 E-gravs. He would black out under a brief force of 76.1 E-gravs or a nearly instantaneous shock of 103 E-gravs.

All this was in his medfiche.

So why retest?

Sten decided that it was just part of the applied sadism that every school he had attended, back to the factory world of Vulcan, had put him through.

But of all the test methods he hated, a centrifuge was the worst. His brain knew that there was no way his body could tell it was being spun in a circle to produce gravitic acceleration. But his body said "bet me" and heaved.

Of course Phase One used a centrifuge.

Sten curled a lip at the stainless steel machinery craning above him in the huge room.

"You look worried, Candidate Sten." It was Mason.

Sten hit the exaggerated position that the IPs called attention. "Nossir. Not worried, sir."

"Are you scared, Candidate?"

Great roaring clichés. Sten wished that Alex was with him. He knew the chubby heavy-worlder would have found a response—probably smacking Mason.

Sten remembered, however, that Kilgour had already gone through flight school. Since Sten hadn't heard anything, he assumed that Alex had graduated—without killing Mason.

Sten decided that Kilgour must have been sent to another Phase One than this one, made a noncommittal reply to Mason, and clambered up the steps into one of the centrifuge's capsules.

Later that night, Sten's stomach had reseated itself enough to feel mild hunger.

He left his room, still feeling most tottery, and went for the rec room. One of the food machines would, no doubt, have something resembling thin gruel.

Sh'aarl't, Bishop, and Lotor sat at one of the game tables in complete silence. Sten took his full cup from the slot and sat down beside them. Lotor gave him the news.

"They washed Victoria today."

Sten jumped, and the soup splashed, unheeded, in his lap.

Bishop answered the unasked question. "She failed the gee-test."

"No way," Sten said. "She was a clotting gymnast. A dancer."

"Evidently," Sh'aarl't said, "vertigo is not uncommon—even in athletes."

"How many gees?"

"Twelve point something," Bishop said.

"Clot," Sten swore. Even mild combat maneuvers in a ship with the McLean generators shut down could pull more than that.

He realized that all of them spoke of Victoria in the past tense. Phase One may have been sadistic in some ways, but when a candidate was disqualified, he was immediately removed. Sten was a little surprised that the three had any idea at all on what had flunked the woman.

He also realized that with Victoria, their talisman for possible graduation to the next phase, gone, none of them felt any hope of making it.

CHAPTER TEN

THE BULLETIN DISPLAY in the barracks' lobby was known, not inappropriately, as "The Tablet of Doom." Sten read the latest directive as it flashed for his attention: 1600 hours, this day, all candidates were directed to assemble in the central quadrangle. He wondered what new form of mass torment the IPs had devised. There were, after all, only a few days left in Phase One, and there were still survivors in the program, including Sh'aarl't, Bishop, and Lotor.

Then he caught the kicker.

DRESS UNIFORM.

Sten was in a world of trouble. He had been quite correct hiding his ribbons upon entering the school. He noticed that those with more decorations or rank than the IPs felt appropriate seemed to get far more than their share of attention and harassment. Thus far, in spite of Mason's evident personal hatred, Sten had managed to run somewhat silent and somewhat deep.

Oh, well. All good things seize their bearings eventually.

"My, don't we look pretty, Candidate," Mason crooned. "All those ribbons and bows."

Sten had considered not putting the medals on. But he knew that under the current circumstances it was an offense of basic regulations for a soldier not to wear the decorations to which he was entitled. It would be just like the IPs to look up everyone's record jacket, then check chests or sashes for exactitude and use any difference to bust another candidate out.

Sten yessired Mason while marveling at Chief Instructor Pilot Ferrari. So much for the theory that fat slobs only get promoted to warrant officer. That might be his current serving rank, but Ferrari was now wearing the stars of a fleet admiral, with decorations banked almost to his epaulettes.

Sten noticed, in spite of his awe, that there appeared to be a soup stain just above Ferrari's belt line.

"If I'd known you had all those hero buttons, Candidate," Mason went on, "I would have given you more attention. But we still have time."

Fine. Sten was doomed. He wondered how Mason would nuke him.

Minutes later, he found out.

Ferrari had called the class to attention and congratulated them. The formal testing was complete. Any of them still standing was successful. All that remained was the final test.

"Do not bother," Ferrari said, "going through your notes and memories in preparation. The end test we are quite proud of, not the least because it has everything yet nothing to do with what has gone before. You have twenty-four hours to consider what such an examination might be. We find that suspense is good for the soul. The test, by the way, will be administered singly. Each instructor pilot will choose candidates, and it is his responsibility at that point."

And now Sten knew how Mason was going to get him.

CHAPTER ELEVEN

THE AIRCRAFT—AT least Sten guessed it was an aircraft—
was the most clotting impossible collection of scrap metal
he had ever seen. It consisted of a flat metal platform about
two meters in diameter, with two seats, two sets of what
Sten thought to be controls, and a windscreen. The platform sat atop two metal skids. Behind it was some sort of
power plant and then a long spidered-metal girder that
ended in a side-facing fan blade. Above the platform was
another fan, horizontal to the ground, with twin blades each
about six meters long. The device sat in the middle of a
wide, completely flat landing ground. Two hundred meters
in front of the aircraft, a series of pylons sprouted.

Sten and Mason were the only two beings on the landing
field. Sten turned a blank but—he hoped—enthusiastic
face toward Mason.

"We got a theory here in flight school," Mason said. "We
know there are natural pilots—none of you clowns qualify,
of course—and also a lot of people have flown a lot of
things.

"No sense testing someone for basic ability if we put
them on their favorite toy, is there? So what we came up
with is something that, as far as we know, *nobody* has flown
for a thousand years or so. This pile of drakh was called a
helicopter. Since it killed a whole group of pilots in its day,
when antigrav came around they couldn't scrap-heap these
guys fast enough.

"You're gonna fly it, Candidate. Or else you're gonna
look for a new job category. I hear they're recruiting planetary meteorologists for the Pioneer Sectors."

"Yes, sir."

"Not that we're unfair. We're gonna give you some help. First you get two facts: Fact number one is that this helicopter, unlike anything else I've ever heard of, really doesn't want to fly at all. It won't lift without bitching, it glides like a rock, and it lands about the same if you don't know what you're doing. Fact number two is it's easy to fly if you're the kind of person who can pat his head and rub his stomach at the same time."

Sten wondered if Mason was making his notion of a joke. Impossible—the man was humorless.

"Next, you and me are gonna strap in, and I'm gonna show you how the controls work. Then you'll take over, and follow my instructions. I'll start simple."

Right, simple. Ostensibly, the few controls were easy. The stick in front controlled the angle of the individual fan blades—the airfoil surface—as they rotated. This stick could be moved to any side and, Mason explained, could make the helicopter maneuver. A second lever, to the side, moved up and down, and, with a twist grip, rotated to give engine speed and, therefore, rotor speed. Two rudder pedals controlled the tiny fan at the ship's rear, which kept the helicopter from following the natural torque reaction of the blades and spinning wildly.

The first test was to hover the ship.

Mason lifted it, lowered it, then lifted it again. It seemed easy.

"All you got to do is keep it a meter off the ground."

He told Sten to take the controls.

The helicopter then developed a different personality and, in spite of Sten's sawing, dipped, bounced the front end of the skids on the field, then, following Sten's over-controlling, reared back . . . then forward . . . and Mason had to grab the controls.

"You want to try it again?"

Sten nodded.

He did better—but not much. Power . . . keep that collective in place . . . real gentle with that stick.

Sten didn't prang it this time, but the required meter altitude varied up to about three.

Sten's flight suit was soaked with sweat.

Again.

The variable came down to plus or minus a meter.

Mason was looking at Sten. "All right. Next we're going to move forward."

Mason moved the helicopter forward about fifty meters, turned, and flew back, then repeated the whole maneuver.

"I want you to hold two meters altitude and just fly down there in a straight line. I'll tell you when to stop."

The helicopter porpoised off. He scraped his skids twice, and his flight toward those distant pylons was a sidewinder's path. Mason took over and put Sten through the same routine three more times. Sten had no idea if he was about to be trained as a pilot or a weatherman.

The next stage took the helicopter all the way down to the pylons and S-curved through them. The first time Sten tried it, he discovered he had straight and level flight somehow memorized—the helicopter clipped every single pole as it went down the course. By the fourth try, Sten managed to hit no more than four or five of them.

Mason was looking at him. Then Mason signaled—he had it.

Sten sat back and, per orders, put his hands in his lap.

Mason landed the ship back where it had started, shut down, and unbuckled. Sten followed, stepping off the platform and ducking under the rotors as they slowed.

Mason was standing, stone-faced, about thirty meters away from the helicopter. "That's all, Candidate. Report to your quarters. You'll be informed as to your status."

Sten saluted. Clot. So much for the Emperor's ideas about Sten.

"Candidate!"

Sten stopped and turned.

"Did you ever fly one of these things before?"

And Sten, through his honest denial, felt a small glint of hope.

CHAPTER TWELVE

A DAY LATER, Sten's name, as well as Bishop's, Sh'aarl't's, and Lotor's, went on the list: *Phase One. Accepted. Assigned to Imperial Flight Training, Phase Two.*

In Phase Two, they would learn how to fly.

There should have been some kind of party. But everyone-was too tired to get bashed. Of the 500 candidates, fewer than forty had been selected.

According to the clichés, graduation should have been announced by the IPs lugging in cases of alk and welcoming the candidates to the thin, whatever-colored line. Instead, Sh'aarl't, Sten, and Bishop split a flask of herbal tea while they packed. All they wanted was away.

Waiting near the sleds that would take the candidates to their ships were Ferrari and Mason.

Again according to cliché, there should now have been understanding on one hand and acceptance on the other. But Mason's expression was exactly that of the first day— he looked as if he was sorry that any of them had made it. And he turned an even harder stare on Sten.

Sten returned it.

Clot forgiveness and understanding—he wanted to meet Mason in an alley behind a hangar sometime and give him a scar to match the first one. Preferably across the throat ...

CHAPTER THIRTEEN

THE LABEL "the Fringe Worlds" suggests some sort of geographical or political cohesiveness to the spattered cluster that occupied space between the Empire and the Tahn System. There was almost none.

The cluster had been slowly settled by Imperial pioneers. They were not the radicals or the adventurers who had explored, for instance, the Lupus Cluster. They were people wanting things to be a little more simple and peaceful. A large percentage of them were retired military or civil servants starting a second, or even third, career. Others wanted a chance to establish themselves in comfort as small manufacturers or business people.

But if there were no hero pioneers, there also were none of the villains that pioneering creates. Not, at least, until the expansion from the Tahn empire brought new, and somewhat different, immigrants.

What government there was in the Fringe Worlds mirrored the settlers themselves. Whether confined to a single world or including a half dozen or so systems, it was generally some species of parliamentarianism, ranging from mildly liberal to mildly authoritarian. Since prospective tyrants went elsewhere, what armed forces existed were somewhere between customs police and coastal guards. The only unifying political force the cluster had was an economic summit that met to iron out modern problems every five years or so. It was a backwater cluster, content to remain as it was.

Until the Tahn.

The Tahn who immigrated into the Fringe Worlds were financially backed by their leaders, as the Tahn birth rate

and political ambitions clamored for Lebensraum. These
were true pioneers, looking for more. Since their culture
encouraged communal economics, they naturally had an
advantage over the ex-Imperialists. And so the situation
escalated into violence—riots and pogroms.

The Imperial settlers were there first, so they had a
chance to modify the government. Tahn were not permitted
extensive freeholds. They were excluded from voting. They
were physically ghettoized into enclaves either rural or
urban.

The Tahn settlers' resentment was fed by the Tahn Empire itself, which wanted the cluster added to its holdings.

The revolutionary movement was not only popular but
well backed by the Tahn. And the Empire had done little to
solve the problem. After all, backwater areas with minor
problems—riots, no matter how bloody, are not as bad as
active genocide—get minor attention.

The Imperial garrisons assigned to the Tahn worlds were
fat and lazy. Instead of being peacekeepers, the officers and
men tended to agree with the settlers. The Tahn, after all,
were different—which meant "not as good as."

There had been a brief time, not long before, when the
confrontation between the Empire itself and the Tahn might
have been prevented. Some of the more farsighted Tahn
revolutionaries had recognized that if the confrontation occurred, they were liable to be crushed in the middle. Very
secretly they had sent the head of the organization to Prime
World. Godfrey Alain had been murdered in a plot that was
aimed against the Emperor himself. Final negotiations between the Empire and the peace faction of the Tahn Council
had also ended in blood.

The war drums were not even slightly muted, especially
on the Fringe Worlds.

But no one in the cluster seemed to know how close
Empirewide war was.

CHAPTER FOURTEEN

THE DUSTY GRAVCAR sputtered feebly over a country lane. It was an elderly design: long, boxy, with an extended rear cargo area. And the way it was balking, it was plain that it had been under constant and varied lease since it had left the factory.

The salesman hunched over the controls seemed as weathered and as old as the vehicle. He was a large man with a broad, friendly face and bulky shoulders that strained at his years-out-of-date coveralls. The man hummed peacefully to himself in an off-key voice timed to the sputtering McLean drive engine. As he drove in apparent complete ease and relaxation, his eyes swiveled like a predator's, drinking in every detail of the landscape.

This was poor land, pocked with rocks and wind-bowed clumps of trees. It seemed to be one dry gale away from becoming a permanent dust bowl.

During the course of the day, the salesman had skimmed past a half a dozen sharecropper farms tended by a few hollow-eyed Tahn immigrants. He had hesitated at each place, noted the extreme poverty, and gone on. None of them were places where a normal being would have even asked for a friendly glass of water. Not because of the hostility—which was real and more than apparent—but because if it had been given, it might have been the last few ounces of water left on the farm.

In the distance he spotted a sudden shot of green. He shifted course and soon came upon a large farm. The earth seemed comparatively rich—not loam, but not rock either —and was heavily diked with irrigation ditches. In the middle of the spread were big shambling buildings surrounding a small artesian pond. This would be the source of wealth. Several people were working the field with rusted, creaking machinery.

Still humming, the man eased the gravsled to a stop next to a cattle guard. He pretended not to notice the instant freezing of the people in the field. He casually got out under their burning stares, stepped over behind a bush, and relieved his bladder. Then he struck a smoke, gazed lazily about, and walked over to the fence railing. He peered with mild interest at the men and women in the field—one pro judging the work of others. He gave a loud snort. If he had had a mustache, the honk would have blown it up to his bushy eyebrows. The snort seemed to be both a nervous habit and a comment on the state of things.

"Nice place," he finally said. His voice hit that perfect raised pitch that a farmer uses to communicate to a companion many rows away.

The group drew back slightly as a middle-aged Tahn, nearly the salesman's size, strode forward. The salesman smiled broadly at him, pointedly ignoring the others who were picking up weapons and spreading slowly out to the side.

"Wouldn't think you could grow kale crops in these parts," the salesman said as the Tahn drew closer. He looked more closely at the fields. " 'Course they do look a little yellow-eyed and peaked."

The man stopped in front of him, just on the other side of the fence. Meanwhile, his sons and daughters had half ringed the salesman in. He heard the snicks of safeties switching off.

"Next town's about forty klicks down the road," the farmer said. It was an invitation to get the clot back in the gravcar and get out.

The elderly salesman snorted again. "Yeah. I noted that on the comp-map. Didn't seem like much of a town."

"It ain't," the Tahn said. "Next Imperial place gotta be two, maybe two and a half days go."

The salesman laughed. "Spotted me, huh? What the hell, I ain't ashamed. Besides, being a farmer is the only citizenship I claim."

The man stared at him. "If you're a farmer," he said, "what you doin' off your spread?"

"Gave it up after eighty years," the salesman said. "You might say I'm retired. Except that wouldn't be right. Actually, I'm on my second career."

The farmer's eyes shifted, checking the positions of his brood. He inspected the horizon for any possible Imperial reinforcements. "That so?"

Death was whispering in the salesman's ear.

"Yeah," he said, unconcerned. "That's so. Sell fertilizer gizmos now. My own design. Maybe you'd be interested in one."

He pulled out a much-used kerchief and honked into it. Then he looked at the kale fields again. He noted some blackened areas in the distance; this was just one of many Tahn farms, he understood, that had been hit by roving gangs of Imperial settlers.

"Wouldn't help with the withering, but one of my fellas sure as hell would take the yellow out."

"Mister," the farmer said, "you're either a damn fool, or—"

The salesman laughed. "At my age," he said, "I've gotten used to a lot worse things than being called a fool."

"Listen, old man," the farmer said. "You're Imperial. Don't you know better than to come near a Tahn place?"

The salesman snorted. "Pish, man. You're talkin' politics. Never gave a damn about politics. Only thing I got in common with politicians is what I sell. Matter of fact, fertilizer's a lot more useful. And my stuff don't stick to your boots, either."

He turned to the cargo compartment of his gravsled. Instantly weapons came up. The salesman just pulled several small bottles out of a carton. He held one out for the farmer, his face total innocence.

"My calling card," he said.

Cautiously, the Tahn farmer reached over the fence and took one of the bottles. He looked at the printing on the side. The salesman figured that the time was ripe for introductions.

"Ian Mahoney," he said. "Fine cider and fertilizer . . . Go

ahead. Try it. Whipped that batch up myself. A little raw, but it'll do the job."

The farmer opened the bottle and sniffed. The sweet smell of apples drifted out. And underlying it, there was the sharp odor of alcohol.

"It's nothing serious," Mahoney said. "Maybe seventy-five proof or so. Take a shot."

The farmer sipped, then sucked in his breath. It was good stuff all right. Without hesitation, he chugged down the rest of the bottle.

"That's damn fine cider," he said.

Mahoney snorted. "You oughta see my fertilizer. Nothing clotting organic in it. All pure, sweet-smelling chemicals. Great for the plants, and you don't have to worry about the kids getting ringworm—long as you keep 'em away from your cattle."

The farmer laughed. Mahoney noted the weapons being lowered. Then, with some relief, he saw the Tahn wave his hulking children over to him in a friendly gesture.

"Say, mister," the farmer said. "You got any more of that cider?"

"Sure thing."

And with a honk of his nose, a grin, and a scratch of his behind, Major General Ian Mahoney, commander of the Imperial First Guards Division, reached into the back of his gravcar to buy the boys a drink.

CHAPTER FIFTEEN

IT WAS A COUNTRY inn—large, gleaming white, with exposed stained beams of expensive wood. The gravcars lined up outside were all reasonably new and worth many, many credits. For kilometers around, the farmland was sleek and water-proud. The name of the place was the Imperial Arms Inn.

Bloody figures, Mahoney thought as he reached for the door.

He heard voices shouting from within in heated debate.

"Clottin' low-life Tahn. Up to me, police'd clear out every one of them."

"Clot the police. We gotta take care of our own business. A being oughta kill his own snakes. I say we all get together one night and—"

Mahoney was spotted instantly as he walked inside. A church-hall hush fell over the room. Mahoney automatically honked into his handkerchief—cursing mentally to himself that he had ever dreamed up that touch—and strolled over to the bar.

He eased his bulk into a stool. "Shot and a beer, friend," he told the bartender.

All around him, every person was listening intently to each word he said. The bartender filled up a mug and placed it before him. A second later, a shot glass chinked beside it.

"Traveling through?" the bartender asked, sounding way too casual.

"Sure am," Mahoney said. "But real slowly, today. Hell of a hangover."

He took a sip of his beer and chased it with the full shot. The bartender refilled it.

"Party too hard, huh?"

Mahoney groaned. "You don't know the half of it," he said. "I happened by the McGregor place, yesterday. You know the spread—maybe thirty klicks out?"

The bartender nodded, as did the rest of the room. Everyone knew the McGregors.

"They just married off their last kid," Mahoney said. That was far from news to the crowd in the inn. "I showed up just at reception time. Hit it right off with those nice people. They made me stay and filled me right up with all I could eat and drink." He snorted through his increasingly reddening nose. " 'Course, they didn't have to twist my arm much."

Mahoney felt the room relax. A moment later it was all a-babble again. The bartender even bought him the next shot. Mahoney sipped at it and peered about the bar, just one friendly face looking for another.

A well-dressed, overstuffed man strolled over to him, carrying his drink. He sat down beside Mahoney.

"You look like you might be in sales," the man said.

Mahoney laughed. "Hell, does it change a fellow that quick? Farmed two-thirds of my life. Now I'm into sales. Sorta."

"What do you mean by sorta?"

Mahoney instantly warmed to the man. He began dragging out circulars and brochures.

"Fertilizer plants is my game," he said. "Look at these boys. Small, cheap, and you get an output for anything from a kitchen garden to a big sucker of a farm."

The man seemed genuinely interested. "Say, maybe we could use something like that."

Mahoney peered at him through his old man's bushy eyebrows. "No offense, but you don't seem the farmin' type."

"No offense taken," the man said. "I'm into hardware. Got thirty-two stores and growing."

"Say, you *are* a find. Let me tell you about these little guys." And Mahoney went into what he called his dancing-bear act. It took many drinks and the good part of an hour. Other men joined the conversation. And soon Mahoney was handing out bottles of his "calling card."

By now his mission had taken him to eleven or more Fringe World planets in nearly that many systems. He had his cover story fine-tuned. Now he was winding up on the Empire's capital world for the Fringe System: Cavite.

Mahoney was passing himself off as an elderly farmer who had spent most of his life tending a large, rich spread on one of the key Imperial agricultural systems. He was also a habitual tinkerer, constantly inventing little devices to solve problems that irritated him.

Fertilizer was one of his big bugaboos. Mahoney could go on for hours about the rotten quality and expense of the average fertilizer—and he frequently did, to the dismay of casual dinner guests. Anyway, Mahoney the farmer had invented the dandy little fertilizer plant, then put his own money up to found a small company.

Presently, he was acting as his own advance man, touring agricultural areas to brag about his wares. The fact that he wasn't asking for any money out front but was merely asking people if one of his salesmen could visit in a month or so eased the suspicions of even the overly hostile settlers of the Fringe Worlds.

Mahoney also thought his homemade cider was a nice touch, as was his old man's chatter, with his knowledge of farming trivia and the ability to bore just about anyone. His only regret was the snort he had adopted to go with the act. Now he couldn't stop, and he was wondering if he would ever be able to cure himself of the self-made habit. He was also bemoaning the fact that his constant snorting was turning his nose bright red.

"Sounds great to me," the hardware man said. "Government give you any trouble in the licensing?"

Mahoney snorted a particularly snotty blast. "Licenses? Government? What kind of fool you think I am? Clot, dealt with the damned government all my life. Do everything they can to wreck a farm, if you let them."

There were angry mutters of agreement from the gathered farmers.

"Besides, I only got maybe thirty years or more in me. Time I got through those licensing butt bungs, I'd be long dead."

The logic was ancient and irrefutable.

"What about shipping? They givin' you any trouble about that?"

"Well, I ain't shippin' just yet. Right now, I'm gettin' to know people, show off my plants. Why? You think I'll have any trouble in these parts?"

The hardware man exploded. "Clottin' right! I got orders stacked all over the place. Cash orders. And with all this business of the Tahn going on, I'm about ready to go broke."

He went into a long litany of complaints, which were

added to and spiced up by comments from a slowly growing crowd with Mahoney at its center.

They told him about the sneaky, lazy Tahn, about the attacks on their property and their counterattacks. They told him about an economy that was almost paralyzed, and about incompetent cops and worse than incompetent Imperial garrison troops.

They went on about their suspicions: mysterious lights over Tahn enclaves, probable stockpiling of weapons, and professional Tahn troops slipping in to reinforce their filthy brethren.

The Imperial settlers, of course, were blameless. They had tried so hard to bear up under the burden. Everyone in the bar had made a personal sacrifice, hadn't he? Why, they had even dipped deep into their bank accounts to buy weapons to protect their farms and Imperial property.

Through it all, Mahoney allowed his face to become grimmer and grimmer in agreement. He rarely interrupted, except to snort or to buy another round of drinks.

By the time the night was over, he could have filled an entire fiche with his report.

He was also beginning to realize that the situation with the Mercury Corps was even worse than he had told the Emperor. The intelligence he was getting was at complete odds with what the Emperor had been hearing. In the Fringe Worlds, the corps had been pierced, corrupted, and broken.

It was enough to swear a good Irishman off drink.

CHAPTER SIXTEEN

"... SO THEN WE told this Imperial piece of drakh to put his back taxes where the star don't shine and get the clot out of our county."

The big Tahn woman howled with laughter at Mahoney's story and pounded him on the back.

"Only way to deal with them," she said. She gave a huge beery belch and peered out into the night. "Turn here."

Mahoney did as directed, and soon he was topping a rise. Just before them was the glow of the Tahn communal farm that his companion was headwoman of. Mahoney had met her at a local watering hole. Frehda was a big middle-aged woman who had spent most of her years managing the fortunes of a large Tahn enclave. Over vast quantities of beer, chased by a dozen bottles of his cider, they had become fast friends.

Mahoney had readily accepted her invitation to spend a few days at her enclave "to see how we do things in these parts." She assured him it would be an education. Mahoney had other reasons to believe her; little prickles of rumor and bar talk had led him in this direction.

Even at night the enclave was impressive. As they approached, Mahoney could see many large steel barracks surrounded by what seemed to be a fairly sophisticated security system and nasty razor-wire fencing. As he approached the gated main entrance, the figures of two heavily armed Tahn farmers loomed out.

Frehda shouted a few friendly obscenities at them by way of greeting.

"Who's the fella, boss?" one of them wanted to know.

"Salesman pal," Frehda said. "Good man. Drink anybody 'cept maybe me under the table."

There were chuckles at this. Mahoney gathered that alcohol consumption was just one of many things Frehda was noted for. He had secretly used up nearly half of his ready supply of sobriety pills during the evening to keep even vaguely straight.

"I'll put him up at my place," Frehda went on. "Maybe one of you can give him a look-see around in the ayem."

"Anything in particular you wanna see, mister?" one of the Tahn asked. Mahoney caught an undertone of suspicion. Frehda might be the boss lady, but she was way too drunk for someone to take her at her word on a stranger.

"Got any pigs?" he asked.

" 'Course we got pigs. What do you think we are, sharecroppers?"

Mahoney snorted. "No," he said. "Just that I got a soft spot for pigs. Been studying all my life. I could write volumes on pigs."

"He can talk them, too," Frehda said. "Just about wore my ear out till I got him drunk enough to go on to somethin' else."

The two Tahn guards relaxed. They chuckled among themselves and waved the gravcar through.

Mahoney came awake to blinding sunlight piercing the barred windows of his room, and loud, barked shouts. His head was thumping from last night's excess—he hadn't been able to get away from bending elbows with Frehda for hours.

There were more shouts. They had a peculiar quality to them. Like commands? Giving an automatic snort that burned his delicate nose membranes, Mahoney got out of his cot and started dressing. Let us see, Ian, what we can see.

Mahoney blinked out of Frehda's portion of the barracks. And the first thing he noted surprised even him.

Several men were putting twenty or more teenage Tahn through what seemed to be a very militarylike obstacle course. Ho, ho, Mahoney, me lad. Ho, clotting ho. He wandered over by one of the men and watched the kids go at it. Whenever any of them slowed or got tangled in an obstacle, there were immediate shouts of derision from the adults.

"Whatcha got here, friend?"

The man looked at him. "Oh, you the salesman guy staying with Frehda, right?"

Mahoney snorted an affirmative.

"To answer your question, mister, we're just givin' the kids a little physical training. Whittle off some of the baby fat."

Riiight, Mahoney thought.

"Good idea," Mahoney said. "Kids these days are lazy little devils. Gotta keep the boot up."

He looked over at a coiled barbed-wire fence that a large farm boy was vaulting over.

"What's that contraption?" he asked.

"Oh, that's a hedgehog. About the same size as all the fencing around here."

Mahoney had to grab himself by the throat to keep from reacting in some obvious way. So, you call it a hedgehog, do you, mate? Mahoney *knew* that the man standing next to him was no poor Tahn farmhand. He was a professional soldier sent out by the Tahn military to train young meat for the slaughter to come.

"Must be hell on the britches," Mahoney joked, rubbing an imaginary sore spot on his behind.

The man thought this was pretty funny. "Least you can sew up pants," he said.

Mahoney spent the next two days lazily touring the farm —which was well off even by Imperial settler standards— making casual talk and casual friends and wolfing down the enormous meals the communal farm kitchen shoveled out.

Except for that first obvious soldier he had met and possibly one or two others, everyone seemed to be exactly as he appeared. What he had here were several hundred hard-working Tahn farmers who had gotten tired of the poverty imposed on them by the Imperial majority. So they had pooled their talent and funds to make a life of it.

From some of the stories he heard over the table, their success had not set well with the local gentry and rich Imperial farmers. There had been many attacks, some of them quite nasty.

Mahoney could understand why the farmers had fallen so easily for the infiltrating soldier boys. Now they could protect themselves. Also, from their comments, Mahoney realized that they saw this as only a temporary solution. Sooner or later, unless events intervened, the commune would fall. Mahoney got the idea that the Tahn soldiers were promising an eventual rescue by their empire system. Tahn warships would someday come screaming in over the horizon, and the settlers would all rise up in support of their genetic friends of the cradle.

Mahoney knew from experience that in reality all those kids and their fathers and mothers would be used as a bloody shield for the pros.

Hadn't he done it himself back in his Mantis Section days?

The farmers had given him free rein. He was allowed to go anywhere he wanted—except one place. Every time he had come near it, he had been edged away. About half a klick from the pig creches was a large, fairly modern—for the Fringe Worlds—grain silo. It was prefab, but still, it was an expensive thing to import and then to build.

At first Mahoney expressed interest in it, just to keep up his role. Actually he didn't give a clot.

"Oh, that," his guide had said. "Just a silo. You seen better. Always clottin' up on us one way or the other. You ain't interested in that. Now, let me show you the incubators.

"Bet you never seen so many chicks crackin' shells in your life."

This was not a chick ranch. The birds were used only for local consumption. Therefore, the incubator was far from a machine to delight a tired old farmer's eyes.

So, what was with the silo? Mahoney casually brought it up. And each time he was guided away. Ian, he told himself, it's time you risked your sweet Irish ass.

* * *

He slipped out the last night of his stay, ghosting across the farm past the obstacle run and then the grunts of the pigs. It was easy. He picked up one of the soldiers snoring away in his hidey-hole on the path to the silo. Rotten discipline.

He circled the position, and soon he was inside the silo. A primitive sniffer was the only security, and he quickly bypassed it before he entered.

The silo was suspiciously empty. There were only a few tons of grain. Considering the bulging storage areas spotted about the farm, the space was much needed.

A Mantis rookie could have found the arms cache in a few minutes. Mahoney caught it almost as soon as he peeped his flashbeam around the inside of the structure.

In one corner was a large, busted-down bailer. One doesn't bail grain, and this was hardly the place to put a temporary mechanic's shop. The bailer was a rust bucket, except for the joint of one leg, which was shiny with lubricant. Mahoney gave a couple of test twists and pulls and then had to jump back as a section of the floor hissed aside.

Beneath the bailer was a room nearly the size of the silo floor. Carefully stacked in sealed crates were every kind of weapon that a soldier could need. About half of them were things that no farmer with the kind of training Mahoney guessed these people were getting could use. This stuff was for pros.

He caught the slight sound of a small rodent just behind him and to his left. Rodent? In a modern silo?

Mahoney back-flipped to his right as a hammer blow just grazed the side of his head. He half rolled to his left, then rolled to the right, hearing the chunk of something terribly heavy and sharp smash down.

As he came to his feet, he could sense a large blackness rushing at him. He fingertipped out a tiny bester stun grenade, hurled it, and then dropped to the floor, burying his head in his arms. His shoulders tensed for the blow, and then there was an almost X-ray flash through his hands.

It took Mahoney many shaky seconds to come up again. He woozily tried to figure out what had happened.

The bester grenade produced a time blast that erased very

recent memory and time to come for some hours. As near as Mahoney could figure, he was missing only a few seconds.

He peeped his beam to the dark shape slumped near him. Oh, yes. It was the soldier who had been sleeping on duty. There must be some other alarm system besides the one he had dismantled.

Mahoney found it and disarmed it. He dragged his peacefully snoring opponent out and tucked him back into his bushes where he belonged. Then he rearmed both systems and slid back to his room.

He made loud, cheery good-byes to his new Tahn friends the next day, passing out presents, jokes, and kisses where kisses belonged.

Mahoney gave the snoozing sentry a few extra bottles of cider, and the man beamed broadly at him, clapped him on the back, and told him to be sure to stop by if he was ever in the area again.

The invitation was sincere.

CHAPTER SEVENTEEN

"I COULD TELL you how to solve your Tahn problem," the farmer said, "and we don't need the damned government to do it!"

The farmer was a short man with an expansive waistline and soft hands. His spread was many times larger than the Tahn communal farm Mahoney had recently visited, and from what Ian could gather, the Imperial settler spent his days tapping in figures on his computer or huddled with his bankers.

Mahoney beetled his brows in deep interest. He was seated at the dinner table with the man, his tubby pink-cheeked wife, and their large brood of obnoxious children.

One of the snotty so-and-sos was trying to get his attention, tapping his sleeve with a spoon dripping with gravy.

"A moment, son," Mahoney soothed, "while I hear what your father has to say." Little clot, he thought, I'll wring your bloody neck if you touch me with that thing again.

"Go on," he told the farmer. "This is a subject that concerns all of us."

"Clottin' right," the farmer said. "The Tahn are lower than drakh and bleeding us all."

"Please, dear," his wife admonished. "The children." She turned to Mahoney. "I hope you'll forgive my husband's language."

Mahoney gave an understanding smile. "I've heard worse."

The woman giggled back. "So have I. Still . . . If you had to *live* with these Tahn, you'd understand why my husband becomes so heated. They really are—" She leaned closer to Mahoney to make her point. "*Different*, you know."

"I can imagine," Mahoney said. He settled back with their good after-dinner port to listen to the farmer expand on his subject. It was enough to chill the blood of a tyrant.

Mahoney was absolutely sure what was going to be in his report to the Eternal Emperor. But he had decidedly mixed feelings about it. Like, who were the heroes and who were the villains?

"Yes, please," he said. "Another splash of port would go down just fine."

CHAPTER EIGHTEEN

IMPERIAL FLIGHT SCHOOL, Stage or Phase Two, began in deep space. Sten and the others in his class, now referred to as "mister," regardless of sex or whether they were even human, started with pressurized spitkits—space taxis.

Learn...learn in your guts...which direction to apply force. Understand when to brake. Learn how to calculate a basic orbit from point A to (radar-seen) point B. Then do it again.

Once they were competent, the next step put them in actual ships. More time passed as they learned, still in space, the use of the secondary—Yukawa—drive.

As they grew proficient, the navigational bashing intensified. A ship under AM2 drive, of course, could hardly find its "course" under any but mathematical conditions.

Sten, in spite of his worries about calculating, was getting by. He still needed occasional offshift coaching from Bishop, but things were coming more easily.

One thing that helped, Sten thought, was that he was hardly a raw recruit. During his time in Mantis, he had gone through a great deal of real combat, from mass landings to solo insertions to ship-to-ship combat. There was a large mental file based on personal experience backlog that made it easier for Sten to translate raw numbers into a clotting great asteroid that he would rather not intersect orbits with.

On the other hand, Sten's experience also made it hard for him to keep his mouth shut on occasion.

Phase Two of flight training differed from Phase One in that the IPs seemed as if they wanted all the students to graduate. But it was far from being perfect.

Too much of the tactics was theoretical, taught by IPs who had never flown combat in their lives or who were reservists called back as part of mobilization.

A lot of what was taught, Sten knew from experience, was a great way to suicide. He wondered about the teachings he didn't have a reference point on—were they equally fallacious?

It was a great subject for B.S. But only Bishop and he could really debate the point; with the others it quickly became a great excuse to slander whichever IP was on the "Most Hated" list for the week.

Training progressed. All the students were rated as at least acceptable in deep space.

Then the hard part started: landings, takeoffs, maneuvers on worlds with various atmospheres, weather, and gravitation. Thus far training had washed out only a dozen cadets and killed just three.

But then it got dangerous.

Lotor had one bad habit—and it killed him.

A somewhat talented pilot, he stood above midpoint in the class standings. His failing, Sten learned later, was not uncommon.

Lotor felt that a flight was over and done with when he had his ship within close proximity of its landing situation. Sh'aarl't had told him repeatedly the old cliché that no flight is complete until one is sitting at the bar on one's second round.

Lotor's oversight couldn't be considered very dangerous in a time when antigravity exisited. He probably could have flown privately or even commercially through several lifetimes without problems.

The Empire trained for emergencies, however.

Situation: A combat team was to be inserted on a near-vacuum world. The ground was silicate dust pooled as much as twenty meters deep. Sharp boulders knifed out of the dust bowls.

Requirement: The combat team had to be inserted without discovery; a landing on Yukawa drive would stir up enough dust to produce a huge cloud that would hang for hours and surely give the team away. Also, the ship had to be landed in such a manner as to leave no lasting imprint in the dust.

Solution: Hang the ship vertically about fifty meters above the surface. Cut Yukawa drive and back down on the McLean generators. Hold centimeters above the surface long enough for the mythical combat team to unload, then take off.

The IP gave the situation to Lotor, who analyzed it and found the correct solution.

The two of them were in a Connors-class delta-winged light assault ship. Flight training not only taught emergency situations but, very correctly, sometimes used unsuitable ships. Sten agreed with that—he'd spent enough time in combat to know that when one desperately needed a wrench, sometimes a pair of pliers would have to make do.

But the wide wings were the final nail.

Lotor nosed up and reduced Yukawa drive. The ship dropped a meter or so, and he caught it on the McLean generators. He slowly reduced power, and the ship smoothed toward the dust below.

The trap of an antigravity screen, of course, is that "down" is toward the generator and bears no relationship to where "real" vertical should be.

The ship was three meters high and, to Lotor's senses, descending quite vertically. Close enough, he must have decided, and he slid the generator pots to zero.

The ship dropped a meter, and one wing hit a protruding boulder. The ship toppled.

According to the remote flight recorder, at that moment the IP hit the McLean controls at the same instant that Lotor figured out that something was very wrong.

Lotor kicked in the Yukawa drive. By the time he had power, the ship had already fallen to near horizontal. The blast of power, coupled with the McLean push, pinwheeled the ship.

Cycloning dust hid most of the end. All that the cameras recorded was a possible red blast that would have been produced as the cabin opened like a tin and the ship's atmosphere exploded.

It took most of the planet day for the dust to subside. Rescue crews felt their way in, looking for the bodies. Neither the corpse of Lotor nor the IP was ever recovered.

Sten, Sh'aarl't, and Bishop held their own wake and attempted to sample all the beers that Lotor had not gotten around to trying before his death.

CHAPTER NINETEEN

OTHERS IN THE class were killed, some stupidly, some unavoidably. The survivors learned what Sten already knew: No amount of mourning would revive them. Life—and flight school—goes on.

The barracks at Imperial Flight Training were not as luxurious as the psychologically booby-trapped ones in Phase One. But passes were available, and the pressure was lightened enough for cadets to have some time for consciousness alteration—and for talk.

A favorite topic was What Happens Next. Sten's classmates were fascinated with the topic. Each individual was assuming, of course, that he would successfully get his pilot's wings.

They were especially interested in What Happens Next for Sten. Most of the cadets were either new to the service or rankers—they would be commissioned, on graduation, as either warrant officers or lieutenants. Sten was one of the few who was not only already an officer but a medium-high-ranking one. The topic then became what would the navy do with an ex-army type with rank.

"Our Sten is in trouble," Sh'aarl't opined. "A commander should command at least a destroyer. But a destroyer skipper must be a highly skilled flier. Not a chance for our Sten."

Sten, instead of replying, took one of Sh'aarl't's fangs in hand and used it as a pry top for his next beer.

"It's ambition," Bishop put in. "Captain Sten heard somewhere that admirals get better jobs on retirement than busted-up crunchies, which was all the future he could see. So he switched.

"Too bad, Commander. I can see you now. You'll be the only flight-qualified base nursery officer in the Empire."

Sten blew foam. "Keep talking, you two. I always believe junior officers should have a chance to speak for themselves.

"Just remember . . . on graduation day, I want to see those salutes snap! With all eight legs!"

Sten discovered he had an ability he did not even know existed, although he had come to realize that Ida, the Mantis Section's pilot, must have had a great deal of it. The ability might be described as as mechanical spatial awareness. The same unconscious perceptions that kept Sten from banging into tables as he walked extended to the ships he was learning to fly. Somehow he "felt" where the ship's nose was, and how far to either side the airfoils, if any, extended.

Sten never scraped the sides of an entry port on launch or landing. But there was the day that he learned his new ability had definite limits.

The class had just begun flying heavy assault transports, the huge assemblages that carried the cone-and-capsule launchers used in a planetary attack. Aesthetically, the transport looked like a merchantman with terminal bloats. Sten hated the brute. The situation wasn't improved by the fact that the control room of the ship was buried in the transport's midsection. But Sten hid his dislike and wallowed the barge around obediently.

At the end of the day the students were ordered to dock their ships. The maneuver was very simple: lift the ship on antigrav, reverse the Yukawa drive, and move the transport into its equally monstrous hangar. There were more than adequate rear-vision screens, and a robot followme sat on tracks to mark the center of the hangar.

But somehow Sten lost his bearings—and the Empire lost a hangar.

Very slowly and majestically the transport ground into one hangar wall. Equally majestically, the hangar roof crumpled on top of the ship.

There was no damage to the heavily armored transport. But Sten had to sit for six hours while they cleared the rubble off the ship, listening to a long dissertation from the instructor pilot about his flying abilities. And his fellow trainees made sure it was a very long time before Sten was allowed to forget.

CHAPTER TWENTY

STEN LOVED THE brutal little tacships. He was in the distinct minority.

The tacships, which varied from single- to twenty-man crews were multiple-mission craft, used for short-range scouting, lightning single-strike attacks, ground strikes, and, in the event of a major action, as the fleet's first wave of skirmishers—much the same missions that Sten the soldier was most comfortable with.

That did not logically justify liking them. They were overpowered, highly maneuverable—to the point of being skittish—weapons platforms.

A ship may be designed with many things in mind, but eventually compromises must be made. Since no compromises were made for speed/maneuvering/hitting, that also meant that comfort and armor were nonexistent in a tacship.

Sten loved bringing a ship in-atmosphere, hands and feet dancing on the control as he went from AM2 to Yukawa, bringing the ship out of its howling dive close enough to the surface to experience ground-rush, nap-of-the-earth flying under electronic horizons. He loved being able to hang in space and slowly maneuver in on a hulking battleship without being observed, to touch the LAUNCH button and see the battlewagon "explode" on his screen as the simulator recorded and translated the mock attack into "experience." He delighted in being able to tuck a tacship into almost any shelter, hiding from a flight of searching destroyers.

His classmates thought that while all this was fun, it was also a way to guarantee a very short, if possibly glorious, military career.

"Whyinhell do you think I got into flight school anyway?" Bishop told Sten. "About the third landing I made with the Guard I figured out those bastards were trying to kill me. And I mean the ones on *my* side. You're a slow study, Commander. No wonder they made you a clottin' officer."

Sten, however, may have loved the tacships too well. A few weeks before graduation, he was interviewed by the school's commandant and half a dozen of the senior instructors. Halfway through the interview, Sten got the idea that they were interested in Sten becoming an instructor.

Sten turned green. He wanted a rear echelon job like he wanted a genital transplant. And being an IP was too damned dangerous, between the reservists, the archaic, and the inexperienced. But it did not appear as if Sten would be consulted.

For once Sh'aarl't and Bishop honestly commiserated with Sten instead of harassing him. Being an IP was a fate —not worse than death but pretty similar.

Sten's fears were correct. He had been selected to remain at Flight Training School as an instructor. Orders had even been cut at naval personnel.

But somehow those orders were canceled before they reached Sten. Other, quite specific orders were dictated— from, as the covering fax to the school's commandant said, "highest levels."

The commandant protested—until someone advised him that those "highest levels" were on Prime World itself!

* * *

The biggest difference between the army and the navy, Sten thought, was that the navy was a lot more polite.

Army orders bluntly grabbed a crunchie and told him where to be and what to do and when to do it. Or else.

Naval orders, on the other hand . . .

You, Commander Sten, are requested and ordered, at the pleasure of the Eternal Emperor, to take charge of Tac-Div Y47L, now being commissioned at the Imperial Port of Soward.

You are further requested and ordered to proceed with TacDiv Y47L for duties which shall be assigned to you in and around the Caltor System.

You will report to and serve under Fleet Admiral X. R. van Doorman, 23rd Fleet.

More detailed instructions will be provided you at a later date.

Saved. Saved by the God of Many Names.

Sten paused only long enough to find out that the Caltor System was part of the Fringe Worlds, which would put him very close to the Tahn and where the action would start, before he whooped in joy and went looking for his friends.

He was going to kiss Sh'aarl't.

Hell, he felt good enough to kiss Bishop.

Graduation from Phase Two was very different from the last day in Selection.

The graduates threw the chief IP into the school's fountain. When the school commandant protested mildly, they threw him in as well.

The two elderly officers sat in the armpit-deep purple-dyed water and watched the cavorting around them. Finally the commandant turned to his chief.

"You would think, after all these years, that they could find *something* more original to do than just pitch us here again."

The chief IP was busily wringing out his hat and didn't answer.

Sh'aarl't, Bishop, and Sten bade leaky farewells, vowing to write, to get together once a year, and all the rest of the bushwa service people promise and never do.

Sh'aarl't was still awaiting orders. Bishop's orders were exactly what he wanted—pushing a large, unarmed transport around the sky from one unknown and therefore peaceful system to another.

Sten wondered if he would ever see either of them again.

CHAPTER TWENTY-ONE

THERE WAS NO pomp and there was carefully no ceremony when Lady Atago transferred her command from the battleship *Forez* to the infinitely smaller *Zhenya*.

Admiral Deska had spent a good portion of his military career studying his superior. She despised the frills and displays of military recognition. All that she required was that one do exactly as she indicated without hesitation. She became very thoughtful about any icing upon that requirement.

Despite their size, the *Zhenya* and her sisterships were a major tech miracle for the Tahn. The design and development of the ships would have cost even the Imperial naval R&D staff a good percentage of its budget.

The *Zhenya* was intended for mine warfare of the most sophisticated kind, a type of combat that the Imperial Navy had given little attention.

It had been a very long time since the Empire had fought a war with an equal. Even the brutal Mueller Wars were, ultimately, a limited uprising. Mines were used in positional warfare to deny passage to the enemy or to provide stationary security for one's own positions. They could also be laid to interdict the enemy's own ship lanes. Mines simply hadn't seemed relevant to the navy strategists.

The other reason for the navy's lack of interest in mine warfare was its unromantic nature. A mine was a heavy clunk of metal that just sat there until something made it go bang, generally long after the minelayer had departed. Mine experts didn't wear long white scarves or get many hero medals, even though mines, in space, on land, or in water, were one of the most deadly and cost-efficient ways of destroying the enemy.

The Tahn were less interested in glamour than in any and every method of winning a war. The *Zhenya* was one of the keys to their future.

Sophisticated space mines, of a kind never seen before, could be laid with impossible speed by the *Zhenya*. Each mine was basically an atomic torpedo that was immediately alerted to any ship in its vicinity. A "friendly" ship would be transmitting on its Identification–Friend or Foe com line, and the mine would read the code and ignore that ship. An enemy ship or one not transmitting the current code to the mine would find a very different reaction. The mine—and any other mines within range—would activate and home on the enemy ship. With thousands of mines in any one field, even the most heavily armed Imperial battleship would be doomed.

The Tahn had also solved another problem. Space warfare, even one with established battle lines, was very mobile and its conditions changed rapidly. Retreating or attacking through one's own minefield could be lethal, even if the mine had identified the oncoming ship as friendly. It still was a large chunk of debris to encounter at speed. And if battle conditions changed, the minefield might have to be abandoned—it took a lot of time and caution to sweep a field and then re-lay it.

The *Zhenya* could retrieve and redeploy mines almost as fast as it could lay them. It was an interesting way to be able to create, define, or modify the field that the enemy would be forced to fight on—in theory.

The *Zhenya*-class ships had yet to be proved. In the Tahn's haste to add the ships to their combat fleets, there had been many failures—all ending with the deaths of the entire crew.

Deska was confident that all the problems with the *Zhenya* and her sister ships had been solved, but not so confident that he felt safe risking the Lady Atago's life. He explained this to her, and she listened with seeming interest. She thought for a moment.

"Assemble the crew," she said finally.

Although it was a small crew, gathered together they filled the *Zhenya*'s mess hall. The Lady Atago waited quietly until everyone was available and then began to speak.

"Our task today," she said, "is to prove the worth of the *Zhenya*. On our success, much is dependent. You understand this, do you not?"

No one said a word. The audience barely breathed. But there was a stiffening of attention.

"Previous trials have ended in disappointment," she continued. "This is why I am with you today. If you die, I die. It is therefore required that every one of you perform his individual task to his supreme abilities."

She swept the room with her never changing eyes of absolute zero.

"It goes without saying," she hammered home, "that if there is a failure today, it would be best for any of you not to be among the few survivors."

She dropped her eyes and flicked at a crumb left on the otherwise spotless mess table in front of her. The crew was dismissed.

The drone tacship drove toward the *Zhenya* at full power. Between the robot and the minelayer hung a cluster of the newly developed mines. Lady Atago stood behind the mine control screen, watching closely.

"Report."

"All mines report incoming ship as friendly."

"Change the recognition code."

Sweat beaded one tech's forehead. It was at this point that the accidents had occurred. All too often, when the IFF code was changed, the mine either refused to attack a no-longer-friendly—according to the recognition code— ship or launched on every ship within range, including the minelayer.

This time the control board barely had time to report the change in status and register that the mine was reporting an enemy ship before six mine-missiles launched.

The drone tacship fired back with antiship missiles. Two of the mines were exploded.

The third mine hit the robot and tore out its hull. Less than a second later, a score more were hunting the debris. The rest made note of the kill and returned to station.

"Did the mines show any response to the drone's electronic countermeasures?" Atago asked.

The tech consulted a nearby screen. "Negative. All transmissions from the enemy were ignored once it had been identified."

The Lady Atago turned her attention from the screen to Admiral Deska. She allowed one perfect eyebrow to raise a millimeter.

"You may inform the council, Admiral," she said, "that we will begin full production."

A half hour later the flagship was once again the *Forez*.

Lady Atago went quietly back to her maps and battle plans.

CHAPTER TWENTY-TWO

STEN LANDED ON Cavite, central world of the Caltor System, as a commander without a fleet.

Among the other shortcomings of the tacships was that their tiny supply holds limited their range. Their delicate engines also required far more frequent maintenance intervals than did most Imperial craft. So the four tacships that were to be Sten's command had been berthed in a freighter and now were somewhere between Soward and Cavite.

Sten made the long haul from Prime to Cavite as a liner passenger. He spent the voyage going through pictures, sketches, abstracts, and envelope projections, as besotted with his new assignment as any first lover.

Part of the time he devoted to a quick but thorough study of what was going to be his base planet. Cavite was about two-thirds the size of Prime World and sparsely settled. There was little industry on Cavite—mostly it was an agriculture-based economy, with a little fishing and lumbering. The climate was also similar to Prime—fairly temperate, with a tendency to snow a bit more than on Prime.

The rest of the time Sten pored over details involving his ships. It did not matter that at present his command consisted only of four brand-new Bulkeley-class vessels and himself. He was to man his ship on arrival on Cavite.

Under separate covers, a fax had gone to Admiral Doorman, requesting full cooperation.

Sten had arrived on Soward just before his four ships were "launched." There wasn't a great deal of ceremony— the hull builder had signed the ships over to a secondary yard, a transporter gantry had picked up the ships, complete less armament, electronics, controls, and crew compartment, and had lugged them across the huge plant.

Incomplete as they were, Sten was in love the first time he had seen the sleek alloy needles sitting on their chocks. To him, the entry in the new *Jane's* update fiche was poetry:

6406.795 TACTICAL ASSAULT CRAFT
Construction of a new class of tactical ship by the Empire has been rumored, but as this cannot be confirmed at present, this entry must be considered tentative. Intelligence suggests that these ships are designed to replace and upgrade several current classes now considered obsolescent.
It has been suggested that these ships will bear the generic class of BULKELEY. Development of this class is considered to be under construction, with no information as to the number of ships contracted for, commissioning dates, or deployment dates.
To repeat, All information must be considered quite tentative.

Sten figured that the editor of *Jane's* was practicing the age-old CYA, since the rest of the data was entirely too clotting accurate for his comfort:

* * *

CHARACTERISTICS:
TYPE: Fleet patrol craft
LENGTH: 90 meters est. (actually 97 meters)
D: Approx. 1400 fl.
CREW: Unknown
ARMAMENT: Unknown, but theorized to be far heavier than
any other ships in this category.

The rest of the entry was a long string of unknowns. Sten
could have filled in the details.

Each ship carried a crew of twelve: three officers—CO,
weapons/XO, engineering—and nine enlisted men.

And they *were* heavily armed.

For close-in fighting, there were two chainguns.
Medium-range combat would be handled by eight launchers
firing Goblin VI missiles, now upgraded with better
"brains" and a 10-kt capacity. There were three Goblins for
each launcher.

For defense there was a limited countermissile capability—five Fox-class missiles—but a very elaborate electronic countermeasure suite.

Bulkeley ships were intended either to sneak in unnoticed or to cut and run if hit. But the Bulkeley class craft
were designed as ship killers.

Main armament was the Kali—a heavy, 60-megaton missile that was almost twenty meters long. Packed inside the
missile's bulbous skin was a computer nearly as smart as a
ship's and an exotic ECM setup. The missile was launched
in a tube that extended down the ship's axis. Three backup
missiles were racked around the launch tube.

Crew space, given all this artillery and the monstrous
engines, was laughable. The captain's cabin was about the
size of a wall closet, with pull-down desk and bunk. It was
the most private compartment on the ship, actually having a
draw curtain to separate the CO from the rest of the men.
The other two officers bunked together, in a cabin exactly
the size of the captain's. The crew bunks were ranked on
either side of the ship's largest compartment, which doubled as rec room, mess hall, and kitchen.

The only cat that could have been swung inside the ship would have been a Manx—a Manx kitten.

Big deal. If Sten had wanted luxury, he would have opted for Bishop's plan and flown BUCs.

CHAPTER TWENTY-THREE

STANDARD OBSCENITY PROCEDURE: When an officer arrives at his new duty station, he reports to his new commanding officer.

In the Guard this had meant that one was to show up at the unit's orderly room in semidress uniform. Officer and his new fearless leader would size each other up; the newcomer would be given his new responsibilities and whatever trick tips the old man chose to pass on and set in motion.

The navy, Sten had learned, was slightly more formal.

The "invitation" to meet Admiral van Doorman had been hand delivered. And was printed. On real paper. That, Sten figured, meant full-dress uniform. Whites. Gloves. Clot, even a haircut.

By scurrying and bribing, Sten had gotten the batman assigned to his temporary bachelor officer's quarters to electrostat-press his uniform and borrow or steal a pair of white gloves from someone. The haircut was easy, since Sten kept his hair about two centimeters from shaven.

The card requested the pleasure of his company at 1400 hours. Sten gave himself an extra hour for the civilian grav-car to wind through the packed streets of Cavite City. Even then, he arrived at the main entrance to the naval base with only twenty minutes to spare.

His mouth dropped when the sentry at the gate checked only Sten's ID, then in a bored manner waved the gravcar forward.

Nice, Sten thought. Here we are on the edge of everything, and the taxi drivers can go anywhere they want. Great security.

He paid the driver at dockside, got out, and then goggled.

The flagship of 23rd Fleet was the Imperial Cruiser *Swampscott*. Sten had looked the ship up and found out that it had been built nearly seventy-five years previously; it was periodically upgraded instead of being scrapped. The description gave no inkling of just how awesome the *Swampscott* had become—awesome in the sense of atrocious.

The cruiser evidently had been built to the then limits of hull design, power, and armament. Upgrading had started by cutting the ship in half and adding another 500 meters to the midsection. The next stage had added bulges to the hull.

After that, the redesigners must have been desperate to meet the additions, since the *Swampscott* could now be described as a chubby cruiser that had run, very hard, into a solid object without destruction.

As a grand finale, there were twin structures atop the hull, structures that would be familiar to any Chinese Emperor of the T'ang Dynasty of ancient Earth.

Since the *Swampscott* had never fought a war, these excrescences did not matter. The ship, polished until it glowed, was used for ceremonial show-the-flag visits. It would settle down in-atmosphere in as stately a manner as any dowager queen going down steps in a ball gown. If a planetary assault had ever been required, the *Swampscott* would either have spun out of control or wallowed uncontrollably. In a wind tunnel, a model of the *Swampscott* might have been described as having all the aerodynamics of a chandelier.

Sten recovered, checked the time, and hurried into the lift tube.

Exiting, he saw not one but four full-dress sentries and one very bored, but very full-dressed, officer of the deck.

He saluted the nonexistent and unseen "colors"—toward the stern—and the OOD, then gave the lieutenant a copy of the invitation and his ID card.

"Oh, Lord," the lieutenant said. "Commander, you made a real mistake."

"Oh?"

"Yessir. Admiral Doorman's headquarters are downtown."

Downtown? What was that navalese for? "Isn't this the flagship?"

"Yessir. But Admiral Doorman prefers the Carlton Hotel. He says it gives him more room to think."

Sten and the lieutenant looked at each other.

"Sir, you're going to be very late. Let me get a gravsled out. Admiral Doorman's most insistent about punctuality."

This was a great way to start a new assignment, Sten thought.

Admiral Doorman may have insisted on punctuality, but it applied only to his subordinates.

Sten had arrived at the hotel in a sweaty panic, nearly twenty minutes late. He had been escorted to the lower of Doorman's three hotel suites, reported to the snotty flag secretary at the desk, and been told to sit down.

And he waited.

He was not bored, however. Awful amazement would have been a better description of Sten's emotional state as he eavesdropped on the various conversations as officers came and went in the huge antechamber:

"Of course I'll try to explain to the admiral that anodizing takes a great deal of work to remove. But you know how he loves the shine of brass," a fat staff officer said to a worried ship captain.

"Fine. We have a deal. You give me J'rak for the boxing, and I'll let you have my drum and bugle team." The conversation was between two commanders.

"I do not care about that exercise, Lieutenant. You've already exceeded your training missile allocation for this quarter."

"But sir, half my crew's brand-new, and I—"

"Lieutenant, I learned to follow orders. Isn't it time you learn the same?"

Real amazement came as two people spilled out of a lift tube. They were just beautiful.

The ship captain was young, dashing, tall, handsome, and blond-haired. His undress whites gloved his statuesque body and molded his muscles.

His companion, equally blond, wore game shorts.

They were laughing, enjoying the free life.

Sten hated their guts on sight.

Chattering away, the two sauntered past Sten, down a corridor. The woman suddenly made some excuse, stopped, put her foot upon a chair arm, and adjusted the fastener on her sports shoe. And her eyes very calmly itemized Sten. Then she laughed, took her companion's arm, and disappeared. She had a figure that made it nearly impossible not to stare after. So Sten stared.

"That's definitely off limits, Commander," the flag secretary said.

Not that he cared, but Sten raised a questioning eyebrow.

"The lady is the admiral's daughter."

Sten wanted to say something sarcastic, but he was saved by the buzzing of the annunciator. He was escorted into the admiral's office.

The term "office" was a considerable understatement. The only chambers that Sten had seen more palatial were some of the ceremonial rooms in the Imperial palace. Always the cynic, he wondered if the suite had been furnished with Doorman's private funds or if he had fiddled something.

Fleet Admiral Xavier Rijn van Doorman was equally spectacular. This was a man whose very presence, from his white coiffed mane to his unwavering eyes to his firm chin to his impressive chest, shouted command leadership. This was a leader men would follow into the very gates of hell. After ten minutes of conversation, Sten had a fairly decent idea that was where most of them would end up.

It could have been said about van Doorman, as it had

been about another officer centuries earlier, that he never allowed an original thought to ruin his day.

But still, he was the very image of a leader: fit to address any parliament, soothe any worried politician, address any banquet, or show any banner—and totally incompetent to command a fleet that Sten knew might be only days from being the first line of defense in a war.

Van Doorman was a very polite man, and very skilled in the minefields of social inquisition. He must have scanned Sten's fiche before Sten had entered the room. Certainly he was most curious about Sten's previous assignment—at the Imperial palace itself, as CO of the Emperor's Gurkha bodyguard.

Van Doorman was proud that he had managed to attend several Empire Days and had once been presented to the Emperor himself as part of a mass awards ceremony.

"I'm sure, Commander," Doorman said, "that you'll be able to bring us up to speed on the new social niceties. The Fringe Worlds are somewhat behind the times."

"Sir, I'll try . . . but I didn't spend much time at ceremonial functions."

"Ah, well. I'm sure my wife and daughter will help you realize you know more than you think."

Clotting great. I am gong to have to be polite to the whole family.

"You'll find that duty out here is most interesting, Commander. Because of the climate, and the fact that all of us are so desperately far from home, we make allowances in the duty schedule."

"Sir?"

"You will find that most of your duties can be accomplished in the first watches. Since I don't want my officers finding this station boring—and boredom does create work for idle hands—I make sure that qualified officers are available for those necessary diplomatic functions."

"I'm not sure I understand."

"Oh, there are balls . . . appearances on some of the minor worlds . . . we have our own sports teams that compete most successfully against the best our settlers can field. I also believe that all duty makes Jack a very dull officer. I approve of my officers taking long leaves—some of the native creatures are excellent for the hunt. We provide local support for anyone interested in these pursuits."

"Uh . . . sir, since I've got brand-new ships, where am I going to find the time for those kinds of things?"

"I've received a request to provide as complete cooperation as possible to you. That goes without saying. I'll ensure that you have a few competent chiefs who'll keep everything Bristol fashion."

Sten, at this point, should have expressed gratitude and agreement. But as always, his mouth followed its own discipline.

"Thank you, sir. But I'll still have to pass. I'm afraid I'll be too busy with the boats."

Seeing van Doorman's expression ice up, Sten cursed himself.

Doorman picked up a fiche and dropped it into a viewer. "Yes. The boats. I'll be quite frank, Commander. I have always been opposed to the theory of tactical ships."

"Sir?"

"For a number of reasons. First, they are very costly to run. Second, it requires a very skilled officer and crew to operate them. These two conditions mean that men who should be serving on larger ships volunteer for these speedcraft. This is unfair to commanders of possibly less romantic craft, because men who should become mates and chiefs remain as ordinaries. It is also unfair to these volunteers, since they will not receive proper attention or promotion. Also, there is the issue of safety. There is no way I can be convinced that service on one of your, umm, mosquito boats could be as safe as a tour on the *Swampscott*."

"I didn't know we joined the service to be safe and comfortable, sir." Sten was angry.

And so, even though it showed only as a slight reddening around his distinguished temples, was van Doorman. "We differ, Commander." He stood. "Thank you for taking the time to see me, Commander Sten. I've found this conversation most interesting."

Interesting? Conversation? Sten got up and came to attention. "A question, sir?"

"Certainly, young man." Doorman's tone was solid ice.

"How will I go about crewing my ships, sir? I assume you have some SOP I should follow?"

"Thank you. All too many of you younger men lack an understanding of the social lubrication.

"You'll be permitted to advertise your needs in the fleet bulletin. Any officer or enlisted man who chooses to volunteer will be permitted—after concurrence from his division head and commanding officer, of course."

Clot. Clot. Clot.

Sten saluted, did a perfect about-face, and went out.

Van Doorman's last, when translated, meant that Sten could recruit his little heart out. But what officer in his right mind would allow a competent underling to volunteer for the boats?

Sten knew he'd get the unfit, the troublemakers, and the square pegs. He desperately hoped that the 23rd Fleet had a whole lot of them.

CHAPTER TWENTY-FOUR

SPACE IS NOT BLACK. Nor can spaceships creep along. Nevertheless, that was what Commander Lavonne visualized his ship, the Imperial Destroyer *San Jacinto*, doing as it moved into the Erebus System.

He was a spy, slithering slowly through the night.

The DesRon commander had detailed the *San Jacinto* for this mission. The navy prided itself on never volunteering for, but never rejecting, a mission, no matter how absurd or suicidal.

Officially, the assignment was not that out of the ordinary. Imperial destroyers were designed for scouting capabilities.

But only under wartime conditions. And not when, according to every bit of club poop that Lavonne had heard, every single specially designed spy ship that had entered the Tahn sectors disappeared tracelessly.

Orders, however, are orders.

Lavonne had spent some time planning his tactics before he plotted a course. This included shutting down every possible machine that could possibly be picked up by an enemy sensor—from air conditioning to the caffmachines in the mess. He theorized that the spy ships had been discovered because their course had originated from Imperial or Fringe worlds. So he'd selected a course that first sent the *San Jacinto* toward an arm of the Tahn Empire. The course then moved from the second point of origin farther into solidly Tahn-controlled clusters. His third course sent the destroyer back "out," closing with the Erebus System he had been directed to recon.

On a galactic and null-time scope, the *San Jacinto*'s course could be plotted as a hesitation forward.

For short periods of time the ship would enter AM2 drive. Then it would drop out and hold in place. During that holding, every normal sensor, plus the specially installed systems provided, was used to see if the *San Jacinto* might have been detected.

Lavonne knew that Imperial sensors were superior to anything the Tahn had. Since no Tahn ship had been detected by his screens, he felt he was still hidden in the shadows.

The *San Jacinto* hesitated toward the dying sun of Erebus.

And he found what he was looking for.

Input flooded. The system was a huge building yard and harbor. There were more Tahn ships in this one sector than intelligence estimates provided for the entire Tahn Empire.

Lavonne, at this point, should have closed down the sensors and scooted. He had far more data than any other infiltrating Imperial ship had gotten. Possibly, if he had fled, his ship could have survived.

Instead, Lavonne, hypnotized by what he was seeing, crept onward. After all, Imperial forces had a secret—AM2, the single power source for stardrive, provided only by the Empire, was modified before being sold to other systems. On the *San Jacinto*'s screens, Lavonne knew, any Tahn ship's drive would show purple.

Lavonne did not know that certain Tahn ships had their drive baffled. The power loss was more than compensated for by their indetectability.

So when the screens went red and every alarm went off, the *San Jacinto* was far too close.

Lavonne slammed into the control room as the GQ siren howled and read the situation instantly: To their "right" flank, a minefield had been detected; ahead lay the central Erebus worlds; and coming in from the "left," at full drive, was a Tahn battleship, schooled by cruisers and destroyers.

At full power, Lavonne spun the *San Jacinto* into a new orbit. Their only chance was flight—and Lavonne's canniness. The emergency escape pattern led not out of the Erebus System toward the Fringe Worlds but rather toward the center of the Tahn Empire. Once he lost his pursuers, he could reset his course toward home.

Lavonne had a few minutes of hope—a new Imperial destroyer such as the *San Jacinto* should be able to outdistance any battleship or cruiser. The worst that Lavonne should face would be the Tahn destroyers.

Those few minutes ended as an analyst reported in properly flat tones that the battleship was outdistancing its own escorts and closing on the *San Jacinto*. Within five hours and some minutes, he continued, the battleship, of a previously unknown type, would be within combat range of the *San Jacinto*.

The battleship was the *Forez*. Admiral Deska paced the control room as his huge ship closed on the destroyer. He, too, was computing a time sequence.

Could the *Forez* come within range of the Imperial destroyer before it could conceivably escape?

If the Imperial spy ship survived, all of the elaborate Tahn plans, from improved ship design to construction to obvious strategy, would be blown.

He considered the ticking clock. There would be no problems. The Imperial ship was doomed.

At four hours and forty minutes, Commander Lavonne realized the inevitable.

There was one possible chance.

Lavonne ordered the ship out of AM2 drive, hoping that the Tahn battleship would sweep past. Their response was instantaneous.

Very weil, then. Lavonne sent his ship directly at the *Forez*.

Sometimes the lapdog can take on the mastiff.

Lavonne ordered flares and secondary armaments fired at will. He hoped that the explosions, and whatever clutter his ECM apparatus could provide, might be some kind of smoke screen.

Lavonne knew that the *San Jacinto* was doomed. All he could hope was that his ship might inflict some damage on the huge Tahn battlewagon now filling the missile station's sights.

He was only light-seconds from coming into range when the *Forez* launched its main battery.

Six Tahn missiles intersected with the *San Jacinto*'s orbit as Lavonne's finger hovered over the red firing key.

And there was nothing remaining of the *San Jacinto* except a widening sextuplicate bubble of gas and radioactivity.

BOOK TWO

LET ALL DRAW

CHAPTER TWENTY-FIVE

THROUGHOUT THEIR HISTORY, the Tahn were always a bloody accident waiting to happen to anyone unfortunate enough to pass their way. It was a civilization born in disaster and nurtured by many battles.

Even the Eternal Emperor could barely remember the feud that had started it all. The origins of the Tahn lay in a huge civil war occurring in a cluster far from their present homelands. Two mighty forces lined up on opposing sides and went at it for a century and a half. The cluster in question was so peripheral to the Emperor that it was more than convenient for him to ignore the whole thing and let them settle it themselves.

Eventually, the people who were to become the Tahn suffered a final crushing defeat. The winners gave the survivors two choices: genocide or mass migration. The Tahn chose flight, an episode in their history that they never forgot. Cowardice, then, became their race's original sin. It was the first and last time the Tahn ever chose life over even certain death.

Almost the entire first wave of the massive migration was composed of warriors and their families. This made the Tahn a group of people unwelcome in any settled society they approached. No one was foolish enough to invite them to share his hearth. This was another factor in the Tahn racial memory. They considered themselves permanent outcasts, and from then on they would treat any stranger in kind.

The area they finally settled was one of the most unwanted sectors of the Empire. The Tahn put down roots in a desolate pocket surrounded by slightly richer neighbors and began to create their single-purpose society. Since it was military-based, it was no wonder that it was so sharply stratified: from the peasant class to the ruling military council was as distant as the farthest sun.

The greatest weakness of the Tahn, however, became their greatest strength. They prospered and expanded. Their neighbors became edgy as the Tahn neared the various borders. Most of them tried to negotiate. In each case, the Tahn used negotiation only as a tool to gain time. Then they would attack with no warning. They would throw their entire effort into the fray, ignoring casualties that would have given pause to almost any other being.

The Tahn fought continually for over three hundred years. In the end they had eliminated their neighbors and carved out an empire. It was no matter that they had lost nearly eighty percent of their population in doing so. They had rebuilt before, and they could do it again.

The Eternal Emperor was now facing a revitalized Tahn Empire many many times its original size. The explosive growth had created a host of problems for the Tahn: there were more dissidents than ever before, and frequent and bloody ousters from the Tahn High Council were increasingly common.

Unwittingly, the Emperor had solved this for them. The Tahn were once again united in purpose and in their bitter world view.

CHAPTER TWENTY-SIX

A FEW WEEKS later, Sten was no longer a commander without a fleet. His four Imperial tacships, the *Claggett, Gamble, Kelly,* and *Richards*, had been off-loaded and lifted into temporary fitting-out slips in the huge Cavite naval yard.

But he remained a commander without a crew. The aftermath of the interview with Admiral van Doorman had produced exactly what Sten anticipated—zero qualified volunteers showed up.

But the 23rd Fleet *did* have its share of malcontents and such. After twenty interviews, Sten thought of the punch line from a long-forgotten joke of Alex's: "Great Empire, not *that* shaggy."

If Sten had been put in command of a destroyer, he might have been able to fit those applicant-losers into ship's divisions without problems. But not with four twelveman ships plus a skeleton maintenance staff.

Time was running short. On three occasions he'd had a "friendly" visit from one of van Doorman's aides.

The man had sympathized with Sten over his problems and had promised he would do everything possible to keep things from van Doorman's attention—just a favor from one officer to another. Sten surmised that the aide couldn't get his gravcar back to van Doorman quickly enough to report how deep in drakh this young misfit was.

Or maybe Sten was getting paranoid. It was quite conceivable—all his time was spent on the tacships. When he remembered to eat, he opened a pack of something or other, heated it, and ate absentmindedly, his mind and fingers tracing circuitry, hydraulics, and plumbing across the ships' blueprint fiches.

This particular day he had climbed out of the greasy boiler suit he had been living in, pulled on a semidress uniform, and set out to do war with the 23rd Fleet's logistics division.

Every military has a table of organizations and equipment giving exactly how many people of what rank are authorized in each command and what items of equipment, from battleships to forks, are also allowable. The organization with too many or too much can get gigged just as badly as one that's short of gear.

Sten had found out that the 23rd Log authorized one day's basic load for ammunition and missiles—that being the amount of firepower a ship, in combat, would use up at maximum. Resupply in time of war for Sten's tacships would mean breaking off their patrol routine and returning to Cavite's enormous supply dumps.

Sten had tried to reason with the officer, starting with the logical point that the aborting of patrols when the weapons ran dry was hardly efficient and ending with the possibly illogical point that maybe, in time of war, those supply dumps might just get themselves bombed flat.

The officer didn't want to hear about patrol problems, shook his head in irritation at the mere mention of possible hostilities, and laughed aloud at the idea that Cavite couldn't destroy any attacker long before it had time to launch.

It was shaping up to be one of those days.

Sten set his sled down outside the security fence surrounding the fitting-out slips and absently returned the sentry's salute at the gate.

"Afternoon, Commander." The sentry liked Sten. He and his fellow guards had a private pool as to when van Doorman would relieve the commander and send him back to Prime for reassignment. It would be a pity, but on the other hand, the sentry's guess was only a couple of days away, and drink money was far more important than the fate of any officer.

"Afternoon."

"Sir, your weapons officer is already onboard."

Sten was in motion. "Troop, I want the guard out. Now."

"But—"

"Move, boy. I don't *have* a weapons officer!"

The guard thumbed the silent alarm, and within moments there were five sentries around Sten, nervously fingering their loaded willyguns.

Sten took out the miniwillygun he always carried in the small of his back and started for the *Claggett*, the only ship with an entry port yawning.

A saboteur? Spy? Or just a nosy Parker? It didn't matter. Sten put his six men on either side of the port and went silently up the ladder.

He stopped, listening, just at the mouth of the ship's tiny lock. There were clatters, thumps, and mutters sounding from forward. Sten was about to wave the guards up after him when the mutter became distinguishable:

"C'mon, y' wee clottin' beastie. Dinnae be tellin't me Ah cannae launch twa a' once."

Sten stuck his head out the port. "Sorry, gentlemen. I screwed up. I guess I do have a weapons officer. I'll file a correction with the OOD."

The puzzled sentries saluted, shrugged, and walked away.

Sten went forward.

"Mr. Kilgour!" he snapped at the hatch into the control room, and had the pleasure of seeing a head bang in surprise into a computer screen. "Don't you know how to report properly?"

Warrant Officer Alex Kilgour looked aggrieved, rubbing his forehead. "Lad, Ah figured y'd be off playin't polo wi y'r admiral."

Alex Kilgour was a stocky heavy-worlder from the planet of Edinburgh. He'd been Sten's team sergeant in Mantis Section, and then Sten had gotten him reassigned to the palace when Sten commanded the guard. Kilgour had made the mistake of falling in love and applying for a marriage certificate, and the Emperor had shipped him off to flight school months ahead of Sten, also commissioning him in warrant ranks.

Sten had no idea how or why Kilgour was on Cavite—but he was very clotting glad to see him, regardless.

"It wasn't much of a task t' be assigned to y'r squadron, young Sten," Kilgour explained over two mugs of caff in the closet that passed for the *Claggett's* wardroom.

"First, Ah kept tabs, knowin't y'd be runnin' into braw problems y' c'd no handle. Then a word here, a charmin't smile there, an' whiff, Kilgour's on his way. But enow a' young love. Clottin' brief me, Commander. Where's th' bonny crew?"

Sten ran through the problems. Alex heard him out, then patted Sten's shoulder in sympathy, driving the deck plates down a few centimeters.

"Noo y' can relax, wi Kilgour here. Y'r problem, son, is y' dinnae be lookin't for volunteers in the right places."

"Like hell! I've been recruiting everyplace but the cemeteries."

"It'll no get s' bad we'll hae to assign the livin't dead, Commander. You hae nae worries now. Just trust me."

CHAPTER TWENTY-SEVEN

"DINNAE THEY BE a fine bunch," Kilgour said proudly.

Sten looked askance at the thirty-odd beings glowering at him, then behind him at the firmly sealed portals of the prison. "How many murderers?"

"Nae one. Twa manslaughters wa' the best Ah could do. Th' rest—"

Sten cut Kilgour off. He would have time later to agonize over the fiches. Suddenly the prisoners in front of him appeared as—at least potentially—shining examples of sailorly virtue. The problem was that Sten, never adept at inspiring speeches, was trying to figure out what to say to these beings to convince them that they did not want to remain in the 23rd Fleet's safe, sane stockade.

Alex leaned closer to him to whisper. "Ah could warm 'em up, if ya like, lad. Tell 'em a joke or three."

"No jokes," Sten said firmly.

Alex's response was immediate gloom.

"No even the one about the spotted snakes? Tha's perfect for a braw crew such as this."

"You will *especially* avoid the one about the spotted snakes. Kilgour, there are laws about cruel and unusual punishment. And if you even dream spotted snakes, I'll have you keelhauled."

Still glaring, Sten turned his attention to the task at hand. The glare must have had a great deal of heat behind it, because the men instantly stopped their shuffling and shifting.

Oh, well. At least he had their attention. Now all he had to do was some fancy convincing. Basic speechmaking—always talk to a crowd as if it were one person and choose one being in that crowd to address directly.

Sten picked out one man who looked a little less dirty, battered, and shifty than the others and walked up to him.

"My name's Sten. I'm commissioning four tacships. And I need a crew."

"Y' comin' here, you're scrapin' the bottom," another prisoner said.

"Sir."

The prisoner spat on the ground. Sten stared at him. The man's eyes turned away. "Sir," he grunted reluctantly.

"No offense, sir." That was the prisoner whom Sten had picked as the centerpiece. "But what's in it for us?"

"You're out. Your records'll get reviewed. I can wipe your charge sheets if I want. If you work out."

"What 'bout rank?" yet another prisoner asked.

"You qualify for a stripe, you'll get it."

"What'll we be doing?"

"Running patrols. Out there."

"Toward the Tahn?"

"As close as we can get."

"Sounds like a clottin' great way to get dead."

"It is that," Sten agreed. "Plus the quarters'll make your cells here look like mansions, the food would gag a garbage worm, and my officers'll be all over you like a dirty shipsuit. Oh, yeah. You'll be lucky to get liberty once a cycle. And if you do, it'll probably be on some planetoid where the biggest thing going is watching metal oxidize."

"Doesn't sound like there's much in it."

"Sure doesn't, sir." This was a fourth prisoner. "Can I ask you something? Personal?"

"GA."

"Why are *you* doin' it? Tacship people are all volunteers. You lookin' for some kind of medal?"

"Clot medals," Sten said honestly. Then he thought

about what he was going to say. "You could probably get my ass in a sling if you told anybody this—but I think that we're getting real close to a clottin' war."

"With the Tahn." Sten's target nodded.

"Uh huh. And I'd a lot rather be out there moving around when it happens than sitting on my butt here on Cavite. Or, come to think about it, sitting here in this pen."

"I still think any of us'd be clottin' fools to volunteer."

"Just what I'm looking for. Clotting fool volunteers. I'll be in the head screw's—sorry, warden's—office until 1600 if any of you feel foolish."

To his astonishment, Sten got seventeen volunteers. He never realized that the final convincement was his slip of the tongue—only somebody who had been a jailbird or on the wrong side of the law would call the warden a screw.

CHAPTER TWENTY-EIGHT

"HOW MANY GENERATIONS has your family been warriors, Lieutenant Sekka?" Sten asked with some incredulity.

"For at least two hundred," the man across from him said. "But that was after the Sonko clan emigrated from Earth. Before that, we Mandingos, at least according to legend, had been fighting men for another hundred generations. That's not to say that all of us have been just warriors. We have been military scholars, diplomats, politicians . . . there was even one of us who was an actor. We do not often discuss him, even though he was reputedly excellent." Sekka laughed. His baritone chortle was just as pleasing to the ear as the man's perfect voice.

Sten looked again at Sekka's fiche. It looked very good —there were just enough reprimands and cautions from superior officers to match the letters of merit and decorations.

"You like taking chances, don't you?"

"Not at all," Sekka said. "Any course of action should be calculated, and if the potential for disaster is less than that for success, the choice is obvious."

Sten put the fiche back in its envelope and shoved a hand across the tiny folding desk. "Lieutenant, welcome the hell aboard. You'll skipper the *Kelly*. Second ship on the left."

Sekka came to attention, almost cracking his skull on the overhead. "Thank you, sir. Two questions. Who are my other officers?"

"None, yet. You're the first one I've signed up."

"Mmm. Crew?"

"You have four yardbirds and one eager innocent. Assign them as you wish."

"Yessir."

"Lieutenant Sekka? I have a question. How'd you hear about this posting?"

Sekka lifted an eyebrow. "Why from the admiral's note in the current fleet proceedings, sir."

Sten covered. "Right. Not thinking. Thank you, Lieutenant. That's all. On your way out, would you ask Mr. Kilgour if he would report to me at his convenience?"

"Kilgour. You didn't."

"Ah did."

"How?"

"The typsettin' plant th' shitepokes who run tha' lyin't publication hae na in th' way ae security."

"So you blueboxed into it, and phonied the admiral's own column?"

"Is tha' nae aye harsh way t' put it?"

Alex, ever since his scam back on Hawkthorne and later with the prisoners, fancied himself quite the recruiter.

Sten changed the subject. "Is there any way he could trace who did it?"

"Trace me, lad? Th' man wha' solved a conspiracy again' our own Emperor?"

Sten put his head in his hands. "Mr. Kilgour. I know the navy is dry. But would there, by some odd chance . . ."

"By an odd chance, there is. Ah'll fetch the flask."

CHAPTER TWENTY-NINE

ALEX LIKED SOME rain, like the nearly constant gray drizzle of his home world. But the tropical buckets that came down on Cavite tried his patience sorely. He counted unmarked alcoves down the narrow alleyway, found the correct one, and tapped on the barred door. From the inside his tapping probably sounded like a sledgehammer warming up.

"What is the word?" a synth-voice whispered.

"It's aye wet oot here, an Ah am lackit th' patience," Alex complained. Not particularly angry, he stepped back and rammed a metal-shod bootheel intó the door.

The door split in half, and Alex pulled the two halves out of his way and entered.

He had time to notice that the inside of the brothel was quite nice, if one fancied red velvet and dark paintings, before the first guard came down the corridor at him. Alex batted him into the wall with one of the door halves. His mate came dashing toward Alex, was picked up, and went back up the corridor, in the air, somewhat faster than he had come down.

"Ah'm looki't for a Mister Willie Sutton," he announced.

"Do you have a warrant?" the synth-voice asked.

"No."

"Are you armed?"

"What kind of ae clot y' thinkit Ah am? A course."

"Please keep your hands in plain sight. There are sensors covering you. Any electronic emission which is detected will be responded to. You will be constantly in the field of fire from automatically triggered weapons. Any hostile act will be responded to before you could complete such an action."

Alex sort of wanted to test his reflexes against the robot guns, but he was trying to be peaceful.

"You will continue down to the end of the corridor, past the entrance to the establishment proper. At the end of the corridor, you will find stairs. Continue up them, and then down the hall to the second door. Enter that room and wait, while we determine whether a Willie Sutton is known to anyone on the premises."

Alex followed instructions. As he walked past, he looked into the whorehouse's reception area, fell in love twice, smiled politely at those two women, but continued on.

Kilgour was on duty.

The room was more red velvet and more elderly paintings, dimly lit by glass-beaded lamps. The furniture was unusual, consisting of three or four wide, heavily braced hassocks. Kilgour stood with his back close to one wall and waited.

The door on the other side of the room opened.

"Would my thoughts be correct in assuming you are interested in applying for work as my bodyguard?"

"Willie Sutton" waddled into the room. It was a spindar, a large—two meters, choose any direction—scaled creature that looked like an oversize scaly pangolin with extra arms. Since spindars' own names were not pronounceable by the *Homo sapien* tongue, they generally took on a human name, a name prominent in whatever field the spindar chose to excel in.

Kilgour had no idea who Willie Sutton had been, but he was fairly sure that the human had not been a philanthropist.

"Warrant Officer Alex Kilgour," he identified himself, not answering the question.

"You, then, are a deserter, as I am?"

"Na, Chief Sutton. But Ah hae consider't it."

"You are not from the military police. Certainly not,

from your grimace. How might my establishment and myself be of service to you? I am assuming, for the sake of argument, that you mean me no harm."

"We want you to come back."

The spindar chuffed and sat back on its tail. "To the fleet? Hardly likely. During the years I served, I experienced enough courts-martial to find the experience irritatingly redundant."

Sutton was telling the truth. There probably had been no supply specialist in the Imperial Navy who had been tried so many times, almost always on the same offense: misappropriation of imperial supplies and equipment.

There also probably had been no supply specialist who had been promoted back up from the ranks so many times, again almost always for the same accomplishment: Due to the outstanding performance and support of (insert rank at time) Sutton, (insert unit or ship name) accomplished its mission well within the assigned limits in an exemplary fashion.

"We need a thief," Kilgour said.

The spindar chuffed twice more. Alex explained the problems that he and Sten faced.

The spindar, thinking, extruded claws from a forearm and raked part of the carpet beside him into shreds. Alex noted that the carpet was torn up in other parts of the room.

"What about the present charges that, shall we say, made it desirable for me to absent myself from my last duty station?"

Kilgour took two fiches from inside his shirt and handed them to Sutton. "Tha first's y'r real service record. Tha original. Consider tha a present."

The spindar scratched himself.

"Tha second's a new record, which, dinnae wish t' be't braggin't, Ah helped create. Couldnae be cleaner. You report back, and Ah'll hae tha in th' records in minutes."

"An entirely fresh beginning," the spindar marveled.

"M'boss say't there's a slight condition. If y' thinkit y' could be worryin't th' same scam on us, bad things c'd happen. About those, Ah'll say nae more."

"The mechanics of pandering and prostitution," the spindar said, almost to himself, "have become most predictable. You humans have such a limited sexual imagination. Return to duty." He chuffed. "What a peculiar proposition." Chuff. "Tell your commander I shall provide an answer by this hour tomorrow."

CHAPTER THIRTY

STEN LOLLED BACK in his chair. His feet were stretched out lazily, crossed at the ankles, measuring the width of his desk. Inside he was tense, coiled, waiting for the hammer to fall. Outside he was doing his best to appear to be the cool, uninvolved navy commanding officer.

Personally, Sten thought he probably looked like a damned fool. All he needed right now was a knock of urgency on his door to spoil the entire persona.

The door *was* knocked upon. The raps were urgent; equally urgently, the door slammed open. Sten nearly compacted his knees getting his feet off the desk. Wildly, he thought for an instant which face he should present—bored CO indifference or calm CO concern. There was no stop-action camera there, or time to show the twists in his face as Alex and the spindar, Sutton, burst in.

"What seems to be the—" Sten started.

"Sir!" Sutton blurted. "We've been taken!"

Sten reflexively glanced about. Was the *Gamble* being boarded? Was Cavite being invaded? The admiral's daughter violated? Taken? By whom? Sten skipped the why and where and assumed the now.

Mostly, what Sten was really worrying about was how he was going to untangle his feet and leap into position. Alex saved his behind by sort of explaining.

"Wha' Mr. Sutton, here, is sayin't, Commander, is we

been busted. I dinnae care t' guess wha for, but we been pushin't the motive a wee bit a' late."

Sten buried a laugh. He had a pretty good idea what was going on. But Alex had been running on his luck a great deal. It was time for Sten to run it back. He placed a look of great concern on his face. He almost *harummphed*. With as much dignity as could be mustered in a three by two-meter space, Sten rose to his feet.

"What, gentlemen, could possibly be the problem?" His voice was very casual and cool.

"We're trying to tell you, sir," Sutton said. "We're being invaded by the cops!"

Sten allowed himself to be drawn out the door.

At dockside, drawn up before the *Gamble*, was a phalanx of Black Marias with five police gravsleds per side and two cops per vehicle.

"I told you, sir," Sutton said. "We've been taken." He turned to Alex with accusation in his eyes and an angry quiver in his voice. "You turned me in."

"You? Who th' clottin' hell are you? Dinnae hae reference of grandeur, lad. They're bleedin' bustin' us all!" Alex gave Sten a glance. "I dinnae suppose we hae good graces here. But, if w' do, Ah'd be serious usin' them now, Sten!"

Sten maintained his superiority of silence. Oddly enough, it did seem to have an effect on the two beings next to him. There was an agonizing moment, then a hiss from the lead sled in the column. The driver's door opened, and an enormous member of the Cavite police force unreeled himself out. There was another moment for brushing of tunic and flicking at stray hairs. Then measured bootheels advanced toward Sten. There was an official piece of paper held in his thrust-out hand.

"A warrant, Ah'll ween," Alex whispered.

Sten was silent.

The cop marched up to Sten, tossed him a smart salute, and handed him the document. Alex peered over at it, his face breaking into amazement.

"You dinnae?" he said.

"I did," Sten said. "Thank you, Constable Foss," he said formally.

"With pleasure, sir," Foss said. "Now, begging your pardon, sir, but we're all on Ten-Seven. Can you process twenty recruits in less than an hour? Or should some of us come back?"

Alex finally came through. "Twenty of you, aye? Come in, come in, said the cider to the fly."

Moments later, he and Sutton were lining up the cops.

"So, thae be what it's come to, then?" he whispered to Sten. "Recruitin' clottin' fuzz."

Sten gave Alex his best and most practiced CO look. "Ain't war hell?"

First Lieutenant Ned Estill was a miracle captured in amber. He looked sharp! Sounded sharp! Was sharp! And his résumé was as crisp and clean as his dress whites. He snapped Sten a knife-edged salute, heels clicking like a shot.

"If that will be all, *sir!*"

Sten had rarely been confronted with such perfection. Estill was the kind of officer who made even a commander feel the grime around his collar. The comparison was especially pertinent because Sten and Alex were dressed in filthy engineer's coveralls. Estill's interview had been impromptu—an interruption of a greasegun's-eye tour of the ship. Sten had as much difficulty in dismissing the man as he and Alex had in quizzing him. How do you deal with a naval recruiting poster?

"We'll be gettin' back to you, Lieutenant," Alex said, solving Sten's immediate gape. Sten almost had to physically hold up his jaw as Estill wheeled 180 perfect degrees and clicked—not walked—down the gangway.

Sten sagged back against the hull in relief.

"Who sent him?" Sten wanted to know. "He's gotta be a spy, or something. Nobody, but nobody that good would ever volunteer for our dinky little boats."

"He nae be a spy," Alex said, "alto' he be a Doorman lad his whole career. The wee spindar checked him out."

"Okay," Sten said, "but look at his record. Honors, awards, medals, prized exploration assignments. Personal commendations from every superior officer."

"All peacetime, lad," Alex reminded. "Also, nae *one*

good word from his ultimate superior—Doorman himself."

"Estill's too good," Sten said. "I don't trust him."

"We got crew enough for the four ships," Alex said, "but we're still lackin' two captains."

Sten mulled that over for a bit, wondering if Lieutenant Estill was an answer to his prayers or the seeding bed for future nightmares. Besides, did Estill have . . .

"Luck, Ah wonder if the lad has luck?" Alex said, completing Sten's thought. "How desperate are we?"

"If I could put a good first mate with him . . ." Sten mused.

There was a thrumming of engines overhead, and a loud voice crackled through a hailer across the docks. "Hey, you swabbies get off your butts and give a lady a hand!"

Sten and Alex looked up to see a rust bucket of a towship hovering overhead. The tow pilot already had one ship dangling from its cradle and was moving into position over the *Gamble*. Long, slender robo arms snaked out and started unfastening the dock lines.

"What in the clot do you think you're doing?" Sten yelled up.

The woman's voice crackled out again. "What's it look like? Moving your ship to the engine test stands. You are on the schedule, aren't you? Or doesn't your captain keep the ranks informed of what's going on?"

"You can't move two ships at once!" Sten shouted back.

"Wanna clottin' bet? Hell, on a good day I can pull three. Now, get cracking with that line, mister!"

A bit bemused, the two men did what the woman said. And then they watched in awe as she maneuvered *Gamble* into a sling below the first ship in a few seconds flat. The tow engines roared to full power, and she started away.

"That lass is *some* pilot, young Sten," Alex said. "Ah've rarely seen the likes of her."

But Sten was paying him no mind; he was already running along the docks after the tow as it wound its way toward the test stands. By the time he reached the yard, the pilot was already transferring the *Gamble* over into the work berth.

"Hey, I'm comin' aboard!" Sten yelled, and without

waiting for permission he swarmed up the netting to the towship.

A little later, he found himself squeezed into the tiny pilot's cabin. In person, the woman was even more stunning than her obvious flying talents. She was slender and tall, with enormous dark eyes and long black hair tucked into her pilot's cap. She was looking Sten over, speculatively and a bit amused.

"If this is your way of asking a lady out for a beer," she said, "I admire the clot out of your gall. I get off in two hours."

"That isn't what I had in mind," Sten said.

"Oh, yeah? Say, what kind of a sailor are you, anyway?"

"A *commander* type sailor," Sten said dryly.

The woman gave him a startled look, then groaned. "Oh, no. Me and my big ensign yap. Well, guess there goes my job. Ah, what the clot! I was lookin' for one when I found this gig."

"In that case," Sten said, "report to me tomorrow at 0800 hours. I got an opening for first mate."

"You gotta be kidding." The woman was in shock.

"Negative. Interested?"

"Just like that, huh? First mate?"

"Yep. Just like that. Except from now on you gotta call me 'sir'!"

She chewed that over, then nodded. "I guess I could get used to that."

"Sir," Sten reminded.

"Sir," she said.

"By the way, what's your name?"

"Luz, Luz Tapia. Oh, clot, I mean Luz Tapia, sir."

With one shot, Sten had solved the problem of the *Richards* and his doubts about Estill.

Only the problem of a skipper for the *Claggett* remained. But so far the last hurdle seemed insurmountable. Alex and Sten gloomed over the few remaining names on their list.

"What a sorry lot," Alex said. "Ah wouldnae mak ae of these clots cap'n ae a gravsled."

Sten had to agree. To make matters worse, he was

quickly running out of time. And Doorman hadn't been making things easy for him. His aides had been swamping Sten with regular calls asking for status reports and issuing thinly veiled threats.

For one of the few times in his life, Sten found himself stumped.

There was a loud scratching at the door.

"In!" Sten shouted.

There was a pause, and then the scratching came again, louder than before.

Sten jumped to his feet. "Who the clottin hell..." He slapped at the button, and the door hissed open. Sheer horror looked him in the face. Sten whooped with delight.

"What the clot are you doing here?" he yelled.

"Heard you were looking for a captain," the horror replied.

And Sten fell into Sh'aarl't's arms and arms and arms.

CHAPTER THIRTY-ONE

EVEN AS HE walked under the baroque gates into the officer's club grounds, Sten began calling himself several kinds of a dumb clot. Across the vast pampered garden—which Sten was sure was tended by poor swabbies pressed into service by their superiors—he could see the palatial and sprawling building that housed the club.

Even by Prime World standards it would be considered posh. The building was many-columned and pure white. It was lit by constantly playing lights. The central structure had a copper-yellow dome that looked suspiciously as if it had been gold-leafed. Sten gritted his teeth as he thought how many ships could have been outfitted at the obvious cost.

He could hear the sounds of his partying brother and sister officers. Somehow the laughter seemed a little too loud, the howls of enjoyment a little too shrill.

Sten almost turned back. Then he thought, To hell with it. He had come here to celebrate with a by-God decent meal and a few too many drinks. He walked on, determined to have a good time. Besides, everybody on van Doorman's staff couldn't be clots, could they? There were sure to be a few interesting beings, right?

Just to his left was a large tree, cloaked in darkness. As he passed it, a figure came out of the shadows toward him. Sten pivoted, his knife sliding into his palm. The figure seemed to lunge for him, and just as Sten was about to strike, he smelled a strange mixture of strong alcohol and heady perfume. Instead of striking, he caught—and his arms were suddenly filled with surprising softness.

The young woman bleared up at him and then gave a slightly twisted grin of faint recognition. "Oh, s'it's you," she giggled. "Come to give me a cuddle, huh?"

It was Brijit van Doorman. The admiral's daughter. And she was quite drunk.

Sten desperately tried to push her upright and away— doing his best, but failing, to keep from touching places he ought not to touch. Visions of firing squads danced in his head.

"Was'a matter?" Brijit protested. "Din't ya ever see a girl get a tiddle little, I mean a little tiddly, before?"

"Please, Ms. van Doorman . . ." Sten fumbled.

She collapsed against him; as Sten clutched at her, she slid out of his arms as if she were greased and tumbled to the lawn. She was suddenly stricken by a mixture of laughter and hiccups.

"Had a *hic* con—con—contest. Drinking con—*hic*— test. I won."

"So I see," Sten said.

"He didn't like it."

"Who's he?" Sten asked.

Brijit became very formal. "*He* is my fiancé. Old whatis-bod. Rey. Right, Rey Hall—uh, Halldor. My true true true love."

The firing squad disappeared from Sten's mind to be replaced by a small figure being keelhauled. The figure looked very much like Sten.

"Why don't I go get Rey?" Sten said.

"No, no, no. He's with Daddy. Daddy doesn't like me to drink either."

This was all just as clotting wonderful as it could get. At least that was what Sten thought until Brijit started to cry. Not nice, soft little ladylike sobs either, but a loud bawl. Sten saw several people peering curiously out the window.

"Let me take you home," Sten said.

She stopped crying immediately. She gave him a little conspiratorial look. "Right. Home. Then nobody will ever know."

"Absolutely," Sten said. "No one will know. Okay, up we go, now."

It took him a good five minutes to get her to her feet. But that didn't do much good, as she kept sagging toward the ground each time. Finally, Sten picked her up and carried back along the path and through the gates to his gravcar.

He had barely cleared the ground when she lapsed into total unconsciousness. Sten was about ready to explode. Of all the clotting little...Ah, what the hell. He'd find the way. He punched her name into the gravcar's directory, found her address, and set the autopilot.

As they swept through the city, he took a good look at her. Except for a slight flush in her features and a bruised look about her mouth, no one could tell she had a load on.

What the hey, so she got a load on? Sten imagined that it wasn't very pleasant being related to van Doorman. So she wanted to kick her heels up a little? She had a right to, didn't she?

Asleep, Brijit seemed very peaceful, little-girl-innocent and...and...Get a hold of yourself, Sten. So she's a knockout. She's also the admiral's daughter, remember? Do not think those thoughts. Do not think them at all.

Brijit never woke up when they reached her house, and Sten had to carry her in and tuck her into bed. He palmed a switch to turn off the lights, sighed, and let himself out.

He found a furious blond man waiting for him at his gravsled. The man was in uniform and wore the insignia of a commander. The last time Sten had seen him had been outside van Doorman's office—he'd been wearing shorts and accompanying Brijit. It did not require much of Sten's deductive powers to figure out who the man was.

"So, there you are, you clot! I'll teach you to—"

The man swung at Sten, starting at his knees and coming straight up. Sten stepped back lightly, and the man almost fell from the force of the swing.

"You must be Rey Halldor," Sten said. "Brijit's fiancé."

"You're clotting right I am," Halldor said, swinging again.

Sten ducked, holding out both hands, trying to make peace. "Listen, Halldor. I didn't have anything to do with it. She got drunk. I found her. I took her home. Period. That's it. Nothing else happened."

Halldor charged, windmilling. Sten tried to dance aside, but one of the blows caught his ear. It hurt like hell.

"Okay, you clot," Sten said.

One arm stiffened. A hand connected, and the man found himself lying on his back, looking foolishly up at Sten.

"You . . . you hit me," said an astonished Halldor.

"You're clottin' right I hit you, Commander," Sten said. "And if you get up, that's not all I'll do."

"I want your name. Now, you clot."

"The clot you are speaking to is Commander Sten, at your service."

"This isn't the end of it," Halldor said.

"Right."

Sten vaulted into his gravcar. He almost broke the control panel punching in the code that would take him home.

I just love how you meet people, young Sten. Isn't it just wonderful how you got all the rough edges polished off on Prime World?

CHAPTER THIRTY-TWO

"HEY, CHIEF. I think I got something," Foss said.

Warrant Officer Kilgour, in spite of his years with the less-than-militarily-correct Mantis teams, was offended. "The term is Commander or Sten, son. And that is not the way to report."

Sten, amused, didn't bother to wait for Foss to rejargon. He was instantly across the *Gamble*'s command deck—easily done, since it measured four meters on a side—and was staring at the screen.

"Well," he said, waiting for the ship's computer to give him a better analysis than a blip, sector, and proximity, "we have something. I guess it ain't birds."

Foss flushed.

Sten's flotilla was on its third week of shakedown. It had not been a thrill a minute.

Combine hardened felons with a naval background with policemen with no military background with eager volunteers with fairly virginal officers, then add to that four state-of-the-art patrolcraft. State of the art is correctly redefined by any engineer or technician with field service as: It will promise you everything and deliver you very little. Under stress or when you really need it, it will break. The Bulkeley-class tacships fulfilled these requirements very exactly.

Sten and Alex had managed twenty hours of sleep each since the *Gamble*, *Claggett*, *Kelly*, and *Richards* had launched from Cavite Base. The launch, intended to be a smooth soaring out of atmosphere, had been a limp toward space. The AM2 drive on Sh'aarl't's ship, the *Claggett*, had refused to kick in on command, and the formation had crawled into a holding orbit on Yukawa drive. It took hours of circuit running before they discovered that someone at the builder's yard had left his lunchtime tabloid—headline: "Emperor to Finally Wed? Escorts Beauty from Nirvana to Ball"—between two filter screens.

Sten's comment about birds was not a joke—the ship's screens had identified one of Cavite's moons as aquatic waterfowls, and the identification had been confirmed by the ship's *Jane's*. Still worse, the suggested response from the weapons computer had been bows and arrows. Of course, the professionally paranoid recruits from Cavite's police department saw signs of sabotage and Tahn sympathies among the builders. Sten knew better—over the years he'd learned that the more sophisticated a computer was, the more likely it was to independently develop what in humans would be called a sense of black humor. Foss had managed to find the glitch and recircuit it within a day.

Eric Foss was a rare find. If he hadn't been the initial source of recruitment from the police, Sten and Alex might have passed him over. He was a large, red-faced young man just barely old enough to join the military, much less the police. He'd spent his few short months on the Cavite force as a traffic officer.

Despite his bulk, the young man was so quiet, so calm, that he almost seemed asleep. But his test scores on communications of all kinds were awesome and not to be believed. Sten had personally tested him again—and the scores had improved. If Sten had been a superstitious man, he might have thought Foss a sensitive. But instead, he put him in charge of flotilla communications.

Shakedown had continued, always interesting in a morbid sort of way. The fire-system nozzles had been misaligned and filled the weapons compartments with foams; fuel-feed passages were warped; the galley stoves took a Ph.D. to understand, and the refreshers were worse.

On the other hand, all of the ships had power beyond the manufacturer's specs; target acquisition was superfast, and the missile-firing tests went flawlessly.

Unexpectedly, the crewmen and women managed to meld fairly painlessly. The only incident had been one of the ex-cons pulling a knife on an ex-policeman in an argument over the last piece of soyasteak. But the ex-cop had broken the man's arm in six places, snapped the knife in two, and told the officer of the watch that the other poor fellow must have tripped over something.

Even the command ranks were working into shape. Sh'aarl't, on the *Claggett*, was just as good as Sten had anticipated. Lamine Sekka, on the *Kelly*, was awesome, and Sten understood how the man's family had survived all those generations as warriors. Lieutenant Estill, backed by Ensign Tapia on ther *Richards*, was coming along. He still had a tendency to follow slavishly on its anticipation every order, but Sten had hopes.

At least no one had fed himself into the power chamber, and no one had rammed anything. Both Sten and Alex, maintaining their public air of "not quite right, guys, try it again," were pleased.

But sleep was becoming an increasingly attractive future.

Seven more ship-days, Sten had promised himself. Then we are going to practice landing and concealment on the prettiest and most deserted world we can find and practice deep Zen breathing.

At that point, the contact alarm went off. The screen changed from a blip to a blur of words:

OBJECT IDENTIFIED AS NON-NATURAL. OBJECT IDENTI-FIED AS AM2-POWERED SPACECRAFT. OBJECT ON PROJECTED ORBIT...(NONCOLLISION)...NO *JANE'S* ENTRY CONGRUENT WITH SHIP PROFILE...SHIP OUTPUTTING ON NO RECEIVABLE WAVELENGTH...SHIP *TENTATIVE*...*TENTATIVE*...OPERA-TING UNDER SILENT RUNNING CONDITIONS...

The words became an outline of the oncoming ship. Sten and Alex eyed the screen.

"Ugly clot, wha'e'er she be," Alex said.

"Almost as ugly as the *Cienfuegos*," Sten said, referring to a spy ship, camouflaged as a mining explorer, on which they had almost managed to get themselves killed during their Mantis days.

Alex got it. "Wee Foss, gie her a buzz on the distress freak."

Before Foss could key the frequency, the screen changed again:

ANALYSIS COMPLETE OF DRIVE EMISSION—DRIVE CODING SUGGESTS SHIP FROM TAHN WORLDS.

Sten keyed the mike. "Unknown ship . . . unknown ship . . . this is the Imperial Tactical Ship *Gamble*. You are operating in a closed sector. I repeat, you are operating in a closed sector. Prepare for inspection."

Without waiting for a response, he reached over Foss's shoulder and keyed the com to the "talk between ships" circuit. "*Clagett, Kelly, Richards*, this is *Gamble*. All ships, general quarters. All weapons systems on full readiness. All ships slave-link to my flight pattern. All commanders stand by for independent action. This may not be a drill. If fired on, return fire. I say again, this may not be a drill. *Gamble* out."

A speaker bleated. "Imperial Ship *Gamble*, this is the *Baka*. Do not understand your last, over."

There was another frequency change. "*Baka*, this is *Gamble*. I say again my last. Stand by for boarding and inspection."

"This is *Baka*. We wish to protest. We are a civilian exploration ship under correct charter. If there has been any error in our course, we will accept escort out of the restricted sector. We do not wish to be boarded."

"This is *Gamble*. We are warping parallel orbit. You will be boarded within . . . eight E-minutes. Any attempt to evade boarding or resistance will be met with the appropriate countermeasures. This is *Gamble*. Out."

Sten turned to Alex. "Mr. Kilgour. You . . . me . . . sidearms. Four men with willyguns. Move!"

Sten's crew may not have been fully trained as sailors, but they were fairly skilled at breaking and entering. Breaking was not necessary—the *Baka* had its lock extended and ready. The entrance slid open. Two men were on either side of the tube, willyguns held—not quite—leveled. The other two flanked Sten and Alex. They started down the tube, and their stomachs jumped a little as they crossed from their own artificial gravity field to that of the *Baka*.

The *Baka*'s inner port opened.

Sten expected to be met with fuming and shouts. Instead there was quiet outrage.

The ship's CO introduced himself as Captain Deska. He was a man of control—but a man who was most angry. "Captain... Sten, this is totally unwarranted. I shall lodge a protest with my government immediately."

"On what grounds?" Sten asked mildly.

"We have been hijacked merely because we are Tahn. This is rank discrimination—my company has nothing to do with politics."

My company? A ship's captain working for someone would hardly have said "my." Sten decided that this Deska wasn't terribly good at fraud. "You are in a forbidden sector," he said.

"You are incorrect. We have the correct clearances and permission. In my cabin."

Sten smiled politely. He would be most interested in inspecting said clearances.

Deska led the way to his cabin. The ship corridors, unlike those of a normal exploration ship, were immaculate and freshly anodized. The crew members were also unusual—not the bearded loners and technicians that normally made up a long-cruise explorer but clean-shaven, cropped-haired, and wearing identical coveralls.

It did not take Sten long to peruse the clearances. He snapped the fiche off and stood up from the small console in Deska's Spartan quarters.

"You see," Deska said. "That permission was personally requested and cleared by your own Tanz Sullamora. If you have not heard of the man—"

"I know who he is. One of our Imperial biggies," Sten said. "As a matter of fact, I know him personally."

Was there a slight flicker from Deska?

"Excellent," Deska said heartily.

"Interesting ship you have here," Sten went on. "Very clean."

"There is no excuse for lack of cleanliness."

"That's my theory, too. Of course, I'm not a civilian..." Sten changed the subject. "Your crew's sharper than mine. You run a taut ship, Captain."

"Thank you, Commander."

"I don't think you want to feel too grateful. This ship, under my authority as an officer of the Empire, is under custody. Any attempt at resistance or disregard of my orders will be countered, if necessary, by force of arms. You are instructed and ordered to proceed, under my command, to the nearest Imperial base, in this case Cavite, at which time you are entitled to all protection and recourse available under Imperial law."

"But why?"

Sten touched buttons on two small cased pouches on his belt. "Do you really want to know, Captain Deska?"

"I do."

"Fine. By the way, I just shut off my recorder and turned on a block. I assume you have this room monitored. Nothing else we say will be picked up, I can guarantee you.

"Captain, you are busted because I think you're a spy ship. No, Captain. You asked me, and I'm gonna tell you. Every one of your men looks like an officer—and you do, too. Tahn officers. If I were a sneaky type, I'd guess that you are some kind of high-level commander. And you came out here, with a pretty good forgery to cover yourself, to check out the approaches to Cavite. Just in case the balloon goes up. Am I wrong, Captain?"

"This is an outrage!"

"Sure is. But you're still busted. And by the way, even if you manage to convince Cavite you are innocent, innocent, innocent, all the hot poop your scanners have been picking up will be wiped before we release you."

Admiral Deska, second-in-command of Lady Atago's combined fleet, just looked at Sten. "You are very, very wrong, Commander. And I shall remember you for a very, very long time."

CHAPTER THIRTY-THREE

"YOU DID WHAT?" Sten blurted. He did not even notice that he had forgotten to say "sir." Not that van Doorman needed an excuse to get angry.

"I did not ask you for a comment, Commander. I merely took the courtesy of informing you as to my decision. Since you are slightly deaf, I shall repeat it:

"After considerable investigation by my staff, supervised by myself, we have determined that the boarding of the Tahn Scientific Ship *Baka* was in error. Admittedly, they had accidentally entered a proscribed area of space, but their commanding officer, a Captain Deska, told me that their charts were out of date and in error."

"Sir, did you personally examine those charts?"

"Commander, be silent! Captain Deska is a gentleman. I saw no reason to question his word."

Sten, heels locked, stared glumly down at Doorman's desk.

"I also personally commend an apology to his superiors and to his company headquarters on Heath, which is the capital of the Tahn System."

Sten, once again, did not know when to keep his mouth shut. "Sir. One question. Did you at least have techs wipe the ship's recorder systems?"

"I did not. How could he have navigated home if I did?"

"Thank you, sir."

"One further point. You should consider yourself lucky."

"Sir?"

"Since it would prove an embarrassment to the officers and men of the 23rd Fleet if Imperial headquarters were to hear of this debacle, of course there is no way that I can place the correct letter of reprimand in your personal fiche."

Translation: van Doorman hadn't reported the incident to Prime World.

"I shall tell you something else, young man. When you were first assigned to my command, I had my doubts.

"The navy is a proud and noble service. A service composed of gentlebeings. You, on the other hand, were formed by the army. Necessary types, certainly. But hardly correct from the navy point of view.

"I hoped that you would change your ways from the examples you would see around you, here on Cavite. I was most incorrect. You not only have isolated yourself from your peers, but have chosen to associate with, and I am not exaggerating, scum from the lowest circles of our society.

"So be it. You came from the gutter...and choose to swim in it. At my first opportunity, the first time you make the most minor error, I shall break you, Commander Sten. I shall dissolve your entire unit, have you court-martialed, and, I most earnestly hope, send you to a penal planet in irons. That is all!"

Sten saluted, pivoted, and marched out of van Doorman's office, out of the hotel, and deep into the grounds—where, behind a tree, he laughed himself back into sanity. Admiral van Doorman probably believed he had stuck Sten's guts on a pole and waved them high overhead. He really should have taken lessons from the most polite Mantis instructor.

Scum Sten headed back for his ships. Not only did he want a drink, he wanted to find out—Alex would know—what the clot "irons" were.

CHAPTER THIRTY-FOUR

"BOSS, YOU LOOK like you could use a drink."

"Many," the Emperor said. "Drag up a pew and a bottle, Mahoney."

Building drinks was simple—it consisted of grabbing a bottle of what the Emperor called scotch from the old rolltop desk and half filling two glasses.

"What," Mahoney asked after slugging down his drink and getting a refill, "is burning Sullamora's tubes? He's stomping around the anteroom like you just nationalized his mother."

"Clot," the Emperor swore. "I told him I know he's innocent six times already. Of course the *Baka*'s papers were forged. I went and told him very clear, I went and shouted in his ear."

Mahoney just gave him a puzzled look.

The Emperor sighed. "Never mind. I guess when you leave I'll have to pat his poo-poo again."

"Speaking of that, sir."

"Yeah. I know."

The matter at hand was the boarding and subsequent release of the *Baka*. Van Doorman may not have filed a report, but one of Mahoney's agents, put in place in the days when Mahoney had run Imperial Intelligence—Mercury Corps—had.

"First thing we've got to do, sir, is bust that clotting Doorman down to brig rat third class."

"I've never been able to figure out if beings become soldiers because they're simple, or whether wearing a uniform makes them that way," the Emperor said. He paused and drank. "Van Doorman has got six—count them, six—of

126

my idiot members of parliament who think he's the most brilliant swabbie since Nelson."

"You're just going to leave him running amok with the 23rd Fleet?"

"Of course not. I am going to amass, most carefully, a very large stone bucket. At the appropriate time, I'll run some of my pet politicos out to the Fringe Worlds on a fact-finding mission. They'll come back and tell me how terrible things are. After that, I'll be reluctantly forced to give Doorman another star and put him in charge of iceberg watching somewhere."

"Sir, I don't think we have that kind of time. Both my agent and Sten agree that every swinging Richard on the *Baka* was a Tahn officer. They are getting ready to hit us."

"Forget Doormat for a minute, refill my goddamned glass, and tell me what you want to do. And no, I am not going to authorize a preemptive first strike on Heath."

"That," General Mahoney said, following orders, "*was* going to be one of my options."

"Remember, Ian. I don't start wars. I just finish them."

Mahoney held up a hand. He had heard time and again the Emperor's belief that no one wins in a war and that the more wars that are fought, the weaker the structure of the society fighting them becomes. "What about this one, sir? What about—"

"You tried that one before, General. And I am *still* not going to redeploy your First Guards on the Fringe Worlds. We are, right now, about one millimeter from going to war with the Tahn. I am doing everything I goddamned know to keep that from happening. I plonk your thugs out there, and that would be it."

Mahoney framed his sentence very carefully. The Emperor may have considered Mahoney a confidant and even maybe a friend—but he still was the Eternal Emperor, and one step over the line could put General Mahoney out there looking for icebergs with Doorman. "No offense, sir. But supposing you can't stop the Tahn? Meaning no disrespect."

The Emperor growled, started to snap, and decided to finish his drink instead. He got up and stared out the window at the palace gardens below. "There is that," he said finally. "Maybe I'm getting too set in my ways."

"Then I can—"

"Negative, General. No Guards." The Emperor considered for another moment. "How long has it been since the First Guards went through jungle refresher training?"

"Six months, sir."

"Way too long. I'm ashamed of you, Mahoney, for letting your unit get fat and sloppy."

Mahoney didn't even bother to·protest—the Emperor had his scheming look about him.

"Seems to me I own some kind of armpit swamp out in that part of the universe. Used to be a staging base back in the Mueller Wars."

Mahoney crossed to one of the Emperor's computer terminals and searched. "Yessir. Isby XIII. Unoccupied now except by what the fiche says are some real nasty primordials and a caretaker staff on the main base. And you're right. It's very close to the Fringe Worlds. It'd take me ... maybe a week to transship from there."

"Would you stop worrying about the Fringe Worlds? The solution with those gentle and lovable Tahn will be diplomatic. The only reason I'm punting you out there is to see whether mosquitoes like Mick blood." Then the Emperor turned serious. "Christ, Mahoney. That's the best I can think of. Right now, I'm starting to run out of Emperor moves."

And Major General Ian Mahoney wondered if maybe he'd better make sure his own life insurance policy was current.

CHAPTER THIRTY-FIVE

THE TWENTY-SEVEN MEMBERS of the Tahn Council sat in various attitudes of attention as Lady Atago detailed the progress on Erebus. Even on screen her chilly efficiency cut across the light-years separating her from the Tahn home world of Heath. If there was any deference in her manner to her superiors, it was only to her mentor, Lord Fehrle, the most powerful member of the council.

"...And so, my lords and ladies," she was saying, "in summation, the fleet is at sixty percent strength; fuel and other supplies, forty-three percent; weapons and ammunition, seventy-one percent."

Fehrle raised a finger for attention. "One question, my lady," he said. "Some of the members have expressed concern about crewing. What is the status, if you please?"

"It displeases me to say, my lord," Atago said, "that I can only give you an estimate. To be frank, training has not yet come up to Tahn standards."

"An estimate will do," Fehrle said.

"In that case, I would say we have enough manpower to place a skeleton crew aboard all currently operational ships. There would be gaps in key positions, of course, but I believe these deficiences could be overcome."

"I have a question, if you please, my lady." This was from Colonel Pastour, the newest member of the council. Fehrle buried a groan of impatience and shot a glance at Lord Wichman, who just gave a slight shake of his head.

"Yes, my lord?"

"How long before we can be at full strength?"

"Two years, minimum," Lady Atago said without hesitation.

"In that case," Pastour continued, "perhaps the other members would benefit from your counsel. Do you advise us to proceed with the action under discussion?"

"It is not my place to say, my lord."

"Come, come. You must at least have an opinion."

Lady Atago's glare bored through him. Good, Fehrle thought. She's not going to be caught out by Pastour's seemingly innocent question.

"I'm sorry, my lord. I do not. My duty is to follow your orders, not to second-guess the thinking of the council."

But Pastour would not give up so easily. "Very admirable, my lady. However, as the fleet commander, you must have some estimate of our chances for success if we act immediately."

"Adequate, my lord."

"Only adequate?"

"Isn't adequate enough for any Tahn, my lord?"

Pastour flushed, and there were murmur of agreement from around the table. Fehrle decided to break in. Although the old colonel made him uneasy in his wavering, it was not good to threaten the unanimity of the council.

"I think that will be all for now, my lady," he said. "Now, if you will excuse us, we will be back to you within the hour with our decision."

"Thank you, my lord."

Fehrle palmed a button, and the screen image of Lady Atago vanished.

"I must say, my lord," Wichman said, "that I'm sure that I echo the sentiments of the other members of the council by expressing my pleasure in your choice of Lady Atago to command the fleet."

There were more murmur of agreement, except from Pastour, who had recovered and merely gave a chuckle.

"Right you are," he said. "Except if I were you, Lord Fehrle, I'd keep a weather eye on that woman. She's just a bit too good for comfort."

Fehrle ignored him. Pastour sometimes had a way of saying the oddest things. And at the moment, Fehrle was questioning his own decision to raise the man to the council. Well, no use worrying about that now. The fact was that Pastour was one of the key industrialists in the Tahn Empire. He also had the uncanny ability to raise large guard units—all of which he financed from his own pocket— where seemingly there had been few warm bodies available.

Also, Lord Wichman's supreme militancy—even for a Tahn—served as a counterbalance to Pastour. Wichman was one of Fehrle's master strokes. He was a man who had risen through the ranks of the military and could boast nearly every award for heroism that the Tahn Empire had to offer. More importantly, he had a way with the masses, and in his role as minister of the people, he seemed to be able to get any kind of sacrifice necessary from the working class. How he got that cooperation, no one cared to know.

In another time, the Tahn Council would have been most closely compared to a politburo system of government. Each member represented key areas of society. The various viewpoints were discussed and whenever possible added to the political stewpot. All decisions were unanimous and final. There was never a vote, never any public dissension. Each matter was thoroughly discussed in private, compromises made whenever necessary, and the plan agreed upon. A meeting of the council itself was a mere formality for the record.

And so it was with no trepidation at all that Fehrle addressed his fellow lords and ladies.

"Then, I assume we are all agreed," he said. "We proceed with the attack on the Emperor as planned?"

There were nods all around—except one.

"I'm not sure," Pastour said. "I still wonder if maybe we ought to wait until we are at full readiness. In two years, we'll have the Empire in the palm of our hand."

There was an instant hush in the room. Everyone looked at Fehrle to see how he would react.

Fehrle did his best to keep the impatience out of his voice. "This has all been discussed before, my lord," he said. "The longer we wait, the longer the Emperor has to build more ships. We cannot win a manufacturing war with the Eternal Emperor. You of all people should know that."

"Yes, yes. But what if this operation doesn't succeed? We are risking our entire fleet! Where will we be if we lose that? Back under the Emperor's thumb, that's where, I tell you!"

Wichman instantly shot to his feet, his eyes bulging and his face scarlet with anger. "I will not stay in the same room with a coward!" he shouted.

The room erupted as Wichman began to stalk out. Fehrle slammed his hand down on the table. Wichman froze in midstep. Silence reigned again in the room.

"My lords! My ladies! Do you forget where you are?"

Fehrle glared around at each member. They all squirmed in their seats uncomfortably. Then he turned to Pastour and gave him a frosty smile.

"I'm sure the good colonel misspoke. We all know from his reputation that he is no coward." He glanced over at Wichman. "Don't you agree, my lord?"

Wichman's shoulders slumped, and he walked silently back to his seat. "I apologize for my rudeness," he said to Pastour.

"And I for mine. You must forgive me. I have a great deal more to learn about the workings of the council."

The tension crept away, and Lord Fehrle brought the meeting back to order.

"It's settled, then. We attack immediately!"

Everyone shouted in agreement. Pastour's voice was the loudest of all.

CHAPTER THIRTY-SIX

"MR. KILGOUR," Foss said, wistfully looking at the display in front of him, "can I ask you something?"

"GA, lad." Kilgour checked the time. There was an hour and a half to go before the shift changed—and a little inconsequential conversation might help kill the boredom.

"Look at all those fat freighters down there. When you were young, did you ever want to be a pirate?"

Kilgour chuckled. "Lad, Ah hae input f' ye. When Ah was wee, Ah *was* a pirate. Come frae a long line a' rogues, Ah do."

Foss glanced at Kilgour. He was still not sure when his XO was extending his mandible. He turned back to the screen.

Sten's four ships had been assigned escort duty. Even though the increasing tension with the Tahn had reduced merchant traffic through the Fringe Worlds, there were still certain shipments that had to be routed through the area. The ships were now dispatched in convoys and given integral escort. In addition, during passage near the Tahn sector, Imperial ships were attached for support. Hanging "below" Sten's ships were five tubby merchants from Tanz Sullamora's fleet, one container link with four tugs, two hastily armed auxiliary cruisers, and one archaic destroyer, the *Neosho*, from van Doorman's fleet.

Sten couldn't figure out van Doorman's thinking—if, indeed, the admiral was ever guilty of that. He seemed more interested in keeping his ships on the ground than in space. Possibly, Sten hazarded, the admiral was worried that he would forget them if they weren't in plain sight. Van Doorman was, even though the term's origins were long-lost, a perfect bean counter.

This didn't apply to Sten's tiny flotilla. Van Doorman proved true to his word. He wanted Sten's butt on toast. He evidently thought the best way to crucify Sten was to keep him busy. The *Claggett, Gamble, Kelly,* and *Richards* were used as everything from dispatch runners to chartmakers to the present duty—high escort on this merchant run. Sten didn't think much of van Doorman's plot—if Sten had wanted to ruin someone's career, he would have kept the person underfoot at all times. Sten was also not upset that his ships were kept on the run—he was still shaking his somewhat motley crew down.

The only problem was the wear and tear factor on the delicate engines. If it weren't for Sutton's brilliance in conniving far more parts and even spare engines than authorized, all four tacships would have been redlined by now.

And so the four ships dozed on high escort. The skipper of the *Neosho* had cheerfully agreed with Sten's plan to keep his flotilla above the convoy proper, enabling the Bulkeley-class's superior electronics to umbrella the convoy. He had promptly stuck the *Neosho* at proud point and, as far as Sten could tell from intership transmissions, was spending most of his time on the lead merchantman.

Sten was slightly envious—rumor had it that Sullamora's ships were most plush, and their crews didn't believe in Spartan thinking—but not very.

Sten kept his crews on minimal watch—with one exception. The electronics suite was fully manned and watching. There had been entirely too many nonreports from ships passing through this sector. There were many possible explanations: Merchant ships were notoriously sloppy for transmitting sector-exit reports; accidents did happen; pirates; or Question Mark.

Pirates made no sense. In spite of the livie fantasies, it was impossible for a private individual, given the Imperial control of AM2, to operate a raider for very long. It was the Question Mark that intrigued Sten and Alex.

Four days into the assignment, their question was answered.

General quarters clanged Sten from his cubicle, where he was filling out another of van Doorman's interminable status reports, to the command deck.

The convoy was below and ahead of his ships—Sten noticed that, as always, one freighter was lagging to the rear of the formation. But on the monitor three unknown ships were coming in from "low rear." Sten checked the prediction screen. Their path would intersect that rear freighter in minutes.

Electronics does not necessarily simplify command: Sten, nearly simultaneously, ordered all weapons systems on the *Gamble* to standby; alerted his other three ships; cut to the supposedly open command link between ComEscort and ComConvoy, though he got no answer; braced himself and cut onto the assigned transmission band to all convoy ships; and turned away from the convoy screen.

"Below" him was instant chaos. The *Neosho* and the Commander/Escort's lead merchantman continued, unhearing—Sten guessed it must be a helluva party. Two freighters immediately took evasive action and almost collided. A third freighter sought an orbit directly away from the convoy. The container link began lumping like a giant inchworm, as if all of the tug skippers had suddenly decided to go their own way. The lagging merchantman suddenly and uselessly went to full power, and the two auxiliary cruisers began bleating questions.

Sten was too busy to worry about them.

"All tacships, this is *Gamble*. Switch to independent command. Acquire targets. Please monitor my attempts to communicate with unknown ships. Permission to fire at commander's discretion, over."

He made another switch to the sector's emergency band, which, in theory, every ship should be monitoring.

"Unknown ships...this is the Imperial Ship *Gamble*. Identify yourselves...alter trajectory...or prepare to be attacked."

The com screen stayed blank. Kilgour pointed at another screen, which showed violet haze from all three ships.

"First th' wee *Baka*...noo thae' clowns. Ah thinkit tha Tahn be playin't games."

Another screen had a computer projection of the three incoming raiders.

"Spitkits," Kilgour murmured. "Ah'll hazard tha' raiders be converted patrolcraft. Raiders wi' enough to blast a civilian an' a prize crew for boardin'."

Foss, at the control board, eyed Kilgour. Maybe the man from Edinburgh *had* been a pirate.

"Tacships," Sten ordered, "engage and destroy incoming ships!"

Kilgour had the *Gamble* on an intersection orbit, coming "down" on the incoming ships. Evidently they were intent on the merchantman. "Weapons selection, sir?"

"We won't waste a Kali. Give me firing prox on a Goblin."

Kilgour had the control helmet on. "And six . . . and five . . . and four . . . and three . . . and one. Goblin on th' way, mate."

The first raider never knew what happened. It simply vanished. The second and third split formation—one ship 180-ing on a return orbit at full power. Sten checked an indicator—the raider's top speed was less than two-thirds of that of any of the tacships.

The third ship, perhaps with a brighter skipper, tried another tactic. It launched two ship-to-ship missiles and, also at full power, tried an evasion orbit, one that would lead it within a few light-seconds of the lagging merchantman. Perhaps the raider thought he could lose himself in the clutter around the freighter.

"*Clagget . . . Kelly . . . Richards*," Sten ordered. "You want to nail the one that's homeward bound for me? I'll take the sneaky guy."

"Roger, *Gamble*," came the cultured voice of Sekka. "But you do appear to be allowing yourself all the fun."

"Negative, *Kelly*. While you're at it, maybe you could snag me a prisoner or two? And maybe try to get a back projection on where these guys came from?"

"We'll try. *Kelly* out."

While Sten was talking, Alex had already deployed three Fox countermissiles and produced two satisfactory explosions from the raider's own launch.

"Closing ... closing ... closing ..." came the monotone from Foss.

"Unknown ship, this is the Imperial Ship *Gamble*. Cut power immediately!"

Nothing showed onscreen.

"Puir lad," Alex observed. "Puir stupid clot. Wha' he should'a don wha launch on yon freighter an' hopit we're soft-hearted enough to look for survivors ... Goblin launched. Ah'll try t' takit just the wee idiot's drive tubes ... closin't ... hit ... ah well." The raider became another expanding ball of gas.

"*Gamble*, this is *Claggett*. Raider exploded. No survivors observed."

"All tacships, this is *Gamble*. Resume previous orbit."

"*Gamble*, this is *Neosho*. What is going on, over?" The query was rather plaintive.

Foss correctly left the transmission unanswered while Sten and Kilgour figured out a response that wouldn't get them court-martialed when they returned to Cavite.

CHAPTER THIRTY-SEVEN

STEN CLEARED OFF the small surface that served as his desk, turned on the pinlight/magnifiers, and eased his chair closer. He had determined that this was going to be a perfect evening—one of the rare nights he had absolutely alone to pursue his hobby.

He had given the crews of his ships twelve-hour passes, leaving him relatively free of responsibility. He poured himself a tumbler of Stregg, swirled the crystal liquid around in the glass, and sipped. The fire lit down to his toes.

He sighed in anticipated pleasure, then lifted out the tiny black case and snapped it open. It contained a dozen or more tiny cards, each jammed with computer equations. Sten's passion was holographic models of ancient factories and scenes. One card, for instance, contained in its micro-circuits a complete early-twentieth-century Earth lumber mill, with working saws and gears and belts. Every machine in the mill was controlled by a miniature worker, who went about his individual tasks—as best as Sten could research them—exactly as he had many centuries ago. Sten had completed the mill during his last assignment on Prime World.

He had started his latest model during flight school. It was one of his more difficult moving holographic displays. He slid the card into its slot and palmed the computer on. Small figures working in a sprawling field leapt out onto the desk. What Sten was recreating was an ancient British hops field. From his research he knew that hops—used in the beer-brewing process—were grown on towering tripod poles. When harvest time came each year, men and women were recruited from all over the country. The plants were so tall, with the fruited vines at the very top, that the workers strode through the fields on stilts to pick them.

Thus far, Sten's display consisted of the fields of hops, most of the workers, and the ox-drawn carts used to haul out the harvest. Months of work lay ahead of him before he could complete the rest of the sprawling farm. He tickled a few keys on his computer to call up an incomplete ox cart. Then he got out his light pen to start sketching in a few more details.

There was a tentative scratching at his cabin door. Sten felt the anger rise. For clot's sake, he had given strict orders to be left alone. Ah, well. "In!" he called.

The door hissed open, revealing a badly frightened sentry. "Begging your pardon, sir, but . . ." The man started stumbling over his words. "But . . . uh, there's a lady."

"I don't care if it's the Queen of—oh, never mind. Who is it?"

"I think it's the admiral's daughter, sir."

Clot! That was just what he needed. A drunk for company. "Tell her I'm not here."

The sentry started to back out, hesitated, and then

pushed something forward. It was a single rose and a small gift-wrapped package.

"She said to give you this, sir," the sentry plunged on. "Said it was to say she was sorry. Uh . . . uh . . . I think she'd know I was lying, sir, if I told her what you said."

Sten took pity on the man, accepted the gifts, and waved him out. "I'll be with her in a minute."

He placed the rose to one side, took a hefty snort of his Stregg for courage, and slit open the package. There was a small computer card inside—identical to the ones he used in holography. What in the world . . . He slid it into one of the drives. A three-dimensional model of a tower jumped out on his desk. It was a perfect replica of one of the barns used by the ancient hop farmers! How had she known?

No matter how one looked at it, this was one hell of a way to apologize.

They had a midnight picnic-style dinner at one of the most fashionable restaurants on Cavite. Brijit van Doorman insisted on buying.

Sten almost hadn't recognized the woman when he had met her on deck. The last time he had seen her, she had been beautiful but drunk, with a spoiled pout on her lips. This time there was no pout, just large anxious eyes and a nervous little smile.

"I almost hoped you weren't here," she said in a soft voice. "I'm not very good at saying sorry—especially in person."

"I'd say you're very good at it," Sten said.

"Oh, you mean the little barn." She dismissed the gift with a wave. "That was easy. I just asked your friend, Alex. We've spoken on and off for days."

So that was why the tubby heavy-worlder had gone out this evening, with mysterious chuckles at no apparent jokes and pokes into the ribs of the others.

"I assume he also said I'd be onboard tonight."

Brijit laughed. "Is that such a betrayal?" she asked.

Sten looked at the long, flowing hair and the equally flowing body. "No. I don't think so."

Somehow, the stroll back to her gravcar led to a lingering

talk that neither seemed to want to cut off with a thank you
and good-bye. Which led to the dinner invitation. Which
took them to the restaurant that Sten was sure even Marr
and Senn would envy back on Prime World.

It was an exotic outdoor café perched on the end of a
private landing strip. The center was a beer garden, where
the patrons could gather and drink and converse as the late-
night picnic baskets were packed with their orders.
Surrounding the beer garden were many small opaque
bubblecraft. Each craft was large enough to comfortably fit
the basket and two people.

Sten was not surprised that Brijit had made reservations.
They waited about an hour in the quiet garden, talking, sip-
ping at their drinks, and watching the bubbles silently drift
off into the night to swirl around and around the restaurant
in darting orbits, like so many fireflies.

Sten told her about himself as best he could, skipping
with hidden embarrassment over his Mantis Section years.
Strange that he should feel that way. The lies were so
drilled in and part of him that normally they seemed almost
real. Perhaps his discomfort was just a product of the warm
night and the chilled wine.

Brijit chattered on about herself and her navy-brat up-
bringing, which had involved jumping from system to
system as her father rose through the ranks. Although
unstated, Sten got the idea that she was uncomfortable about the pomp that van Doorman liked to dress his
command with. Uncomfortable, but guilty about her discomfort.

Eventually they were summoned to their own private
bubblecraft. They boarded, the gull-wing port closed softly
in on them, and they lifted away.

There must have been more than a hundred items in the
basket, all bite-sized, with no flavor exactly the same as the
last.

Brijit told Sten the rest of her story over brandy. Of
course, there had been a lover.

"I think he was about the handsomest man I've ever
met," she said. "Don't get me wrong. He wasn't the big-

muscles type. Kind of slight. Wiry slight. And dark." She paused. "He was a Tahn."

It all came together then for Sten. The admiral's daughter and her Tahn lover. Sten could imagine how van Doorman would handle a situation like that. It would be very painful for both parties. It would also be something van Doorman would never let his daughter forget.

"I only have one question," Sten said.

"Oh, you mean Rey?"

"Yeah, Rey. I understand you two are engaged."

"Rey thinks we're engaged. Father *knows* we're engaged. But as far as I'm concerned—" She broke off, staring down at the lights of Cavite.

"Yes?"

Brijit laughed. "I think Rey is a clot!"

"So, what do you plan on doing?"

Brijit leaned back on the soft couch that spanned one side of the bubble. "Oh, I don't know. Play the game, I guess. Until something better comes along."

Sten had heard tones of something like this before. "Aren't white knights a little out of fashion?"

Brijit came up from the couch and snuggled herself under one of his arms. She peered up at him with a mock batting of large liquid eyes. "Oh, sir," she said softly, lifting up her lips. "I don't believe in white knights at all."

A moment later they were kissing, and Brijit was falling back on the couch. Her dress slid up, revealing smooth ivory flesh covered only by a wisp of silk between her thighs that was held in place by a slender gold chain about her waist.

Sten brushed his lips across the softness of her belly. Then he unclasped the chain.

CHAPTER THIRTY-EIGHT

"THIS IS IMPERIAL Tacship *Gamble*. Request landing clearance."

There was no visual onscreen, but Sten could feel the controller down on the planetoid below goggle.

"This is Romney. Say again your last."

"This is the *Gamble*," Sten repeated patiently. "I want to land on your crooked little world."

"Stand by."

There was a very long silence.

"Ah think, young Sten, y're givin't these smugglers more slack'n's warrantable."

"Maybe."

At last the transmitter crackled. "Imperial ship ... this is Jon Wild. I understand you want *landing instructions*."

"Correct."

"Since when does the Empire knock on doors like ours?"

Kilgour relaxed. "You were right, lad. Now we're gettin't somewheres."

"This is the *Gamble*. When we want to trade."

"Trade? There's just one ship up there."

"Correct, Sr. Wild."

"Clear to land. Follow the GCA beam down. I wish I could make some kind of threat if you're lying to me. However ... this conversation is being recorded, I know, and I have a right to counsel, legal advice, and such ..." The voice turned mildly plaintive.

"It would be interesting if you're telling the truth," Wild continued. "A vehicle shall be waiting to transport you to my quarters. Romney. Out."

* * *

Jon Wild was a piece of work—as was his planetoid. Romney was a planetoid hanging just outside anyone's known jurisdiction. It had been domed generations earlier as a transmission relay point. But technology had made the relay station obsolete, and it was abandoned.

It had taken Sten some time to find Romney. Actually, the whole idea had been Kilgour's.

"Lad, wid'y vet m'thinkin't," he had begun. "When y' hae ae dictatorship ae th' Tahn, y' hae violators, human nature bein't wha' it is. Correct?"

"We saw enough of that when we were on Heath," Sten agreed.

"Glad y' concur. If y' hae pimps ae thieves an tha', dinnae it be possible t' hae smugglers?"

Sten got it instantly and put Kilgour in motion. The tacships had gone out beyond the Fringe sectors and hung in space, silently monitoring single-ship movements. None of these reports had gone to 23rd Fleet Intelligence—Sten knew that there would be an immediate order to investigate. Eventually there had been enough data to run progs. Yes, there were smugglers, moving in and out of the Tahn worlds. Yes, they did have a base—actually, less a base than a transfer point for goods coming from Imperial worlds intended for import to the Tahn.

But there are smugglers and smugglers. Sten had swooped on a number of ships heading for Romney, checked cargoes, and interrogated crews. Satisfied, he had marooned, on a conveniently outlying planet sans communications, the smugglers and survival supplies.

He had enough to discuss the state of the galaxy with whoever led or spoke for the smugglers. Evidently that person was Jon Wild. Sten had conjured many pictures of what a master smuggler might look like, from a grossly overdressed and overfed sybarite to a slender fop. He did not expect a man who looked as if he would be most satisfied working in Imperial Long-dead Statistics.

Nor had he expected that Wild's headquarters would resemble a dispatch center. From appearances, the smuggler chief would have been a most satisfactory number two for Tanz Sullamora's trading empire.

Wild had offered alk to Sten and Alex and seemed unsurprised when it was refused. He sipped what Sten surmised to be water, taking his time in his evaluation.

"You wish to trade," he finally said. "For what?"

"You saw my ship."

"Indeed. It appeared most efficient."

"Efficient, but not very comfortable."

"Doesn't Admiral van Doorman supply you properly?" Wild asked with buried amusement. Sten did not bother answering.

"What gives you the impression," Wild continued, "that I might be of help?"

Sten wasn't interested in fencing. He handed over the manifest fiches from the smuggling ships he had seized. Wild put them into a viewer, then took his time responding.

"Let us assume that I had something to do with these shipments," Wild said. "And let us further assume that in some manner I could provide equivalent resupply for your ships, Commander. Briefly—how much of a rake-off are you looking for?"

Kilgour bristled. Sten put a hand on his arm.

"Wrong, Wild. I don't give a damn about your smuggling."

"Uh oh."

"My turn now. I've seized your cargoes just to make sure you weren't moving arms or AM2 into the Tahn worlds. You aren't."

Wild seemed honestly shocked. "One thing I am most proud of, commander. I have no truck with war or its trappings. But if I can manage to provide, for people who have the means to pay for it, some small items that make life more convenient, without forcing my customers through the absurdity of customs and thou-shalt-nots . . . I will pursue the matter."

"Thank you, Sr. Wild. We'll be equally frank with you."

Sten and Alex's plot was fairly simple. They had monitored the smugglers' movements long enough to show that the same ships were coming in and out. Therefore, these smugglers had orbits plotted that did not intersect the intense Tahn patrols. Since they were not trading in guns or fuel, Sten wasn't bothered—obviously the Tahn would be forced to pay with hard credits, credits that would not be spent on their own worlds. Slight though it probably was, this might marginally unsettle the Tahn currency base.

Sten's proposal was most simple—he would like any military information that Wild's men and women came up with. In exchange, so long as they held to the no-war-stuff policy, he would leave them completely alone.

Wild shook his head and poured himself another glass of water. "I don't like it," he said.

"Why not?"

"Nobody's that honest."

Sten grinned. "I said we'd like to trade for good things, Sr. Wild. I didn't say that we'd strike an honest bargain."

Wild relaxed in relief. "I, of course, will have to discuss this with my captains."

"Best y' be doin't it w' subtlety, Wild," Kilgour said. "If y' leak to the Tahn, an' we get ambushed..."

"You may assume subtlety, Warrant Officer," Wild said. "I have been smuggling for half a century, and, thus far, no one has gotten closer to my operation than you two." He stood. "I do not foresee any difficulties from my officers," he finished. "Now, would you care to examine my orbit plots so we may determine the most logical meeting places?"

CHAPTER THIRTY-NINE

"AH THINK WE'RE a wee bit lost, young Sten."

"This is clottin' ridiculous. We both aced navigation school. How can we be lost three klicks outside the base? Lemme look at the map again."

Sten and Alex pored over the map of Cavite City one

more time. The other members of the *Claggett*'s crew hovered nearby, trying not to laugh too obviously at their superiors.

"Okay, one more time," Sten said. "South on Imperial Boulevard."

"We done tha'."

"Left at Dessler."

"Check."

"Then right at Garret."

"We bloody done tha' too."

"Now we should see a skoshie little alleyway' about half-way down Garret. The alley cuts straight through to Burns Avenue. That's the theory, anyway."

"Tha be'it a rotten theory. Tha's nae such street!"

The problem they were having was that Cavite's street system was as much of a warren as ancient Tokyo. To compound their difficulties, half the street signs had been obliterated or ripped out by roving street gangs.

Their journey had started out innocently enough. Sten had decided to reward his people for all their hard work by treating them all to a big bash of a dinner. He had told them to pick out any place at all, and hang the expense. He was mildly surprised when the vote came in. Almost every crew member had elected to chow down at a Tahn restaurant. In particular, they picked the Rain Forest. It was an out-of-the-way little spot that boasted the spiciest Tahn food in the city.

Sten had no objection, but he was curious. "Why Tahn food? What's wrong with the native stuff?"

He was greeted with a chorus of "bleahs," which he took to mean that the best of the native fare boarded on bland greasy. So, the Rain Forest restaurant it was. Sten and his crew had some last-minute refitting to do aboard the *Gamble*, so the plan was for the others to go ahead, to be met at the restaurant later.

Sten was shocked when they reached the center of the city. Imperial started out as a broad, clean street that wound past high-class shops, hotels, and gleaming business offices. Then it became what could best be described as a war zone. The street itself was pitted with gaping holes.

Half the shops were either boarded up or burned out. The hulks of abandoned vehicles lined either side of the street. The few people they saw—except for the seven-man squads of cops in full riot gear—were furtive things that scurried into dark corners when they spotted the *Gamble*'s crew.

"What the clot's going on here?" Sten wanted to know.

Foss, who had been out on the streets of Cavite a great deal more, explained. When the Tahn had started beating their war drums, it had made the locals as nervous as hell. First a few, then a flood began fleeing, leaving their businesses and homes abandoned. Unemployment had become fierce, which had led to a booming membership in street gangs. The Tahn section of the city, moreover, had become an embattled slum ghetto, at the mercy of Tahn-bashing gangs.

"You mean that's where this restaurant is? Smack dab in the middle of a riot area?"

"Something like that, sir."

"Clotting wonderful. Next time we eat bland and greasy."

But there was nothing else to do but press on, following the map that the security guard at the base gate had said was AM2 bulletproof. Sten was now thinking fondly of what strings he could pull to bust that clotting guard down to spaceman second.

Sten shoved the map back at Alex. "We must have taken a wrong turn," he said. "There's only one thing we can do. Go all the way back to Dessler and start again."

Everyone groaned.

"They'll have eaten all the food by the time we get there," Foss said. Then he remembered himself. "Begging your pardon, sir."

"What other choice do we have?"

"Ah could alw'ys tell tha spotted snake story," Kilgour offered. "Just ta keep our spirits up, like."

Before Sten could strangle Alex, a joygirl came around the corner. She was dressed in one of the dirtiest, most revealing costumes Sten had ever seen. Also, unlike the other people they had seen so far that night, she didn't seem to have a drop of fear in her blood. Her walk was cool and casual. She was also wearing, Sten noted, an enormous pistol around her waist.

"Uh, excuse me, miss?"

The joygirl looked Sten up and down. Then she glanced over at the other crew members. "You gotta be kidding," she said. "I'm not taking *all* you swabbies on. I'd be out of work for a week."

"No, no," Sten said. "You got me wrong. I just need a little help."

"I'll bet you do."

Sten finally got her attention by waving a handful of credits at her. He explained the problem. The lady shook her head in disgust at their stupidity and pointed at a sagging gate half-hidden by a rusted-out gravsled.

"Right through there," she said. "Then it's left, left, and then it'll fall on your thick skulls."

Two minutes later they were hoisting foaming mugs at the Rain Forest, doing their best to catch up with their shipmates.

The restaurant was aptly named. Hidden under its small dome *was* a forest. Tables were scattered among trees and beside gentle waterfalls. There was a soft breeze coming from somewhere. Colorful birds and huge insects with lacy wings flitted over the diners. The owner was one Sr. Tige, an elderly, gentle Tahn who seemed honestly to enjoy watching the delight on his patrons' faces when they dug into his food.

The menu was as exotic as the atmosphere, with more than thirty items offered. The food ranged from mild-hot to burn-your-scalp-off and was meant to be washed down with big mugs of a delicate Tahn beer. Most of the dishes were served family style in huge crockery bowls.

Sten groaned, patted the small swell at his belt, and leaned back into his seat.

"One more bite," he said, "and I turn into a hot-air vehicle."

"What's the matter, Commander? Out of training?" Luz grinned at him and began spooning out another mound on her plate.

"Where do you put it?" Sten wasn't joking. He couldn't believe the enormous quantities of food she had piled into that slender figure.

"Would you believe a wooden leg, sir?"

Luz was in civvies tonight, and she was wearing a halter top that just covered her small, shapely breasts and the shortest pair of pure white shorts this side of Prime World. Her legs were long and tawny and smooth. Sten glanced down at her legs—he couldn't help but admire them—and shook his head.

"No. Wood I *definitely* don't believe!"

Then he caught himself and flushed. Watch it, Sten, he thought. You can't be doing what you'd love to be doing! Luz saw the blush and smiled. She knew what he was thinking. She gave his hand a gentle pat and then politely turned away and began chattering nonsense to Sekka. Sten realized that in some odd way he had just been rescued. He loved her for it.

There was a crashing sound and loud shouts. Startled, Sten looked up to see a terrified young couple quivering just inside the door. The man's face was bloodied, and the woman's clothing had been ripped. The man was Tahn. There was a splintering of plas as a heavy weight struck a door.

People outside were shouting. "Throw him out... clottin' Tahn fooling with our women..."

Sr. Tige pointed to a back door, and the couple started running for it. But just then the main door crashed open, and four bully boys burst in. They spotted the couple, howled in glee, and rushed toward them. Sr. Tige put up an arm to stop them, but one man smashed him to the floor. The others, led by a hulking thug swinging an equally large club, advanced on the pair.

"First you, you piece of filth," he said to the young Tahn. "Then your slut."

"You're disturbin' our meal, lad," came a soft Scot voice.

The bully boys turned to see Alex and Sten standing just behind them.

"After you pay the damages," Sten said, "you can go."

The man with the club gave a booming laugh. "More Tahn lovers," he said.

Across the room, Sten saw his crew members coming to their feet, but he waved them back.

"I think he's trying to insult us," Sten said to Alex.

"Aye. He wa' brung up bloody rude, this lad."

Without warning, the big man swung the club at Alex with all his strength. Alex didn't even bother ducking or stepping aside. He caught the club in midswing and plucked it away as if from a child. The force of the swing, however, carried the big man toward Alex. The heavy-worlder grabbed an elbow, spun him around, and booted him toward the door. The kick lifted the man from the floor, and he crashed headfirst into a wall. He slumped to the ground.

Enraged, the other three charged. Sten slipped under a knife thrust and left that man howling on the floor with a broken wrist; he struck out with three fingers at another, catching him in the throat. At the last split instant he pulled the punch just enough to avoid crushing the larnyx. He spun on one heel to deal with the other man. But that was unnecessary. Alex had the man suspended from the floor by his belt buckle and was talking soothingly.

"Now, Ah know ye be'it all drunked up, lad. So we will nae hold it again' ye. Hand over the credits and you can go, peaceful like."

The man was too frightened to respond. Alex was getting impatient, so he upended him, gave him a shake, and credits crashed out to the ground. Then, quite casually, he lofted the man out the door. He and Sten frisked the others, relieved them of their money, and booted them out.

Sten walked over to Sr. Tige, who was comforting the couple. He handed the credits to the old Tahn.

"If this isn't enough, sir," he said, "my crew and I would be glad to take up a collection to make up the difference."

"Many, many thanks, young man," he said. "But you must leave, quickly. Before they come back with others."

Sten shrugged. "So. I think we've got more than enough forces to handle them and their crowd."

The old man shook his head. "No. No. You don't know how it is here . . ."

From outside there was an angry rumbling sound. Sten rushed over to the door. Now he knew what the old Tahn was talking about.

In the short time that had elapsed, a mob of over a hundred Imperial settlers had gathered outside. They were screaming for blood. Down the street Sten could see many more pouring around the corner. The oddest part of the whole scene was the big Black Maria just on the outskirts of the growing crowd. There were a half a dozen cops standing there, jeering and egging the mob on.

Sten felt a tug at his shoulder.

"I know how to deal with this," the old man told him.

A switch to one side of the main door brought thick steel grating crashing down to lock into drilled holes in the floor. Around the dome there was the sound of more clanging steel as grating slid in to close up the windows.

"Out. Out, please," the man said. "We will be safe here. But if you stay, you will be arrested."

Numbly, Sten found himself creeping out the back door with his crew.

"You know, lad," Alex said in a low voice. "Ah'm not too sure we chos'it the correct side."

Sten had not one word of reply.

CHAPTER FORTY

THE NEXT FEW weeks for Sten and the others were paradoxical. They *knew* that the war was moments away. Each report from Wild's smugglers verified their feelings—Tahn ships were being commissioned and assigned to battlefleets daily. The civilians on Heath had already become accustomed to regulated hours and ration chips.

Cavite was the exact opposite. It seemed to Sten that Admiral van Doorman, his officers, and his men retreated further and further into a fantasy world. To the officers, van Doorman's parties became steadily more lavish. To Sten's enlisted men, the other sailors of the fleet grew more and more sloppy and less concerned.

But the times, even in retrospect, appeared golden.

Perhaps, for Sten, an element was his love affair with Brijit. But that was only one element.

Perhaps the linkup with Wild was another part of it. The smuggler was very conscious of his end of the bargain. Sten decided that he and the others were eating better than when he had been assigned to the Emperor's own court. In fact, he was, for the first time in his life, wondering if maybe he was getting fat.

Another factor might have been that there were *none* of the troubles that Sten and Alex had expected from their pickup crew. Even Lieutenant Estill seemed to be fitting in perfectly. What few problems came up were handled quickly by a fat lip applied sensitively by Mr. Kilgour, who had taken on the personal role of flotilla master-at-arms.

But the real reason was that the four tacships, and the people who volunteered for them, were doing exactly as they wanted and as they were supposed to—without anyone shooting at them.

Sten kept his ships off Cavite as much as possible. Even for a major teardown his ground crews would be sardined into the ship they would be tearing down and taken to a completely deserted beach world. Major inspections were regarded as nightmares, and no one in Cavite's yard could understand why the engine and hull specialists were coming back with tans and happy smiles.

Sten was an instinctual flier—but the sensation that had struck him was that of speed, of flying low-level with some relatable objects veering up and past him. Now, on those long slow watches, he found another joy.

The tacships spent long shifts just observing, hanging

above a planetary system's ecliptic, possibly correcting starcharts, possibly monitoring Tahn ship movements, possibly evaluating those worlds as Tahn outposts. Sten should have been bored.

He never was. Alex had modified one of the *Gamble*'s Goblin missiles, removing the warhead and replacing it with extra fuel cells.

It was Sten's joy, offwatch, to put on a spare control helmet and float "his" Goblin out into deep space. He knew that the perceptions of a star being "above" or a planet "below" him were the false analogues provided by computer. He also knew that his feelings of heat from a nearby sun, or cold from an iceplanet, were completely subjective. But he still reveled in them. To him, this was the ultimate form of the human dream of flight. It was even better, because he knew that if anything happened, he was really safely on board the *Gamble*.

The shifts and days drifted past. Sten frequently had to check patrol time by the ship's log. If the supplies would have held out, Sten thought he might have remained in space forever, beyond human reach or response.

It was after such a fugue that Sten encountered the *Forez* for the first time, and Admiral Deska for the second.

The *Kelly* and the *Gamble* had been attempting to plot a meteor stream's track. Lieutenant Sekka had insisted that the meteors came from a single exploded planet. Sten had argued that merely because the boulders were somewhat oversize didn't necessarily indicate anything. But, in amusement, he had authorized a backplot on those rocks.

Every alarm siren in the universe brought the fun and games to an end. Alex and Sten, on the *Gamble*'s command deck, and Lieutenant Sekka, on the *Kelly*, stared at the screen.

"Wha' we hae here," Kilgour finally said, "is the biggest clottin' battlewagon Ah hae ever seen. Imperial or Tahn. An' tha's nae entry in *Jane*'s f'r it."

"Stand by, emergency power," Sten said. He checked their position. They were supposedly in a neutral sector, although Sten had a fair idea that if the Tahn were feeling feisty, that wouldn't help.

There was a com blast that sent the readings into the red. "Foreign ship. Identify or be blasted."

"Impolite clots," Kilgour muttered.

Sten went to the closed circuit to Sekka. "*Kelly*, if the shooting starts, get out of it."

"But—"

"Orders."

He changed channels.

"Imperial Tacship *Gamble* receiving."

The screen cleared. It took Sten a moment to recognize the Tahn officer, in full-dress uniform, standing behind the communications specialist. But he did.

"Captain Deska. You've gotten a promotion."

Deska, too, was puzzled—and then he remembered. He did not seem pleased at the memory. He covered nicely. "Imperial ship . . . we are not receiving your transmissions. This is the Tahn Battleship *Forez*. You have intruded into a Tahn sector. Stand by to be boarded. You are subject to internment."

"I wish," Sten said to Alex, "we had Ida with us."

Alex grinned. Their gypsy pilot in Mantis Section had once hoisted her skirts, with nothing underneath, after hearing a similar command.

Sten, not being good at repartee, shut down communication. "*Kelly*. Return to Cavite at full power. Full report. Keep it under seal for forty-eight E-hours or until my return, whichever comes first."

"I did not accept command in order to—yessir."

That got one worry out of the way—the *Kelly* was several light-minutes behind Sten's ship, and Sten figured there was no way that Sekka could get caught.

He thought for a moment. "Mr. Kilgour."

"Sir."

"I would like a collision course set for this *Forez*."

"Sir."

"Three-quarters power."

Someone on the *Forez* must have computed Sten's trajectory. The emergency circuit yammered at him. Sten ignored it.

"Lad, thae hae a great ploy. But hae y' consider't we may be ae war already? Tha' Tahn'd know afore we did."

Sten, as a matter of fact, had not. It was a little late to add that into the equation, however.

"New orbit . . . get me a light-minute away from that clot . . . on count . . . three . . . two . . . now!"

An observer with systemwide vision would have seen the *Gamble* veer.

"Tahn ship appears to have weapons systems tracking," Foss said.

"Far clottin' out. Foss, I want that random orbit of yours . . . on count . . . two . . . one . . . now!"

Foss had come up with a random-choice attack pattern that Sten had used to train the Fox antimissile crews. Foss swore it was impossible for anyone, even linked to a supercomputer, to track a missile using such an orbit.

There were two considerations: The *Gamble*, no matter how agile, could not compare to a missile. Also, its effects on the crew, despite the McLean generators, were unsettling.

Sten took it as long as he could. Then he had a slight inspiration. "New trajectory . . . stand by . . . I want a boarding trajectory!"

"Sir."

"Goddammit, you heard me!"

"Boarding trajectory. Aye, sir."

The two ships bore toward each other again.

"Mr. Kilgour, what honors do you render a Tahn ship?"

"Clot if Ah know't, Skipper. Stab 'em in tha' back ae tha' be a Campbell?"

Sten swore to himself. It would have been a great jape. He had never worried about the *Forez*. At least not that much. First, he thought that if war had been declared—or had even begun sans declaration—Admiral Deska would have ground Sten's nose in it. Second, he assumed that the *Forez*'s missiles were probably larger than the *Gamble* herself. And third, tacships do not attack, let alone reattack, battleships.

The *Forez* and the *Gamble* passed each other barely three light-seconds apart. It was not close enough, in spite of Kilgour's claims, to chip the antipickup anodizing on the *Gamble*'s hull.

A ship in space, with its McLean generators on, had no true up or down, so the *Forez*'s response to the close pass would have been known only to the officers and men on its bridge and navcenter. But Sten, watching in a rear screen, was most pleased to see the huge Tahn battleship end-over-end-over-end three times before it recovered.

"Emergency power, Mr. Kilgour," he said, and was unashamed of a bit of smugness.

"Lad," Alex managed. "Y're thinki't y're entirely too cute t' be one ae us humans."

CHAPTER FORTY-ONE

STEN, HEELS LOCKED and fingers correctly curled at the seams of his uniform, wondered which of his multifarious sins van Doorman had discovered. For some reason, however, van Doorman seemed almost cheerful. Sten guessed that it was caused by the maze of painters and carpenters he had threaded his way through entering the admiral's suite at the Carlton Hotel.

"Commander, I realize that ceremony evidently means little to you. But are you aware that Empire Day is less than seventy-two hours from now?"

Sten was. Empire Day was a personal creation of the Eternal Emperor. Once every E-year, all Imperial Forces not engaged in combat threw an open house. It was a combination of public relations and a way of showing the lethality of the usually sheathed Imperial saber. "I am, sir."

"And I am mildly surprised. I wanted to issue instructions for the proper display of your ships and men."

"Display, sir?"

"Of course," van Doorman said, a trace irritably. "The entire 23rd Fleet will be open to visitors, as usual."

"Uh . . . I'm sorry, sir. We can't do it."

Van Doorman scowled, then brightened. Perhaps this might be the excuse he needed to gulag Sten. "That was not a request, Commander. You may take it as a direct order."

"Sir, that's an order I can't obey." Sten sort of wanted to see how purple his admiral would get before he explained but thought better of it. "Sir, according to Imperial Order R-278-XN-FICHE: BULKELEY, all of my ships are under a security edict. From Prime World, sir. There's a copy in your operations files, sir." Sten was making up the order number—but such an order *did* exist.

Van Doorman sat back in his chair after probably rejecting several comebacks. "So you and your crew of thugs will just frowst about on Empire Day. Most convenient."

And then Sten had his idea, inspired by the thought of Empire Day—and the Emperor, who loved a double-blind plan. "Nossir. We'd rather not, sir, unless that's your orders."

Before van Doorman could answer, Sten went on. "Actually, Admiral, I had planned to set an appointment with your flag secretary today, to offer a suggestion."

Van Doorman waited.

"Sir, while we can't allow anyone close to our ships, there's no reason that they can't be seen. Everyone on Cavite's seen us take off and land."

"You have an idea," van Doorman said.

"Yessir. Is there any reason that we could not do a flyby? Perhaps after you deliver the opening remarks?"

"Hmm," van Doorman mused. "I *have* watched your operations. Quite spectacular—although as I have said before, I see little combat value in your craft. But they are very, very showy."

"Yessir. And my officers are very experienced in in-atmosphere aerobatics."

Van Doorman actually smiled. "Perhaps, Commander, I have been judging you too harshly. I felt that you really did not have the interests of our navy at heart. I could have been mistaken."

"Thank you, sir. But I'm not quite finished."

"Go ahead."

"If you would be willing to issue authorization, we could provide quite a fireworks display as part of the flyby."

"Fireworks aren't exactly part of our ordnance."

"I know that, sir. But we could draw blanks for the chainguns and remove the warheads on some of the obsolete missiles we have in storage."

"You are thinking. That would be very exciting. And it would enable us to get rid of some of those clunkers, before we get gigged for having them at the next IG."

Sten realized that van Doorman was making a joke. He laughed.

"Very well. Very well indeed. I'll issue the authorization today. Commander, I think you and I are starting to think in the same lines."

God help me if we are, Sten thought. "One more thing, sir."

"Another idea?"

"Nossir. A question. You said the *entire* fleet will be on display?"

"Outside of two picket boats—that is my custom."

Sten saluted and left.

The war council consisted of Sten, Alex, Sh'aarl't, Estill, Sekka, and Sutton and was held in one of the flotilla's engine yards.

"This is to be regarded as information-only, people," Sten started. He relayed what had happened at the meeting with van Doorman. The other officers took a minute to absorb things, then put on their what-a-dumb-clottin'-idea-but-you're-the-skipper expressions.

"Maybe there's madness to my method. I got to thinking that if I were a Tahn, and I wanted a time to start things off with a bang, I could do a helluva lot worse than pick Empire Day.

"Every clotting ship our wonderful admiral has is gonna be sitting on line. Security will be two tacships and shore patrolmen on foot."

"Tha's noo bad thinkin'," Alex said. "Th' Tahn dinna appear to me t'be't standin't on ceremony like declarations of war or like that."

"And if they hit us," Sh'aarl't added, "I'd just as soon not be sitting on the ground waiting."

"Maybe I'm slow, Commander," Estill said. "But say you're right. And we're airborne when—and if—they come in. But with, pardon me, clotting fireworks?"

Alex looked at the lieutenant with admiration. It may have been the first time he had used the word "clot" since being commissioned. Being in the mosquito fleet was proving salutory for Estill's character.

"Exactly, Lieutenant," Sten said. "We're going to have great fireworks. Goblin fireworks, Fox fireworks, and Kali fireworks. Van Doorman's given us permission to loot his armory—and we're going to take advantage."

Tapia laughed. "What happens if you're wrong—and ol' Doormat calls for his fireworks?"

"It'd be a clottin' major display, and we'll *all* be looking for new jobs. Vote?"

Van Doorman would probably have relieved Sten on the spot just for running his flotilla with even a breath of democracy.

Kilgour, of course, was all for it. As was Tapia. Sekka and Sh'aarl't gave it a moment of thought, then concurred. Estill smiled. "Paranoiacs together," he said, and raised his hand.

"Fine. Get work crews together, Mr. Sutton, and some gravsleds."

"Yes, sir. By the way, would you have any objections if some of my boys happen to be terrible at mathematics and acquire some *extra* weaponry?"

"Mr. Sutton, I myself could never count above ten without taking my boots off. Now, move 'em out."

CHAPTER FORTY-TWO

SR. ECU FLOATED just above the sand, which had been sifted to a prism white—a white even purer than the minuscule sensors that whiskered from his wings. He settled closer to the garden floor, shuddered in disgust, and gave a faint flap to a winglet. A puff of dust rose from the sand, and he was in position again.

Lord Fehrle had kept him waiting for nearly two hours. The impatience he felt now had little to do with the length of the waiting. Sr. Ecu was a member of a race that treasured the subtle stretchings of time. But not now, and not in this environment.

He supposed that he had been ushered into the sand garden because the Lord Fehrle wanted to impress him with his sense of art and understanding. Besides patience, the Manabi were noted for their sensitivity to visual stimulation.

The sand garden was a perfect bowl with a radius of about a half a kilometer. In this area were laid exactly ten stones, ranging in size from five meters down to a third of a meter. Each stone was of a different color: earth colors varying from deep black to a tinge of orange. They had all been mathematically placed the proper distance apart. It was the coldest work of art that Sr. Ecu had seen in his hundred-plus years. During the two hours of waiting he had considered what may have been in Lord Fehrle's mind when he created it.

The thinking was not comfortable. If one stone had been ever so slightly out of place or if a patch of sand had not been as perfect as the rest, he would have felt much better.

He had tried to change the shape of it all with his own presence.

Sr. Ecu's body was black with a hint of red just under the wing tips. His tail snaked out three meters, narrowing to a point that had once held a sting in his race's ancestral past. He had tried moving himself around from point to point, hovering for long minutes as he tried physically to break up the cold perfection that was the garden. Somehow he kept finding himself back in the same place. If nothing more, his physical presence in the perfect spot added to the psychological ugliness of the place.

Even for a Tahn, on a scale of one to ten, Lord Fehrle rated below zero as a diplomat. This was an estimation that Sr. Ecu could make with authority. His own race was noted for its diplomatic bearing—which was the reason Fehrle had requested his presence.

In any other circumstances Sr. Ecu would have left in a diplomatic huff after the first half hour. Anger at insult can be a valuable tool in intrasystem relations. But not in *these* circumstances. He was not sure that the Manabi could preserve their traditional neutrality, much less a future, if the Tahn and the Empire continued on their collision course.

So he would wait and talk and see in this obscenity of a garden that perfectly illustrated the Tahn mind.

It was another half hour before Lord Fehrle appeared. He was polite but abrupt, acting as if *he* had been kept waiting instead of the Manabi. Fehrle had sketched in the current status of relations between the Empire and the Tahn. All of this, except for smaller details, the Manabi knew. He dared Fehrle's impatience by saying so.

"This is a textbook summation of the situation, my lord," he said. "Most admirable. Almost elegant in its sparseness. But I fail to see my role."

"To be frank," Fehrle said, "we intend to launch a full-out attack."

All three of Sr. Ecu's stomachs lurched. Their linings had been sorely tested in the past, to the point where he had been sure he would never be able to digest his favorite microorganisms again. This, however, was true disaster.

"I beg you to reconsider, my lord," he said. "Are your

positions really so far apart? Is it *really* too late to talk? In my experience . . ."

"That's why I asked you here," Fehrle said. "There is a way out. A way to avoid total war."

Sr. Ecu knew the man was lying through his gleaming teeth. However, he could hardly say so. "I'm delighted to hear that," he said. "I suppose you have some new demands. Compromises, perhaps? Areas of concern to be traded for firm agreements?"

Fehrle snorted. "Not at all," he said. "We will settle for nothing less than total capitulation."

"If I may say so, that is not a very good way to resume negotiations, my lord," Sr. Ecu murmured.

"But that is where I intend to begin, just the same," Fehrle said. "I have a fiche outlining our position. It will be delivered to you before you leave for Prime World."

"And how much time shall I tell the Emperor's emissaries they have to respond?"

"Seventy-two E-hours," Lord Fehrle said flatly, almost in a monotone.

"But, my lord, that's impossible. It would take a miracle for me to even *reach* Prime World in that time, much less to set up the proper channels."

"It's seventy-two hours just the same."

"You must listen to reason, my lord!"

"Then you refuse?"

Now Sr. Ecu understood. Fehrle wanted a refusal. Later he could say that he had done his best to avert full war but that the Manabi would not undertake the mission. He had to admire the plan, as in a way he admired how perfectly ugly the man's garden was. Because there was no way in his race's coda that Sr. Ecu could undertake the mission.

"Yes, my lord. I'm afraid I must refuse."

"Very well, then."

Lord Fehrle turned without another word and stalked off across the white sand. Sr. Ecu rippled his wings and in a moment was soaring away, his own self-esteem and his race's neutrality shattered.

CHAPTER FORTY-THREE

THE WEATHER REPORT for Empire Day was disappointing: overcast with occasional rain, heavy at times. Rotten weather for a holiday—but it would save the lives of several thousands of beings on Cavite and, perhaps, be responsible for Sten's survival on that day.

Sten had restricted his crews to the flotilla area twenty-four hours beforehand. There had been grumbles—Empire Day for the 23rd Fleet was not only show-and-tell day but a rationale for some serious partying. Not that there was much time for bitching—they were too busy loading and resupplying the ships. And quickly the crew members, seeing live missiles and ammunition being not only loaded but racked and mounted, figured that something very much out of the ordinary was going on.

The ships were ready to launch at 1900 hours. Sten was amused to see that the final load actually was fireworks, acquired by Sutton from some of his black-market contacts. Sten put everyone under light hypno sleep and tried for a little rest himself—without result.

Wearing a slicker against the occasional spatters of rain, he spent the middle hours of the night pacing around his ships and wondering why he had ever wanted to be the man in charge of anything.

He roused his people at 0100.

The *Kelly, Claggett, Gamble*, and *Richards* lifted near-silently on Yukawa drive at 0230. Dawn would be at 0445. Admiral van Doorman would open the ceremonies at 0800.

* * *

163

The Tahn, too, had their timetable. It was based around that of the 23rd Fleet.

A month earlier, a Tahn working inside fleet head-quarters had copied the Empire Day schedule fiche, and it had been immediately relayed offworld. The fiche occupied a small screen on one side of the *Forez*'s bridge. Neither Lady Atago nor Admiral Deska needed to consult it.

Nearby hung a second, newly completed battleship—the *Kiso*—of the same class as the *Forez*. The Tahn battlefleet waited just on the edge of Cavite's stellar system. Nearly numberless cruisers, destroyers, attack ships, and troop-ships filled out the fleet.

Other battlefleets, equally massive, had been assigned other targets in the Fringe Worlds. Lady Atago was to destroy the 23rd Fleet and its base on Cavite.

On the tick, Atago ordered the attack.

Remote sensors scattered offworld were destroyed, jammed, or given false data to transmit. To make sure there was no alert, at 0500 five squads of commando Tahn, some of whom had been trained on Frehda's farm, hit the 23rd Fleet's SigInt center. Other Tahn, correctly uniformed as Imperial sailors, took over the center.

At 0730, the main elements of Atago's battlefleet were just out-atmosphere. The two picket boats, their crew members hung over and their screens focused, against orders, on the display field below, barely had time to see the incoming Tahn destroyers before they were destroyed.

On the field, Admiral van Doorman, flanked by Brijit and his wife, checked the time—ten minutes—and then started up the steps of the reviewing stand.

Staff officers and civilian dignitaries were already wait-ing.

In the ionosphere, the Tahn assault ship opened its bays, and small attack craft spewed downward.

Sten's problem, after lift, was where to hide. If he was correct and Cavite was about to be hit, it would be hit hard. He had full confidence in his tacships—but not in an orbital situation where he might be facing a battleship or six.

Nor was the cloud cover the answer, as any ship attacking from offworld would be using electronics. The clouds wouldn't even show up on most shipscreens.

Sten's best solution was to take his flotilla out over the ocean, some twenty kilometers away from Cavite, and hold at fifty meters over the sea. He figured that he would probably be buried in ground clutter and very hard to pick up.

Foss was the first to pick up the attacking ships.

"All ships," Sten ordered. "Independent attacks. Conserve munitions and watch your tails. We're at war!"

Kilgour had the *Gamble* at full power, headed back for Cavite.

The first V-wing of Tahn launched air-to-ground metal-seeking missiles at 1000 meters, pulled momentarily level, and scattered frag bombs down the length of the field.

The parade ground became a hell of explosions.

Van Doorman had time enough to see the missiles, gape once, and throw himself on top of his wife and daughter before all thought vanished and sanity became trying to hold on to the pitching ground under him.

The Tahn ships lifted, banked, and came back on a strafing pass. Most of the dignitaries and staff officers not killed by the bombs were shattered with chaingun bursts.

Van Doorman lifted his head and saw, through blood, the ships coming back in. That was all he remembered.

He didn't see the *Richards* and *Claggett* come in on the flank, their own chainguns raving, or the thinly armored Tahn ships cartwheel into the field, their pinwheeling wreckage doing as much damage to the 23rd Fleet's ships as the missiles had.

Seeing the *Richards* and *Claggett* pull ahead of him, Sten changed his mind and his tactics. He ordered the *Kelly* into wingman's slot and climbed for space.

The Tahn assault ship was not expecting any response from the maelstrom below and was an easy target. The *Gamble*'s weapons systems clicked through Kali choice to Goblin, and Kilgour fired.

The hull of the ship gaped, and red flame seared out.

In the *Kelly*, Sekka had taken away his weapons officer's

control helmet—*he* was the warrior of generations. The chant he was muttering went back 2,000 years as his sights crossed and settled on the huge bulk of the *Forez*. Without orders, he launched the Kali.

Even under full AM2 power, the *Kelly* jolted as the huge missile chuffed out the center launch tube, and its own AM2 drive launched it.

For Sekka, there was nothing but the growing bulk of the Tahn battleship in his eyes as he became the Kali.

The missile was well named. It struck the *Forez* on a weapons deck. Two-hundred-fifty Tahn crewmen died in the initial explosion, and more were killed in the blast of secondary explosions.

Sekka allowed himself a tight smile as he pulled off the helmet, seeing, onscreen, four attacking Tahn destroyers. That was nothing. And if they killed him, what was death to a Mandingo warrior?

It was possible that the two Tahn cruisers did not ever expect attack from a ship as small as the *Gamble*. Certainly they seemed to take no significant evasive action and launched only a handful of countermissiles before Kilgour had Goblins at full power, targets locked.

Sten knew that the Goblins could injure a cruiser, but he did not expect the nearly simultaneous explosions; seeing the screen begin flashing NO TARGET UNDER ACQUISITION, Alex lifted his weapons helmet.

"Lad, wha's th' matter wi' their blawdy cruisers?"

Sten, seeing a pack of destroyers coming in, too late to save their charges, was busy with evasive action.

Lady Atago, on the bridge of the *Forez*, braced herself as the battleship shuddered under another explosion. Part of her brain was pleased—in spite of catastrophe, the men and women she had trained were responding efficiently and without panic.

"Your orders?"

Atago considered the choices. There was only one. "Admiral Deska, cancel the landing on Cavite. We cannot proceed with only one capital ship. The other landings on the secondary systems may proceed. You and I shall transfer our flags to the *Kiso*. Order the *Forez* to proceed to a forward repair base."

"Your orders, milady."

Sten saw the Tahn fleet begin its withdrawal as he and his ships returned to base.

It wasn't much of a victory. Below on Cavite, the 23rd Fleet, the only Imperial forces in the Fringe Worlds, was almost completely destroyed.

The Tahn war had just begun.

BOOK THREE

ON THE WIND

CHAPTER FORTY-FOUR

THE ATTACK ON the Caltor System and Cavite was not the actual beginning of the war. That had occurred one E-hour earlier in an attack against Prime World and the Emperor himself.

Nearly simultaneously, thousands of Tahn ships savaged the Empire. Missions varied from invasion to base reduction to fleet battles. At the end of the initial phase, the Tahn estimated their success at better than eighty-five percent. It was one of the blackest days in the Empire's history.

The attack coordination had been exceedingly complex, since the Tahn wanted to reap the maximum benefits possible from Empire Day. Technically the minute of vengeance —what more prosaic cultures might call D-day—was at the same tick of the ammonium maser clock that each fleet commander had on his or her bridge.

Actually, of course, there were adjustments, since each of the Imperial worlds used its own time zoning. There also were readjustments to keep the attacks within a close enough time frame to prevent the Empire from coming to full alert.

Almost more important to the Tahn was a "moral" readjustment. Somehow the Tahn felt it perfectly legitimate to begin a war without the usual roundelay of escalating diplomatic threats but dishonorable to not strike at—their phrase—the throat of the tiger.

Prime World.

The Eternal Emperor.

The choice of Empire day to begin the war was made for several reasons. The Tahn correctly assumed the Imperial military would be collected and relaxed; there would be, if the attacks were successful, an inevitable lowering of Imperial morale; and, finally, because this was the one day of the year when everyone knew where the Emperor was—at home, expecting visitors.

Home was a oversize duplicate of the Earth castle Arundel, with a six- by two-kilometer bailey in front, surrounded by fifty-five kilometers of parkland. Housed in the bailey's V-banked walls were the most important elements of the Empire's administration. The castle itself contained not only the Emperor, his bodyguards, and considerable staff but the command and control center for the entire Empire. Most of the necessary technology was buried far under Arundel, along with enough air/water/food to withstand a century-long siege.

The visitors the Emperor was expecting were his subjects. Once a year the normally closed-off castle was opened up for a superspectacle of bands, military displays, and games. To be invited or somehow to wangle a ticket to Empire Day at the palace was an indication of signal achievement or purchase.

It had taken four years for the Tahn to prepare for their attack on Arundel. The only possible assault that could be made was a surgical strike—there was no way that the Tahn could slip a fleet or even a squadron of destroyers through the Empire's offworld security patrols.

Except for Empire Day, the airspace over Arundel was sealed. All aerial traffic on Prime World was monitored, and any deviation from the flight pattern put the palace's AA sections on alert. An intrusion into the palace's airspace was electronically challenged once and then attacked. It was equally impossible to approach the palace on the ground—the only connection between Arundel and the nearest city, Fowler, was by high-speed pneumosubway.

Except for Empire Day...

On Empire Day huge troop-carrying gravlighters were used to move tourists from Fowler to the palace. The security precautions were minimal—all passengers were, of course, vetted and searched. The lighters themselves were given a fixed flight pattern and time, in addition to being equipped with a IFF—Identification–Friend or Foe—box linked to the palace's aerial security section.

These precautions were ludicrously easy to subvert.

Oddly enough, the Tahn may have felt it dishonorable not to attack the Emperor—but, on the other hand, they preferred to do the dirty work through a cutout. "Honor" in a militaristic society is most often Rabelaisian: "Do what thou wilt shalt be the whole of the law."

Three highly committed Tahn immigrants—revolutionaries from the late Godfrey Alain's Fringe World movement —had been chosen and moved into position by Tahn intelligence two years previously. One was instructed to find a minor job at Fowler's port, Soward. A second found employment as a barkeep. The third was hired as a gardener by the occupants of one of the luxurious estates that ringed the Imperial grounds. He was an excellent gardener —the merchant prince who employed him swore he had never had a harder or more conscientious worker.

The method of attack would be by missile, a rather specially designed missile. The Tahn surmised correctly that Arundel was faced with nuclear shielding, so a conventional nuke within practical limits would not provide complete destruction. The final missile looked most odd. It was approximately ten meters long and was configured to provide a very specific sensor profile, a profile closely matching that of a much larger Guard gravlighter.

Inside it were two nuclear devices. Tahn science had figured out how to utilize the ancient shaped-charge effect— the Munro effect—with atomics. For shrouding and cone they used imperium, the shielding normally used to handle Anti-Matter Two, the Empire's primary power source. Behind the first device was the guidance mechanism, and back of that was the second device. The missile's nose was sharply pointed, less for aerodynamics than for blast effect.

Besides the guidance system, the missile also contained a duplicate of the IFF box that would be used by the gravlighters on Empire Day.

The missile had been smuggled, in three sections, onto Prime World some months previously, transported to a leased warehouse, assembled, and set in its launch rack by a team of Tahn scientists.

The three Tahn from the Fringe Worlds were never told the location of the missile; they were merely instructed to be in certain locations with certain equipment at a certain time.

Two days before Empire Day, the Tahn who was a ramp rat at Soward installed a small timer-equipped device in a specified gravlighter's McLean generator.

One day before Empire Day, the controller for the three men boarded an offworld flight and disappeared.

At 1100 on Empire Day, the three men were in place.

The gardener sat ready behind the controls of one of his employer's gravsleds. No one in the mansion would notice —two canisters of a binary blood gas had seen to that.

The other two were atop a building in Soward, near the launch site, one watching a timer, the other counting gravlighters as they lifted off toward Arundel.

Number seven was "theirs."

On the field, the pilot of the sabotaged gravlighter applied power. The lighter raised, belched smoke, and clanked down. The field's dispatcher swore and ordered a standby unit up to cross-load the passengers.

On the building, the timer touched zero, and the first man fingered a switch on his control box. At the warehouse, explosive charges blew a ragged hole in the roof. McLean-assist takeoff units lifted the missile into the air, then dropped away as the Yukawa drive cut in and the missile smashed forward at full power.

Kilometers away, the third man also went into action. At the commanded time, he lifted the gravsled straight up. His mouth was very dry as he hoped that the palace's aerial sensors would be a little slow.

His own control panel beeped at him—the missile was within range. He focused the riflelike device toward Arundel, dim in the morning haze, and touched a switch. A low-power laser illuminated Arundel's gateway. A second beep informed him that the missile had acquired the target.

For the three Tahn, their mission was accomplished.

Now their orders were to evade capture and make their way to a given rendezvous point outside Soward. Of course, Tahn intelligence had no intention either of making a pickup or of leaving a trail. Both the launch and the aiming control boxes contained secondary timers and explosive charges. Seconds after the missile signaled, they went off.

No one saw the explosion that vaporized the Tahn as they scurried toward a ladder, but a watch officer at Arundel saw the gravsled ball into flame and pinwheel down. His hand was halfway to an alert button when the automatic sensors correctly interpreted that the gravlighter headed for the palace was moving at a speed far beyond reason and screamed warning.

The Eternal Emperor was in his apartments alternately cursing to the head of his Gurkha bodyguards about the necessity to wear full-dress uniform and pinning on various decorations. Captain Chittahang Limbu was half listening and smiling agreeably. Limbu was still somewhat in awe of his current position. Formerly a Subadar major, he had been promoted to Sten's old job as head of the Emperor's bodyguard. This was the highest position a Gurkha had ever held in Imperial history.

He was fondly remembering the celebration his home village had thrown for him on his last leave, when the overhead alarm bansheed its warning.

The Emperor jumped, sticking himself with a medal pin. Limbu was a stocky brown blur, slapping a switch on the panel at his waist and then manhandling the Emperor forward, toward a suddenly gaping hole in the wall.

Whatever was happening, his orders were clear and in no way allowed for the Gurkhas' love of combat.

The missile's impact point was almost perfect. The thin nose squashed as designed, allowing the missile to hang in place for a microsecond. The first nuke blew, and its directional blast tore through the shielding. The missile continued to crumple, and then the second bomb exploded.

And Arundel, heart of the Empire, vanished into the center of a newborn sun.

CHAPTER FORTY-FIVE

STEN ITEMIZED CHAOS as he slowly steered his combat car over the rubble that had been Cavite City's main street. This was not the first city or world that he had been on when the talking stopped and the shooting started. But this appeared to be the first time he had been in on the ground floor of a Empirewide war.

Experience is valuable, he reminded himself, which avoided his worry about Brijit.

Sten had brought his miraculously undamaged ships down onto Cavite Base at nightfall. Sometimes dishonesty pays—he had located his supply base in a disused warehouse in the test yards. As a result, the weaponry and supplies that Sutton had acquired had not been touched by the Tahn attack.

He ordered his boats to resupply and return to low orbit immediately. He would try to find out from fleet headquarters how bad things really were.

Cavite Base was a boil and confusion of smoke and flame.

Sten commandeered a combat car and headed for the Carlton Hotel. If it still stood, he assumed that what remained of van Doorman's command staff would be there.

Cavite City hadn't suffered major damage, Sten estimated. Imperial Boulevard—the central street—had absorbed some incendiary and AP bombs or rockets, but most of the buildings still stood. There weren't any civilians on the night-hung streets other than rescue workers and fire-fighting teams. Contrary to legend, disaster generally made people pull together or retreat into their homes—rioting in the streets had always been a myth.

Sten veered the combat car aside as a gravsled, hastily painted with red crosses on the landing pads, whistled past. In the distance, he could hear the sounds of combat. That was the storming of the SigInt center—since the Tahn had not been able to land, those revolutionaries who had occupied the center had died to the last man.

Sten did not know, or much care, what the shooting signified—the situation was bad enough right now for him. He grounded the combat car outside the Carlton and started for the entrance.

Security, he noted wryly, had improved—three sets of SP men checked him before he hit the main doors. But some things did not change. The two dress-uniformed patrolmen still snapped their willyguns to salute as he came up the steps. Sten wondered if either of them realized that their uniforms were now spattered with muck, blood, and what appeared to be vomit.

If Cavite City was chaos, Admiral van Doorman's headquarters was worse. Sten desperately needed to know how bad the damage was and what his orders should be. He started at the fleet operations office. It was dark and deserted. Only the computer terminals flashed and analyzed the disaster of the day. A passing tech told him that all operations personnel appeared to have died in the attack.

Fine. He would try fleet intelligence.

Sten should have known what was going on when he saw that the door to the intelligence center yawned wide, with no sentries.

Inside, he found madness—quite literally.

Ship Captain Ladislaw sat behind a terminal, programming and reprogramming. He greeted Sten happily and then showed him what dispositions would be made on the morrow, moving the gradated dots that were the ships of the 23rd Fleet across the starchart covering one wall.

The Tahn would be repelled handily, he said. Sten knew that most of the ships he was chessboarding around were broken and smoking on the landing field at the base.

He smiled, agreed with Ladislaw, then stepped behind him, one-handed a sopor injection from his belt medpak, and shot it into the base of the ship captain's spine. Ladislaw folded instantly across his printout of impossibilities, and Sten headed for van Doorman's office.

Admiral Xavier Rijn van Doorman was quite calm and quite collected. His command center was an oasis of peace.

Sten saw Brijit peering in from the half-open door that led to van Doorman's quarters and thanked Someone that she was still alive.

Van Doorman was studying the status board over his desk. Sten glanced at it and winced—the situation was even worse than he had anticipated. For all intents and purposes, the 23rd Fleet had ceased to exist.

At dawn that morning, the 23rd Fleet strength consisted of one heavy cruiser, the *Swampscott*, two light cruisers, some thirteen destroyers, fifty-six assorted obsolete patrol-craft, minelayer/sweepers, Sten's tacdiv, one hospital ship, and the usual gaggle of supply and maintenance craft.

The status readout showed one light cruiser destroyed, and one heavily damaged. Six destroyers were out of action, as were about half of the light combat ships and support elements.

The oddness was that the *Swampscott* was untouched. It had survived because of Sten's attack on the *Forez*. The *Swampscott* had been one of Atago's self-assigned targets.

Sten's orders were simple—to keep his tacships in space. Van Doorman would provide any support necessary until the situation straightened itself out. Sten was given complete freedom of command. Any assistance Intelligence or Operations could provide was his for the asking—one madman, and corpses.

Just wonderful, Sten thought.

Yessir, Admiral.

His snappy salute was returned with equal fervor. He saw the blankness in van Doorman's eyes and wondered.

In the corridor, Brijit was in his arms and explaining. Her mother had died in the attack. There was nothing left. Nothing at all.

Probably Sten should have stayed with her that night. But the coldness that was Sten's sheath, the coldness that had come from the death of his parents years before on Vulcan, the coldness that had seen too many drinking friends die, stopped him. Instead there was a hug, and he was hurrying toward the com center. He wanted the *Gamble* in for a pickup.

As the *Gamble* flared in, settling in the middle of the boulevard outside the Carlton, Sten found time to be amazed at van Doorman's ability to control himself.

That was another cipher. But one to watch very carefully, Sten thought, as the *Gamble's* port yawned and he ran toward it.

He had already forgotten van Doorman, Brijit, and the likelihood that he and his people would die in the Caltor System.

His mind was hearing only "independent command . . ."

CHAPTER FORTY-SIX

THE ETERNAL EMPEROR spotted something and waddled, bulky in his radiation suit, through the nuclear ruin that had been one of his rose gardens. Behind him, willyguns ready, moved two suited Gurkhas—Captain Limbu and a naik. Above and to their rear floated a combat car, guns sweeping the grounds.

Limbu had been successful in shoving the Emperor into the McLean-controlled slide tube that led 2,000 meters into the underground sanctuary and control center under the castle, then had dived after him. Radiation-proof air locks had slammed closed as they fell.

Very few others aboveground had lived—there were only a handful of Gurkhas, less than one platoon of the newly reformed Praetorian guard, and fewer than a dozen members of the Imperial household staff. Arundel and its immediate grounds were leveled. The outer layer of the bai-

ley walls had been peeled, but there had been little damage
to the administrative offices inside them.

The only structure still standing inside the palace
grounds was the Imperial Parliament building, some ten
kilometers from ground zero. This was ironic, because
its survival was owed to the fact that the Emperor, not wishing to look at his politicians' headquarters, had built a
kilometer-high mountain between the palace and the
Parliament building, a mountain that successfully diverted
the blast from the twinned bombs.

Civilian casualties on the planet were very slight, most of
the destruction having been restricted to the Emperor's
own fifty-five-kilometer palace grounds.

The Emperor bent, awkwardly picked something up
from the ground, and held it out for the Gurkhas' admiration. Somehow, one solitary rose had been burnt to instant
ash yet had held together. The Gurkhas looked at the rose,
faces expressionless through their face shields, then spun,
hearing the whine of a McLean generator. Their guns were
up aiming.

"No!" the Emperor exclaimed, and the guns were lowered.

Floating toward the Emperor was a teardrop. Through
its transparent nose, the Emperor recognized the black and
tinted-red body of a Manabi. Given the circumstances, it
could only be Sr. Ecu.

The teardrop hovered a diplomatic three meters away.

"You live." The observation was made calmly.

"I live," the Emperor agreed.

"My sorrows. Arundel was very beautiful."

"Palaces are easy to rebuild," the Emperor said flatly.

The teardrop shifted slightly in a breeze.

"Are you speaking for the Tahn?" the Emperor asked.

"That would have been their desire. I declined. They
wished me to deliver an ultimatum—but without allowing
me sufficient time to travel from Heath to Prime."

"That sounds like their style."

"I now speak both for the Manabi. And for myself."

Most interesting, the Emperor thought. The Manabi almost never spoke as a single culture. "May I ask some questions first?"

"You may ask. I may decline to answer."

"Of course."

Ecu shifted his suit so that he appeared to be looking at the Gurkhas.

"Never mind," the Emperor assured him. "They won't talk any more than you will."

That was most true—neither a Gurkha nor a Manabi would release any information unless specifically ordered. And both races were impervious to torture, drugs, or psychological interrogation.

"I have just arrived on Prime. What are your estimates of the situation?"

"Lousy," the Emperor said frankly. "I've lost at least half a dozen fleet elements; forty systems, minimum, have either fallen to the Tahn or are going to; my Guard divisions are being decimated; and it's going to get a lot worse."

Ecu considered. "And your allies?"

"They are," the Emperor said dryly, "still conferring about the situation. My estimates are that less than half of my supposed friends will declare war on the Tahn. The rest'll wait to see how things shake out."

"What are your ultimate predictions?"

The Emperor considered the ashen rose for long moments. "That question I shall not answer."

"I see. I now speak," Ecu said formally, "for my grandsires, my fellows, and for those generations yet to be conceived and hatched."

The Emperor blinked. Ecu was indeed speaking for the entire Manabi.

"We are not a warlike species. However, in this struggle, we declare our support for the forces of the Empire. We shall strive to maintain an appearance of neutrality, but you shall be permitted access to any information we have gathered or shall gather."

The Emperor almost smiled. This was the only good news in an otherwise tragic universe.

"Why?" he asked. "It looks like the Tahn will win."

"Impossible," Ecu said flatly. "May we speak under the rose?"

"I already said—"

"I repeat my request."

The Emperor nodded. A metalloid rod slid from Sr. Ecu's suit—the Emperor again motioned down the Gurkhas' weapons—and touched the Emperor's helmet.

"I think," Ecu's voice echoed, "that even your most faithful should not hear the following.

"Would you agree that the Tahn believe that Anti-Matter Two is duplicatable or that, given a Tahn victory, they could learn the location of its source?"

Again there was long silence. Where and how AM2 had come into being was the most closely held secret of the Empire, since only AM2 held the Empire together, no matter how tenuously.

"That may be what they're thinking," the Emperor finally admitted.

"They are wrong. Do not bother responding. We believe that the only—and I mean only—source of AM2 is yourself. We have no knowledge or intelligence how this occurs, but this is our synthesis.

"For this reason, we predict there can only be two results from this war: either you shall be victorious, or the Tahn shall win. And their victory will mean the total destruction of what low level of civilization exists."

The probe collapsed, and its tip brushed the edge of the rose.

Dry, powdery ash dusted the Emperor's gauntlet.

CHAPTER FORTY-SEVEN

"HOW COMPLETELY ARE you willing to interpret Admiral van Doorman's orders, Commander?"

Sten waited for Sutton to elaborate. The four tacship skippers, plus Sutton and Kilgour, were attempting to plot their tactics for the weeks to come, although none of them believed the Tahn had any intentions of letting the ruins of the 23rd Fleet survive that long.

They were gathered in the crammed supply warehouse that Sutton had cozened for storing the division's supplies.

"I am ... humph ... growing most fond of these ships of ours," the spindar continued. "They remind me all too much of my species' own offspring. Even after they are no longer biologically connected to the pouch, they must remain within close range of it, or perish."

Sten caught the analogy. His tacships, due to their cramped quarters and limited ammunition/food/air supplies, were most short-ranged.

"The Tahn'll be hitting Cavite again," Sh'aarl't said. "Maybe just carpet bombing, maybe invasion. I'd rather not have our supplies just sitting here waiting."

"Not to mention," Sekka added, looking around at the mad assemblage of explosives, munitions, rations, and spare parts, "what would happen if one mite of a bomb happened to come through the roof."

"Quite exactly my point," the spindar chuffed. "Cavite Base is not my idea of a burrow/haven."

"First problem," Sten said. "No way will van Doorman approve us moving the boats, the supplies, and your support people offworld."

"Do you plan on telling him?"

"I don't think he'd even notice," Estill put in.

"Agreed. Second problem—how can we move all this drakh? We don't have enough cargo area as it is on the boats."

"I foresaw our dilemma," Sutton said. "It would seem that there is a certain civilian who owes me a favor. A very enormous favor."

"Of course he has a ship."

"Of course."

"How," Sh'aarl't asked skeptically, "has he been able to keep it from being requisitioned?"

"The ship in question is, harrumph, used to transport waste."

"A garbage scow?"

"Somewhat worse than that. Human waste."

Sten whistled tunelessly. "The swabbies are gonna love it when they find out they're traveling via crapper."

"Tha'll dinna mind, Skipper," Kilgour said. "Considerin't tha believ't tha're in't already."

"Very funny, Mr. Kilgour. I'll let you pass the word down."

"No problem, lad. One wee point. Does any hae an idea where we'll be hiein' twa?"

"Poor being," Sh'aarl't sympathized, patting Alex on the shoulder with a pedipalp. The heavy-worlder was so used to her by now that he didn't even flinch. "Where else would we go but among common thieves?"

"Ah'll be cursit! Y'r right, Sh'aarl't. M' mind's gon't."

"Romney!" Sten exclaimed.

"Exactly," Sh'aarl't said. "If anybody's able to stay invisible to the Tahn, it'll be the smugglers."

"Wild must've zigged when zaggin' wae th' answer," Alex said soberly.

Sten didn't answer. He was bringing the *Gamble* closer to Romney's shattered dome. The other three ships and the transporter waited a planetary diameter out.

"Negative elint, sir," Foss reported.

If the Tahn were waiting in ambush, Foss's instruments

would have picked something up. Sten reduced Yukawa drive power, and the *Gamble* dropped slowly through the tear in the dome.

Romney was a graveyard.

Sten counted six—no, seven—smashed ships around the landing field. Where Wild's headquarters had been was only a crater. The other buildings—com, living quarters, hangars, and the enormous storage warehouses—were blasted ruins.

"Bring the other ships in," he ordered. "I want them dispersed around the field. I want all hands suited up and in front of that first hangar in one hour."

"Gather around, people," Sten said.

The formation broke and formed a ragged semicircle around their CO.

"Foss . . . Kilgour. What'd you find?"

"It looks," the electronics tech said cautiously, "like Wild and his smugglers did get hit by surprise."

"An' by th' Tahn," Alex added. "W' found' it three unblown't project'les."

"Bodies?"

"Na, there'd be th' weirdness. Noo a one. An' th' warehouses be't emptied flat."

"Couldn't the Tahn have landed and looted the place?"

"Wi'oot takin't Wild's weaponry wi' 'em?" Kilgour pointed to where a seemingly untouched SA missile battery sat abandoned. Sten nodded. Foss's electronics analysis and Kilgour's Mantis-trained estimate agreed with his own.

"Fine. Troops, this is going to be our home away from home. Mr. Sutton, I want that transport unloaded ASAP. All hands. Second, full power back to Cavite. You'll have the *Richards* for escort. I want you to scrounge all the bubbleshelters you can find. Foss, let Mr. Sutton know what you'll need to set up a detection station from Cavite, and how much of Wild's electronics you can salvage.

"Here's the plan, friends. This is still going to be our forward base. We'll move bubbles *inside* the hangars and warehouses. We'll move some of those smaller buildings around, wreck 'em up a bit, and use them for overhead cover. Even if the Tahn decide to recheck Romney, they're still going to find a dead world."

Assuming, Sten continued mentally as he dismissed his unit, they go by visuals and self-confidence only. If they put sniffers or heat sensors inside the dome—that'll be all she scrolled.

But it was still better odds than they had on Cavite.

CHAPTER FORTY-EIGHT

THE BIGGEST QUESTION the beings of the 23rd Fleet kept asking themselves was why the Tahn hadn't hit Cavite again.

The damage done by Sten's tacships—the destruction of two cruisers and assorted in-atmosphere ships, plus the damage to the *Forez* and an assault ship—was hardly enough to discourage the Tahn. Probably only complete obliteration of Lady Atago's entire fleet would have done that.

Certainly the 23rd was no longer a threat. With the exception of Sten's tacdivision, van Doorman's shattered force was mainly impotent.

The same question was being asked by Atago's crew members as well.

The outsystem landings had been very successful. Atago and Admiral Deska had been restructuring their invasion plans for Cavite when orders arrived. Lady Atago was to report to the Tahn Council at once for further instructions. Her fleet was ordered to consolidate existing gains but to make no major attacks on Imperial forces.

Admiral Deska spent the time waiting for Atago's return driving the repair crews working on the *Forez* even harder and staring at a wallscreen that showed the extent of the

Tahn victories—at least, those either the Empire or the Tahn had chosen to report.

On the screen Deska had assigned orange to the Tahn galaxies, blue to the Empire, and red for the Tahn conquests. On a time-sweep, it was most impressive, as the Tahn spread red tentacles out and out, sweeping deeply into Imperial space. Only a handful of systems still showed cerulean, and those at the base of Deska's screen—worlds yet to be attacked.

The blue glimmer that represented the Caltor System was shameful to Deska. He had failed. And the Tahn did not welcome failure of any sort.

A cursory examination of their language was adequate proof, as well as being an illustration of the problems that any nonmilitaristic culture faced in trying to deal with the Tahn. Since the Tahn "race" or "culture" was an assemblage of various warrior societies, their language was equally an assemblage of soldierly jargon and buzzwords. Still worse—the first Tahn Council had decided that their race needed a properly martial manner of communication. So skilled linguists had created what was known as a semivance tongue, in which the same word had multiple definitions. In this manner, an emotional connation was automatically given.

Three examples:

The verb *akomita* meant both "to surrender" and "to cease to exist"; the verb *meltah* was both "to destroy" and "to succeed"; the verb *verlach* was defined as "to conquer" and "to shame."

There was an excellent chance, Admiral Deska knew, that Lady Atago, in spite of Lord Fehrle's protection, might be ordered to expiate the disgrace of her fleet with ritual suicide. He doubted, given her rank, that any worse penalty could be assessed. In that event, Deska knew, he would share her fate.

He forced himself into a fourth-level dhyana state, no-mind, no-fear, no-doubt, as he waited for the battle cruiser that bore either Lady Atago or his new fleet commander to couple locks with the *Kiso*.

The lock irised, and Lady Atago boarded the *Kiso*.

Deska allowed himself a moment of hope. He enlarged the monitor pickup until Atago's face filled his screen. Of course there was no expression on her classic mask features. Deska snapped the monitor off. In her own time, Atago would tell him.

And in her own time, Atago did.

Indeed, the Tahn Council was not pleased with the failure. Other admirals who had failed to fully complete their instructions had already been cashiered, demoted, or removed. Atago, Deska surmised, had also been scheduled for relief. But the continued existence of the Imperial presence on the Caltor worlds suggested an alternative plan. Deska was surprised that the plan came not from Lord Fehrle, Atago's protector, but from Lord Pastour.

"This is not as we expected," the industrialist had said, though Lady Atago did not report the conversation to Admiral Deska, "but there may be harvest buds in this weed."

"Continue."

"I would think," Pastour went on, staring at the wallscreen that was a larger and more up-to-date version of what Deska had projected for himself, "that this Caltor System shines as much for the Emperor as for us."

"Probably," Lord Fehrle agreed.

"We agree that one of the biggest factors for our eventual success is that the Emperor makes his assessments as much through emotion as logic?"

"You are rechewing old meat. Of course."

"Bear with me. Not being a senior member of the council, not as skilled as yet in decision making of this scope, sometimes I must reason aloud.

"So we have agreed on one fact. Now, fact B is that the Emperor might be seeking some kind of success to convince those beings who have not yet cast in with us to remain faithful."

"We shall accept that as a fact," Lord Wichman said.

"Given these two facts, I would suggest that we allow at least three—no, correction, four—reliable intelligence sources to leak to the Empire that the reason for the failure in the Caltor System was due to inept command and the use of second-line forces."

"Ah." Wichman nodded.

"Yes. Perhaps we might convince the Emperor to commit more forces than this shabbiness of a fleet that we have already demolished. Once these reinforcements are landed —we close the net."

"There is soundness to your idea," Lord Fehrle said. "Another fact. We know that the—" he touched a memcode button "—23rd Fleet is poorly led and has filed specious intelligence in the past. So of course we must make no changes in our own forces that might cause this van Doorman to sound an alarm. The plan is excellent. I admire Lord Pastour for his battle cunning."

His eyes swept the other twenty-seven members. There was no need for a vote.

"I will make one addition," Lord Wichman added. "Might we not be advised to reinforce Lady Atago with one of our reserve landing fleets? Thus the Imperial forces shall not simply be defeated, but completely annihilated." He glanced across the chamber for Lord Fehrle's approval.

"So ordered. And sealed," Fehrle said. He turned to the screen showing Lady Atago. "That is all, Lady Atago. A full operations order shall be couriered to you when you return to your fleet."

Her screen blanked. Fehrle stared at the smooth grayness. And you had better have the luck of battles with you this time, he thought. Because if you fail once more, there shall be no way I can protect you.

Orders went out before Atago's battle cruiser could take off from Heath—three full Tahn landing forces, with supply, support, and attack craft, would be committed to her fleet, and the intelligence plants would be made at once.

None of this was necessary. The Eternal Emperor had already ordered Major General Ian Mahoney and his First Guards to establish a forward operating base on the world of Cavite.

CHAPTER FORTY-NINE

THE ONLY HOPE of survival that Sten and his four tacships had was never to be where or when they were anticipated. Even a Tahn corvette, forewarned, had more than enough armament to obliterate any of the Bulkeley-class ships. Sten's constant counsel was for them to think like a minnow in a school of sharks.

The next stage after finding a semihidden base of operations was to pick a target that the ships could hit and get out of with some expectation of survival.

The three systems nearest to Caltor swarmed with Tahn ships, all on constant alert and looking for glory. What Sten's people had to do was to hit where they weren't expected—and to hit where the maximum damage could be done.

That meant the Tahn supply route.

Of course the Tahn would have their supply lines more heavily guarded near the Caltor System. But what about farther out, closer to their own systems? It seemed unlikely that the Tahn would waste fuel, ships, or men, since the only Imperial forces within reach were the remnants of van Doorman's fleet. And they must think that the tacships that had worked over the Cavite landing force were far too short-ranged to reach deep into their own empire.

Indeed, the tacships *were* short-ranged—in terms of rations and armament, not fuel. Each of them had onboard enough AM2 to fuel their drives for half a year.

Sten hoped the Tahn were as logical as he was.

And so the four tacships became parasites. A survey ship whose drive mechanisms had been destroyed in the Tahn's first attack was borrowed, lifted off Cavite by the tacships—Tapia's tug experience was most valuable—and packed with supplies on Romney. Then, with Sten's own boats still linked to the survey ship, they took off.

Their initial course took them far to one side of the worlds now occupied by the Tahn. Somewhere between nowhere and lost, they reset their course toward the heart of the Tahn worlds.

They advanced very slowly, their sensors reaching out, hour after hour, keeping watch-on, watch-off. They knew —semi-knew/hoped like hell—that any Tahn ship could be picked up by them before they showed up on the Tahn screens. They were not searching blindly. Sten had assumed that at least one supply route would lead from Heath, the Tahn capital world, toward the newly occupied systems near Cavite. He projected that route as a line, and other, unknown routes coming toward those worlds.

Two weeks out, they made their final resupply from the survey ship, stuck it into a tight orbit around an uninhabited world, and crept on. By then, the small, overworked air recyclers in the tacships were groaning for relief, leaving the ships and crew smelling like very used socks. Sten wondered why none of the war livies ever pointed out that soldiers stink: stink from fear, stink from fatigue, stink from uncleanliness.

And then dual alarms shrilled. The four ships went to general quarters and waited for orders.

Four transports lined across one of Sten's screens. Their drives were, of course, unshielded, so the purple flare from the ships told Sten instantly that they were Tahn. But more interesting were a series of tiny flickers from another screen.

"Shall we take them?" Sh'aarl't asked from the *Claggett*.

"Negative. Stand by."

Sten, Kilgour, and Foss studied those flickers.

"Too wee t' be't ships," Alex said.

"Navaids," Foss suggested.

"Not this far out," Sten said. "Are they broadcasting?"

Foss checked his board. "Negative, sir. We're picking up some kind of low-power static. Maybe activating receivers on standby?"

"Some kind of transponder? Or a superantenna?"

"Bloomin' unlikely," Kilgour said.

Sten wanted a closer look. He slid behind Kilgour's weapon's console and put on a control helmet. "I want a Fox launch. Keep the warhead on safe."

Kilgour reached over his shoulder and tapped a key.

Sten, "seeing" space through the countermissile's radar, moved it toward the light flicker, keeping the missile barely above minimum speed. The flickers grew, and his perspective changed as his "vision" went to radar. He perceived dozens of the objects, now solid blips. Sten reversed the missile and applied power until he was no longer approaching the objects, then re-reversed and waited for some kind of analysis from his ship, which now seemed to be far behind him, even though he still sat motionlessly at the console.

"There's no interconnection between them," Foss said. "Physical or electronic. At least not in its present state."

"What it looks like," Sten said slowly, "is a minefield."

"Y're bonkers, lad. E'en th' Tahn whidna put out mines in th' void on th' zip chance some wee unfortunate'd wander into it."

"Do mines have to be passive?"

"Mmm. Strong point."

Sten lifted the helmet off and turned to the other two on the command deck. Foss was thinking, tapping his fingernails against his teeth.

"Maybe that static is from their receivers. You know, it wouldn't be too hard to set up. Sure. You could build it on a breadboard."

Electronics jargon hadn't changed all that much over the centuries...and still managed to leave Sten and Kilgour blank.

"I meant, sir, it'd be easy to jury-rig. You put a missile out there, with a receiver-transmitter. Your own ships have some kind of IFF, so the missile knows not to go after them. Anybody else comes within range, the missile activates and goes after them. If you wanted to get tricky, you could even program your missiles to move around or sweep themselves if you wanted to. Probably the circuit'd look something like this . . ." Foss blanked a screen and picked up a light pen.

"Later wi' the schematics, lad," Kilgour said. "The question is, What are we going to do about them?"

"Maybe they're not set to go after something as small as a tacship," Sten said.

"Will y' b' willin't t' bet on that?"

"My momma didn't raise no fools."

"Which means we cannae go down agin' th' convoys like a sheep ae th' fold, then."

"Not necessarily. And maybe we don't even need to. Mr. Kilgour, have the mate break out three shipsuits."

"A lad could get killed doin't this," Kilgour growled. The three men hung inches away from one of the Tahn mines.

Once Sten, Foss, and Kilgour had exited the *Gamble*, turning the deck over to Engineer Hawkins, they had used an unarmed Goblin and its AM2 drive to bring them closer to the mine. Sten was fairly sure the small Goblin wouldn't present enough mass to activate the mine. Fairly sure, he reminded himself, could get one fairly dead.

Half a kilometer away from one of the mines, Sten parked the Goblin, and the three used their suit drives to close in.

The mine was about five meters long and cylindrical, with drivetubes at one end. It was nested inside its launch/monitor/control, a doughnut-holed ring with a diameter of about six meters.

The three orbited the mine until they were sure they saw no obvious booby traps, then moved in toward what they hoped was an inspection panel. Foss unclipped a stud drive from his suit's belt.

"Okay to try it, sir?"

"Why not?"

Sten opened his mike to the *Gamble* and started a running description of what was happening. If Foss erred and the mine went off, the next team to try it—if there was a next team—wouldn't make the same mistake.

Foss touched the drive to a stud and applied power.

"We're pulling the first stud, lower left side, now . . . it looks standard. Any resistance? The first stud is out. Second stud, upper right. It's free. Third stud, lower left, also out. All studs removed. The panel is free. We are moving it out two centimeters. There are no connections between the panel and the mine."

All three men peered through the narrow access port while Foss probed the interior with his helmet spot.

"What do we have?"

"Sloppy work, sir."

"Foss, you aren't grading an electronics class!"

"Sorry, sir. If we're right . . . the way they've got the plates rigged . . . yeah. Pretty simple."

"This is Sten. Going off for a moment. Clear." Sten shut down the tight beam to the *Gamble* and motioned the other two away from the mine. "Can we disarm these brutes, Foss?"

"Easy. Cut any of three boards I spotted out, and all these'll be good for is ornamental wastebaskets."

"So all we have to figure is what kind of range the mines have, defuse enough so we've got operating room, and we're back in business."

Kilgour clonked a heavy arm three times on Sten's helmet. The clonks, evidently intended as sympathetic pats on the head, sent them pirouetting in circles. They ended staring upside down at each other.

"Puir lad," Alex sympathized. "It's aye the pressure cooker a' command. T' be't so young an' so brainburned."

"You have a better idea?"

"Ah do. An *evil* plan. Worthy ae a Campbell. Best ae all, it means we dinnae e'en hae t' be around t' be causin't braw death an' destruction."

"GA."

"If y' buy't, can Ah tell the lads ae th' wee spotted snakes?"

"Not even if your plot'll win the war single-handed. Come on, Kilgour. Stop being cute and talk to us."

Kilgour did.

The Tahn convoy was made up of eight troop transports, each carrying an elite battalion landing force, intended to augment the Tahn Council's planned trap in the Caltor Sys-

tem, plus three armament ships and a single escort. The
escort was a small patrol craft intended to be more a guide
than protection.

Their course led them within light-seconds of a certain
minefield. The convoy commander, a recently recalled re-
servist, was very uncomfortable.

As a merchant service cáptain, he had become convinced years ago that machinery was out to get him. The
bigger the machine, the more homicidal its intentions. He
tried to keep machines with explosives inside them well
clear of his nightmares.

That tiny superstitious part of him was not surprised
when a lookout reported activity in the minefield. And then
the reports cascaded in—the mines had activated themselves and were closing in.

Convinced that his Identification–Friend or Foe was
dysfunctional, the convoy commander ordered his ship to
be closed up with another.

The move had no effect.

He screamed for condition red on the all-ships channel.
Crews raced for action quarters stations, and collision
panels closed on the transports.

The missiles hammered toward the convoy, their speed
increasing by the second.

Fifteen of them impacted on the eleven transports. The
mine-missiles were designed to be able to sardine-can a
warship, and so the thin-skinned transports simply became
flame, then gas, and then nothing except expanding energy.

What Sten's crew had done, working under the diabo-
lism of Kilgour and Foss, was not simply to defuse the
mines. Instead, Foss had analyzed what the IFF broadcast
from the Tahn ships would be, then reprogrammed the
mines to use that as a firing and homing signal.

The convoy had vanished, except for the tiny patrolcraft. Sten had not needed to be so cautious; the mines
were, indeed, set to ignore small craft.

Six missiles had been launched that did not find their
targets in time. They orbited aimlessly, without instructions.

The captain of the patrolcraft would have been best advised to put on full power and get out to report. Instead, he opened fire on one of the missiles—which activated a secondary program: if fired on by any ship of any size, seek out that target.

There was a final explosion—and the beginnings of a mystery. How could a convoy entirely vanish in a perfectly secure and guarded sector?

Sailors do not like mysteries but love to talk about them. Very shortly, the word was out—the Fringe Worlds were jinxed. Better not ship out with that destination, friend.

The convoy disappearance also forced the Tahn to divert badly needed escorts from the forward areas both for escort duty and to hunt for what the council theorized was some kind of Q-ship, an Imperial raider masquerading as a Tahn vessel.

Sten countermined four more fields before he ordered the tacships back to Romney.

They had begun to fight back.

CHAPTER FIFTY

"COMMANDER STEN," Admiral van Doorman said, turning away from the screen that showed Sten's after-action report, "my congratulations."

"Thank you, sir."

"You know," van Doorman said, as he stood and paced toward one of the screened windows in his command suite, "I am afraid that it's just too easy in this navy to adopt a particular mind-set. One becomes set in his ways. You decide that there is only one group of standards. You think that the smaller the ship, the less capable it is. You think that a show of force is all that's needed to maintain Imperial security. You think—hell, you think all manner of things.

And then one day you find that you are wrong."

That, Sten thought, was a fairly honest and accurate summation and indictment of the admiral. Maybe add in a love for bumf and spit and polish, and a streak of stubborn stupidity. Now will this make van Doorman do something sensible, like resign, or maybe take poison like the Tahn do when they custer the works? Ha. Ha.

"I have decided to award you the Distinguished Service Order, and authorize you to award four Imperial Medals to any members of your division whose actions you deem outstanding."

"Thank you, sir." Sten would rather have had two spare engines for his tacships and a full resupply of missiles.

"I would like you and whichever four you choose back at this headquarters by 1400 hours. Dress uniform."

"Yessir. May I ask why?"

"For the award ceremony. I'll arrange to have full livie coverage. And a conference afterward for the media."

"Sir . . . I, uh, don't think that's a good idea."

"Don't be modest, Commander! You have won a victory. And right now Cavite—not just Cavite but the entire Empire—needs some good news."

"I am not being modest, sir. Sir . . . there are four more booby-trapped minefields out there. If we put the word out on what happened . . . sir, that'd foul up the whole operation."

Van Doorman actually considered what Sten had said. He reseated himself at his desk and rubbed his chin in thought. "Would it be possible that a, shall we say, different explanation of the action be provided?" Translation: Can we lie?

"Possibly, sir. But . . . won't the livie people want to talk to my crew? I don't think they could carry it off. They aren't trained in disinformation."

Kilgour would slaughter Sten if he knew he had said that —Alex was one of the best liars in the line of duty whom Sten had ever met.

"It would be chancy," van Doorman agreed. "Perhaps you're right. I'll postpone the media conference for the moment." He changed the subject. "Commander, one further thing. I don't wish to change your orders—you're doing admirably as an independent. But I'd like you to consider a more immediate focus for your future actions."

"Such as?"

"Whenever possible, I would appreciate your division hitting the closer Tahn-occupied systems."

"That could be difficult, sir. Their cover is pretty tight."

"This is most important."

"A question, sir. Why the change?"

"I am preparing to mount an operation within the next few weeks that will need full fleet support. Unfortunately, I can't be more specific at present—we're operating under total security."

So much for van Doorman's brief flash of reality. Sten could have mentioned that he probably had a higher security clearance than anyone in the 23rd Fleet, including its admiral. Or that it was clottin' hard to support an attack—a retreat?—if one didn't know what was going on. Or that total security for the clotpoles on van Doorman's staff probably meant that it was all over the officer's club by now.

"Yessir," Sten said. "My staff and I will prepare some possible scenarios for you."

"Excellent, Commander. And again, my congratulations."

Sten highballed the admiral and left. He was wondering if van Doorman was contagious. Scenario? And staff? That would consist of four officers, one warrant officer, and a spindar plotting over a bottle. He started looking for Brijit.

Sten hoped to find her in some romantic setting—perhaps in a flowered glen out of sight and sound of the war. He also hoped that Brijit would have recovered from her mother's death enough to have a bit of lust in her heart.

He found her ninety feet underground, wearing a blood-spattered set of coveralls and maneuvering a gurney past a rockchewer.

Someone on van Doorman's staff had an element of brains and cunning. The Empire Day attack had packed Cavite's hospitals solidly, and this unknown planner evidently knew enough about the Tahn method of waging war to realize that putting the ancient red cross on a hospital roof provided an excellent aiming point. So the base hospital had gone underground into solid rock. It was also directly under the building that had been, years before, the Tahn consulate for the Fringe Worlds.

Sten helped Brijit slip the casualty into an IC machine, then asked when she got offshift. Brijit smiled tiredly and told him tomorrow. Sten would be long offworld by then. So much for romance.

Brijit managed another smile, one with some empathy. She had a fairly good idea what Sten had in mind. Instead, she took him to the crowded staff mess hall and fed him a perfectly vile cup of caff.

She had volunteered for the hospital the day after her mother's funeral. The prewar world of whites, boredom, and garden parties was burnt away.

Sten was most impressed and was about to say something, when he started really listening to Brijit's exhausted chatter.

It was Dr. Morrison this and Dr. Morrison that, and how hard Dr. Morrison was working, and how many lives had been saved. Brijit, Sten gathered, was Dr. Morrison's main OR nurse. And he realized that even if he were in that flowered glade with Brijit, all that would happen was that she would possibly ask him to make a garland for Dr. Morrison.

Oh, well. Sten couldn't honestly evaluate himself as being anyone's ideal main squeeze, even ignoring the fact that a tacship commander's life span is measured in mayflies.

Brijit's features suddenly softened and then brightened. Sten remembered that she had looked that way at him not too long ago.

"There she is now! Dr. Morrison! Over here."

Commander Ellen Morrison, Imperial Medical Corps, was, Sten had to admit, almost as beautiful as Brijit. She greeted Sten coolly, as if he were a prospective patient, and sat down. Brijit, almost reflexively, took Morrison's hand.

Sten talked for a few more minutes about inconsequentialities, finished his caff, made his excuses, and left.

War changes everything it touches. Sometimes even for the better.

A few days later, van Doorman got his famous victory, courtesy of the Imperial Tacship *Richards*, Lieutenant Estill, and Ensign Tapia. Or at least everyone except Tapia thought he did.

They were a week out of Cavite when they got their target. It was one of the monstrous Tahn assault ships that were the launch base for the in-atmosphere attack craft. The ship, according to the *Jane's* fiche, would be lightly armored and, if hit before the bulkheads that subdivided the hangar deck could be closed, should become an instantly satisfactory torch.

The problem was that the ship was escorted by one cruiser and half a dozen destroyers, and no one on the *Richards* was in a particularly suicidal mood that watch.

Tapia let Estill run up and knock down half a dozen attacks on the computer before she made her suggestion. Even though it was extremely irregular, Estill was learning from his time in the tacdiv. He turned the deck over to her and announced that if her idea worked, he would "fly" the Kali on the attack.

At full power the *Richards* sped ahead of the Tahn ships, made a slight correction in course, and then went "dead" in space, directly intersecting what Tapia calculated the Tahn ships' course to be. She shut down all power, including the McLean artificial-gravity generator. Then anything that wasn't armament was pitched out a port—chairs, rations, metalloid foil configured to provide excellent radar reflection, and even the two spare shipsuits.

Then they waited. With even the recirculators off, the air got thick very quickly.

Their passive detectors picked up the Tahn sensing beams.

They continued to wait.

A single Tahn destroyer flashed out from the pack and figure-eighted, its computer obviously analyzing just what was dead ahead.

"This'll be interesting," Tapia whispered unnecessarily to Estill.

Interesting was one way to put it. If their camouflage as a wreck didn't work, they would be staring at that destroyer on an attack run. Tapia didn't know if either their reflexes or the *Richards*' power would get them away in time.

The *Richards*' passive screens went dead, and Tapia started breathing again. If the ruse had failed, the screens would have told her that a ranging computer was on the tacship. "Any time you're ready, Lieutenant."

Estill nodded. Tapia fed power to his board. Estill put out a narrow ranging beam to the Tahn assault ship. Closing... closing... in range.

Tapia slammed her power board on... buzzed the engineer, who did the same... and the *Richards* came alive. Two seconds later, Estill launched his Kali.

Alarms blared on the Tahn ships. The destroyers went into an attack pattern, and the cruiser full-powered to protect her charge. The assault ship went to an emergency evasive pattern.

Tapia was too busy to see what was going on. She had full power on the *Richards*, an eccentric evasion orbit fed in, and was now interested in survival.

The Kali was only a few seconds from strike when the Tahn assault ship fired its forward bank of antimissiles.

They should have been useless.

Standard doctrine for any weapons officer using the control helmet on a missile was to stay with the bird through contact. But somehow to Estill this meant a kind of death. At the last moment he hit the firing contact and jerked the helmet away.

The explosion blanked the rear screens of the *Richards*.

"We got it!" Estill shouted. The helmet went back on, and he launched a flight of Goblins to track to their rear.

Tapia read a proximity indicator—there were Tahn missiles coming at them. Closing... negative. The *Richards* was outrunning them.

Tapia had only a moment to check the main screen for a blink. And that blink showed her the same number of Tahn blips as had been there ten minutes before.

No one believed her—except the Tahn. The Kali had indeed detonated on an antimissile. Four main frames of the assault craft were warped, but the forward Tahn repair yards would have the assault ship back in commission within days.

Tapia tried—but no one wanted to hear the truth.

Lieutenant Ned Estill was an instant hero. Van Doorman awarded him the Galactic Cross, even though technically the medal could be given only on direct Imperial authority. The livie people went berserk—Lieutenant Estill could not have been more of a hero if they had been able to custom design one. His face and deeds were blazoned Empirewide within hours.

Tapia privately reported to Sten what she thought had actually happened. Sten considered, then told her to forget it. He didn't give a damn about medals, the Empire could do with a few hero types, and Estill honestly believed that he had destroyed the assault ship.

He did order, though, that all officers and weapons specialists renew their capabilities in a simulator. Once was an error. If Estill made the same mistake again, he could end up very dead.

And Sten couldn't afford to lose the *Richards*.

Lieutenant Lamine Sekka still seethed. The conversation with Sten had started in acrimony and gotten intense from there. What made it worse was that the original idea had been Sekka's.

Sten had attempted to follow van Doorman's vague instructions to harry the nearby worlds as much as possible. Harrying required intelligence. Specific—such as which worlds were occupied by what forces in which conditions.

The tacdiv spent too many hours as spy ships before anyone could start determining targets.

Sekka had found one of the juiciest.

A distinguishing feature of one planet was a river many thousands of kilometers long. Above its mouth, which looked more like an estuary, was a huge alluvial plain. It was a perfect infantry staging base for the Tahn. They had put an estimated two divisions of troops on the floodplain, using it as a temporary base until the landing in the Caltor System.

Sekka had even been able to determine where the divisions' headquarters were most likely sited.

Sten was congratulatory. "Now. Go kill them, Lieutenant."

"Sir?"

Sten was very tired and a little snappish. "I said—take ship. Put armament on ship. Destroy Tahn."

"I am not a child, Commander!"

Sten took a deep breath. "Sorry, Lamine. But what's the problem? You found yourself a cluster of bad people. Take care of them."

"Maybe I'm not sure what—exactly—you want me to do."

"Let's see." Sten ran through his arsenal mentally. "Here's what I'd suggest. First yank your Goblin launchers. Put eight more chainguns in their slots. Get rid of all but two of the Fox countermissiles. You'll need extra canisters of projectiles.

"Take the Kali out. There's a busted-up close-support ship over in the boneyard. It should still have a belt-fed Y-launcher. Turn that around and mount it nose first down the Kali tube.

"You'll want to use two-, maybe three-kt mininukes. When you come in, I'd suggest you put the launcher on a five-second interval."

"Is there anything else, Commander?" Sekka's voice was shaking.

"If I knew where we could get some nice, persistent penetrating nerve gas ... but I don't. I guess that's all." Sten was deliberately not noticing Sekka's reactions, hoping he would not be required to respond. He was wrong.

Sekka was on his feet. "Commander, I am not a murderer!"

Sten, too, was up. "Lieutenant Sekka, I want you at attention. I want your ears open and your mouth shut.

"Yes. You are a murderer. Your job is to kill enemy soldiers and sailors—any way you can. That means strangling them at birth if somebody would invent a time machine!

Who the hell do you think operates those ships you've been shooting at? Robots?"

"That's different."

"I said shut up, Lieutenant! The hell it is! What did you expect me to tell you to do? Wait until those troops load into their tin cans and then hit them? Would that make things more legitimate? Or maybe wait until they land here on Cavite?

"Maybe your family has been living on legend too many generations, Lieutenant Sekka. You had best realize that if it wasn't for war, every *warrior* would be tossed in the lethal chambers for premeditated homicide.

"That's all. You have your orders. I want you offplanet in forty E-hours. Dismissed!"

"May I say something, sir?"

"You may not! I said dismissed!"

Sekka brought up a perfect salute, pivoted, and went out. Sten slid back down into his chair. He heard a low chuckle from the other entrance to *Gamble*'s mess hall.

Alex walked in and found another chair.

"I'm not running a combat unit," Sten groaned. "This is a clottin' divinity school!"

"Puir tyke," Alex sympathized. "Next he'll be thinkin't tha be rules a' war. P'raps it'd cheer y' lad, if Ah told th' story ae th' spotted snakes again."

Sten grinned. "I'd keelhaul you, Alex. If I had a keel. Come on. Let's go put our Rover Scouts to bed."

Sekka had followed orders and lifted off. His insertion plan had worked perfectly—and its perfection tasted like ashes. He had brought the *Kelly* in-atmosphere at night and under cover of a storm, far below the horizon, at sea. He had submarined his tacship into the river's mouth and then carefully navigated upriver until his ship sat on the bottom, directly next to the Tahn base. The Tahn did not bother to run any sea or river patrols on the world, which was in a highly primitive stage of evolution.

His crew members were as grim and quiet as he was.

Sekka had decided that what he had been ordered to do was wrong—but he would do it as perfectly as he knew how. Remembering his own days in training, he decided that the most vulnerable time any army has is about an hour after dawn. Even if the unit practices dawn and dusk stand-tos, an hour later everyone is busy with personal cleanup, breakfast, and evading whatever noncoms are looking for drakh details.

At the time click he brought the *Kelly* out of the water and, at full Yukawa drive, on a zigzag pattern crossing directly over the headquarters areas. He had the ship set for contour flying at four meters.

When he crossed the perimeter, he ordered the crew members manning the additional chainguns to open fire. He personally triggered the Y-launcher and saw the small nuclear bombs arc thousands of feet into the air before they started their descent. By the time they hit and exploded, he would be many kilometers away.

Sekka had all rear screens turned off. He was a murderer. Possibly Commander Sten was right and *all* warriors were murderers. But he did not need to be a witness.

The attack, by one small ship, lasted for twenty minutes. At its end, when the *Kelly* climbed for space and went to AM2 drive, one divisional headquarters was completely destroyed and the second had taken forty percent casualties. Of the 25,000-plus Tahn soldiers, nearly 11,000 were dead or critically wounded. Both divisions had ceased to exist as combat formations.

Lieutenant Lamine Sekka refused a proffered medal, requested a three-day pass, and stayed catatonic on drugs and alcohol for the full three days.

Then he treated his hangover, shaved, showered, and went back to duty.

Sh'aarl't had found herself a great target. The problem was that no one could figure out how to destroy it without getting blown out of the sky in the process.

It was a Tahn armaments dump. The Tahn had found a wide cliff-ringed valley. They had studded the rim of the valley with antiaircraft missiles and lasers and maintained overhead patrols as well as an armed satellite in a synchronous orbit just out-atmosphere. To make the situation worse, the world—Oragent—was under almost complete and constant cloud cover.

Sh'aarl't had tracked Tahn resupply ships to the world and figured out their approximate landing point. There had been more than enough traffic to arouse her interest. She assumed some kind of supply dump, since very few of the ships landing or taking off from Oragent were combat craft.

To narrow the field further, she stalked a single unescorted ship, bounced it, and launched a single missile, carefully steered to just remove the ship's power train. Then she had planned to dissect the ship with Fox missiles until she found out what it was carrying.

The missile exploded—and the Tahn ship was obliterated.

"We may theorize," Sh'aarl't told her weapons officer, "that barge wasn't carrying rations."

"Dunno, ma'am. The Tahn like their food spicy."

"Bad joke, mister. Since you're being bright today, how are we going to snoop and poop into that arms depot?"

It was a good question. Finding out what was under those clouds by manned recon could well have been fatal. Any other intelligence gathering would have to be done without alerting the Tahn.

Sh'aarl't put the *Claggett* down on one of Oragent's moons and thought about the problem.

Step one was to set up a stabilized camera with a very long lens. Infrared techniques and computer enhancement helped a little. She now could see the vaguely circular area that was the depot. She chanced a few laser-ranging shots and got enough input to suggest that the depot was in a valley. A series of infrared exposures, taken over time, also showed blotches of heat emanation from one area of the valley floor—what probably was the landing field—and occasional spatters from the cliff walls. AA lasers, most likely.

At that point, she returned to Romney and consulted with Sten and Kilgour.

It was pretty easy to determine what *couldn't* be done. Dumping a missile straight down at the dump wasn't very likely to be successful. Even a MIRVed Kali—and nobody was sure that the missile could be so modified—wouldn't get past the satellite, let alone the ring of AA batteries.

Possibly a specialized Wild Weasel ship might be able to suppress the target acquisition systems long enough for a raid—but Wild Weasels were just one of the many craft the 23rd Fleet was fresh out of.

"The problem is," Sh'aarl't said, "there's no way in."

"Correction, lass," Alex said. "Tha's noo high-tech way in. An' Ah'll wager th' Tahn are thinkit th' same ae you."

Sten got Alex's hint. "Maybe," he said doubtfully. "But first I don't think Doorknob's gonna loan us any of his marines for a landing force. And even if he does, you want to bet they're any more ept than the rest of his people?"

"Ah was noo thinki't aboot borrowin't misery when there's need for but twa of us."

"Us," Sh'aarl't snorted. "Who is us?"

"Why, me an' Fearless Commander Sten, ae course."

"I'll assume you aren't trying another bad joke."

"Nope. Ah'm bein't dead straight."

"That's drakh, Mr. Kilgour," Sh'aarl't said. "You two aren't supercommandos. I don't know what you did before, Kilgour, but our death-defying leader was just a straight old Guards officer. Remember?"

Yes. Well, that was the cover that both Sten and Alex had on their service record to hide their years in Mantis.

"Y're noo hesitatin', are y'? Worri't aboot keepin't up wi' an old clot like me, Commander? Or p'raps y're feelin't soft. Ah hae noticed your wee paunch a' late."

To Sh'aarl't, this was rank insubordination. She waited for the thunder. Instead, Sten looked injured.

"I am not getting fat, Kilgour."

"Ah, you're right, lad. It's naught but the hangin' ae y'r coverall."

"You two are serious!"

"Maybe it's the only way to do it," Sten said.

"You know that Imperial regulations has an article saying that an officer has the duty to relieve his commander in, and I quote, 'instances of incapacitating injury, failure to perform the ordered mission, or'—my emphasis—'mental injury,' end quote?"

"In this fleet ae th' damn't, lost, crazy, an' brainburnt, Lieutenant, who'd be th' judge?"

"All right. One more try. There's no way that two swabbies can take out an entire arms depot. That only happens in the livies."

Sten and Alex looked at each other. A clotting arms depot? Hell, there were several system governments that had found Sudden Change thrust upon them courtesy of a couple of Mantis operatives.

"I assume that you've got a plot more than just going in cuttin' and thrusting?" Sten asked.

"Ah dinnae hae a plot a' yet," Alex admitted. "But som'at'll come to mind."

"Dinnae fash, Mr. Kilgour. A thought has occurred to me."

"Thinkit, noo. We're in th' crapper for sure."

"On your way out, would you ask Foss to haul his butt in here?"

Sh'aarl't looked at them analytically. She was not stupid. "Very interesting," she observed. "Either both of you have gone bonkers—or somebody's lying to me."

"Pardon?"

"I remember somebody told me once that when somebody gets scooped up by the Imperial sneakies, their service record gets phonied up. Any comments?"

"Great story, Sh'aarl't. We'll have to talk about it sometime. Well, Mr. Kilgour? Time's a-wastin'."

The implementation of Sten's plan would be low-tech, but the method of attack was exceedingly technical. Or possibly antitechnical.

Sten would not have known what a petard was if one had been set off in his air lock—but he, along with Hamlet, hoped that it would indeed be great sport to hoist the Tahn by their own.

The possible solution lay in the sophistication of current fire-control and antiaircraft systems.

The days of brave, keen-sighted gunners crouched behind their weaponry and opening up on overhead aircraft were long gone. A missile launch site or laser blast would be remoted to a central, fixed operation fire-control center. This center—Sten theorized it would be located in the valley's center—would have a current sitrep on aerial traffic, fed in by radar, the orbital satellite, and other air- or ground-based sensors.

If the controlled airspace was intruded on, the fire-control system would evaluate the threat, bring the antiaircraft complex to alert if necessary, allocate targets to the various weapons, and open fire.

The individual weapons might or might not have the capability of local control in the event of the center's destruction. But the maximum crew the individual guns would have could be a gunner or two, certainly a couple of service techs, and possibly a few guards for ground security.

Since the weapons would be remotely aimed and fired, positioning them required a bit more work than just exact geographic siting. It was also necessary to program each gun with a no-fire zone, so that regardless of what an attacking aircraft might be doing, it would be impossible for any gun to fire, for instance, across the valley if another weapon was in its line of fire. Also, since the guns overlooked a highly explosive ammo dump, under no circumstances would it be possible for any weapon to fire down into the valley.

Sten proposed to alter those circumstances.

Blueboxing a local fire-control system was, Foss said, as easy as going to sleep listening to one of Kilgour's stories. The problem would be hooking it up.

Fortunately, not all of the Tahn ships shot down on Cavite on Empire Day had been completely destroyed. Sten and Foss grubbed through the wreckage, carefully examining all possible connections the Tahn used. They also examined the abandoned weaponry—Sten assumed it would have come from Tahn sources—on Romney.

Fortunately, there were no more than a dozen options. Foss also assumed that there would be a certain number of similarities between Imperial weapons controls and those of the Tahn.

The final device, dubbed by Foss a "fiendish thingie," consisted of one control box, anodized the same color as the electronic boxes found in the wreckage, dangling cables, and a separate power source. They fit into two backpacks and weighed about twenty-five kilos each.

Sutton managed to find in some storehouse two sets of the phototropic Mantis-issue camouflage uniforms that semifit Alex and Sten. A combat car was given a radar-absorbing anodizing and fitted with a sensor-reflecting overhead cover. Neither of them would work perfectly, but Sten was working from Alex's original supposition—that the Tahn wouldn't be looking that hard in his direction. He hoped.

Sh'aarl't insisted that the *Claggett* make the insertion— she had found the target, and even if she wasn't going to mount the attack, it was still her eggsac. Sten couldn't tell whether her ruffed hair meant that she was angry, convinced that her CO was mad, or worried.

She brought the *Claggett* in-atmosphere on the far side of the satellite, then contour flew until the tacship's sensors began picking up the signals from the Tahn depot. Again, she assumed the superiority of the Imperial sensors.

Sten and Alex unloaded and broke the combat car out of the slung cargo capsule below the *Claggett*. Their pickup point would be the same, two planetary days away.

Sh'aarl't waved a mournful mandible, the lock hissed closed, and the *Claggett* hissed away.

Sten and Alex boarded the car and, very slowly, floated, barely a meter above the ground, in the general direction of the arms depot. Their course was not plotted as a direct line but zigged toward the valley. If the unknown object that was their combat car was picked up by the Tahn, possibly a route that didn't point directly at the valley could be disarming.

Both men were lightly armed—if the drakh came down, their only plan would be to throw down a base of fire and then go to ground.

They had miniwillyguns and four bester grenades. Sten and Alex both carried kukris—the curved fighting knife they had learned to use and admire while serving with the Gurkhas—and Sten had his own tiny knife buried in the sheath under the skin of his forearm.

Sten landed the combat car when they were about ten kilometers away from the valley and waited for darkness. Through the twilight, he could see the mountain ring surrounding the valley. The view through binocs suggested that the valley might be an old volcanic crater. Certainly the mountain walls around it were very steeply sloped. That was all to the good—maybe no one would expect visitors from that direction.

At full dark, Sten crept the car forward, grounding it finally at the base of the walls. They pulled on hoods fitted with light-enhancing goggles, shouldered their packs, and started up.

The climb was a hard scramble, but they didn't need to rope up. The biggest problem was the loose shale underfoot. A slip not only would send them broadsliding back down but probably would set off alarm devices. Their preplotted course led them up toward one of the laser blasts near the canyon mouth.

It seemed as if Kilgour's tactical thinking was correct—no one would be looking for some stupid foot soldiers to try an insertion.

The first alarm was wholly primitive—a simple beam break set about a meter above the ground. Whatever smaller creatures inhabited the world could pass under the beam and not disturb any guard's somnolence.

Sten and Alex became smaller creatures and did the same.

The second line of defense might have taken a bit longer to circumvent, consisting of a series of small hemispherical sensors intended, most likely, to pick up an intruder of a certain physical type—it could be preset to go off when it picked up something moving of a certain size, a certain body temperature, or even by light ground disturbances set off by body weight. Kilgour was ready to subvert that sensor with a standard-issue Mantis bluebox, the so-called Invisible Thug transmitter. That proved to be unnecessary—the system wasn't even turned on. But just to make sure it wouldn't be turned on after they passed, Sten slid his knife out of his arm, slit the sensor's metalloid housing open, and stirred its electronic guts vigorously.

So far, the mission was very standard—a recruit halfway through basic Guard training could have infiltrated the site.

Next should have been a contact alarm set of wires. It was, and was carefully stepped through by the two men.

They shut the power down on their see-in-the-dark hoods, lay on their stomachs inside that wire, and started looking for the sentry. Ahead of them was the cliff rim, and bulking above it the laser gun, and beside it two mobile vans that would house the crew.

Sten scanned the area with his binocs set for light amplification, passive mode. If someone else was using a scope, the binocs would pick it up first. Negative. He switched to active mode.

He found the guard. He was sitting on the steps of one of the vans, his projectile gun leaning against the van walls. His attention seemed to be focused on the ground between his boots.

Sten could imagine Alex mentally purring "No puhroblem." They turned their hoods back on and slid forward the laser.

Kilgour found the fire-control center input leads to the laser and, after making sure they weren't alarm-rigged, disconnected them. They sorted through the octopus of leads on their own bluebox. Luck was in session—one of Foss's leads fit perfectly.

The new lead was fed down the gun and under its base plate. Bluebox and backup power sources were then bonded to the base plate. Alex loosened the lock on the bluebox's one external readout, and it glowed dimly. If everyone was right, they were go, and the petard was hissing.

Sten and Alex became part of the night again and slithered downslope to the combat car. Sten knew this would not work—nothing that sneaky ever performed vaguely up to expectations.

The next stage, after and if they were picked up by the *Claggett*, might be interesting.

The *Claggett*'s command deck was armpit to elbow, since both Sten and Alex had insisted on witnessing the results, if any, of their great ploy.

Sh'aarl't had brought her tacship in-atmosphere at a distance carefully calculated to be just within the range of the Tahn satellite's sensors, then dived for the ground.

That, they hoped, would put the antiaircraft systems on full alert.

Then Sh'aarl't launched two remote pilot vehicles that had been modified to give sensor returns matching the tacship. Sh'aarl't and her weapons officer each wore control helmets—Sh'aarl't's looked more like a figure-eight safety mask that sat just above her eyes—and sent the RPVs streaking for the valley.

Four kilometers distance . . . Sh'aarl't murmured, "They have us" . . . three kilometers . . . and the fire-control system ordered all tracking weapons to open fire.

One of those tracking weapons, of course, was the laser that Sten and Alex had boogered. It swung, not away from the valley but toward its center. Its bell depressed, unnoticed, toward the valley's floor. The RPVs were two kilometers away from the valley when the cliff walls exploded into flame and violet light, as did a seventy-five-meter-high by 200-kilometer-square stack of ship-to-ship missile containers. The fireball rolled across the flatland, and two other dumps went up.

The fire-control system wasn't concerned with what was happening inside the valley. It continued firing. One RPV was hit by two laser blasts and three missiles. It vanished, and Sh'aarl't, back in the *Claggett*, swore and pulled her control helmet off.

An analysis computer—part of the fire-control system's backup—realized that one laser gun was dysfunctional and cut it out of circuit. That triggered the bluebox's own power source and activated a second program. On quickfire, the laser pulsed light beams back and forth across the valley.

Alarms in the gun's mobile vans clanged up and down. The techs darted out and saw that their gun was systematically destroying what it had been intended to protect.

They ran toward the override controls just as the second

RPV, almost inside the valley's mouth, veered in flames into a cliff wall, and the entire arms depot blew.

Sh'aarl't had the *Claggett* screaming for space, one set of eyes scanning screens for any Tahn interceptions but most of her attention focused on the screen that showed a boil of flame and smoke on the horizon, blasting almost to the fringes of the atmosphere.

Sten and Alex looked at each other.

"It worked," Sten said in some surprise.

"Aye. When dinnae a ploy ae mine *ever* misfire?"

"Of *yours*?"

"Ah, leave us no be't choosy. A plan't *ours*."

"Well," Sten said resignedly. "I guess I should be glad he's giving me some of the credit."

CHAPTER FIFTY-ONE

FLEET ADMIRAL Xavier Rijn van Doorman's battle plan was ready to implement. He'd dubbed it "Operation Riposte." Sten might have named it "Lastgasp," but he guessed it wasn't apropos to disillusion one's heroes before they trundled into the valley of death.

Not that van Doorman had been particularly optimistic when the briefing began.

There had been eight beings in the room: van Doorman; Sten's instant enemy, Commander Rey Halldor; four captains; two lieutenants; and Sten. The captains were destroyer skippers; the two lieutenants helmed minesweepers.

Van Doorman had introduced everyone, then said that his initial appreciation was not to go beyond the briefing room under any circumstances. Probably quite correctly, since what he said was completely depressing. Most accurate, but still depressing.

The Tahn, he had begun, must be only days away from mounting a second invasion attempt on Cavite. If such an assault was made, van Doorman admitted frankly that the 23rd Fleet would be unable to stop it.

But it was intolerable to just sit and wait to be hit.

Van Doorman's strategy was not unlike Sten's operations—he wanted to hit the Tahn now and get them off guard. It was possible that what was left of the 23rd Fleet might be able to keep the Tahn off guard until the Empire could support Cavite, and then drive the Tahn off the Fringe Worlds.

From the intelligence operations Sten had seen, the Empire might be a long time in doing that.

But at least van Doorman had a plan, Sten had to admit. It was not, surprisingly, all that bad—at least in the briefing.

"I propose," van Doorman began, "to detach four of my destroyers to be the main striking element of what I have named Task Force Halldor." He nodded at the commander beside him. "Commander Halldor will be in direct charge of the combat maneuvering. Commander Sten and his tactical division have determined that the Tahn are moving planetary assault forces to the following systems." A wallscreen lit up, showing the immediate space around Cavite. Four systems gleamed. "The Tahn are taking no chances—they're moving their troop and assault ships in system, using the system ecliptics for screens, and moving close to the planets themselves, thereby utilizing them for cover. While they are providing heavy escort for these convoys, Commander Sten reports escort elements are very light between the convoys and the planets themselves. Gentlebeings, that gave me the plan."

The plan was for the task force to lurk just out-atmosphere of one of the planets that lay on the Tahn convoy route. There should be enough screen clutter to prevent the task force from being detected by the oncoming Tahn escorts.

"This will be," van Doorman went on, "the attack configuration to be used."

Another screen lit.

The two minesweepers would be in front of the destroyers, which would be spaced out in finger-four formation. This, van Doorman admitted, was not the ideal attack configuration. But with only six destroyers still intact, and having committed four of them to the task force, he was very unwilling to lose any of them to a Tahn minefield.

Sten's tacships would provide flank security for the destroyers. Van Doorman hoped that the task force could get inside the escort screen before they were discovered.

"If we are lucky," he said, "such will be the case. In that event, Commander Sten, you are additionally tasked with giving the alert when the Tahn ships *do* attack."

At least, Sten thought, he hadn't been ordered to stop the Tahn. A Tahn destroyer could obliterate a tacship with its secondary armament and without thinking. Heavier ships . . . Sten decided he didn't want to compute that event.

The destroyers were ordered to go for the transports and to avoid battle with combat ships.

"Get in among 'em," van Doorman said, a note of excitement oozing into his orders. "Like a xypaca in the poultry."

The destroyers were to make two passes through the convoy, then retreat. Sten's tacships were then to take advantage of any targets of opportunity before withdrawing. Sten was instructed to plot the retreating destroyers' courses and avoid them in his own retreat—the minesweepers would be laying eggs in that pattern.

"Finally," van Doorman said, "I shall be waiting one AU beyond the area of engagement with the *Swampscott* to provide cover. I would prefer to accompany the attack. But the *Swampscott*—" He stopped. Sten finished mentally: couldn't get out of its own way; had never been in a fleet engagement; had spiders in the missile launch tubes; would conceivably blow up if full battle power was applied. At least no one could say van Doorman lacked courage.

Van Doorman finished his briefing and passed out fiches of the operations order. Then, very emotionally, he drew himself to attention and saluted his officers.

"Good hunting," he said. "And may you return with your prey."

Prey. Sten had the same pronunciation if not the same spelling.

He stopped Halldor in the corridor. "When you attack," he started diplomatically, "what plots will you be using?"

"I'll provide your division with my intentions," Halldor said, most coolly.

Great, Sten thought. Brijit's in the arms of Morrison, both of us are losers, and you can't let it go. "That wasn't going to be my question," he went on. "Since my boats'll be out there on the flanks, and I guess you'll be launching missiles in all directions, I wanted to make sure none of my people get in the way of a big bang."

Halldor thought. "You could put your IFFs on when we go in . . . and I'll have your pattern programmed into the missiles."

"Won't work, Commander. We're squashable enough when the big boys play. Holding a flare in the air won't make us any more invisible. Maybe you could feed a size filter into them. So they won't want to play tag with us teenies."

Halldor looked Sten up and down. "You're very cautious, aren't you, Commander?"

Prod, prod, Commander. How would you like a prod in the eye? Sten just smiled. "Not cautious, Commander Halldor. Cowardly."

He saluted Halldor and went back to brief his people.

The battle off the planet of Badung might possibly have gone into Imperial history and fleet instructional fiches as a classic mosquito action.

That wasn't what happened.

Napoleon supposedly said, when one of his generals was up for a marshal's baton, after listening to a reel of the man's victories, "The hell with his qualifications! Is he lucky?"

And whatever van Doorman's other attributes were, being lucky was not among them.

The battle began perfectly. The task force was able to position itself close to Badung without discovery.

A Tahn convoy did appear—five fat and happy transports escorted by six destroyers, a cruiser, and assorted light patrolcraft.

Halldor ordered the attack.

And things went wrong.

Halldor's own destroyer was hit by something—a mine, space junk, never determined—in the weapons space and holed. He remoted command to a second destroyer while his own ship limped toward the cover of the *Swampscott*. The other three destroyers continued the attack.

Sten winced, staring at the main screen on the *Gamble*. He didn't need to look at the battle computer to see what had happened and what was—or in this case was not—going to happen.

The three destroyers launched their shipkillers at extreme range. The reasons were many—with the exception of Sten's people, none of the 23rd Fleet's weaponeers had seen much combat. In peacetime they would perhaps be permitted to live-fire one missile per year, and despite manufacturer's claims, simulators do not properly simulate.

Another reason might have been the rumors about the Tahn's own antiship missiles. Supposedly they had heavier warheads, superior guidance, and speed greater than that of most commissioned warships. None of those stories were true, although the Tahn shipkillers were very, very fast. The Tahn ships were lethal simply because their men and women had been thoroughly trained for years before the war started.

A third reason was the rapidly spreading rumor that there was something very wrong with the Imperial missiles. They did not go where directed, they did not compute as programmed, and they did not explode when or where they should. That rumor was absolutely true.

The three Imperial destroyers therefore swept only halfway through the Tahn convoy before reversing their action. Seconds later another destroyer was hit and destroyed. The after-action report claimed that the destroyer had been hit by an antiship missile launched by the cruiser. Sten, however, from a position of vantage, had seen the flare of a short-range missile from one of the transports. Evidently the Imperial cruiser's ECM crew wasn't paying attention or wasn't fast enough to acquire the target.

Two down.

The remaining two destroyers went to full power, retreating. As they fled toward the barely comforting umbrella that the *Swampscott* would provide, they launched three missiles each—untargeted as far as the computers on Sten's tacships could determine.

Later, they claimed hits. According to their reports, one Tahn destroyer was obliterated, the cruiser took a major hit, two transports were destroyed, and another Tahn destroyer was lightly hit. Five hits for six launches.

Unfortunately, all claims were wrong.

None of the Imperial officers or sailors reporting hits were lying—they saw missile explosions on their screens, near or fairly near the blips of Tahn ships, and assumed the best. That has always been the case in battle—people see what they want to believe.

There was only one hit.

Possibly Halldor had failed to relay the orders to put a size screen on the missiles, although he claimed otherwise. Or possibly the missile itself lost the program.

But that single missile hit perfectly, directly amidships on the *Kelly*.

Lieutenant Lamine Sekka, warrior of 200 generations, died with all his crew before his spear had been more than bloodied, along with two officers and nine sailors.

A quarter of Sten's command was gone in that one blinding flash.

CHAPTER FIFTY-TWO

THE RETURN TO Cavite was a glum limp. Not only had the task force gone zero-zero, Sten knew, but his crews were still in shock. Tacship service was not unlike the Mantis teams—normally they took very light casualties, being specialists in getting out of the way of the heavy artillery. But inevitably the numbers caught up, and when they did, very few friends would make it to the wake.

The task force limped home because, moments after the surviving ships rendezvoused with the *Swampscott* and the withdrawal started, *Swampy* had blown out one of her aged drivetubes. The tacships and the destroyers ended up escorting the cruiser back to Cavite.

To their surprise, Cavite was a boil of spacecraft. Huge ships—transports, assault landing craft, combat fleets—filled the skies and packed the fleet's landing grounds. Two battleships hung on the outer reaches of the atmosphere.

For a moment Sten thought that the Tahn had pulled an end run and landed on Cavite while the Imperial forces were stalking the convoy. And then his computer growled at him and began IDing the ships.

There was a full Imperial fleet plus landing and support ships for an entire Guards division.

Sten and Alex exchanged glances. They didn't say anything—Foss and his ears were on the command deck. But the thought was mutual—perhaps they weren't all doomed. Maybe this war was not going as badly as they thought. With these reinforcements, they might be able at least to hold the Tahn.

The icing on the cake was finding out that the unit was the First Guards, perhaps the best of the Imperial elite, headed by General Mahoney, Sten and Alex's old boss in Mantis.

They landed and ordered Sutton and the ground crews to get the three boats fueled, supplied, and armed for immediate takeoff. Kilgour made a slight change. Ground crews always felt as much a part of their assigned craft as any combat crew person. And Alex knew that the support teams of the *Kelly* would not only be mourning but endlessly wondering if something they had done quickly or maybe not exactly could have contributed to the ship's destruction. The *Kelly*'s ground crews were taken off duty and given six hours liberty.

Liberty in shattered Cavite City wasn't much. Large portions of the city, still occupied by Tahn settlers, were off limits and most chancy to enter with anything other than an armored gravsled. Half of the stores owned by Imperial immigrants were shuttered or burnt out, and their proprietors had fled.

Passage price on any of the merchant ships that were daring enough to make the passage to Cavite and skillful enough to evade the Tahn patrols was simply set—How much do you own in liquid assets? Only the quite rich need apply for a corner space in a stinking cargo hold.

Sten filed his immediate after-action report. Then he and Kilgour freshened up, put on their least tired sets of coveralls, and started looking for Guards headquarters.

They found General Mahoney in a cacophony of underlings. Division headquarters was set up in a collection of armored carriers half a kilometer from the landing field. Sten wondered why Mahoney wasn't working out of his command assault ship.

Mahoney spotted them standing outside his personal carrier. Four gestures in sign language: Stand by. Ten minutes. I'm in the drakh.

It took twenty minutes before the last officer had his orders and was scurrying away. And then Mahoney brought them up to speed.

There may have been icing, but there wasn't any cake, the general informed them rather grimly.

"Quite a fleet," he said, indicating a monitor screen.

"Admire it real fast, gentlemen. Because it's only going to be around for another fourteen hours or so. I don't know what they nomenclature this kind of operation in Staff College, but I'd call it Dump and Depart."

"An' there's a reason?" Alex asked. "Or is the wee navy afeard a' gettin' their tunics messed?"

"Clot yes, there's a reason," Mahoney said. "And if I didn't have a staff conference in . . . twenty minutes, I'd pull up a bottle and give you all the gory details. But I'll give you an overall.

"First of all, the Empire's up against it. Bad. I assume you two thugs have accessed van Doorman's 'Eyes-only' sitreps from Prime?"

They had—Sten through a computer tap and Alex by making friends with a semilovely cipher clerk on the *Swampscott*. The reports were uniformly disastrous.

"The real status is even worse," Mahoney said. "This big chubby fleet that's all around us? Maybe it'd give you a start if somebody said it's the only still-intact strike force for a quarter of this galaxy?"

Sten blinked.

Mahoney smiled grimly. "The Tahn, and all their new allies who're scrambling aboard, haven't missed much. Two things you might find interesting—so far we haven't been able to mount one single offensive. Not against Tahn systems, not even to recover any of the systems we've lost. The fleet gave my transports cover—and as soon as we're off-loaded, they're going to load up every dependent and any Imperial settler whose got brains enough to evacuate. Then everything except a few of the assault ships and patrol boats haul ass for safety."

Sten grimaced.

"There aren't a whole clottin' lot of other options," Mahoney said. "The Empire can't take the chance of losing this fleet."

"It's none of my business, sir. But why're you here? Seems to me," Sten said, "like all that's going to happen is the First Guards'll go down the sewer pipe with the rest of us."

"Your CO's a cheery sort," Mahoney commented.

"Aye, sir. He's thinkit tha's a sewer pipe to go doon."

"Okay. This—like the rest of the drakh I've said—is classified. We're supposed to hold Cavite. Sooner or later what goes around'll come around. And the Empire will need a springboard to strike back from."

"What brainburn came up with *that*?"

"Your ex-boss," Mahoney said.

Sten backwatered—even though this was most informal, he didn't think it quite bright to be insulting the Eternal Emperor. "Sorry, sir. But I still don't think it's going to work."

Even though there was no one else in the carrier, Mahoney lowered his voice. "I don't either, Commander. I think the Emperor still thinks that he's got time to play with. Because sooner or later, we're going to win. He's putting his chips on sooner."

"Personal question, sir. What's your opinion?"

"I think that you and I and the Guards and van Doorman's fleet are going to end up providing some top-quality martyrs for Imperial recruiting," Mahoney said frankly. "Oh, well," he finished. "I guess things aren't going to get much worse."

Mahoney was wrong.

Three hours later, even before the fleet had finished offloading Mahoney's supplies, two Tahn destroyers hit Cavite Base. Missiles killed one of them, and the second was battered into retreat by one of the battlewagons.

But the fleet admiral had absolute orders. If the Tahn made *any* attack, he was to abort and withdraw at once, regardless of mission status on Cavite.

Ports hissed shut, and the Imperial fleet whined into the air and vanished into AM2 drive, leaving the skies of Cavite as bare as they had been before—leaving more than 7,000 Imperial civilians abandoned.

Two days after that, Tahn bombs thundered down on Cavite. The invasion bombardment had begun.

CHAPTER FIFTY-THREE

THE FIRST ATTACK was successful. Too successful.

Forty nonnuclear bombs had been skip-launched by Tahn ships, darting into the upper reaches of Cavite's ionosphere and then away. All of them had similar targets—Imperial communication and/or computer centers. Thirty-one of them hit on target, or close enough to cause significant damage. Six more sent the com centers offline for at least an hour. Two were destroyed by a very alert Guards surface-to-air missile team, and the last was blown out of the sky by a patrol boat.

Of course the bombs had to have been guided. Mahoney and his superskilled Guard technicians had less than three hours to make their analysis.

Could the bombs have been remote-flown by operators in the Tahn ships? Highly unlikely, because not only were the fixed centers of the 23rd Fleet hit—including two strikes on the critical SigInt center—but three of Mahoney's semimobile sites were hit as well. It would be almost impossible for any human operator to have reflexes fast enough to spot the antenna array and significantly divert a downward-plunging bomb quickly enough to make a hit.

Also, none of Mahoney's ECM experts had picked up any transmission on any band aimed at the bombs.

Van Doorman, whose electronics ability stopped just short of understanding how electrical current in a cable can alternate and still work, had his own theory: The Tahn had developed a secret weapon.

Unsurprisingly, all estimates from fleet technicians

echoed his theory. They knew on which side their circuit boards were buttered.

Mahoney listened to the admiral's theory politely, made noncommital noises, and got off the com. He already had his own ideas—and teams—in motion.

Any military is a juggernaut in more ways than the amount of force it can exert. It also tends to stick with any plan that has worked once or twice until it is proved that the enemy is on to it. That translates to friendly casualties, sometimes appallingly high, and sometimes even then the lesson is not learned.

For instance, during one of Earth's periodic wars, Earth Date A.D. 1914–1918, the military situation stalemated itself into trench warfare, with both sides fighting from fixed positions dug into the earth. The commander on one side, a certain Haig, ordered his troops to attack front-ally and in parade-ground lines. Sixty thousand men were killed on his side in the first day alone.

After that, anyone not entirely gormless would have either relieved himself for terminal stupidity or else found a different set of tactics. But with only a few exceptions, that same battle plan was used until the war ground to an exhausted halt—each time with a casualty rate almost as catastrophic.

The Tahn were guilty of this mental laziness as well. Their system of using an agent in place to laser-guide either a bomb or a missile had worked extraordinarily well previously on a hundred or more worlds. There was no need to come up with a different method for the initial bombardment of Cavite that would precede the invasion. Especially when there were Tahn agents in place and many trained and eager members of the various Tahn revolutionary organizations available, despite the losses taken after the failure of Empire Day.

Habit was certainly part of Lady Atago and Admiral Deska's decision to use aimed bombs. A second factor may have been their quite justified contempt for the Imperial forces. But there was a vast difference between the sloths and recruits of the 23rd Fleet and the hard men of the First Guards. The Empire might not have fought a major war for many years—but the First Guards were very experienced as the Empire's fire brigade. Most of the men of the Guard were careerists, and almost half of them had more than twenty years of combat experience, off and on.

Among their specialties were city fighting and security sweeps. There were more than fifty bomb controllers in place around Cavite City, hidden in attics or unused buildings or operating from long-set-up mole holes in offices or apartments.

Two battalions of Guards were deployed. They worked in five-person teams, five-finger machines. The first man knocked or rang on the door, standing to its side. Two more crouched, weapons ready to either side. The last two were back and to either side to provide covering fire or to keep anyone from sniping out a window. Any resistance, or refusal to answer, and the door came down. Any supposition that General Mahoney had a tendency to disregard civil liberties when it was expedient was most correct. Besides, any investigating commission would be set up only if they held Cavite, and only after the war was won.

Direction-finder gravsleds swept down the streets and over the buildings themselves.

Before the next wave of Tahn tacships came in for the launch, forty-seven guidance sites had been found; either the sites were eliminated along with their operators, or the Tahn fled, leaving their gear behind. The dozen or so left were IDed and removed after they attempted to illuminate the bomb targets.

The bombs scattered across the city. Harmlessly, if looked at from the military sense—only three significant targets were damaged. But they shattered Cavite City. There were 6,000 civilian casualties. The military defines its terms most selfishly.

The Tahn, however, did not escape unscathed. Sten's three tacships and a flight of patrolcraft were waiting on an anticipated orbit pattern. Twelve Tahn tacships were destroyed. The Tahn, expecting that their attacks would disrupt Cavite's air defenses, had sent in second- and third-class ships.

Three more waves came in, again at the Tahn-dictated interval of three hours. All three attacks were decimated.

All three bombing missions went wild. And more citizens, both Imperial and Tahn, died.

Then Lady Atago changed her tactics.

So did Sten.

> *"She's gane till her father's garden,*
> *And pu'd an apple, red and green;*
> *Twas a' to wyle him, sweet Sir Hugh,*
> *And to entice him in."*

Alex stopped muttering and looked at Foss. What're y' gawkin't a', swab?"

"Didn't know you spoke any foreign languages, sir."

"Dinna be makin't fun ae th' way Ah speak. Ah hae yet t' makit up thae fitness report."

"So? 'There'll be no promotion/This side of the ocean/So cheer up my lads/Clot 'em all,'" Foss also quoted. "Sir."

The person to be wiled was of course not Sir Hugh, but the Tahn commander. And Sten was not planning to use an apple, either green or red. Instead, hung under each of the three tacships was a long, streamlined pod. It contained a full, destroyer-intended ECM suite, far more powerful if not as sophisticated as the countermeasure equipment on the Bulkeley-class tacships. Signals were fed from the pods and the tacships own electronics down a half-kilometer-long cable to strange and wonderfully configured polyhedrons below. The tacships hung about 200 meters above the main landing field.

"D' y' really thinkit this'll go?" Alex asked.

"Why wouldn't it?" Sten said.

"Ah. Try a differen' way. Supposin't it works aye too well?"

"We go boom."

"Ah no mind bein't expendable—but thae's no joy in bein't expungeable."

Sten had figured that when the operator-guided bombing missions failed, the next approach would be more conventional.

It was. Four Tahn destroyers multiple-fired operator-guided missiles from in-atmosphere, 1000 meters above the ground and about 400 kilometers away from Cavite City.

"I have a launch... I have multiples..." Foss suddenly announced in a monotone, his eyes pinned to a screen.

Equal reports chattered in from the *Claggett* and the *Richards*.

"All ships... stand by," Sten ordered. "On my order, activate... now!"

Foss touched a switch, and the electronic countermeasure pod hummed into life.

The Tahn operators were navigating their missiles with both radar and visual sensing fed into their control helmets. The visual range was extraordinarily easy to jam. Without excitement, the Tahn controllers put full attention on their radar guidance.

Their sensors punched through the clutter that was Cavite looking for their targets: large metallic objects. This strike was after what was left of the 23rd Fleet and the few ships Mahoney had remaining.

The skilled Tahn controllers found targets... their weapons computers kept all missiles from homing on a single ship... and the targets grew in the operators' radar eyes.

Narrow beams kept any of them from seeing those stationary ships move.

"Half speed," Sten ordered.

The tacships climbed.

"Do you have them?"

"Uhh... that's an affirmative. All missiles homing as projected."

"Full power... now! Drive power... now!

The tacships bolted into space.

The missiles were very close to the Imperial ships—or so the operators thought. What they were closing on were the radar-spoofing polyhedrons instead of the 23rd's grounded ships. Almost all of the missiles had their own automatic homing mechanisms active and, therefore, tried to follow the ships.

Stabilizing guidance systems tumbled, and the missiles spun out of control. A few, still under operator control, lost their targets and kept on keeping on while the controllers tried to figure out what had happened. A warship cannot vanish tracelessly.

Six of the missiles managed to track the false targets for a few moments until their fuel ran out and the missiles self-destructed.

A few AUs out, Sten ordered power cut, counted noses, and realized that they had gotten away with it. But that, he knew, would be a one-time-only gimmick.

He wondered what would happen next.

CHAPTER FIFTY-FOUR

TIME BECAME A blur for Sten and his crews. Their clocks and calendars were events half-remembered in mumbled exhaustion: That was the day we ran that recon patrol. No. We were escorting the sweepers then. Remember, that's when the *Sampson* blew up? You're full of drakh. We were out on a doggo ambush then.

No one knew for sure. Any of them would have traded their chances on an afterlife for two shifts of uninterrupted sleep, a meal that wasn't gobbled cold from a pak, or—don't even whisper it—a bath.

The ships stank almost as much as the sailors did, smelling of fear, fuel fumes, ozone, sweat, and overheated insulation. They were also starting to wear out. The Kali launcher on the *Richards* was kaput. That did not matter too much—there were only three of the giant missiles left. Both chainguns on the *Claggett* were capable of only intermittent fire, and its tell-me-thrice battle computer had lost a lobe. Sten's own ship, the *Gamble*, had only six Goblin launchers that still tracked.

All of the Yukawa drive units needed teardown—they were many, many hours outside the regulated service intervals. The AM2 drives still functioned, unsurprisingly since they had approximately as many moving parts as a brick.

But the navcomputers were all causing problems—projected courses had to be run four times and averaged. When there was time, at least.

And the Tahn forces kept getting stronger and bolder. Sten almost hoped for the day of invasion to come.

In the meantime, there were the missions. Escort X ships . . . patrol Y sector . . . escort Guard Unit Z and provide cover until its forward firebase is secure . . .

Routine missions.

It was on one such "routine" mission that they encountered the ghost ship.

A stationary sensor had reported an inbound transport following a highly abnormal course. The transport did not respond to any communication attempts, nor did its IFF give the correct automatic responses for the assigned time period. Both radar and a flash visual identified the ship, however, as a standard-design Imperial fleet tender.

Sten assumed some sort of Tahn trap.

He positioned the *Gamble* and the *Claggett* at an intersection point on the transport's orbit and waited. The *Richards* was grounded, partially torn-down on Romney. Sutton and his crew were sure that this time they had figured out what was wrong with the Yukawa drives and promised a quick fix.

The transport broke the detector screens a few hours later. The two tacships waited. Sten expected that a couple of Tahn destroyers would be lurking somewhere behind the tender. But there was nothing. The *Gamble*'s *Jane*'s fiche identified the transport as an Atrek-class tender, the IFT Galkin.

Sten chanced challenging the transport. The automatic IFF response was weeks out of date. Foss could not get any sort of response other than that, nor was the transport broadcasting on any wavelength that could be received by the *Gamble*.

Sten launched his eye-modified Goblin to have a closer look. Possibly the transport was a dummy.

There was no response.

Sten matched orbits with the transport, put a recorder on, and circumnavigated the ship. Both locks and all cargo ports were sealed. There was no sign that any of the lifeships had been launched. Finally Sten brought the Goblin in until one fin touched the outer lock door. If the transport was a booby trap, that should set it off.

The detectors still reported no other ships onscreen. Still, Sten had a crawling feeling that the *Galkin* might be the bait for a nasty Tahn surprise.

He opened the tight beam to the *Claggett* to discuss the situation with Sh'aarl't. She was in complete agreement with him. It smelled very much like a trap. There was only one way to find out. Someone had to board the ship.

"Sh'aarl't . . . Kilgour and I are boarding. I want you about a light-second off, on the transport's back orbit."

Sh'aarl't came back at him instantly. "That doesn't sound too wise to me, Sten," she said. "If we are jumped, the *Claggett* would be outgunned by almost anything the Tahn threw at us—practically down to a lifeboat."

She had a strong point. Sh'aarl't and her weapons officer, Ensign Dejean, would check things out. The *Gamble* would play rear guard. Kilgour moved the ship into position and they both watched the screen as the *Claggett*'s AM2 drive flared. A few moments later, the *Claggett* was docking with the *Galkin*.

Even at close range, there was nothing strange noted visually by either Sh'aarl't or Dejean. Their suit sensors also showed nothing beyond the normal. Sh'aarl't keyed her mike. "We're boarding."

Sten buried the instinct to say something stupid, like "be careful." Instead, he bent his head closer to the monitor, listening to the crackle of the two voices.

Dejean, expecting a bolt of lightning to leap from the ship to his suit glove, touched the outer lock control. It obediently irised open. Sh'aarl't and Dejean hesitated, then entered. Sh'aarl't's perceptions swung as the *Galkin*'s McLean gravity generators provided a new "down" for them. Their boots touched the inside of the lock—again there was no sudden explosion.

"My suit shows normal atmosphere," Dejean reported. "But I have no intention of trusting it."

They kept their suit faceplates sealed. Sh'aarl't touched the inner lock control. It, too, opened.

She increased transmitter output power enough to punch

through the ship's atmosphere and outer hull. They rhinoceros waddled in their armored combat suits into the *Galkin*.

They found nothing. The ship, from machinery spaces to the engine room, was completely deserted. None of the lifeships had been launched. All spacesuits, from survival type to the small, two-person work capsules, were racked.

Both beings found it more comforting to continue the search with weapons ready. Sh'aarl't turned on a recorder at her waist and fed the information back to the *Gamble*.

They checked the crew quarters. Not only were they deserted, the lockers that should have held the crew's personal effects were empty.

Dejean checked the ship's stores. They were bare, as if the *Galkin* had never been supplied before it took off.

Sh'aarl't ignored the crawl of fear down her back spine and went to the control room. She found the ship's log and ran it back. The Imperial Fleet Tender *Galkin*, Captain Ali Remo in command, had taken off from the planet of Mehr some six cycles previously. Complement forty-two officers, 453 enlisted. Captain Remo carefully noted they were six officers, thirty-four men under authorized complement.

The *Galkin* had been ordered to reinforce the 23rd Fleet on Cavite.

She key jumped to the log's last entry:

IMPERIAL DATE...SHIP DATE 22, THIRD WATCH. OFFICER OF THE WATCH: LT. MURIEL ERNDS, SECOND OFFICER ENSIGN GORSHA, ENGINE ROOM CHIEF ARTIFICER MILLIKEN. COURSE AS SET, NO UNPLOTTED OBJECTS DETECTED. 2240 SHIPS HOURS GENERAL QUARTERS DRILL ORDERED PER CAPTAIN'S INSTRUCTIONS. TIME TO FULL READINESS 7 MINUTES, 23 SECONDS. STAND DOWN FROM DRILL ORDERED, 2256 SHIPS HOURS. 2300 STANDARD REPORT INPUT

...and the log automatically recorded the readout monitoring the *Galkin*'s condition.

Sten paced the control room of the *Gamble*, listening intently to everything Sh'aarl't said.

"It all looks perfectly normal," she reported. "Except for the fact that sometime after 2300 hours, every man, woman, and being on the *Galkin* decided to vanish."

Sten looked at Alex. The stocky Edinburghian looked very unhappy.

"Ah noo believe he ghosts," he said, "but—"

"Wait a minute! I think we got something!" Sh'aarl't's voice crackled excitedly over the monitor.

Sten waited much longer than a minute. He became impatient. "Report, Sh'aarl't! What *have* you got?"

"Well, according to the log—"

There was an eerie silence as her voice stopped in midsentence. It was if the *Gamble*'s com system had gone dead. Before Sten could say a word, Foss sat bolt up in his chair.

"Skipper! I don't understand it! They're gone!"

Sten rushed to his side and looked at the screen. The large blips that had represented the *Claggett* and the *Galkin* had disappeared.

"It's gotta be some kind of malfunction with the system," Sten said, knowing even as he said it that it wasn't so.

"Not a chance, sir," Foss said, his voice cracking.

It wasn't necessary to give any orders—within bare moments, the *Gamble* was at battle stations, the drive at instant readiness. Foss ran every test and every electronic search pattern in the book, plus a few more he had invented.

Once again: nothing.

There was nothing on the radar, nothing on the intermediate or deep sensors, and no directional pickup on any broadcast frequency, including emergency. At one lightsecond, the two docked ships should have been on visual. But the screens were blank.

"Quarter power," Sten ordered. "Bring us up over that ship real slow."

All inputs remained negative.

"Back-plot the orbit. Mr. Kilgour, I want a figure-eight search pattern. Half speed."

"Aye, sir."

They searched in a gradually widening moving globe pattern for three full E-days. But the *Claggett*, Sh'aarl't, her two officers, and nine enlisted had vanished along with the *Galkin*.

There was no explanation. And there never would be one.

CHAPTER FIFTY-FIVE

THREE HOURS OUT of Romney, the com began yammering onscreen, the message sent en clair:

ALL SHIPS . . . ALL SHIPS . . . CAVITE UNDER ATTACK. INVASION BY TAHN UNDER WAY. ALL SHIPS RETURN TO HOME BASE. ATTACK, REPEAT ATTACK.

Foss already had the fiche in the navcomputer.

"On command," Sten said. "Commit."

"Attack repeat attack," Alex snorted. "Tha' dinnae be a command! Thae's an invite t' Culloden."

Kilgour was right. No *Claggett* . . . no *Kelly* . . . Sten assumed the *Richards* was getting slapped back together on Romney. Sten had no intentions of plummeting his very thin-skinned tacship—or, come to think about it, his own rather thin-skinned body—into the middle of a fleet melee.

He turned the intercom on and read the broadcast from Cavite to his crew without allowing any emotion to enter his voice. Then he said equally flatly, "If anyone's got an idea on what we do when we hit Cavite, input, please."

Alex reached across and kept his finger on the intercom button. "A wee modification as wha' our commander's sayin'. Ideas tha' dinnae win ae of us medals what be posthumous. Mr. Kilgour's mum dinnae be boastin' as her lad comes home ae a box."

There weren't any ideas.

"Great," Sten muttered. "We're about as thick in the tactics department as van Doorman."

"Dinnae fash. We'll do flash fakin't it."

Lady Atago and Admiral Deska had made very sure that there was no possibility of the invasion failing a second time. More than 500 ships swarmed the Caltor System. The Imperial 23rd Fleet wasn't outmanned so much as buried.

Mahoney had stationed Guard detachments on every world and moonlet of the system. Each detachment was given as sophisticated a sensing system as possible. That was not much, even though every detector that could be found had been stripped out of downed or civilian ships, and emplaced. The strike-back weaponry was equally jury-rigged.

Everything from missiles to private yachts to out-atmosphere runabouts to obsolete ships had been hung in space and linked to the improvised guidance systems. Even Ensign Tapia's tug had been roboticized, its control room a deserted spaghetti of wiring.

Most of these improvised missiles were either destroyed long before they found a target or went wonky and missed completely.

But some of them got through.

"Go for the transports," Mahoney had told his guardsmen. They tried. Troopships were ripped open, sardine-spilling Tahn soldiers into space or sending them pinwheeling and igniting like meteorites into atmosphere.

But the Tahn were too strong.

Mahoney watched from his new headquarters, burrowed a hundred meters into a hillock near Cavite Field as, one by one, his com teams lost contact with the off-Cavite detachments. Mahoney's face was quite impassive.

A tech glared down at her general from a com set on one of the balconies above the central floor. Solid imperium, she thought in fury. The clot doesn't even care.

In actuality, Mahoney *was* trying to analyze what he felt. Not one report, he thought with approval, of any of my people breaking. What about you, Ian? You've taken...

let's see, about twenty-five percent casualties. What does that feel like? Not too bad, he thought. No worse, say, than getting your right arm amputated without anaesthetic. Don't feel sorry for yourself, General. If you do something dumb like crying or swearing, your whole division could break.

What arrogance, he marveled. And what would it matter if they did? This is the last time around, isn't it? There isn't going to be enough left of the First Guard to compose a suicide note.

Like you told Sten, he thought. All we're doing is building martyrs for the cause. And enough of that, Ian. You have work to do.

Mahoney pointed to an operator and was instantly linked to all surviving detachment commanders. "They're still coming in, people. Get your reserves out of their holes and ready to go."

The ground around Mahoney shuddered suddenly, and the lights flashed twice before finding a functioning emergency circuit.

The Tahn were hitting Cavite itself.

The lead elements of Tahn ships were unmanned strafers. As ordered, the naval and Guard antiaircraft teams held their fire. Ammunition and missile reserves were almost nonexistent. Wait, they had been told, for the real targets: manned ships. That was expected to be the second wave.

But Atago's tactics were different.

The second element was made up of twenty small assault transports. The transports broke up, and from each ship, six troop capsules dropped toward the city below. In each capsule was a team of Tahn commandos.

Unlike the larger Imperial troop capsule that used wings and tear-away chutes for braking, these capsules were fitted only with retrorockets, set to fire when the capsule was pointed downward and very close to the ground.

Some of them never corrected, and the rockets sent the capsules pinwheeling before they crashed at full speed.

Even the ones that functioned correctly only slowed the capsules down to approximately 50 kph. The internal shock bracing was supposed to provide the rest of the cushioning —of a sort. Thirty percent of the commandos were able to stumble out of their wrecked capsules, form up, and head for their assigned objectives.

That was quite satisfactory—Lady Atago had anticipated and allowed for an eighty percent loss on landing. The Tahn cynicism had gone still further—*none* of the assigned objectives were expected to be taken. This had not been told to the commandos at their briefing. Nor was their real mission revealed—to pinprick the Imperial defenders, to distract them from the main force landings.

One team of commandos did reach its objective—the Carlton Hotel that Atago had theorized might still be used by the 23rd Fleet headquarters. But it had been abandoned weeks ago—van Doorman had returned to the *Swampscott*, which was sitting in the deep revetment near Cavite Field. And the commandos were distracting, but only to the Guard teams who had been ordered to maintain street patrols. The Tahn commandos failed, but in failing they caused casualties and ammunition expenditures. The Empire could afford neither.

The third wave was the heaviest. Four battleships, including the now-repaired *Forez*, Atago and Deska's flagship; twenty cruisers; and a horde of destroyers raved fire at the planet. In the center of the formation were seventy-five fat-bellied assault transports.

Previously hidden Imperial missile launchers rose from bare ground, out of buildings and sheds, and even, in the case of one particular inspired team, from an abandoned double-decked transport gravsled. It was almost impossible to miss.

But it was equally impossible to hit all of the Tahn ships. Sixty-three of the transports grounded in a ring some 400 kilometers outside Cavite City, and their sides clamshelled and Tahn assault troops stormed out.

Lady Atago allowed herself a smile of satisfaction. To her, all that remained was mopping up.

CHAPTER FIFTY-SIX

THE *GAMBLE* HUNG in space, hopefully hidden from the Tahn forces landing on Cavite by one of the world's moons. Sten's entire crew, less Foss, who was minding the sensors, was crammed onto the tiny mess deck reviewing the options.

The problem was that neither Sten nor Kilgour could figure out an attack plan against the Tahn that did not include their own destruction. As Alex pointed out, "As far ae Ah can ken, th' job description dinnae ken kazikami, or wha'e'er th' word is."

Sten might have accepted the military necessity of a suicide mission, given a strategic target that might stop the Tahn. But every idea that was suggested and run up on the battle computer showed that the *Gamble* had a ninety-nine-point-more-nine's chance of never getting through the Tahn outer destroyer screen; setting up and making an attack run on one of the Tahn heavies looked to be impossible.

"What about slingshotting?" Contreras, ex-cop, now the *Gamble*'s bosun's mate, asked. "Full power around this moon, then around Cavite and hit 'em when we come back through."

"Won't work," Sten said. "The Tahn'll pick us up the minute we come out from shadow. That'll give them more than enough time to set up a prog and nail us on the way in."

Contreras tugged at her ear and sank back into thought.

"We can't just sit here, sir." McCoy said. An ex-jailbird, he was now master's mate, engine room.

"Do we have any idea what's left of our fleet?"

"We're still picking up broadcasts that Foss says are

238

from the *Swampscott*. And there seem to be a couple destroyers still in the air."

"Maybe we do wait," McCoy tried. "Sooner or later, somebody down on Cavite's gonna try one. We hit the Tahn from the other side when they do."

Sten gnawed a fingernail. "Crappy plan," he said finally. "Anybody got a better one?"

There were negative head shakes all around.

"Okay, McCoy. We'll give it a shot. Everybody not on watch get their heads down."

Hypno-conditioning let any of them go instantly to sleep and return to full alertness at command. But the ship's detector alarms went off before any of them had made it to their bunks.

Sten sprinted to the command deck. Foss indicated one screen with a solitary blip to one side.

"That's the *Richards*, sir. Correct IFF response. And that..."

Sten didn't need an explanation—the second screen showed another, larger indication. Tahn, of course. Probably a heavy destroyer.

Foss touched keys and moved the two images onto the larger center screen. "It's closing on the *Richards*."

Sten had the mike open and broadcast power at full, breaking com silence. The Tahn ship would certainly pick up his broadcast, but he might be able to save the *Richards* now and worry about his own skin later.

"*Richards...Richards...*this is *Gamble*. Bogey on intersection orbit. Closing on you. Bogey location—"

The *Richards* cut in. "*Gamble...*we have him. I shackle...X-ray delta...Two. Unshackle. Over."

Lieutenant Estill—Sten noted that his voice stayed quite calm—was using a simple voice code. X-ray: main engine. Delta: damaged. Two: fifty-percent power loss.

"This is *Gamble*. Heading yours, over."

Sten hit the GQ alarm. "I want an interception course, Mr. Foss. Engines!"

"Ready, sir."

"Primary drive full emergency. Secondary drive full standby."

"Sir."

"All weapons stations report launch readiness."

"All live stations ready, sir."

"Mr. Foss. What do we have?"

There was now a third blip on the main screen. A red line threaded from the third blip—Sten's ship—toward the Tahn destroyer and the *Gamble*. Suddenly the dot on the screen that was the *Richards* shimmered, coming out of AM2 drive.

"*Gamble* . . . this is *Richards*. Status now I shackle X-Ray delta four. I say again four, over."

Main drive out completely.

"AM2 drives *can't* break down," Foss said.

"Th' hell they can't," Alex said. "Tha's one that did. Now shut up and mind your screens."

"This is *Gamble*. I shackle Yankee alfa one break Mike tango echo, over."

Yankee: secondary—Yukawa drive. Alfa: engage. One: full power. Mike: maneuver. Tango: toward. Echo: enemy.

"This is *Richards*. I shackle. Yankee also delta. Three."

Sutton hadn't been able to repair the *Richards*, or his repairs hadn't worked for long.

There were three points of view: To the Tahn destroyer, the *Richards* appeared to come to a halt as the destroyer closed. To Sten, both ships moved across his main screen. A stationary observer, hanging in space, would not have mental reactions fast enough to perceive any of the three ships as they went past at many times light-speed.

Foss superimposed two time ticks on the main screen. The left was the estimated number of seconds before the Tahn ship would come within launch range of the *Richards*. The right showed time before Sten could attack the destroyer. The seven-second differential could doom the *Richards*.

"Kali. Stand by."

"Ah'm ready."

"Foss. Distress flares ready to launch."

"Distress . . . yessir. Ready."

"Flares . . . fire! Kali! Launch!"

The huge missile slid out of the *Gamble*'s nose just as two distress flares bloomed, radiating through broadcast, radar, and visual wavelengths.

One second later the Tahn ship launched two antiship missiles at the *Richards*.

"Alex... don't worry about what I'm doing. Get that destroyer."

"Lad, Ah'm in a world ah m' own. Dinna fash."

"Distress signals again... launch!"

Sten was hoping that the flares would shake up the Tahn. Maybe the destroyer's weaponeers would divert their missiles toward the *Gamble*. They didn't. The *Richards* was far too sitting a quacker to ignore.

But the failure wasn't complete. Possibly the controllers' attention was broken for a critical quarter second. Because the first missile missed the *Richards* completely—not too hard, since the tacship wasn't that much bigger than the missile was. The second missile went off close enough to the *Richards* to blank its blip on Sten's screen.

Clear screen—and the *Richards* was still there!

"Ah now th' worm'll turn," Kilgour murmured—and triggered the Kali.

Sixty megatons blew the Tahn ship in two. One-third of the destroyer—its midsection—ceased to exist except as raw energy. Some of the stern, pouring sparks and a flash of flame, pinwheeled on. The remnants of the bow started on a tangented orbit toward Sten.

"*Richards... Richards...* this is *Gamble*. Over."

Dead air.

"This is *Gamble*. Are you receiving me?"

Foss saw an ancillary meter flicker. "Sir... there's a 'cast from a suit radio on the *Richards*. Stand by." He added another frequency.

"... this is the *Richards*. I say again, this is the *Richards*." It was Tapia's voice.

"This is the *Gamble*. The destroyer's killed. Give status, over."

"*Richards*. Seven dead. Three wounded. XO in command."

"This is *Gamble*. We're matching orbit. Stand by for pickup."

"Negative on that," Tapia said. "The main lock's crushed. We can't reach the emergency. And our secondary drive is going any second now. Stand clear, *Gamble*." Tapia's voice was a monotone.

"*Richards* . . . this is *Gamble*. Are survivors in suits?"

"That's affirmative."

"Can you reach the Kali inspection hatch?"

With the *Richards*'s Kali launcher down, the tacship's centerline launch tube was empty.

"We can. Can you open the outer hatch? We have no weapons."

"The can opener is on the way, over." Sten closed the com. "Alex?"

Alex diverted control to a Fox countermissile and launched. The small missile sped far beyond the *Richards* at full launch speed before Alex could cut its power and bring it looping back toward them.

"We'll try quarter speed," he said—and sent the Fox into the *Richards*. Even with the warhead on safe, the Fox still ripped nearly a meter off the tacship's nose.

"Ah would'a made a braw surgeon," he said proudly.

Sten reopened the com. "Come on out."

Five suited figures oozed out of the launcher and drifted through space. It took only seconds for Sten to maneuver the *Gamble* alongside. McCoy was already suited and out of the lock. A magnetic line lassoed the survivors of the *Richards*.

Sten sent the *Gamble* away from the *Richards*.

How long it was and how far away they were when the *Richards*'s Yukawa units blew varied in the later telling, depending on the audience's credulity and how many alks the teller was into the evening.

The five survivors were pulled onboard and treated. Sten personally unsuited Ensign Tapia and half carried her to his own bunk. He was being solicitous, he told himself, because she was a very capable officer and a friend as well. Not even his conscious mind believed that rationalization. But again, there wasn't time.

He had to return to Cavite. Without his main armament, there was little good he could do in space.

So all he had to do was slip through the Tahn net off Cavite, maneuver through the attacking forces, find a safe landing at Cavite Base, and then scuttle for a bomb shelter.

No problem, he desperately hoped. We're a lucky ship.

The *Gamble*'s luck ran out eight miles high above Cavite. A six-ship flight of interceptors jumped the *Gamble*. Sten tried to climb for space—but the battle computer showed three destroyers that could intercept.

The interceptors had speed and maneuverability on the *Gamble*. Sten sent his ship at speed toward the ground, zigging in a random pattern.

Kilgour sent three Fox countermissiles to the rear. Two interceptors sharded, and then the rest of the flight was in range. Sten saw the tiny silver flickers of light under the interceptors' main airfoils.

"I have seven...no...observed launches," Foss said, his voice starting to crack. "Intercept time..."

And three of the missiles hit the *Gamble*. Sten heard the hammer blows, saw flame flare from the control panel, noted the mist-hung mountains below filling the frozen main screen, and felt the manual controls go dead.

The Tahn interceptor flight commander pulled out of his dive and half rolled. He watched the smoke-pluming Imperial tacship vanish into the mist, then ordered his squadron to return to the mother ship.

It had been a very good day for him. Five...no, this would be the sixth Imperial his flight had downed. He determined to order an issue of spirits as a reward.

BOOK FOUR

TAKE EVERY MAN HIS BIRD

CHAPTER FIFTY-SEVEN

THE ETERNAL EMPEROR considered what would adequately describe his current mood. Angry—no. Far beyond that. Enraged. Not that—he wasn't showing any emotion. At least so he hoped. Standard Galactica wasn't helping much. He ran through some of the more exotic languages learned from equally unusual beings.

Yes. The Matan word "k'loor" applied, which could be loosely translated as a state compounded equally of worry, unhappiness, hatred, and anger, a state whose existence, though, allowed extreme clarity of thought and an ability to instantly reach and act on a conclusion.

Self-description didn't, however, improve the Imperial mood.

A lot of his ire was self-directed. He had miscalculated serially on when the Tahn would be ready to fight, the state of his own armed forces, and how weasely some of his most trusted allies would prove.

Add to that the fact that he was pacing back and forth outside a sports palace, in front of a stern-faced and geriatic guard armed with a huge, studded club that he had trouble lifting. Time was wasting.

Once again, the delay was his own fault.

The Eternal Emperor had set himself up with many fall-back positions. Even if, for instance, the entire command center under Arundel had been destroyed, duplicate centers existed on a dozen worlds. There were also three secret centers known only to the Emperor.

He had allowed for other secondary centers, personnel,

and instructions for the other elements of his administration. He had missed only one.

Perhaps hopefully, perhaps cynically, he had established no secondary hall for his Parliament. Possibly he had hoped that if the building were destroyed, it would contain the legislators whose presence he found mostly abhorrent. But the building on the other side of the mountain was intact, if somewhat radioactive. And only a handful of parliamentarians had been in it when the Tahn missile struck.

Until the building was decontaminated, one of Prime World's sports centers had been commandeered.

That did not explain the Emperor's wait outside its doors. But that, too, was of his own making.

The Eternal Emperor felt that his people should get some flash and filigree with their government. So he had stolen a ceremony from one or another ancient Earth government.

In theory he was allowed to attend Parliament only at the indulgence of the majority. That meant that ceremonial guards would bar his entrance, he would insist on his right to enter as Emperor, and he would be refused. He would then insist on his right to enter with force of arms. Again he would be refused. Only on the third, humbly worded polite request would he be allowed in. All of the above drakh was done with flowery speech and equally absurd pirouettings.

The Emperor had been proud of this. He thought ceremony an idle tide of pomp and avoided it as much as possible. Entering Parliament was necessary only a couple of times a year for carefully choreographed occasions. The real work of governing was done at the palace, in committee meetings or by carefully negotiated edict.

But now, when he was forced by emergency to address Parliament, he was faced with this—this foofaraw of his own invention.

He looked behind him at Captain Limbu and his second Gurkha bodyguard, daring them to show a slight glint of humor. The Emperor was well aware that the Nepalese found almost everything funny, especially if it involved a superior and embarrassment. Their faces were mahogany. The Emperor grunted and turned back to the front. Probably, he thought, just before the doors swung open and the ancient guard saluted with the mace, almost dropping it in the process, probably they were angry because they had been forced to disarm.

Again he was wrong. The Gurkhas merely had excellent poker faces. And the loss of their normal willyguns, grenades, and the kukri knife wasn't important—both men had tiny miniwillyguns in their tunics, guns that Imperial Intelligence guaranteed would pass through any inspection other than a complete shakedown.

The Emperor waited outside the semicircle of seats while the prime minister ceremoniously welcomed him, assured him of the undying support of his subjects, and then invited him to enlighten them with his wisdom.

Undying support, the Emperor thought as he walked down the aisle. Less than half of the legislators were present. Entire galaxies that had been loud in their prewar support had now declared their neutrality and withdrawn from the government or announced for the Tahn.

The Emperor wore a plain white uniform with the five stars and a wreath on each epaulette that designated him commander in chief/naval forces. He could have worn a thousand different uniforms of the various Imperial forces he was CIC of but chose, again, simplicity.

There was a single decoration on his left chest—the emblem of a qualified ship's engineer. Of all the awards that had been made, this, he once told Mahoney, was the one he was proudest of. It was, he continued, the only one that he had earned instead of being bribed with.

The Emperor spoke, looking straight at the audience—not at the Parliament but at the red light on the livie camera mounted above and beyond the legislators. That was the real audience. His speech would be transmitted within minutes Empirewide, sim-translated into half a million different languages.

"One cycle ago," he began without preamble, "our Empire was knifed in the back by those whom we treated honorably as equals. The Tahn struck without cause, without warning, and without mercy. These are beings who worship their own gods with bloody hands—gods of disease, destruction, and chaos.

"I will not lie to you, my fellow citizens. They struck for our vitals. Not without success. They should welcome this brief candle. Because their success will be brief, indeed.

"War is the ultimate evil. But sometimes it must be fought. And even those wars fought for the most selfish of goals are given noble reasons. The most brutal tyrant will find, somewhere, a spark of decency in his heart, a spark that justifies his slaughter.

"But not the Tahn. Some of you may have seen their pirate propaganda 'casts. What do they want?

"They want the overthrow of our Empire.

"They want my destruction.

"But what do they offer? What do they promise?

"According to the Tahn, their victory will allow all beings an equal share in glory. What is this glory they promise? It is not more food. It is not greater security. It is not the knowledge that generations yet unborn will not be subject to the perils of this time. No. None of that is spoken of.

"Just this glory. Sometimes they call it the destiny of civilization. They mean *their* civilization.

"Those worlds and those peoples that have fallen to the Tahn and groan without hope or witness under their lash could tell us what this destiny brings.

"Despair. Degradation. And finally death. Death that is the only boon that the Tahn really grant, because only death will grant freedom from their tyranny.

"I said before that the Tahn have had their victories. I also said that these victories should be savored by them in haste. Because now the tide is on the turn.

"I speak now to those peoples subjugated by the Tahn. Be of good heart. You are not forgotten. The Tahn will be driven out. Peace will return.

"Now I wish to turn my attention to those who have listened to the blandishments of the Tahn, like dogs drawn to the sweetness of putrefaction. Consider the Tahn and their ways. Before this war, any alliances they made were shattered as soon as it became convenient. The only alliance the Tahn recognize is that between master and slave.

"Study their past. And think of an ancient saying: 'He who wishes to sup with the Devil should bring a very long spoon.'

"Next, I wish to speak directly to the enemy.

"You are very loud in your boasts of your strength. You blazon your winnings. You babble of the closeness of victory.

"Boast as you wish. But you shall find, as you reach out for this final conquest, that it shall recede and recede again from your grasp.

"Your soldiers and sailors will find nothing but death in all its unpleasantries. They will face not just an enemy armed and terrible in his armor in the battle lines, but the deadly anger of those they have outraged in their arrogance. The plight of your noncombatants will be great. They shall never see their young return. And, in time, their own skies will be flames.

"The Empire will return, with fire and sword.

"And finally, I am speaking to the warlords of the Tahn, whose ears are probably sealed in disdain from my words. You sowed this wind. Now you shall reap the whirlwind.

"Those who know me know I do not promise what I cannot fulfill. Therefore, today, I make but one promise. One generation from now, the word 'Tahn' shall be meaningless, except for historians walking the dark corridors of the past.

"You began this war. I shall finish it. The Tahn, with all your might and circumstance, shall lie forgotten in the dust!"

The Eternal Emperor pivoted and stalked from the podium.

He knew it was a good speech when he had written it.

He had upgraded it—the entire legislature was up and applauding. They'd clottin' better, he thought. And then he noticed that even the livie techs, the most jaded of observers, were shouting, their recorders abandoned.

Now all the Eternal Emperor had to do was find a way to keep his promise.

CHAPTER FIFTY-EIGHT

THE *GAMBLE*'S DAMAGE-CONTROL computer found a semi-damaged redundant circuit, and Sten felt the ship's controls come vaguely back to life.

The tacship was less than 1,500 meters above the ground, ground quite invisible through the hanging fog that the ship was plummeting through. Sten's hands blurred over the control board. Nose thrusters—full emergency. Main Yukawa drive—full emergency.

Various blaring alarms and flashing indicators suggested to Sten that the controls' life span would be mayfly brief. He had time to kick the McLean generators to full power before the *Gamble*'s board went dead again. The problem to be pondered was: If the *Gamble*'s plummet was halted before it crashed, the ship would blast straight back up, into the probably waiting sights of the Tahn interceptors. If not, the possibilities were various in their unpleasantries. Sten slammed the impact lock on his control chair's safety harness and braced.

The *Gamble* was almost vertical when it struck.

Ship luck had returned for one final moment. Given the probabilities of hitting a mountainous crag, a glacier, or a scree field, the *Gamble* slid, tail first, into a high-piled snowfield. The snow compressed and melted, braking the *Gamble*'s speed.

Another panel clanged into red life. DRIVE TUBES BLOCKING was the central catastrophe. Sten's hand was poised over the emergency power cutoff breaker when the ship's computer decided that it might be dying but preferred something less Wagnerian than what would happen, and beat Sten to it.

All power cut, and the *Gamble* shuddered to a halt.

There was very complete silence, except for the dim hissing as the hot shipskin was cooled by the melting snow around it.

In blackness, Sten fumbled toward a cupboard and found a batterypak light. Pearly light illuminated the battered control deck.

"All compartments—report." That was another virtue of a ship as small as the *Gamble*—Sten's shout could be heard in most compartments and was quickly passed to even the stern drive station. Sten unsnapped his harness and started to his feet. Suddenly there was a rumble, and Sten staggered. The rumble grew louder, and then the *Gamble* shuddered and pitched a few more degrees to the side.

There was alarm from crew members, then silence again.

"What the hell was that?" Sten asked.

"Ah dinnae ken," Alex said. "Prog some'at nae good, though."

Sten waited for something else to happen.

It did not. The *Gamble* was evidently in its final resting place.

Sten took stock.

Things were not good. One of the wounded sailors from the *Richards* had been killed in the crash. Of Sten's own crew, McCoy, the engine master's mate, had been electrocuted when one of his engine monitor boards short-circuited. Two other sailors were dead, and Sten had two sailors with major injuries. Everyone else had bangs, bruises, or minor breaks.

The ship was dead. The only transceivers functional were the shipsuits and the tiny individual rescue units, and Sten was not about to use them. First of all, he assumed that whatever was left of the Imperial Forces would be somewhat busy at the moment, and he also would rather not have any Tahn units homing on any broadcast.

They would have to rescue themselves.

Sten told Kilgour to break out the emergency gear while he and Tapia, who was now semifunctional, attempted to figure out how much rescuing they would need.

It looked to be considerable. The main lock was crushed

history. Sten managed to muscle the emergency lock open slightly, then swore as icy water jetted into the ship.

They weren't trapped, at least. They could put on space-suits, put the casualties in bubblepaks, and get out of the *Gamble*. Which would leave them in very cold water—not a problem in spacesuits—but the water must be refreezing rapidly.

"So we swim out," Sten said.

"Looks like it, sir."

"And we better full-drive it. I don't think any of us except for Kilgour can bash through an ice cube."

Sten and Tapia found Kilgour in a bashing mood. He had just finished going through the ship's emergency supplies. For some reason, sailors never believe they may actually have to abandon ship. And so their emergency kits tend to be maintained perfunctorily and sometimes raided for necessities. The sailors of the *Gamble* were no different.

"We'll worry about that when we get to the surface," Sten said, "Move them out."

With everyone in the shipsuits and the casualties bubble-pakked, the emergency port was opened fully. Water flooded the compartment. Sten and the others had death grips on anything sturdy. The current boiled around them, and then the water rose over the sailors' heads into the next level.

Kilgour was the first to exit the ship. He held one of the two cutting torches from the *Gamble*'s tiny machine shop. He set it at full power, aimed it up, and cut in his suit's rockets. He started slowly upward through the solidifying sludge of the rapidly freezing lake around the *Gamble*. A line was snap-linked from his suit to the other crew members.

Sten was the last man out. He hung in the black water outside the port for a moment. This was the end of his first command. At least, he told himself, we went out fighting, didn't we, lady?

Then the line went taut, and Sten started upward. There was something wrong with his suit's cycler. His vision was a bit blurred. That was the explanation. No rational being becomes sentimental over inanimate metal, of course. Definitely something had gone wonky with the environmental controls.

Kilgour's suit rockets, intended for use offworld, gave him just enough power to overcome the spacesuit's neutral buoyancy and drift him toward the surface.

"Be a mo," his voice suddenly crackled in Sten's headphones. "The situation's clottin' strange. Ah seem't to've hit air. But . . . Skipper, Ah'd like a wee consultation."

Sten unclipped from the line and put more power on his suit rockets. He broke through a few centimeters of ice, surfaced beside Alex, and shone his suit light around.

The scene *was* strange. They floated in a small, rapidly freezing lake created from the water melted by the *Gamble*'s drive and skin heat. Next to them was the battered nose of the *Gamble*, protruding about half a meter above the ice scum.

That alone was not too strange—but just a couple of meters overhead arced a low, icy ceiling.

"This makes no sense at all," Sten thought out loud.

Tapia surfaced beside him. "Maybe it does," she said. "Do you know anything about snow, sir?"

That wasn't one of Sten's specialities—most of his experience with the stuff came from the snowscape mural that his mother had hocked six months of her life for, back on Vulcan. There had been a couple of Mantis assignments on frozen worlds, but the weather had been just another obstacle, not worth analyzing.

"Not a clottin' lot," he admitted. "As far as I'm concerned, it's just retarded rain."

"That rumble we heard? Maybe that was an avalanche."

"So now we're *really* buried?"

"Looks like it."

Tapia was exactly right. What had happened was that the *Gamble* had buried itself in the deep, perpetual snowfield. Its nose was within a few meters of the surface. But 500 meters above the valley, the ship's driveshock had weakened a snowy cornice. It broke free, and a thousand cubic meters of snow and rock avalanched down and across the valley.

The wreckage of the *Gamble* was buried more than forty

meters below the snowfield. When they had opened the emergency port, the water pouring into the ship had lowered the level of the minilake around the *Gamble*. The ice that had formed at the base of the snow slide now formed the roof of the dome above them.

"Th' problem then," Alex said, "is how we melt on up. Th' suits dinnae hae power enow to gie us airborne. An' tha' snow up there dinnae be load-bearin't."

There was a solution—one that had all the neatness of a melee.

They paddled clumsily, towing the bubblepaks toward the edges of the under-snow lake. Paddling became crawling atop the ice, breaking through, crawling on again, until eventually the surface was solid enough to hold them.

From there, all they had to do was tunnel.

Being in spacesuits, they fortunately didn't have to worry about smothering. Kilgour half forced, half melted his way, curving upward. "Y' dinnae ken Ah wae a miner in m' youth," he said, burning a particularly artistic hairpin bend in the snow.

"Are you sure we're headed up?" Sten asked.

"It dinnae matter, lad. Ae we're goin't up, we'll hit air an' be safe. Ae we're goin't doon, we'll hit sheol an' be warm an' in our rightful place."

Sten scraped snow from where it was icing up on one of his suit's expansion sleeves and didn't answer. Then he noticed something. There was light. Not just light from their suit beams or Kilgour's cutting torch but a sourceless glow all around them.

Seconds later, they broke free onto the surface of Cavite.

Sten unsealed his faceplate. The air tasted strange. Then he realized that he had not breathed unfiltered, unrecycled air for . . . he realized he couldn't remember.

Helluva way to fight a war, he thought.

And speaking of war, the next step would be finding their way down out of the mountains. And the question was, Would their suit power last long enough for them to hit the warm flatlands? An unpowered suit was as useless as the *Gamble*, ruined in the ice below them.

One catastrophe at a time, he told himself. Probably his

sailors, who had less than no experience at ground combat, would get jumped and massacred by a Tahn patrol first.

It would be warm, at least. Sten turned back to his people and started organizing them for the long march.

CHAPTER FIFTY-NINE

ON THE THIRD day after the Cavite landings began, Lady Atago transferred her flag from the *Forez* to a mobile command post on the planet itself. Her headquarters were in a monstrous armored combat command vehicle—dubbed Chilo class by Imperial Intelligence. The huge—almost fifty meters wide by 150 meters long—segmented ACCV traveled on forty triad-mounted three-meter-high rolligons, cleated, low-pressure pillow wheels that gave the vehicle amphibious capabilities as well. Any obstacle the rolligons couldn't pad their way over caused the triad mount to rotate, bringing another wheel into use atop that obstacle. Also, the ACCV was segmented and could twist both vertically and laterally.

It rumbled forward, escorted by a full squadron of tanks and armored ground-to-air missile launchers only a few kilometers behind the fighting lines.

The few Imperial ships still airworthy would never be able to penetrate the AA umbrella—but Atago chose to take no chances. The site she had chosen for her next CP location had several advantages—it was very close to the most promising salient that had been punched through the Tahn lines, there were open areas for ship landings nearby, and there was no need for elaborate camouflage.

The camouflage would be provided by a very large building. It had formerly been a university library in one of Cavite City's satellite towns. And under the new Tahn rule, neither repositories of Imperial propaganda nor education would be necessary.

Six McLean-powered gravsleds were positioned just under the building's eaves, and then the ACCV reversed into the building. Three floors crunched and fell around the vehicle's mushroom dome, but the building held. From the air, Atago's command post was invisible. She was sure that her support ECM units would successfully spoof Imperial detectors.

Also, the tacship division that had plagued the Tahn had been destroyed. Lady Atago was mildly sorry that the division commander, Sten, had not been captured. A show trial could have been arranged, with a suitable punishment broadcast over Imperial com channels. That might have served to discourage some of the more aggressive officers still resisting the Tahn.

But still, Lady Atago was not particularly pleased with the course of the invasion.

The Tahn did have the main Imperial fighting units sealed in the perimeter around Cavite City and were slowly closing the noose. The perimeter had shrunk to less than 200 square kilometers. There were scattered Imperial forces still resisting elsewhere on Cavite, but their destruction would be accomplished within a few days.

The Imperial area now enclosed just Cavite City—and Tahn penetration patrols were already reaching the outskirts of the city—the naval base, and the heights beyond it. Tahn subaqua units had already interdicted any possible retreat by sea.

But the cost was Pyrrhic.

Three complete Tahn landing forces—about the equivalent of four Imperial Guard divisions—had been landed, together with their support units.

They had been decimated. No, Lady Atago corrected herself. The casualties were far greater than one in ten. The spearhead force had driven hard toward Cavite City—and had smashed into the Guard defenses. Four assaults had been mounted and then shattered. In such an event, the Empire would have pulled the unit from combat and held it in reserve until reinforcements had brought it back to combat readiness.

The Tahn were more pragmatic. Their units, once committed to battle, were never withdrawn until they were victorious. Otherwise, they continued in the front lines until taking at least seventy percent casualties. The few survivors would be used to reinforce other formations; the unit itself was retired and completely reformed from scratch.

That had been the fate of the spearhead landing force.

The second landing force had been ordered to attack through the survivors. They, too, had been destroyed.

The Tahn had fought too many battles against the unprepared or the unskilled.

The First Guards Division were neither. They fortified every advantageous position. When they were hit, they held until the last minute. Then they fell back—into previously prepared locations. The Tahn, thinking they had won the objective, set about consolidating. And then the Guard assault elements counterattacked.

At the very least, they caused another ten percent casualties. But mostly they retook the position. It was expensive for the Guards, of course. But far more expensive for the Tahn.

Still worse were the battles in towns. The Guard had every position defended, with supporting cross fire.

Battle into one house—and the Guard would retreat. The house would be taken under cross fire from two other linking positions.

There was never a moment when a Tahn commander could say that his position was secure.

Night was the worst time.

Ian Mahoney had trained his troops to double-think. They held and fought every position that the Tahn wanted. But they never considered a fixed position vital. At night, they sent company-size patrols beyond the front, patrols that hit every target of opportunity.

Night attacks by the Tahn were a perplexity. Recon patrols would report that the Imperial lines were lightly held. An attack would be made—and be destroyed.

Contrary to conventional military thought, the First

Guards held their lines very lightly. There was no attempt to completely garrison the front. Tahn patrols could probe and reprobe, finding nothing. Once the Tahn soldiers had broken through, they would be hit from all sides by carefully husbanded reserves, striking from hidden strongpoints.

But the Tahn, by sheer strength of numbers, were winning.

Lady Atago was very sure of that—so sure that, sitting in the privacy of her compartment, she was planning the surrender of the Guards.

A livie team had already been requested from Heath and was standing by. She had full-dress uniforms ready for herself and for the Tahn guard of honor that would escort her.

Admiral van Doorman—if he was still alive—would not be worthy to grant the surrender. But this Mahoney might.

Yes, she decided. It would be a very picturesque ceremony—perfect propaganda for the Tahn war machine. The surrender would be made on the main field at Cavite Base. The livie crews would show the wrecks and damage of that field.

Drawn up would be the ragged remnants of the Imperial Forces. On cue, General Mahoney would advance to meet Lady Atago.

Did he possess a sword? It did not matter, Lady Atago decided. He would have some sort of sidearm. Lady Atago would accept the sidearm and promise graceful treatment to those surrendered soldiers.

Of course that would not be granted—Lady Atago knew that none of those soldiers would appreciate such treatment. Death could be the only award for anyone who was unfortunate enough not to die in battle. But they would be killed in an honorable manner. By the sword.

That also would be recorded by the livie crews. Perhaps, after the Tahn victory over the Empire, those records would be beneficial to future soldiers of the Tahn.

Lady Atago's future was fully planned.

And after the fall of Cavite, she would attack the heart of the Empire itself.

Her mentor, Lord Fehrle, would be pleased.

Or possibly not, she thought, smiling slightly. She had

not been impressed with Fehrle of late. Perhaps he would not be the man who would lead the Tahn to final victory.

Perhaps someone else might be more qualified. Someone who had herself seen the heart of combat.

Lady Atago allowed herself to chuckle. The future at that moment reached very bright and very bloody to her . . .

CHAPTER SIXTY

SAILORS AND AIRMEN have at least one commonality: they think that somewhere in their Universal Rights they're guaranteed No Walking. Sten's people bitched thoroughly enough for a full company of grunts on being told they were going to Hike Out.

The bitching lasted only about seven kilometers. By then no one had enough stamina left for anything beyond lifting foot from snow, pushing leg forward, putting foot down, lifting other foot from snow . . . and, every half an hour, relieving one of the sailors carrying the bubblepak stretchers.

The spacesuits were even more useless than Sten had originally estimated. Never intended for use on a planetary surface, their pseudo-musculature compensated for less than half of the suit's weight. So walking was a herculean chore.

Sten wished they had powered bunnysuits. Or fur coats. If you are wishing, he thought, why not a new tacship?

If the suits had been less heavy or the weight could have been compensated for with McLean generators, they could have floated over the drifts. Or else improvised snowshoes from tree branches. Instead, they waded doggedly onward.

As night dropped down, Sten looked for a bivvy site. At the edge of the valley they were following, there was a huge tree with snow banked up to its lower limbs. Sten remembered a bit of trivia from a Mantis survival course and ordered his people to burrow toward the tree's trunk. The snow had not completely filled the area around the trunk, and there was a small, circular cave. By rolling about, they compressed the snow, enlarging the cave.

Kilgour checked the wounded. Sten was most grateful for Mantis cross-training, since his TO didn't include a medic. Alex was most competent—Mantis emergency med school would have qualified him as a civilian surgeon very easily. Not that there was much that could be done—their medpak was limited. Kilgour changed burn and stasis dressings and narcoed the injured. One of the wounded would die during the next few hours.

They settled in for the night. None of the sailors believed Tapia or Sten when they were told that they wouldn't need the suit heaters at all, until they saw the exhaled heat from their bodies melt the snow around them to water, which quickly became ice. The temperature in the cave made the space almost livable. Sten widened the hole around the tree's trunk for an air passage.

And so the night crawled into day. The mortally wounded soldier had died during the night. They found a rocky cleft, interred the corpse in its bubblepak, and used three willygun rounds to seal the crevice. Then they started out again.

The next day was a constant trade. Walking with faceplate shut made one warm—warm, and rapidly drained the suit's air supply. If the faceplate was opened and atmosphere breathed, the suit's heater went full on, depleting the powerpak and increasing the chance of facial frostbite.

The skies cleared about noon, and Cavite's sun blazed down. That made matters worse—Contreras went temporarily snowblind; she had to close her faceplate and set it for full polarization. And the snow melted.

There was also the increased chance of being spotted by a Tahn ship, although Sten couldn't figure why any Tahn would bother to patrol this white wasteland.

The second night was a repetition of the first, except with less shelter. Alex used the last of the cutter's power to burn a trench in the snow that would at least get them out of the direct blast of the wind.

That night passed hazily. One sailor was constantly on watch. At first light, they swallowed the last of their suits' liquid rations and moved out again.

Sten was somewhat disgusted at himself. He was starting to wheeze a little around the edges. Feeling exhaustion after only two days on the march? That would have been enough to get him returned to unit immediately back in the Mantis Section days. Sten was starting to understand why so many navy types were lardbutted.

Kilgour didn't make it any easier. His home world of Edinburgh was three-gee, and Cavite was E-normal. And somehow, even though he resembled an anthropomorphized beer keg, he had managed to keep in condition. He tanked through the snow as if it weren't there, as if he weren't wearing a shipsuit, and as if he weren't laden down with the front end of a bubblepak and carrying a medpak and two weapons.

Also, he kept making jokes—or trying to. Sten had to threaten him with close arrest to keep him from telling the awesomely imbecilic spotted snake story—Sten had heard it once back during Mantis training—three times too many. Kilgour had other stories that were almost as bad.

"Ha' Ah gie y' aboot in' time Ah were tourin't th' estate," he began cheerily to Ensign Tapia.

"What's an estate?" she growled as she almost fell face first into a drift.

"Ah, wee Sten, pardon, Commander Sten, hae dinnae spoke th' Ah'm th' rightful Laird Kilgour ae Kilgour?"

"I have no idea what you're talking about."

"Ah'm tryin't t' tell y' boot th' pig."

"Pig?"

"Aye. A great mound ae swineflesh, ae were. A' any rate, th' first Ah e'er saw ae tha' pig wae when Ah wa' tourin't th' estate. An' Ah seeit thae great porker. An' it strikit me, for it hae a wooden leg. Three legs an' aye, a peg."

"A three-legged pig," Foss put in suspiciously, having waded up close enough to Tapia to hear the story.

"Aye. A wonderment. So thae's this wee farmer stan-

-din't nigh his fence. An' I begin't an say, "'Tha' pig, mister.'

"An' he speakit, an say, 'Aye, aye. Thae's a pig ae marvel. Three year ago, m' wee lad fall't down. Inta th' pond. Tha' dinnae be anyone around, an' m' heir's a drown't.

"'Doon plung't th' pig, an' pull him out.'

"An' Ah'm listen't, an' Ah say't, 'Tha's ae marvel. But—'

"An once't 'gain he cuts me off. 'Two year gone, m' gran's in th' gravsled, an' the controls go. An' the gravsled lifts an' 'tis headed for yon viaduct.'"

"Viaduct?" Tapia asked.

"Noo, tha's a fair question, lass. Ah'll answer in a bit. T' continue. I agree wi' m' wee tenant. 'Aye, tha's a pig tha's a wonder. But about' . . . an' ag'in he chops me.

"'One year past, 'tis a deep winter. Y' c'lect, Laird Kilgour.' An Ah says, 'Aye, Ah remember.'

"An he says, 'M' croft catches fire. An' we're all asleep ae' th' dead. But this pig, he storm't ae th' hoose an' wakit us all. Savin't our lives.'

"Ae tha' point, Ah hae enough. 'Be holdin't tha' speech, man,' Ah roars. 'Ah 'gree. 'Tis a marvelous hog. Wha' Ah want to know is, *Why th' clottin' wooden leg!?*'

"An th' crofter look't ae me, an' say, 'Why, mon, you dinnae eat ae pig like thae all at once!'"

Tapia and Foss, both thinking indictable thoughts about premeditated murder, continued wading through the snow. That was Alex on the march.

But possibly his worst trait was the inveterate cheeriness—the constant chants of "Only five more klicks, Skipper" grew wearisome. Especially since they were now plowing through snow that was turning to slush.

Slush? Sten looked ahead and realized there weren't any more peaks in front of them. The valley widened out toward foothills. There were now patches of bare rock in the valley center.

They had made it.

Now all Sten had to worry about was getting his noninfantry deckwipes through the Tahn front lines, into Cavite City.

A piece of cake.

CHAPTER SIXTY-ONE

WHEN THE GROUND stayed flat for seventy-five meters and the temperature went above 15°C, they unpeeled. Kilgour choked politely.

"Th' universe smell't mightily a' feet," he observed. "Th' Tahn'll track us by the reek."

He wasn't exaggerating—they collectively stank like a cesspit. But that lasted only until they ran across the first cattle tank. Kilgour shooed off the three scrawny bovines and charged into the water, tearing off his coveralls as he waded. The others were close behind him.

Sten gave them an hour to scrape off the worst before continuing the march. Now they needed rations and a secure place to plan just how they were going to return to friendly lines.

Navigation was easy—they marched toward the columns of smoke on the horizon that marked the battleground around Cavite City. The land was dry, poor grazing country, spotted here and there with ramshackle farms, most of which were deserted. Sten skirted the few that showed signs of occupation—they didn't look to have enough for their owners let alone be able to resupply Sten.

Then they hit prosperity: green fields and, in the distance, farm buildings. But 2,000 meters from the main building, prosperity showed itself as tragedy. The fields around the farm were deserted.

Sten spread his people out and advanced very cautiously. At 500 meters, he put his sailors into a defensive line in one of the many now-empty irrigation ditches that had made the land arable.

He and Alex went forward.

In the center of the farm was a small artesian pond. Scattered along its banks were fifteen or so bodies. Sten and Alex crouched behind a shed and waited.

A door banged from the main building. Sten thumbed his safety off. The door banged again. And again. It was the wind.

They leapfrogged forward to the first of the bodies. Kilgour sniffed.

"Three. P'raps four days now," he said. "Ah wonder if they had a trial first."

The people had not been killed in combat—each of the men and women had his hands wired behind him or her.

Sten rolled a body over. There was a glint of gold visible around the bloated neck of the corpse. Sten used his gun barrel to pry it free. The glint was a neck emblem.

"They were Tahn," Sten identified. "Settlers, by the way they're dressed."

"Wonder who butchered them?"

Sten shrugged. "Imperial vigilantes. Tahn troops. Does it matter?"

"M' morbid curiosity, Commander. Let's tumble the house."

They brought the others into the farmyard. A couple of sailors saw the bodies and threw up. Get used to it, people, Sten thought. From here on out, we won't be fighting a long-distance war.

He, Tapia, and Kilgour went through the main house. It looked as if the building had been picked up, turned upside down, shaken, and then replaced on its foundations. Everything that could be broken was. Anything that could be spoiled was befouled.

"Ah hae a theory. 'Twas no Imperials did this—four days ago, they'd be scuffin' toward Cavite. Tahn soldiers whidny hae ta'en th' time to be't ae thorough." As he spoke, he was stuffing unbroken rationpaks into a plas sack. "My theory," he went on, "says tha' these wee folk were tryin't t' walk the fence before th' war. Which dinnae set well wi' other Tahn. When th' Tahn landed, their bro' farmers settled accounts, an—"

Kilgour stopped and picked up a tiny bottle from where it had rolled next to a sideboard. He tossed the bottle to Sten.

Sten read the label: "Mahoney Cider & Fertilizer Works. Fine Fruit and Poop for 130 Years."

"We'll be walkin't in th' path ae th' master," Alex said mock solemnly.

Tapia couldn't understand why, in the middle of this death, her two superiors suddenly started laughing.

From then, they moved only by night.

And they moved very slowly, not only from caution but because of the sailors' inexperience. Sten had a permanent set of toothmarks in his tongue, trying to keep from exploding in anger.

These people were not Mantis. They weren't Guards. Clot, they weren't even infantry recruits. Shut up, Commander, and quit expecting supersoldiers. But at this rate, the war might be over before they reached Cavite City. So? Are you in some special hurry to get back under siege and get killed, Commander? Shut up and keep moving.

On the fourth night, Contreras stumbled onto Frehda's farm—literally, going sprawling across a concertinaed stretch of razor wire. Fortunately, her coveralls kept the wire from inflicting severe cuts. The others unwound her, pulled back to the shelter of a clump of brush, and considered.

Once again Sten and Alex went forward, going through the layers of wire and sensors without being discovered. They lay atop the hill looking down onto the rows of barracks and discussed the matter, using the sign language that Mantis had developed for situations like this. It was a very simple one. Spread hands, for instance, meant "What is this?"

Mime T—Tahn. Fingers on collar tabs—military? Shake the head. It was obvious—Tahn soldiers would have had far more elaborate security, and probably wouldn't be showing lights.

Sten pointed toward the floodlit barracks and signed a complete question: "Then what're all those clots with guns and gravsleds doing?" He realized he knew the answer—this was a Tahn revolutionary settlement.

Almost certainly there would be a few Tahn troops down there. He figured that the Tahn would be using those revolutionaries for behind-the-lines security, police duties, and so forth. The "so forth" probably included dealing with any of the settlers, either Imperial or Tahn, who weren't firmly committed to the cause.

Sten felt that he had a fairly good idea of who had murdered that Tahn family—and also how to get back to Cavite City.

Kilgour had the same plan. By the time Sten looked back at him, Alex had his two hands held, palms together, next to his cheek and his head slumped against them.

Right. Now they needed a sentry.

They found one about seventy-five meters farther along the wire. He was walking his post and staying out of the floodlight glare, his eyes sweeping the darkness behind. They modified their plan slightly.

Kilgour crept forward until he was within four meters of the sentry.

Sten, also snake flat, went around inside of the man, toward the barracks, then crept back. His fingers curled, and the knife slid into his hand.

Breathe...breathe...eyes down...Sten's legs curled under him, and he was up. Three steps, and one hand curled around the sentry's chin, snapping the man's head back and to one side. The knife, held ice pick fashion, went straight down into the subclavian artery. The man was unconscious in two seconds, dead in three and a half.

That gave them their prop for the sleeping sentry trap. It was based on the assumption that in all armies sleeping on guard duty is considered as grave a sin as committing an unnatural act on one's commanding officer.

They dragged the body against a post, pulled its cap over its eyes, and let it relax. Sten and Alex took flanking positions to either side of the body, ten meters away into the darkness, and waited.

Sooner or later, the commander of the guard should check his posts. And sooner or later, he did.

A combat car hummed up from the barracks and wove its way along the perimeter. Sten and Alex were prone, assuming that both occupants would be wearing light-enhancing goggles.

They were—but they were looking for their sentry, not for two thugs in the deep grass.

The guard commander saw his "sleeping" sentry. Evidently he decided the man needed a lesson, because the car grounded about ten meters away.

Sten slunk toward the combat car.

The Tahn guard officer—one of Frehda's "advisers"—padded toward his sinning sentry. Next he would bend over the man and bellow. Assuming the sentry survived the initial shock, major punishment would follow. The guard officer looked forward to it—he felt that these Tahn farmers were getting mostly slack, merely because the *real* fighting forces were winning.

He bent—and Alex's hand crashed out of the night in a *teisho-zuki* palm strike against his forehead. The blow, delivered by a normal man, would have stunned. With the full force of Kilgour's three-gee muscles behind it, the commander's skull crushed as if it had imploded under pressure.

Kilgour removed the weapons belts from the two men and ran toward the combat car.

Sten wiped the blade of his knife on the late driver's tunic and got behind the sled's controls. He pulled the driver's goggles over his eyes and lifted the car three meters into the air, turned it, and drove it at full power toward where his sailors waited.

They were mobile again.

CHAPTER SIXTY-TWO

THE TAHN COMBAT car gave Sten and his deck apes not only mobility but a cover as well. Sten assumed some logic from the Tahn: all civilian vehicles would be either grounded or impounded, and all Imperial gravsleds would be inside the Cavite City perimeter. Ergo, anything traveling openly must be Tahn.

Sten did cover himself slightly—after he loaded his people, he found the dustiest road around and made three passes down it within centimeters of the surface. Then he lifted for Cavite City, one more harassed combat car driver trying to get his dusty troops toward the lines.

The only potential problem might be police checkpoints just behind the lines—but they'd be checking the trip tickets and IDs of those headed *away* from combat, not toward the sound of guns.

Then they got even luckier. Sten was waved down by a Tahn road security man as a priority convoy of heavy lifters hurtled through. The convoy was keeping lousy interval, with hundreds of meters between its gravsleds. It was simple for Sten to tuck himself into line near the convoy's end and equally simple to bank down a side street once they hit the outskirts of the city.

The Imperial perimeter had gotten much smaller. The Tahn, vastly outnumbering the Empire's forces, were closing the ring. Sten managed to evade three Tahn street patrols before he decided he'd pushed their luck far enough.

Two kilometers from the lines, Sten tucked the combat car into the third story of a shattered building and thought tactically. From this point, the danger would be steadily greater—the Tahn units would be looking for penetration patrols in their own lines, and the no-man's-land between the lines would be even more hazardous.

Finally, there could well be the problem of being shot by their own troops—Sten had no idea what passwords or signals were in use.

The answer to their problem was a white-uniformed security patrolman.

White uniforms, Sten mused. In a combat zone?

"W' hae rank an' idle ceremony," Kilgour observed, lowering his binocs. "Cannae we be usin't tha?"

"You're just looking for an excuse to gash another screw, Kilgour."

"True. But dinnae it be braw?"

It was.

Again, Sten and Alex reconned the situation, going from rooftop to rooftop until they had that security patrolman in plain sight. A second patrolman stood on the other side of what had been a city street and now was a less-rubbled section of ruins.

Behind the two military cops were two double chaingun positions. Further to the rear were tanks and missile launchers, positioned around a cluster of tracks. These were obviously command vehicles—they sprouted more antennae than a nest of young brine shrimp. It was the command post of the armored brigade supporting the Tahn landing forces. And it lay directly between Sten and the Imperial lines.

"Shall w' ring ae second goin' ae th' guard?"

They could—and did.

Less experienced—or less cynical—soldiers might have skirted the CP. But to Sten and Alex, this was opportunity.

Intelligence, either personally observed by the two men or taught them in Mantis training: headquarters units had massive security. The security elements may have been selected for their efficiency at first but inevitably would turn into spit-and-polish orderlies. They would be commanded, most likely, by ambitious or well-connected young officers. Their formations would slowly, and almost imperceptibly, transition from combat-based to parade-oriented.

The troopers in such a unit would be promoted and commended for the gloss on their boots and the shine on their buttons. After hours of such blanco drill, such a man had a certain reluctance to wade through the muck just because he had heard a possibly strange sound.

And finally there was the factor of arrogance—who would *dare* attack the powerful?

Sten and Alex proposed to exploit that arrogance.

Tourists goggle when the military changes guards. It's done in front of palaces, with dress uniforms, en masse, at predictable times, and with much clanging of weaponry—preferably chromed and antique. That isn't the way it should work when there may be bad guys around—but tradition is tradition, even if it's only a week or so old.

Sten and his sailors took full advantage of that.

The changing of the Tahn general's guard consisted of several platoons marching in close order up to each guard post, where, amid shouts and clatter, the old guard would be inspected and relieved by the guard commander. On relief, he would clang the butt of his weapons a couple of times and march to the rear of that platoon. The new guard would be positioned, and the platoons would stomp on to the next post.

Naturally, that guard changing was done on the clock, by the clock.

Sten knew that the lowest point in the human soul is four hours after midnight.

And that is when he moved.

Clangs... clatters... shouted orders... and Sten's thirteen people slipped silently past the newly posted and yawning guard, straight toward the heart of Atago's command post.

Marching in plain sight, in formation—Sten desperately hoped that his swabbies were keeping some kind of march step—they went in unchallenged.

Step one—complete. Step two—find a hidey-hole.

Kilgour picked an armoured supply gravsled, grounded about 150 meters from the command tracks. He slipped through the undogged entry hatch, kukri ready. Sten waited outside as backup.

He heard only one dying gurgle before Kilgour's head

peered back out. The kukri was unbloodied. Not bad, Sten thought. The lad still has his moves.

He waved the eleven sailors inside. And they waited for dawn.

Sten, Foss, Kilgour, and Tapia kept watch on the track's screens. At this point, the plan deteriorated into opportunity. Sooner or later, sometime around nightfall, Sten thought, there should be some sort of troop movement forward. More chaos. No one would question a group of soldiers moving from a command post toward the front lines. He hoped.

They would move in Tahn uniforms. At first, Sten thought that every man-jill would be so outfitted—one of the barges was full of sealed paks labeled "Uniforms, Issue, Mk. 113." But there was further translation: "Full Dress, Temperate Climate (White)."

Sten thought that if he put his swabbies into those uniforms, they'd probably get out of the CP's lines smoothly—but just might have trouble when they encountered their first Tahn combat troopie.

But there would be another option.

In the early afternoon, Sten thought he'd found it. Combat cars hissed in from the lines, and Tahn officers dismounted.

A command conference, Sten guessed. When this breaks up, we should be able to get up and go.

Then there was a rumble, and a large troop-carrying gravsled hissed toward the command center. A thousand meters above it whined two Tahn battle cruisers.

"Clottin' hell," Alex observed. He had been watching the screen over Sten's shoulder. "Th' brass ae surfacin't."

The gravsled grounded, and a ramp dropped. A line of combat-uniformed Tahn soldiers doubled down it.

"Ah dianne ken th' Tahn be raisin't Goliaths!"

The soldiers *were* very tall. And very broad.

The giants formed two lines on either side of the ramp.

And Sten knew what was going to happen next.

He turned away from the screen and looked at Alex. The heavy-worlder's face was pale.

"W' dinnae hae ae choice, do we, lad?" he whispered.

No, Sten thought. We do not.

He picked up the willygun leaning next to the screen's control panel and checked its sights and load. Then he moved toward the entry port and cautiously eased it open.

Sten was a survivor.

He was also an officer of the Empire.

Situation posited: Formally dressed bodyguards in plain view. Waiting. As are assembled high-ranking officers.

Deduction: Someone of high rank will make an appearance.

Question: Who is that someone?

Answer: Lady Atago. Or Deska.

Question: Is the death of Deska desirable—regardless of sacrifice?

Answer: Probably.

Question: Is the death of Lady Atago desirable?

Answer: Absolutely.

Regardless of the cost, Commander Sten?

Regardless of the cost.

Sten took a hasty sling around his arm, braced against the supply sled's port, and aimed, making sure that the muzzle of his willygun didn't protrude into plain sight.

If Atago came down that ramp, she would die.

And shortly afterward, so would Sten and the sailors he had so carefully tried to keep alive.

Kilgour was moving behind him, shaking people into alertness and whispering.

About 150 meters away, the bodyguards and the Tahn officers snapped to rigid attention.

And Lady Atago started down the ramp.

Aim carefully, Sten, he thought. If it's stupid to die, it's even stupider to get killed after you miss.

The cross hairs of his sight moved across Atago's red cloak and stopped on the center of her green tunic. The Anti-Matter Two round would blow a fist-sized hole in that green.

Sten inhaled, then exhaled half the breath. His finger took up the slack in the trigger.

And then Atago's bodyguards moved, as swiftly and skillfully as a corps de ballet, closing around their charge.

All Sten could see was the white of their uniforms instead of green.

He swore, then lifted his eyes.

Atago was still surrounded. And then, still in phalanx, the circle of white giants marched into one of the commandtracks, the Tahn officers straggling behind them.

Sten lowered his willygun.

He was breathing as deeply as if he had just run five kilometers or had sex. And the part of his brain that was and always would be a street criminal was reading him the riot act. You. You're disappointed because you're still alive? What the hell is the matter with you? And then that survival brain chortled. Sorry, cheena. I didn't realize you held fire to make sure you wouldn't get blasted. Didn't mean to get critical.

That thought made it worse.

Maybe he had. Maybe he had.

Sten was very quiet and very thoughtful for the remainder of the day.

Kilgour took over. He stripped uniforms off the bodies of the Tahn crewmen he'd killed and ordered five of the sailors to get into them.

Near dusk, the Tahn conference broke up. Lady Atago returned to her gravsled completely shielded by her bodyguards. There was never a minute when Sten could have tried again.

S'be't, as the Jann would have said. Now to worry about the future—and staying alive.

It was very simple, in the whine and hiss of departing officers and scurrying troops, to move straight out from the perimeter, unchallenged, toward the lines.

Kilgour found a shell crater, where they waited until full dark.

He slid up to Sten. "Lad, dinnae fash. We'll hae a chance again," he whispered.

Sten grunted.

"A wee thing more, Skipper. Ah dinnae how to say—but Ah been hae'in't troubles wi' m' bowels."

"So?" Sten managed.

"Those bales ae white uniforms?"

"GA."

"They nae be white n' more."

Sten came back to reality and managed a smile.

Now for the last worry—getting killed by their own troops.

If he were commanding a Mantis section, Sten thought, the first time the Imperial troops would realize they had been penetrated was when Sten and his people lined up for morning rations.

But these were sailors.

He found a shelter for his people in some ruins and went forward on his own. Alex lifted a bushy eyebrow, but Sten shook his head.

He moved forward like a weasel from patch to patch of darkness. His fingers found a tripflare, and his body lifted over the wire. A booby mine—avoided.

There—a two-man outpost, both men alert, gun barrels questioning the dark.

He went past them.

Then there was the bunker—the reaction element. No. Too trigger-happy. Sten continued on.

A Guard patrol, coming in from the lines, crept past him. Sten followed them at a discreet distance. One hundred meters farther on, there was a gleam of light as the patrol entered their command post to report.

Sten counted: ten seconds for welcome; ten seconds for the patrol to dump their weapons; another ten as they poured caff.

He went down the bunker steps and slipped sideways through the blackout curtain—a torn blanket—before any of the Imperial guardsmen could react. Then, deliberately casual, he said, "I'm Commander Sten. Imperial Navy. I've got some people outside the wire to bring in."

And they were home.

CHAPTER SIXTY-THREE

GENERAL MAHONEY AND Admiral van Doorman were glowering at a holographic situation map that filled most of Mahoney's command track when Sten reported in.

"What took you so long?" was Mahoney's sole reaction. Oh, well. Sten hadn't expected exactly the chubby calf treatment—Mahoney's highest compliment when he had been running Mercury Corps had been "duty performed adequately."

Then he saw Mahoney hide a grin and felt better.

He scanned the map and felt worse—the Empire was between a rock and a hard place.

Mahoney touched a control, and the overall battlefield vanished, to be replaced with a projection of one segment.

"What's left of your command is holding a section of the line—" Mahoney's pointing finger went through a miniscule half-ruined boulevard. "—just here." For some reason, Sten thought the area looked familiar.

"Since we have a, uh, certain surplus of ramp rats without any ships to service, your people became infantry. I put your senior warrant—a Mr. Sutton, I believe—in charge. He's got your unit, plus I scavenged up another seventy-five clerks, chaplain's assistants, PIO types, and so forth."

Sten kept his poker face. Great, he thought. Not only do my combat people get destroyed, but all my wrenches are dead, too.

"Oddly enough," Mahoney continued, "they've done an exceptional job of holding their positions. For some reason the Tahn have only hit them hard a couple of times."

"The navy knows how to fight," van Doorman put in.

Mahoney would not respond to that, especially in front of a lower-ranking officer.

"But since you've decided to rejoin the living," he continued, "I'm going to pull your detachment back. I want you to take over this position."

Again, the table showed another part of Cavite City: a low, bare hillock, not many kilometers from the navy base, surrounded by destroyed housing complexes.

"We thought this was just a park. But one of my G-2 types found out it's an old fort.

"One hundred fifty years ago or thereabouts, whoever was running the 23rd Fleet decided that the base needed additional security. I guess the Imperial appropriations were fat that year. About ten years later the money must've run out, because they abandoned it and let the grass grow. But we think it's still active."

Mahoney turned to another screen and keyed up a projection. This was a cutaway of the hill itself. There were vertical passages leading to flush-mounted turrets and four horizontal levels below them.

"Typical passive defense," Mahoney commented. He hit another button and got a vertical schematic of the fort. "Four AA chaincannon here . . . here. The turrets are pop-up, and the cannon can be swiveled down to fifteen degrees below horizontal. Each of the main turrets has antipersonnel projectile guns. There are twelve missile silos, but you don't want to get near them. These two little mounts have quad projectile mounts. And that's going to be your new domicile. Any questions?"

"Yessir. First, you said you *think* it's defensible?"

"Hope could be better. As far as the records show, the fort was kept as a reserve strongpoint. So it still should have rations, fuel for the gun mounts, and ammunition. I said don't worry about the missiles—they'll be unstable as all hell by now. If there's no ammunition for the guns in the fort, you're drakh out of luck—all the calibers are as obsolete as the *Swampscott*."

Van Doorman *harrumph*ed but didn't say anything.

"Anything else?"

"Why didn't you move my people out there before?"

"Weel," Mahoney said, "there's a slight problem. Seems this fort is about three kilometers inside the Tahn lines. I didn't think your OIC would be a real swiftie at snoop and poop.

"Once you get positioned, give me a full status report. You'll coordinate through this command as to when you begin operations. I'm sure you won't have any trouble finding targets of opportunity."

"Thank you, sir." Sten saluted. So whatever remained of his people was going to be used as a fire brigade.

"One thing more, Commander. I'll let you pick a call sign."

Sten thought a minute.

"Strongpoint Sh'aarl't," he decided.

"That's all."

The first order of business, Sten thought, was finding out how badly the Tahn had savaged his crew of innocent technicians.

He expected a disaster.

Sten and Alex flattened as a Tahn rocket screamed in, scattering multiple warheads across what had been a complex of shops. Shock waves hammered at them, and then the ground decided to stabilize for a moment.

Cavite City lay in ruins, ruins sticking up toward the sky like so many hollow, rotten teeth. The streets were almost unusable for ground traffic, blocked by shattered buildings. And in the city there were only two kinds of people—the dead and the moles. The dead had been either left entombed by the blasts that killed them, or hastily cremated when they had fallen. But the city stank of death.

Everything living was underground. Deep trenches had been dug and roofed against overhead blasts. There was no such thing as a civilian anymore—the Imperial settlers and the few Tahn who had decided to stay loyal to the Empire were now indistinguishable from the fighting troops. They served as medics, cooks, and even fought from the same bunkers as the Guardsmen. And they died—the Tahn were very nondiscriminatory about who was and who was not a combatant.

Anyone with no immediate assignment discovered a new fondness for digging. The shelters got deeper and deeper as the siege lengthened.

Sten thought he saw Brijit vanish into an unmarked trench entrance as he and his twelve people worked their way forward, but he wasn't sure. If the trench housed a hospital, it would not have been marked—the eons-old Red Cross provided the Tahn with an excellent aiming point.

The closer they came to the lines, the worse it became. Sten was prepared for his own personal catastrophe.

Instead he got the first pleasant surprise since...hell, since Brijit had gone to bed with him. This war was becoming burdensome, he thought.

Actually, there was a series of pleasant surprises.

Now Sten saw why he had vaguely recognized the area his support people had been assigned to. It was at the slum end of Burns Avenue. Mr. Sutton had established his command post in the still fairly undamaged Rain Forest restaurant. Still better was the fact that two of Sr. Tige's sons had stayed with their business/home. The old man had disappeared on the third day after the landing. The sons preferred not to speculate but concentrated on cooking.

Even though the dome was shattered, the birds and insects were either dead or had fled, and the waterfalls were now stagnant green pools, there was still the food. Tige's sons managed to make even the issue rations more than palatable.

Mr. Sutton chuffed three times in succession when he saw the thirteen people who had been given up for lost. He went emotionally overboard and patted Alex on the shoulder once—the equivalent, for spindars, of hysterical joy.

And then he reported.

Sten had expected decimation among the motley crew of technicians and chairborne troopers, most of whom were probably slightly unsure of which end of a willygun was hostile and were surely unaware of certain infantry subtleties, like keeping one's head out of the line of fire.

Instead: six dead, fourteen wounded.

"The Tahn mounted—I believe that is the correct phrase —a most determined attack on our second day," Sutton said. "Their tactics were most foolish. They sent three waves of soldiers at us. We did not find it necessary to aim carefully. Their casualties were appalling, Commander. Just appalling.

"A day or so later, they attempted us again. Most half-heartedly. Since then, we have seen very little action. They appear to be terrified of us."

Sten raised an eyebrow—the Tahn were afraid of *nothing*. But there had to be some explanation.

A Guards sergeant commanding an attached support rocket battery provided it. "Our prog's that the Tahn figured your kiddies'd be a walkover, no offense, sir. They come in dumb, and got dead. Next time, they was just probin'. Then—zipburp. We got curious, so I took out a couple of my people and lifted a prisoner. That's a terrible thing to happen to a Tahn, you maybe know. He says the reason your people didn't get wiped is 'cause everybody figures they're elite. Or decoys."

"Say what?"

"Put it to you like this, Commander. Your people go out on patrol. Nobody told 'em you're supposed to blackface. Or you ain't supposed to be showin' lights or smoking herb. Th' Tahn thought they were gettin' set up. Progged that your swabs had big backup. Plus, this Tahn told us, they couldn't believe any line animals'd build such clottin' poor positions. Hadda be some kind of trap. Guess they got somebody over there guilty of thinkin', huh?"

Sten laughed. And made a note to give the real skinny to whoever took over his section of the line; he wondered how the man would take the basic instruction—remember, tell your people to act real stupid. But in the meantime, he had to figure out how he was going to move his merry marauders back through the enemy lines to this probably non-existent fort.

Whatever he did, he figured it would get pretty interesting.

CHAPTER SIXTY-FOUR

AS FAR AS Strongpoint Sh'aarl't went, getting there was not half the fun.

It took five full nights for Sten's troopies to reach the long-abandoned fort. It started with the small problem that his sailors thought they were minor heroes instead of lucky sods. They had a group name—Sutton's Sinister Swabbies—which had been created by a livie journalist who had reported on the Battling Bastards of the Bridgehead. That, of course, had made the Empirewide 'casts—there was very little in the way of good news those days.

Alex and Sten privately dubbed their cocky swabs the Clotting Klutzes of Cavite.

Actually, either label would have fit. Through good fortune, they hadn't gotten instantly wiped out. And so they had survived long enough to learn combat tactics instinctually. Proof—they were still mostly alive.

Sten hoped to keep them that way.

He moved his detachment to the friendly point closest to this possibly mythical fort. They were ordered to delouse, drakh, and degrease.

Once again, Sten and Alex went point.

Sten was very tired of being the first man into danger, but he saw no other option. Fortunately, Kilgour felt the same and didn't bother complaining. But both of them would have traded their chances on salvation for eight uninterrupted hours on a feather mattress.

They slid through the Tahn front lines without problems, two floating ghosts. Finding that hilltop of the hidden fort was equally easy. Mahoney had sent an op-aimed missile onto its crest, a missile whose warhead area carried a nav-beacon.

There were, according to the fiche, several entryways to the fort. Sten picked the least obvious—a supposedly still-standing power line maintenance shed.

The monitor panel was hinged and counterweighted. It lifted away without complaint. Sten allowed himself to hope that this would be painless.

It wasn't.

He and Alex dropped into the underground passage with a splash. They were in thigh-deep muck. One of the filtering pumps must have stopped operation some years earlier. So had the vector killers.

There were vermin in the tunnel, vermin that thought this was their turf and resented the intruding two-legs. They bit. Sten wished that the livie standard, an area blaster, actually existed. Destroying the multiple-legged waste eaters one at a time with AM2 blasts from their willyguns would have taken an eon. Not to mention that the echoing explosions would have left them quite deaf.

Kilgour had the solution. He pitched bester grenades ahead of him as they waded toward the fort. Time loss wasn't ordinarily lethal, but it was when the air-breathing victims collapsed into water and drowned.

Eventually the tunnel climbed upward, and they waded out of mire. Sten found the master control room and, obeying the TF for the fort, turned the power on.

Lights flickered, and machinery hummed.

That was all Sten needed for the moment—the fort was mannable. The next step was to man it. They returned through the lines and slept through the day.

The second night was spent in a detailed recon of the least perilous route to Strongpoint Sh'aarl't. Sten and Alex broke that route down into 300-meter segments. That was more than enough.

On the third night, they positioned their guides. Sten knew that his befuddled sailors, regardless of their self-opinion, couldn't line-cross without discovery. His idea was to take the sailors he'd walked out of the hills with and use them as route guides. Each guide would be responsible for

300 meters of travel. At the end of his or her route, he or she would pass people on to the next guide.

Almost anyone can learn to traverse—blind and quietly —300 meters of terrain in one night. Riiiight!

Sten had also loaded the odds on his side. For two nights now Imperial artillery had brought in crashing barrages exactly at midnight along the route to the fort. He figured the Tahn would be chortling at the Empire's predictability and, equally predictably, diving into their shellproofs at midnight.

On the fourth and fifth nights, he moved his sailors forward. The barrages were still mounted but, for those two nights, aimed to either side of the corridor that Sten and his people would move along.

Too elaborate, he'd told himself. Too true, he'd also thought. But you got a better option?

Neither he nor Alex could come up with anything cuter. And so, at midnight of night four, three-person teams moved out beyond the Empire's perimeter, to be met and hand-held onward by guides.

Sten was betting that forty percent of his people would reach the fort before the Tahn discovered them. If twenty percent made it from there and if most of the archaic weapons in the fort worked, he might be able to hold the position. Anything else was pure gravy.

Sten, by 0400 hours of the fifth night, was gloating.

Every single sailor had made it to Strongpoint Sh'aarl't'. Sten was starting to believe in them. By silent consent, he and Alex retired their private nickname for the swabbies.

"A'er tha'," as Kilgour pointed out. "Ee tha' want to christen th'selves th' Kilgour-Killin't Campbells, Ah'll dinnae fash."

The next task was to find out how much of a white elephant they were fighting from—and how big a fight it would be.

CHAPTER SIXTY-FIVE

THE FORT WAS more of a cement-gray elephant than white, and it wasn't even that much of an elephant. The beings who had mothballed the structure had done a fairly decent job.

Sten found the fort's command center on the second level and sent teams out to investigate the rest of his base.

Foss was staring at the fire and control computer. "Lord Harry," he marveled. "They actually expected people to *shoot* using this beast? Clottin' thing looks like it should have a kick starter."

He pulled an insulated glove on and touched power switches. According to the specs, the sensor antennae were grid-buried in the fort's armor, so no bedsprings should jump out of the park's grass and give things away.

The air stank of singed insulation—but the computer came to life. Foss unfolded a modern hand-held computer, slid the screen out, and started creating a glossary. The computer worked—but the symbols and readouts were those of a long-forgotten age.

Sten had the environment controls on standby. When they went into action, he would turn them on. But until then, he didn't want vent fans showing above the ground. He and his people would just have to live with the odor. The entire fort smelled musty, like a long-ignored clothes closet.

About half of the visual sensor screens were alive. Sten, once again, didn't use any of the controls that would swivel the pickups.

Okay, he told himself. I can aim at something—I think.

Let's see if there's anything working in the bang department.

He went up into the top-level ready rooms. His squad leaders were already assigning troops to them. Sten let them go about their business. He was busy studying the TO boards. Among the missing pieces of data on the fort had been the list of personnel required to man the base. As Sten had suspected, there were supposed to be far more soldiers than he had in his approximately 125-strong detachment.

Sten juggled bodies around. He wouldn't need to worry about the missile crewmen—that helped a lot. Cooks, bakers, and so forth—his people could rustle their own rations. Instead of three shifts, he would run watch on/watch off.

He was still about 400 people short.

Sten continued his inspection, going up the ladders into each of the turrets. Three of the four chaincannon looked as if they would work, and one of the quad projectile mounts would be online.

The maintenance machines had done their work—the cannon gleamed in dust-free, oily darkness. Tapia was studying the guns, trying to figure out exactly how each of them worked. Ideally, they would be automatically loaded, aimed, and fired. But if the command center was hit or the F-and-C computer went down, each turret would have to be capable of independent action.

Tapia was pretty sure that she could test the shell hoists that led from the fourth-level ammo dump up into the turrets without the turrets popping up. Sten told her to run them.

Machinery moaned and hissed. Monitor panels came semialive, informed Tapia they did not like the way the machinery was behaving, then shut up as lubricant hissed through long-disused channels and the hoist/loaders showed normal operating conditions.

Tapia glanced around. She and Sten were alone in the turret's command capsule.

"How do I get a clottin' transfer out of this clottin' henhouse outfit?" she asked.

"Problems?"

"Hell, yes. I don't like having to just sit here and wait to get hit. Clottin' better bein' a moving target. And it says real clear on my records that I got claustrophobia. And," she added, scratching thoughtfully at her neck, "I think I got fleas, too, off that clottin' bunker I was stuck in."

Having blown steam, she went back to her on-the-job training. Sten admired the turn of her buttocks under the combat suit, thought a couple of unmilitary thoughts, and continued on his rounds.

Sutton had found the kitchens and brought them to life. He was assisted by two others—the sons of Sr. Tige. The two Tahn explained that they saw no future in sitting around the ruins of the restaurant waiting to get shelled. Besides, none of Sten's troops could cook their way out of a rationpak. Sten should have figured out some way to send them back through the lines.

They were civilians and if captured by the Tahn would be quite legally executed. But then, on the other hand, if Cavite City fell, they would be executed as collaborators, even though everyone on Cavite was supposedly an Imperial citizen. *If* Cavite City fell? Sten wondered if he was getting sick—there was no reason for any sort of optimism. *When* Cavite City fell.

What the clot—the Tiges were probably in no worse shape with him than anywhere else.

Besides, there was business. Sutton ran down the supply station.

The spindar had personally lumbered down the rows of ammunition on the bottom level. The pumps had kept the dump from flooding, and the rack sprays had lubricated the stored rounds at intervals.

Bedding? Mr. Sutton lifted a rear leg and scratched the back of his neck. Forget bedding—the dehumidifiers on the third level were wonky. The living spaces themselves were almost uninhabitable.

That wasn't a problem. The troops could doss down in the ready rooms.

Water? Again, no problem. The rain collectors were in perfect condition, as were the purifiers.

Rations?

Sutton was outraged. "I am preparing a full report, Commander. Cha-chuff. Whoever was the quartermaster was on the dropsy! An out-and-out crook!"

Sten smiled. Sutton was getting moralistic on him.

"Examine this," Sutton growled, and pointed to a computer screen. "Imperial regulations specify that each serving trooper is to be afforded a balanced, interesting diet. Am I correct?"

"Imperial regulations specify a lot of things that get conveniently lost in the shuffle."

Sutton ignored Sten's reference to his past. "Balanced, interesting, with full provision for nonhumanoid or special diets."

"GA."

"Look at what this unspeakable person did! All that we have warehoused here are paked legumes and freeze-dried herbivore flesh! How can I feed my people on things like this? How can the Tiges manage to keep the rations interesting? We might as well hook ourselves up to a mass converter and be done with it!"

"We live on nothing but beans and beef for a few days," Sten comforted, "we'll all be our own mass converters."

"Not humorous."

"Besides," Sten continued, "The Tahn are going to wipe us out before we get bored."

"Commander, I'm appalled. You have been associating with that Kilgour for entirely too long."

Sten nodded agreement and went back to the command center. It was time to get in touch with Mahoney and tell him that Strongpoint Sh'aarl't was ready for war.

General Mahoney wanted to make very sure that his new fort would remain undiscovered until exactly the right moment. His com line with Sten was via a ground-cable ULF transmitter. Sten responded with previously coded single-dit signals. Other than that, the fort remained completely passive.

It took Mahoney four days to prepare his major offensive.

A battle can have many objectives—to gain territory, to

mask a second attack, etc. Mahoney's attack was designed to kill Tahn soldiers.

He explained his battle plan very carefully to Admiral van Doorman. Once van Doorman understood the plan, he was ecstatic. He was sure that the battle would shatter the Tahn and force them to withdraw from Cavite—or at least to retreat into defensive quarters.

Ian Mahoney wondered how van Doorman had managed to spend so many years in the service and still believe there was a pony in there somewhere.

The most that could happen was that the Tahn juggernaut might be thrown back and stalled for a while. Mahoney saw no other strategy than the one he had begun with—to try to keep fighting until Cavite could be reinforced. This was a possibility that he viewed as increasingly unlikely. But in the meantime, he could make victory increasingly expensive for Lady Atago and the Tahn.

And so, expecting nothing, the Empire attacked.

The Tahn, of course, had air supremacy around the perimeter. Their constantly patrolling tacships made sure that any men or vehicles moving near the lines stood an odds-on chance of being hit.

Farther back, closer to Cavite Base, Mahoney still had enough functioning AA launchers to keep off all but major Tahn air strikes. Under cover of darkness, he moved half of his available launchers forward and positioned them just inside the perimeter sector near Strongpoint Sh'aarl't.

Van Doorman had very few warships left besides the carefully hidden *Swampscott*. But one of them was the destroyer commanded by Halldor, the *Husha*.

The Tahn normally kept their tacships grounded during darkness, maintaining air superiority with destroyers equipped with warning sensors some kilometers beyond the lines. A night sortie by Imperial ships would bring an instant response, but the Tahn ground-support craft would not be worn out by constant patrolling.

At sunrise, the Tahn tacships lifted from their forward bases toward the lines.

At sunrise plus fifteen minutes, the *Husha* bellowed out

of its underground hanger and, at full Yukawa drive, swept toward and then across the perimeter. Weapons yammering, the *Husha* shattered the flotilla of Tahn ships patrolling that sector. By the time the Tahn had cruisers and destroyers over that part of the perimeter, the *Husha* was already grounded and safe.

Lady Atago and Admiral Deska asked why an Imperial ship would have made the sweep. The answer was obvious —van Doorman proposed an attack.

They reinforced their aerial elements and sent them forward over the lines.

The Tahn ships were easy targets as the Empire's AA tracks threw off their camouflage and launched.

More Tahn ships, including one cruiser, were killed. The Tahn infantry was put on full alert.

And the Imperial Forces made their assault.

Atago was surprised—the first wave wasn't made up of Guard forces. Instead, ragtag soldiers of the naval provisional battalions went forward.

For the Tahn landing forces, they were easy targets.

The naval battalions held briefly, then reeled back, back beyond their original positions.

This was the weak point that Atago had been waiting for. This was a chance to drive a spearhead through the Empire's lines and possibly take Cavite Base itself.

The time was close to nightfall.

Atago ordered her forces to consolidate their salient. At dawn, they would attack once more.

Four hours later, both ElInt and SigInt told Atago that Mahoney was reinforcing the defensive positions with armor. What few assault tracks were undamaged appeared, indeed, to be moving toward the perimeter.

Very good, Lady Atago thought. Her own heavy equipment outnumbered the Imperial tracks by ten to one. Now was the chance to completely smash the Imperial Forces on Cavite. She stripped her own units bare, sending armor forward, organized by hastily established combat commands.

The plan, she knew, would be that at dawn she would attack. General Mahoney would counterattack with his tanks. And her own mailed fist would rumble forward.

There were three hours until dawn.

Lady Atago slept the sleep of a heroine.

General Ian Mahoney, on the other hand, slurped caff and snarled.

From his side of the lines, things were very different. The attack by the *Husha* had been very deliberate, intended to destroy not only Tahn tacships but their reinforcements. That assault had indeed been made by naval battalions, but battalions commanded by officers from the First Guards, who had carefully choreographed the events. Attack . . . and then fall back beyond the lines.

The Tahn counterattack reached positions predetermined by Mahoney, positions that were actually indefensible.

The backup armor that Mahoney had moved forward was mostly gravsleds equipped with noise simulators. They broadcast using call signs of the Guards armor and on Guards armor wavelengths.

Only sixteen Guard assault tracks were on the front lines. At dawn, they went forward—and were obliterated.

It was a disaster. But none of the Tahn investigated those smoking hulks and found out that they were remote-controlled. Not a single Guardsman died in those tracks.

Atago sent her armor in to attack through the salient.

The com grid hummed, and outside the Imperial perimeter, hydraulics hissed into motion and gun turrets ripped through turf, their cannon seeking and then locking onto their targets.

Strongpoint Sh'aarl't was alive.

Alive and killing.

CHAPTER SIXTY-SIX

NO ONE INSIDE the fort was entirely sure that the chaincannon, even though they looked functional, wouldn't blow up when the first round went down the tubes. Sten had ordered the crews out of the turrets and the flash doors sealed before he gave the firing command.

The three cannon roared, sounding like, as Tapia somewhat indelicately put it, "dragons with diarrhea." With a rate of fire of 2,000 rounds per minute, the sound was a wall of solid explosions.

The chaincannon had been intended for defense against high-speed aerial attackers. So although the computer may have been primitive by Foss's standards, its ability to acquire the low-speed targets that were the Tahn tanks was infallible.

The shells were supposed to be incendiary, but only about a third of them went off. It didn't matter—the solid sheet of metal simply can-openered the armor.

Sten heard a squeal of "It works! It works!"—probably from Tapia—as he ordered the gun crews back into the turrets.

Strongpoint Sh'aarl't worked very well indeed.

The first wave of tanks was already rumbling through what had been the Imperial outer perimeter when Mahoney ordered the fort to open up. Meanwhile, three-man Guards teams armed with hunter/killer missiles came out of their spider holes and slaughtered the Tahn tracks within minutes.

Sten had more than enough targets in the three kilometers between the fort and the perimeter.

Lady Atago was holding the bulk of her armor back to

reinforce the spearhead. Since the Tahn knew they had air superiority and were out of line-of-sight of the perimeter, they had the tanks stacked up along the approach routes bow to stern.

Sten, or rather, Foss—or rather the fort's computer—let the chaincannon follow those jammed rubbled roads. The computer tabbed sixty tanks hit and destroyed, and then a series of sympathetic explosions sent fireballs boiling down the streets. The computer, a little sulkily, told Foss that it had lost count.

A red light gleamed—the quad projectile turret, Alex in charge, was in action. The Tahn infantry had recovered from the shock of being hit from the rear and were attacking toward the hill. As long as the antipersonnel chaingun kept firing, it would keep the grunts well out of effective range. Nothing hand-held could punch through the fort's armor—or so the archaic specifications promised.

"All turrets. You're on local control. Find your own targets."

Finally Tapia had some power. She sat in the command capsule on the gunlayer's sight. It looked not unlike a padded bicycle sans wheels, with a hood atop its handlebars. The handlebars, backed by the turret's own computer, were slaved to the cannon.

Four tanks blew apart before the attacking column was able to reverse out of sight behind a building. Out of sight —but not safe. Tapia shouted for the cannon's rate-of-fire control to maximum and chattered a long burst along the ruin's base. The building toppled, crushing the tanks.

Tapia experimented. If she kept firing her gun at maximum rate, the fort would run dry—a gauge showed that the ammo lockers for the gun were already down to eighty percent capacity. She learned how to conserve. Set the cannon's rate of fire to minimum (about 750 rpm) and tap the firing key. Exit one tank.

This was interesting, Tapia thought. She spotted six armored fighting vehicles crossing into the open, spun her sights, but was too late as another turret blew them into scrap metal. Tapia swore and looked around the battlefield again.

The fort was surrounded by the hulks of burning tanks. Smoke plumed up into a solid column around the strongpoint. Tapia switched her sights from optical to infrared and found something interesting.

A track—and it ain't shooting at me. Very interesting. The track was in fact a command track housing the Tahn armored brigade commander. Since the CT had required an elaborate communications setup yet its designers hardly wanted the track to be readily identifiable as the brains behind an attack, the main gun had been replaced by a dummy. Tapia chortled, aimed carefully, and . . .

And the fort shook and her ears clanged in spite of the protective muffs all of the sailors wore.

In the command center, Sten hit a red control, and all of the turrets popped down, leaving nothing but a featureless hilltop for the now-positioned Tahn artillery to shoot at. The environmental system had finished venting the fort and had stored air in backup tanks. If Atago deployed a nuke or chemicals, Sten was ready to switch the fort into its own environment.

Sten doubted that would happen—Lady Atago needed this real estate to attack through. And only in the war livies did soldiers choose to fight in the balky, uncomfortable, and dangerous fighting suits if there was any other option.

"All combat stations. Report."

"Turret A. All green."

"Turret C. We're fine. Noiser'n hell, Skipper." That was Tapia, of course.

"Turret D. They're knocking up some dust. No damage."

"No puh-roblems from the shotgun squad, boss," Kilgour reported from the antipersonnel turret.

Sten was starting to be a little impressed with whoever had built this fort, regardless of their obviously moronic inspiration.

A screen lit. It was Mahoney. With the fort in the open, he had reverted to a standard com link with Sten.

"Report!" Mahoney, in midoperation, was all efficiency.

"Strongpoint Sh'aarl't," Sten said, equally formally, "at

full combat readiness. Expended weaponry filed . . . now!
No casualties reported. Awaiting orders."

Mahoney cracked a smile. "Adequate, Commander.
Stand by. They'll be hitting you full-strength next."

"Understood. Sh'aarl't. Out."

The Tahn assault tracks were pulled back out of range of
the fort's cannon. Atago tried air strikes.

Sten, not expecting any real results, switched the fire
and control computer for aerial targets. Now on fully automatic, the guns elevated, whined, and spat fire.

Tahn tacships were sharded out of the skies. This should
not be happening, Sten told himself. I am manning an archaic weapons system. Hasn't technology progressed?

Foss had the explanation. Archaic, was it? The guns
were tracking, and the projectiles' proximity fuses were de-
tonating on, long-abandoned frequencies. None of the Tahn
ships had ECM sets broadcasting on those frequencies.

Sten was starting to feel a certain fondness for his ancient gray elephant.

"Shall we abandon the attack, Lady?"

Atago ran yet another prog on the computer. "Negative."

Deska tried not to show surprise. "The attrition rate
from that one fort is unacceptable."

"This is true. However, consider this. That fort is quite
effective. The Imperial Forces are weak. Therefore, if that
fort can be destroyed, we should be able to punch completely through their lines. And all that is necessary is to
change our tactics. Which I have already done. The first
stage shall commence within moments."

It was fortunate for the Tahn that Lady Atago had tried
to prepare for any eventuality when she structured her battle plans. She hit Strongpoint Sh'aarl't with monitors.

Monitors should not have been part of the Tahn fleet for
the Cavite operation, since there would be no conceivable
use for the single-purpose behemoths.

Monitors were large, bulky warships. They were heavily

armored and carried light secondary antimissile armament.
Their only weapon was a single monstrous launch tube located along the ship's centerline, much as the Kali launch
tubes on the Bulkeley-class tacships were located, but enor-
mously larger. The missile—projectile—fired by the monitors was, in fact, somewhat larger than a tacship.

A monitor was a miniature spacecraft powered by AM2
engines. It was guided by a single operator into its target,
and was intended for offplanet warfare, to be used against
fortified moonlets or planetoids only.

Tahn intelligence had told Atago that no such space forts
existed in the Fringe Worlds. Atago decided, however, to
add two to her fleet, just in case. Now those two monitors
were deployed against Sten's fort.

One monitor hovered, nose down, just outside Cavite's
atmosphere, and fire belched from its nose. The missile
flashed downward.

The reason that monitors weren't used against close-
range targets became obvious. At full AM2 drive, it is almost impossible for the operator to acquire his target and
home the missile in. Automatic homing was also, of course,
too slow. The vast standoff distances of space warfare were
vital for success, especially since the cost of each missile
was just about that of a manned tacship.

Atago was not concerned with any of that—if Cavite's
fall was delayed much longer, Atago's own fall would be
guaranteed.

Still accelerating, the first missile missed the fort by only
500 meters—its operator was very skilled. The shock wave
flattened what ruins were still standing near Strongpoint
Sh'aarl't for almost a kilometer.

Sten was getting out of his command chair when the
missile landed. He found himself sprawled flat against a
wall two meters away, in blackness. A generator hummed,
and secondary lighting went on. Sten was seeing double.
Dust motes hung in the air.

He stumbled back to the board. "All stations. Report!"

And, amazingly, they did.

The impact, of course, had been even more severe up in
the turrets. Tapia was bleeding from the nose and ears. But

her cannon was still battle-worthy, as were Turrets A and D. The video to Kilgour's antipersonnel turret was out, but there was still an audio link to the center.

By the time Sten had his status, Foss had analyzed what had hit them.

"Very nice," Sten said. Ears still ringing, he and everyone else in the fort were talking very loudly. "What happens if they hit us direct?"

"No prog available," Foss said.

"Very nice indeed. Can you give us any warning?"

"Not when they launch. But they'll be bringing those two monitors on and off station to fire. It'll take 'em some time to reload. As soon as they get on-station, I'll hit the buzzer.

"Speaking of which," Foss said, looking at a screen, "that other clot's getting ready to try his luck."

Sten had time to order all turret crews down into the ready rooms before the second missile hit. This one missed by almost a full kilometer, and the shock was no worse than, Sten estimated, getting punched by Alex.

The gun crews recovered and clattered back up the ladders into the turrets. There were targets waiting for them. Atago had started the second stage, sending assault units forward just when she saw the fort's turrets turtle up. Behind the tracks moved waves of assault infantry.

But her plan became a bloody stalemate. The monitor's rounds did drive Sten's sailors from their guns. But they also destroyed anything around the fort that could have been used as cover for the tracks.

And the monitors took a very long time to reload and fire. There was not time enough for the tracks to close on the fort after the missile exploded before Strongpoint Sh'aarl't was blasting back.

They had reached a stalemate. It wasn't livable inside the fort, but it was survivable. And then two things occurred:

The seventh round from a monitor hit about 175 meters from the fort. The blast was enough to smash the lock on the second, unmanned and inoperable, antipersonnel quad projectile turret. The turret popped up—and stayed up.

And on Sten's central control board, no warning light went on.

The second thing was that Tahn Superior Private Heebner got lost.

CHAPTER SIXTY-SEVEN

PRIVATE HEEBNER WOULD never be used on a recruiting poster. He was short—barely within the Tahn minimum-height requirements—somewhat bowlegged, and had a bit of a potbelly. Not only that, his attitude wasn't very heroic, either.

Heebner had been conscripted from his father's orchards most reluctantly. But he knew better than to express that reluctance to the recruiting officer—the Tahn had Draconian penalties for and loose interpretations of draft resistance. He became even more reluctant when the classification clerk at the induction center informed Heebner that the military had no equivalent for "Fruit, Tree, Manual Gatherer of" and promptly made him a prospective infantryman.

Heebner endured the physical and mental batterings of training quietly in the rear rank. Since he expected nothing, he wasn't as disappointed as some other recruits who discovered that an active duty battalion was run just as brutally as basic training. All Heebner wanted was to do the minimum necessary to keep his squad sergeant from striking him, to stay alive, and to go home.

The private was slightly proud of himself for having survived this much of the war. He had an eye for good cover, excellent fear reactions, and an unwillingness to volunteer —mostly. Heebner had made a brilliant discovery during training. Volunteer duties were mostly in two categories—

the extremely hazardous and the extremely dirty. Dirty frequently meant safe.

Heebner specialized in getting on those kind of details—digging holes for any purpose, bringing rations up through the muck, unloading gravsleds, and so forth, since he had learned that they generally weren't done under fire. And so he had survived.

His willingness to accept the drakh details even got him promoted one notch. Heebner now had to be wary—if he continued doing well, they might make him a noncommissioned officer. Which meant, to Heebner, a bigger target. He was contemplating whether he should commit some minor offense—enough to get him reduced in rank but not enough to earn a beating from his sergeant.

That morning the company his squad was part of had been ordered into the attack against the cursed Imperial fort. The Tahn infantry had nicknamed it AshHome: attacking the fort was a virtual certainty that one's cremated remains would be sent out on the next ship—assuming that one's remains were recovered. Many Tahn bodies lay unrescued in the mire around the fort, buried and then resurrected by exploding rounds.

Superior Private Heebner was lagging just behind the line of advancing troops when Tapia opened fire on the two assault tracks supporting his company. He dived for cover, heard shouts from his sergeant to keep moving, picked himself up—and a round from the monitor slammed in. Heebner went down again, stunned. He was still out when his squad advanced—straight into a burst from Alex's antipersonnel quad mounts.

Heebner staggered back to consciousness and his feet. Behind him the tracks billowed greasy smoke. There was no sign of his squad or company. Most of them were dead. Heebner's mind told him that there was no point continuing the attack if everyone else had given up. He should return to his own lines.

He waded through the mire, concentrating on not falling down again. Cannon rounds splattered nearby, and Heebner ate dirt.

Not dirt, he corrected himself. He was lying against

metal. But no one was shooting at him. And there were no cascades of mud falling on him from exploding shells.

Heebner took stock—and moaned in horror. Somehow he had gotten turned around. Instead of finding his way back to his own lines, the Tahn private was lying on the low mound that was the Imperial fort. Next to him was the shiny, if dented, barrel of a gun turret. Heebner considered prayer. But there were no bullets slashing at him. He was lying next to the unmanned antipersonnel turret, the one that the monitor's seventh round had blown open.

Very well. He could just wait here until night and then escape. And then he remembered that great spaceship somewhere up there. One of those shells would spread him like oil over the fort's carapace. Another realization—he could see a gap between the four muzzles sticking out of the turret and the turret itself. He crawled toward it. The blast had bent back the guns' bullet shield.

Sheer panic impelled Heebner to take the next step. He slid through and thunked down onto concrete. As he landed, his brain began working again. You just entered this fort. Where there are Imperials who probably have fangs the size of pruning hooks?

And then another round from the monitor slammed in, and Heebner was out for close to an hour.

He came fuzzily awake, surprised that he was still alive and not resident in one of the Empire's cooking pots. Heebner, like most of the uneducated Tahn soldiers, believed that the Imperial troops ceremonially ate their enemies.

But he was alive. Uninjured.

And thirsty. He drank from his canteen.

He was hungry, too. His company had attacked carrying only ammunition.

Heebner looked around the inside of the turret. There were lockers against the turret. He explored them. Gas suits . . . radiation suits . . . and emergency rations. Heebner fumbled a pak open and sampled. He smiled. Meat. It was something that a Tahn of his class would be permitted only once or twice a year. The next pak was also meat. It joined its brother in his stomach. The third was beans. Heebner sniffed at them, then set the pak aside. Other cans went into his combat pack.

What now?

More of his brain, possibly stimulated by the beef, woke up. They told us this fort was full of soldiers. Why, then, is this position not manned? Was it hit?

There were no signs of damage to the walls.

Heebner found that he had two choices—either he could remain where he was, or he could flee. If he stayed in the turret, eventually that monstrous cannon would kill him.

If he fled back toward the Tahn lines, there would be questions. Why was he the only survivor of his squad? Had he hid? Had he avoided the attack? The penalties for cowardice under fire were most barbaric.

Wait. If he came back with some valuable information, they might not punish him. Such as?

Of course. Fellow soldiers could use this gap in the turret to take the fort! But wait. If all you return with is a way into the fort, won't your officers expect you to guide the assault formation?

Heebner grimaced. That could be an excellent way to become dead. He brightened. If he returned with some very interesting piece of information, they would send him up to higher headquarters with it, while other unfortunates made the attack.

What could he bring back?

The hatchway leading down into the bowels of the fort was nearby. Heebner undogged it and climbed downward.

The ladder ended in a large room with bunks. Heebner looked wistfully at one of them. Even though it smelled, it was still better than anything he had slept on since he had landed on Cavite.

A large room with bunks...a large, deserted room? How many Imperials are in this fort, he wondered? He found the courage to investigate.

Heebner went out of the ready room into a central passageway. Seconds later, another shell from the monitor earthquaked down. It must have missed by a considerable distance. Heebner heard the clatter of feet and peered out. A group of Imperials ran out of another ready room and climbed up into one of the main turrets. Heebner counted. Only ten? How many people *were* there, anyway?

Was it possible that there were only a handful of Imperials holding back the Tahn? So it would appear.

That was enough for Heebner. This would be valuable information. Enough to keep him from being sent forward again. The intelligence might be valuable enough, he hoped, for him to report to company headquarters instead of to his platoon leader. If his company commander still lived. This could be an excellent way to stay out of the assault.

Superior Private Heebner made his way out of the fort, made the nightmare journey back to his own lines, and reported.

And found himself standing in front of Lady Atago, more terrified than he had been inside the fort. He was not required to make the final assault on Strongpoint Sh'aarl't. Instead, he was promoted to fire team leader, given a medal, and reassigned to the rear.

Heebner was safe. That was enough. It did not matter to him that he wasn't mentioned in the livies trumpeting the reduction of the Imperial fort.

That honor went to Tahn Assault Captain Santol, a far more heroic-looking Tahn. And if it was an honor, he earned it.

CHAPTER SIXTY-EIGHT

STEN WONDERED WHAT would come next when the monitors' shellfire stopped. He wondered if they would run out of projectiles but rather dully hoped that both ships had chamber explosions.

Worry about what comes next when it comes next, he said, and ordered dinner—breakfast? lunch?—up for his people. He rotated a third of the crews down to the mess hall to eat. After everyone was fed, he planned to go to fifty percent alert and let at least some of his sailors sleep.

It didn't work that way.

Contreras stepped off the ladder from the command level to the ready room and burped. A full belly led her to consider other luxuries. Sleep...a bath...a clean uniform... hell, she told herself, why not wish for everything. Like a discharge, spending her accumulated pay on a tourist world where the most primitive machine was a bicycle, and falling in love with a handsome officer. Officer? She caught herself. Too long in the service, woman. Clot the military. A rich civilian.

A smile crept across her lips just as the Tahn projectile blew most of her chest away.

The Tahn assault teams had managed to approach the fort without being seen. Since the fort's computer still showed the jammed antipersonnel carrier as being housed, the warning sensors showed no movement in that sector. Actually the beams were being returned—bouncing—off the turret, returning to the transmitter and being automatically disregarded as part of ground clutter.

Lady Atago's analysis from Private Heebner's report was very correct, giving about an eighty-five percent chance that the area beyond that jammed turret would be in a dead zone.

Captain Santol's navigation had been exact—the assault elements closed in on the fort along that sector, no more than two abreast. Between the shifts for eating and the sailors' exhaustion, the Tahn weren't noticed on any of the visual screens still active.

Once inside the turret, Captain Santol put two trusted sergeants in front, armed with riot weapons. Behind them were grenadiers and one tripod-mounted heavy projectile weapon, and then Captain Santol and his senior sergeant behind them.

Contreras wasn't the first to die—two sailors had been jumped from the rear and garrotted. But she was the first to be shot.

The explosion clanged down the corridors of the fort.

Sten bolted up, and his plate spattered beans and beef across the deck. Accidental discharge . . . like hell, he realized, as he saw Tahn soldiers scuttling forward on one of the command center's internal screens.

He slammed the alarm and opened a mike.

"All personnel." His voice was quite calm. "There are Tahn troops inside the fort. All personnel, secure entry to your areas. Alex?"

"Sir?" Even on the com there was a bit of a brogue.

"Can you see how these clots got in?"

There was a pause. "Tha's naught on the screens, sir. Ah'll bet tha'll hae come in frae' a turret."

That left two possibilities: Either of the two inoperable turrets—one, the second antipersonnel quad projectile turret; two, the second Turret B—could be breached. But the computer showed both secure.

"Turret C," Sten ordered. "Local control. Target—Tahn infantry approaching the fort. Fire at will."

He switched to another channel.

"Turrets A and D. Send five troops down to secure your ready rooms. There are no friendlies moving. Kilgour. If you've got anybody loose, get them to the command center."

"On th' way. Wait."

Alex should have stayed at the antipersonnel turret. But it took only one person to fire the quad projectile weapon. He left that one and, with six others, went looking for blood.

Sixteen sailors manning Turret A went out of their turret, headed toward the Tahn. The two forces met in a corridor. The battle was very quick—and very lethal. The AM2 rounds from the willyguns mostly missed. But hitting the concrete walls of the corridor, they exploded, sending concrete shrapnel shotgunning into the Tahn.

Captain Santol lost two squads before he could get a crew-served weapon firing. And then the sixteen sailors went down in a swelter of gore as projectiles whined and ricocheted.

Santol waved a squad forward, over the bodies and up

into the turret. The rest of the sailors assigned to Turret A died there.

A second maneuver element of the Tahn tore into the element from Turret D. The sailors fought bravely—but weren't a match for the experienced Tahn soldiers.

Sten swore as he watched on a screen.

The Tahn were between his command center and the still-fighting Turret C. Sten had Foss and three computer clerks for an assault element. This would be stupidity, not nobility. But again—he had no options.

The Tahn assault company was spread out through the fort's corridors. They were good, Sten had to admit. Their tactic was to spray fire around a corner, send one man diving across the corridor for security, put two men in place as guards, and move on. And still another Tahn company was filing in through the damaged personnel turret.

Then the counterattack hit.

This was not Kilgour's pathetic strike force of seven, which was still moving down the long tube that led to the fort's center. This attack came from underneath—from the storage spaces.

There were five humans, including the two Tahn brothers. They were led by the spindar, Mr. Willie Sutton. They were pushing in front of them a small gravpallet. On it there were fifteen or so tall metal cylinders. Emergency oxygen tanks.

The counterattack came out of an unnoticed hatchway, halfway down a corridor. At the far end was Captain Santol and his command group.

Sutton was bellowing like a berserk siren as he rumbled forward.

"Shoot them! Shoot them down," Santol shouted, and projectiles crashed down the corridor.

The six Imperial sailors were cut down in the blast. The gravpallet drifted on another ten meters before it slowed to a stop.

Santol ran toward the bodies, a reaction team behind him. There would be more Imperials coming out of that hatch.

He slid around the gravsled . . . and Sutton reared up in

front of him. Scales were ripped away, and ichor oozed
from his wounds and mouth. The spindar loomed to his full
height over the Tahn officer.

Santol's pistol was coming up, but late, too late, as claws
sprang out of Sutton's forearm and bludgeoned forward,
ripping away most of the Tahn's face. Santol screamed and
went down.

His soldiers were firing. Sutton staggered back, against
the wall, then forward again. From somewhere, he pulled a
miniwillygun, brought it up, and fired—not at the Tahn but
behind them, at the gravpallet. The round tore a cylinder
open. Oxygen hissed, and then a ricocheting round
sparked.

The corridor exploded, catching the Tahn in a miniature
firestorm created by the exploding oxygen. Half of Santol's
company died along with their commander. The disoriented
survivors fell back toward the entrance.

Kilgour was waiting at a cross-tube. Again, the Tahn
were not expecting an ambush. They fell back still farther.

It was the best chance Sten would have.

He found the nearest wall com. "All stations. All stations. This is Sten. Evac to entry. I say again. Evac to
entry."

He and his four people linked up with Alex's crew and
the one troop that had been left in the AP turret, and set up
a rear guard.

It was not necessary. The CO of the second Tahn assault
company had ordered most of the soldiers out of the fort.
They would regroup and counterattack.

By the time they did, Tapia's entire crew had made it to
the fort's exit.

They went back down the underground passage leading
to the flattened maintenance shed, splashing through the
deep muck. The shed was gone, but the hatch still operated.

Sten stood by it, taking a head count as his surviving
sailors wearily climbed out. There were thirty-two left.

He formed them up and started across the flattened
wastes toward the Imperial perimeter. Half a kilometer
away, Sten took a small transmitter from his belt, snapped
off the two safety locks, and pressed a switch.

Three minutes later, det charges would go, and Strongpoint Sh'aarl't—or Sutton, or Tige, or whoever—was going to be a large crater in the ground.

The Tahn could have the privilege of naming it.

CHAPTER SIXTY-NINE

TWO HOURS BEFORE dawn, Tanz Sullamora's shielded gravsled was cleared to land in the ruins of Arundel Castle.

There were only two man-made objects above ground. One was a transportable shielded landing dome, very common on radioactive mining planets but most incongruous in the heart of the Empire. The second was a very tall flagpole. At its peak hung two flags—the gleaming standard of the Empire and, below it, the Emperor's house banner, gold with the letters "AM2" superimposed over the negative element's atomic structure.

All Imperial broadcasts showed the ruins and the flag as their opening and closing shots. The symbol may have been obvious—but it signified. The Emperor, like the Empire itself, may have been hard-hit, but he was still standing fast and fighting.

Rad-suited guardsmen led Sullamora, also in antiradiation gear, from his ship through decon showers and into one of the drop shafts leading down toward the Imperial command center below the palace ruins.

At the shaft base, Sullamora clambered out of his suit, was decontaminated once more, and was ushered into the center. Two Gurkhas escorted the merchant prince down long paneled corridors that, even at this hour, were filled with scurrying officers and techs. Sullamora caught tantalizing glimpses, through portals that slid open and shut, of prog boards, huge computer screens, and war rooms.

He did not know that his route led through what the Emperor called a dog and pony show. The work was real, and the staff beings were busy—but everything he saw was nonvital standard procedures such as recruiting, training status, finance, and so forth.

The Emperor's own suite had also been carefully decorated to leave visitors with certain impressions. There were many anterooms, capable of holding any delegation or delegate isolated until the Emperor was ready to meet. The walls were gray, and the furniture was two shades above Spartan. Wallscreens showed mysterious, unexplained maps and projections that would be replaced periodically with equally unknown charts and graphs. The Emperor's quirky sense of humor had decided that some of them were battle plans from wars fought thousands of years previously. Thus far, no one had found him out.

The Emperor's own quarters were a large bedroom, a kitchen that resembled a warship's mess area, a conference room, a monstrous computer center/briefing room, and a personal library. These were also fairly simply furnished, not so much to continue the command center image but because the Emperor had little real interest in the tide of pomp and thrice-gorgeous ceremony.

The wallscreens normally showed scenes from the windows of one or another of the Emperor's vacation homes. But now three images formed a motif throughout his rooms: the ruins of Arundel above him, a shot from space showing the Tahn home world of Heath, and a still of the twenty-seven-member ruling Tahn Council. The three images, he explained, helped focus his attention.

Sullamora spent only a few minutes in an anteroom before being escorted into the Emperor's library.

The Emperor looked and was very tired. He indicated a sideboard that held refreshments. Sullamora declined. The Emperor started, without preamble. "Tanz, I've just requisitioned ten of your high-speed liners."

Sullamora's eyes widened, but the capitalist managed to bury any other reaction. The Emperor, after all, had called him by his first name.

"Sir, any of my resources are yours. You have only to ask."

"No drakh," the Emperor agreed. Then he asked, seemingly irrelevantly, "How long have you been arming your merchant ships?"

"Pardon, Your Majesty? Almost all of my ships carry weapons."

"Come on, Sullamora. It's been a long night, and I'd like to get my head down before dawn. You've got some ships booming around out there that're armed better'n my frigates."

"I did," Sullamora admitted, "take the liberty of increasing the weaponry on some of my vessels. Those, you understand, that were routed near any of the Tahn galaxies."

"Good thinking," the Emperor said, and Sullamora relaxed. "And that's why I'm grabbing ten of them. I'll tell you why shortly. The other reason I wanted this meeting is that I'm requisitioning *you*."

Sullamora's response was a not particularly intellectual. "Heh?"

"From twenty minutes ago, you're now my minister of ship production. You'll have a seat on my private cabinet."

Sullamora was startled. He hadn't even known that the Emperor *had* a private cabinet.

"I want you to build ships for me. I don't care which contractors build them or how. Your orders will be A-Plus category. You have Priority One on any raw materials or personnel you need. I need more warships. Yesterday. I don't have time for all this bidding, bitching, and backbiting that's been going on. Pour yourself a drink. I'll have some tea."

Sullamora followed orders.

"We are hurting," the Emperor continued to Sullamora's back. "The Tahn are taking out my fleets faster than I can commission them. You're going to change all that."

"Thank you for the honor, Your Majesty. What kind of administration do I have?"

"I don't care. Bring in all those hucksters and sharpies from your own companies if you want."

"What will my budget be?"

"You tell me when you're running out of credits, and I'll get you some more."

"What about the accounting oversight?"

"There won't be any. But if I catch you stealing too much from me, or buying junk, I'll kill you. Personally."

The Emperor was not smiling at all.

Sullamora changed the subject slightly. "Sir. May I ask you something?"

"GA."

"You said you'd explain why you need ten of my liners."

"I shall. This is ears-only, Tanz." He paused. "I made a bunch of mistakes when this war started. One of them was thinking that my people out in the Fringe Worlds were better than they were."

"But, sir . . . you sent the First Guards out there."

"I did. And they're my best."

"And they're winning."

"The clot they are. They're getting their ass whipped. The Guard—what's left of it—is hanging on to a teeny little perimeter of one world. About a week from now, they'll be overrun and destroyed."

Sullamora swallowed. This was not what the livies had been telling him.

"I put the Guard out there to hold the Caltor System, because sooner or later things are going to change, and I'm going to need a jumping-off point to invade the Tahn systems.

"I blew it. I thought that I'd get more backup from my allies than I have. I also didn't know the Tahn were stamping out fleets of warships like cheap plas toys. Mistakes. Now I've got to save what I can.

"There's a whole bunch of Imperial civilians on the capital world of Caltor, Cavite. I want your liners in to get them out. Get them out—and some other people I'll need."

The Emperor read Sullamora's face and smiled grimly. "Things look different when you're on the inside, Tanz. You're going to see a lot more ruin and damnation in the next few days."

Sullamora recovered. And asked the big question. "Are we going to win this war?"

The Emperor sighed. This was a question he was getting a little tired of. "Yes. Eventually."

Eventually, Sullamora thought. He took that to mean that the Emperor was very unsure of things. "When we do . . ."

"When we do, I shall make very damned sure that the Tahn systems have a very different form of government. I do not ever want them to return to haunt me."

Sullamora smiled. "War to the knife, and that to the hilt!"

"That wasn't what I was saying. I want the way the Tahn run their government changed. I don't have any quarrel with their people. I'm going to try to win this war without dusting any planets, without carpet bombing, or any of the rest. People don't start wars—governments do."

Sullamora looked at the Emperor. He thought himself to be a historian. And just as he collected heroic art, he admired heroic history. He sort of remembered a statement a heroic Earth sea admiral had made: "Moderation in war is absurdity."

He wholly agreed with that. Of course, he wasn't enough of a historian to know that the admiral in question had never commanded his fleet in anything other than a minor skirmish, or that by the time the next war occurred both he and the superships he had ordered built had been obsolete and retired.

"I see, Your Highness," he said coldly.

The Emperor did not understand Sullamora's frigidity. "When the war is over, you'll be given the appropriate awards. I assume some sort of regency appointment might be in order, covering the entire Tahn areas."

Sullamora suddenly felt that he and the Emperor were speaking entirely separate languages.

He stood, leaving his drink barely tasted, and bowed deeply, formally. "I thank you, Your Highness. I shall be prepared to assume my new position within the week."

He wheeled and exited.

The Emperor stared after him. Then he stood, walked around his desk, picked up Sullamora's drink, and sipped at it thoughtfully. Possibly, he thought, Sr. Sullamora and I may not be communicating on the same wavelength.

So?

He set the drink back down, went back to his desk, and keyed the com on for the latest disaster reports. He was worried about his Empire. If he held it together—and in spite of his bluffness, the Eternal Emperor was starting to wonder—he could worry about individual people later.

The hell he could, he realized.

He put the com on hold and activated a very special computer. There was one individual he had to talk to. Even though that conversation would be one-sided.

CHAPTER SEVENTY

GENERAL IAN MAHONEY looked at his reflection in the shattered bits of mirror and considered.

Contrary to what two of the Emperor's favorite and long-dead doggerelists—Mahoney vaguely remembered their names as Silbert and Gullivan—there were *two* models of a modern major general. One was that of the general, immaculate in full-dress uniform, posing, three-quarter profile, some sort of harvesting cutter in hand, in front of his assembled troops, all of them dripping medals. The second would be the same general, in combat coveralls, willygun smoking—they did that only in the livies—grenades hanging from his harness, cheering his men forward into some sort of breach or other, in the face of onrushing hordes of Evil Sorts.

Major General Ian Mahoney was neither.

He was wearing combat coveralls, and he did have a willygun slung over one shoulder. But the seat of his coveralls was ripped out; his willygun, thanks be to his security, hadn't been fired—yet; and his coveralls were stained in mud, pink, and mauve.

The Tahn had finally run cross-locations on the command transmissions, found Mahoney's command center, and sent in an obliteration air strike.

Tahn tacships had either suppressed the few antiaircraft launchers around Mahoney's headquarters or absorbed the few missiles left in their launch racks. Mahoney's headquarters was left naked.

Mahoney had been bodily yanked from his command track seconds before a Tahn missile hit it. He had gone down—into the muck of the street. That accounted for the mud.

As the second wave of Tahn tacships came in, he had pelted for shelter—any shelter. He had found it, diving facefirst into a semiruined women's emporium. Into, specifically, the shatter of the makeup department. That explained the pink and mauve.

The emporium had a huge basement, which Mahoney found convenient for his new headquarters. Backup com links were brought in, and Mahoney went back to fighting his war, morosely scowling at his reflection in the shatter of a mirror lying nearby.

A tech clattered into the room. "Two messages sir. From ImpCen. And your G4 said you'd need this."

ImpCen: Imperial central headquarters. Prime World. And the case the tech held contained one of Mahoney's most hated security tools.

He looked at the messages. The first was a conventional fiche. What was unconventional about it was the case that the tech had brought in with him. That case, set to a fingerprint lock, contained single-use code pads. These were pads that the encipher wrote his message onto, and the receiver would decipher using a duplicate of that same pad. After one use, both sheets of that pad would be destroyed. It was a very old, but still completely unbreakable, code system.

And Mahoney hated coding almost as much as he loathed formal parades.

The other message had been transcribed onto a rather different receptacle. Mahoney's signal branch had only half a dozen of them; they were the ultimate in security, reception fiches sealed into a small plas box. Whatever had been transmitted onto that fiche could be seen only by Mahoney himself. There was a single indentation on the box, keyed to Mahoney's thumb poreprints. Once Mahoney put his thumb in the notch, whatever was on the fiche would begin broadcasting. If he removed it, or thirty seconds after the message ended—whichever came first—the fiche would self-destruct.

Mahoney knew that these messages were important— and almost certainly catastrophic. The first, encoded onto the single-use pad, would most likely be a set of orders. He ignored it for the moment and instead jabbed his thumb down onto the plas box.

Suddenly, in the cellar, standing on a pile of half-burnt dresses, stood the Eternal Emperor. It was a holographic projection, of course.

"Ian," the cast began, "we're in a world of hurt. I know you've thumbed this before you've decoded your orders, so I'll give it to you fast.

"I can't back you up.

"I don't have the ships, and I don't have the troops to send forward.

"I guess you've probably already figured that as a possibility. Hell, a probability—since there haven't been any good guys in your skies for quite a while.

"Real brief, here's what your orders are: I want the First Guards to hold on to Cavite until the last bullet. Only when all possible means of resistance have been exhausted do you have my permission to surrender. Any elements of the Guards that can evade, escape, and continue the struggle as guerrillas have permission to carry on the fight. I may not be able to keep the clottin' Tahn from treating them as partisans, but I'll do my best. You probably expected that.

"I'm sending in ten fast liners to pick up the civilians that are still on Cavite. Get them out. And I want you out with them.

"This is the hard part for you, Ian. I'm going to have to sacrifice your division. But I am not going to sacrifice what the First Guards really is.

"You've got probably six E-days until the liners show up, from the time you've received this. I want you to pull out a cadre. Your best noncoms, officers, and specialists are to be on those liners. The First Guards Division will die on Cavite. But there will be a new First Guards. We'll reform the division on Prime World, and send it out to fight again.

"I said 'we,' and I meant 'we.' You will be the commander of the new First Guards. Which means that I want you on one of those liners.

"That is an order, General Mahoney. I don't expect you to like it, or to like me. But that is what is going to happen. And I expect you to follow orders."

The holograph whirled about itself and disappeared. Mahoney stared at the open space where it had been.

Then he opened his code case and took out the single-use pad—actually a small computer that self-destructed its programming as it went.

Sorry, Your Eternal Emperorship, he thought. I'll follow orders. All of them except the last one.

If you're going to let my Guards die, there is no way in hell I won't be with them.

CHAPTER SEVENTY-ONE

STEN AND THE REMNANTS of his command made it back into the dubious safety of the Imperial perimeter without incident.

He faced a future that was without options. Sten knew that his ragtag band would be resupplied, rearmed, and fed back into the meat grinder as the Tahn continued their attacks. He was morosely wondering who would be the last to die. That was the future—to be killed, wounded, or captured.

Sten was as unused to defeat as the Empire itself. But there were no options.

He was only mildly surprised when the officer in charge of the repple-depple gave him unexpected orders. His detachment was ordered to turn in all weaponry except their individual arms and stand by for a special assignment.

Sten himself was to report to Mahoney's tactical operations center. Before reporting, he managed to scrounge a few liters of water for a shave and a joygirl's bath, and found a fairly clean combat suit that was pretty close to his size.

The TOC was still in the basement of the emporium. Mahoney finished briefing a handful of officers, all of whom looked as battered as their general, and motioned Sten into a small office that had been the emporium's dispatch room.

Waiting for them was Admiral van Doorman.

Mahoney tersely brought Sten current. The ten liners were inbound to pick up the Imperial civilians and "selected elements" of the First Guards. They were escorted by four destroyers—all that could be spared—and were, so far, undetected by any Tahn patrol. Their ETA was four days away.

Suddenly the 23rd Fleet needed its technicians again. There were only four ships still spaceworthy: two destroyers, including Halldor's ship, the *Husha*; one elderly picket ship; and the *Swampscott*.

They were to be made as combat-worthy as possible, immediately. Sten's surviving techs, highly experienced at improvisation, would be assigned to the *Swampscott*.

Just assigned the cruiser, Sten wondered? And he also wondered if he would get an explanation.

Mahoney was about to give him one, when van Doorman spoke for the first time. "General, this man is still under my command. I'd prefer..."

Mahoney stared at the haggard naval officer, then nodded and exited.

Van Doorman leaned against the side of a desk, staring into emptiness. His voice was nearly a monotone. "The problem we all seem to face, Commander, is that the older we get, the less we like things to change."

Sten thought he was beyond surprise—but he was wrong.

"I was very proud of my fleet. I knew that we didn't have the most modern equipment, and that because we were so far from the Empire we didn't always get the finest sailors. But I knew that we were a strong fighting force.

"Yes," van Doorman mused. "It's obvious I thought a lot of things. So when a young flash shows up and tells me that all I have are spit-and-polish marionettes, and my command structure is rigid, bureaucratic, obsolete, and blind, I did not take kindly to that officer."

"Sir, I never said—"

"Just your presence was sufficient," van Doorman said, a slight note of anger entering his voice. "I have made it a rule to never apologize, Commander. And I do not propose to alter that rule. However. The reason I want you, and whatever's left of your command, assigned to the *Swampscott* is that I know the Tahn will hit us hard when we attempt to withdraw with those liners. I assume heavy casualties. Very likely including myself."

A safe assumption, Sten thought.

"I have appointed you as weapons officer of the *Swampscott*. According to the conventional chain of command, you would be fourth in charge, under the XO, the navigating officer, and the engineering officer. This is not a time for convention," van Doorman went on, his voice flat once more. "I have informed all appropriate officers that, in the event of my being incapacitated, you are to assume command of the *Swampscott*.

"Very good, Commander. I was wondering if I would be able to penetrate your poker face.

"The reason is that I no longer have any faith whatsoever in those officers I chose to promote to their present position. I think I selected them more for their social compatibilty and sycophancy than command ability. And I am not sure that any of them can handle crisis adequately. Do you understand?"

"Yessir."

"I have also informed Commander Halldor that, even though he has a certain amount of time in grade over you, if I become a casualty you are to assume command of my fleet.

"My fleet," van Doorman said in mild wonderment. "Two DDs, one museum piece, and a hulk.

"Those are your orders, Commander. I assume if I survive the withdrawal, I shall face a general court-martial. Very well. Perhaps it is warranted. But I am not going to end my career with total defeat. Make sure the *Swampscott* is fought like a combat ship, and not some tired old man's private toy." Van Doorman's voice broke, and he turned his back on Sten.

Sten came to attention, the interview evidently ended.

"Oh, Commander. One more thing. Personal. My daughter sends her greetings."

"Thank you, sir. How *is* Brijit doing?"

"She is still healthy. Still working with her new... friend." His next words were nearly inaudible. "Another thing I shall never understand."

Sten, with nothing to say, saluted the old man's back and got out.

CHAPTER SEVENTY-TWO

THE FOUR SHIPS that were now the 23rd Fleet had gone underground along with the troops and the civilians. The two destroyers were hidden about two kilometers apart in a widened subway tunnel. The picket ship was camouflaged in a ruined hangar. But the ponderous *Swampscott* had been more difficult to hide.

Sten wondered if the engineer who had come up with the

Swampscott's eventual hiding place was still alive. He would like to have bought the man a beer or six—if there was still any beer in Cavite City.

Two of the massive bomb craters from the Tahn attack on Empire Day had been widened, deepened, concrete-floored, and connected. Under cover of night, electronic masking, and a probe by a Guards battalion, the *Swampscott* was moved into those craters. The hole was then roofed with lightweight beams, and a skin was sprayed over them. Plas was then poured and configured to exactly resemble the craters. None of the Tahn surveillance satellites or overflights by their spy ships spotted the change.

Sten figured that he would probably have carte blanche when he reported to the *Swampscott*. He was right. His immediate superiors, van Doorman's appointees, surmised that Sten was the new man and, true benders and scrapers, believed that his every thought was a general order.

Sten carefully scattered the survivors of his own command through every department of the *Swampscott*. If the drakh came down—and Sten agreed with van Doorman that it would—at least there would be one or two reliable beings he could depend on in every section.

He moved the combat information center, which was also the secondary command location and his duty station, from its location in the second, rearmost "pagoda." He buried it deep in the guts of the ship, finding a certain amount of satisfaction in taking over what had previously been the *Swampscott's* officers' dining room.

He also suggested—which became an order—to van Doorman's executive officer that perhaps the ship might be stripped for combat. Somehow, the *Swampscott* still had its beautiful wooden paneling, ruminant-hide upholstery, and fine and flammable dining gear in officers' country.

The loudest objections, of course, came not from the officers but from their flunkies. Sten gleefully reassigned the waiters, bartenders, and batmen from their lead-swinging positions to the undermanned gun sites.

This was a great deal of fun for Sten—until he remembered that sooner or later this hulk would have to go into combat. He estimated that the *Swampscott* would last for four seconds in battle against a Tahn cruiser. Half that, if they were unfortunate enough to face the *Forez* or *Kiso*.

But he had to take his satisfactions where he could get them.

Sten had, at General Mahoney's request, detached Kilgour and put him as coordinator of civilian movement.

When—and if—the liners showed up, they would have only moments on the ground to load the refugees. And both Mahoney and van Doorman agreed that in this area, there was no room for either ego or proper precedent.

Therefore, Kilgour was ordered into civilian clothes and officially given the rank of deputy mayor of Cavite City. Whoever had held that post previously had either died or disappeared, as had the mayor himself.

Kilgour wondered why he had so much support—certain officers and noncoms of the First Guards had been put under his command. Neither he nor anyone else in the Guards—beyond Mahoney's own chief of staff and the heads of his G-sections—knew that Mahoney was systematically stripping his best out of the division to be sent to safety as cadres for the new unit.

And no one except Ian Mahoney knew that their command general was about to violate orders from the Emperor and stay behind on Cavite to die with the remnants of his division.

At first Kilgour thought it would be a hoot to have vastly higher-ranked officers under his command. The hoot was there, but a very minor part of his job.

Alex Kilgour got very little sleep as the civilians were winkled out of their shelters, broken down into hundred-person loading elements, and assigned cargo orders. Each of them was permitted what he, she, or it wore. No more—including toilet articles.

Kilgour stood in one of the assembly areas. There were two scared children hanging onto either leg and a very adorable baby in his arms—a baby, Kilgour realized, that was piddling on his carefully looted expensive tweeds. And he was trying to listen to, regulate, and order from several conversations.

"... my Deirdre hasn't shown up, and I'm very..."

"... Mr. Kilgour, we need to discuss which city records should be removed with ..."

"... I wan' my mommie ..."

"... your behavior is simply incomprehensible, and I want to know the name of your superior, immediately..."

"... since y' be't th' boss, is there anything me an' some of my mates can do to help with ..."

"... since you're our representative, I would like to protest the heartless way that those soldiers ..."

"... when we reach safety, my lawyers will be most interested in the fact that ..."

"Where's Mommie?"

Kilgour rather desperately wanted to be somewhere safe, like on the front lines facing a Tahn human wave assault.

The blurt transmission came through—the rescue force was twelve hours away from Cavite.

Sten was in the engine room of the *Swampscott*, trying to figure out why the ship's second drive unit was not delivering full power.

He was crouched under one of the drive tubes, listening to the monotonous swearing of the second engineer—who was not a van Doorman appointee and who *was* competent —trying to meter unmetered feed lines when he realized that he had been due at a command conference five minutes before.

He slithered out and ran for a port. There would be no time to change out of his grease-soaked coveralls.

Outside, on the concrete, he looked around for the gravsled that was supposedly assigned just to him. The driver had taken a break and was grabbing a quick meal. It took Sten another ten minutes to hunt the woman down.

Sten was very late by the time the sled lifted and hissed

down a communications trench toward Mahoney's TOC. Very late—but still alive.

The Tahn missile was a blind launch.

The Tahn knew, of course, that the Imperial Forces inside Cavite City had gone underground. But they had little hard intelligence on exactly where the vital centers were.

Since they had a plethora and a half of available weaponry, they fired into the perimeter at random. The Imperial stronghold was narrow enough so that almost anything would do some damage.

Assembled under the ruined emporium were the top-ranking Imperial officers. Mahoney knew the dangers of having most command elements in one place—but it was necessary for him to give a final face-to-face briefing.

The Tahn missile was sent in, nap of the earth, across the front lines. It was not detected by any of the Guards' countermissile batteries. Two kilometers inside the lines, following its programming, it lifted and looked for a target.

There wasn't much. The missile might have gone random, reverting to its basic instructions, and smashed in somewhere close to the perimeter's center if its receivers hadn't picked up a broadcast fragment.

The broadcast came from one of Mahoney's brigade officers, who had sent a "Received-Acknowledged" signal on his belt transponder before entering the TOC.

But that was enough for the missile to target.

Mahoney was beginning. "Six hours from now, most of you will be on your way out. Here's what's going to happen—"

And then the hardened rocket smashed through the upper floors of the emporium, through the shielding atop the basement, and exploded, centimeters above the basement itself.

Sten arrived to a charnel house.

The emporium was a smoking disaster. One of Mahoney's bodyguards stumbled toward him, leaking blood and muttering incoherently. Sten burst past him, down into the basement.

He found death and dying. Major General Ian Mahoney lay on his side, his jaw smashed, his face covered in gore, slowly strangling.

Sten's fingers curled, and his knife slid out of his arm and into his hand, as he rolled Mahoney onto his back. Very carefully, his knife V-incisioned into Mahoney's throat, cutting through the windpipe about three centimeters. He made another cut, Vd to meet the first, then thumbed the tissue out of the tracheotomy.

Mahoney was breathing again, with a gargle and bubble of blood.

Sten grabbed a power cord, cut it through, and ripped the center wires out of the cover. That hollow cover was forced into Mahoney's windpipe, and then Sten covered the incision with the outer foil cover, a dressing sealant from Mahoney's own aidpak.

Mahoney would live—if his other wounds were treated.

He *would* live. Ironically, since Mahoney had planned to stay and die with his Guardsmen. Instead, he would be evacuated as a casualty on the liners.

Sten stood as med people ran into the building.

He took stock.

Fleet Admiral Xavier Rijn van Doorman grinned down at him.

Sten thought that the admiral really didn't have that much to smile about, since the top of his brain case was missing, and gray tissue—almost matching the late admiral's hair color—was leaking out. Also, van Doorman was missing certain components, such as his right arm, his left hand, and, more importantly, his body from the rib cage downward. What little was left of his body was strung on a ruptured pipe.

I suppose I have a ship, Sten thought to himself. Now let's see if van Doorman's flunkies follow their orders.

He didn't have to worry about that—the XO, nav officer, and chief engineer were also dead in the ruins.

Commander Sten was now in charge of the 23rd Fleet.

Two hours later, the rescue liners signaled that they were approaching Cavite.

CHAPTER SEVENTY-THREE

FOR THREE DAYS the air around Cavite City somewhat resembled gray noodle soup. It was part of the deception plan for the evacuation. Not only did the liners have to slip through the Tahn patrols beyond the Fringe Worlds—which they had successfully done—but then they had to land and remain undetected long enough to load the evacuees.

The Tahn total air superiority helped slightly. Since there were seldom any Imperial ships in the air, the Tahn aerial monitors and scanners were only cursorily checked.

The boil of smoke and haze over the Empire's perimeter radically reduced visual observation, and the "noodle soup" blanked almost all other detectors.

The "soup" was chaff, an invention that even predated the Emperor himself. Chaff originally had been thin strips of aluminum, designed to block radar screens. It was cut in lengths one-half that of the wavelength it was intended to interfere with and was dropped from aircraft. On a detector screen the chaff showed up as a solid, impermeable cloud.

This chaff was far more sophisticated, capable of blocking not only radar but infrared and laser sensors. And it was nearly invisible—many thousands of the strips could be fed through the eye of a needle.

Blasted into the upper atmosphere, the canisters exploded, and the strands drifted slowly down toward Cavite City. They may have been almost invisible, but they did not make breathing any more of a pleasure.

The Tahn had gone to full alert when their sensors suddenly became inactive, but as time passed, they decided that this latest tactic was merely a ploy to slow down the inevitable final assault on the city. They certainly did not need sensors—they knew where the Empire's troops were. And so the chaff clouds became nothing more than an annoyance.

And then other alarms went off.

Offplanet patrols suddenly reported enemy forces. The screens showed, unbelievably, that two full Imperial fleets were heading toward Cavite, fleets that Tahn strategic intelligence said could not exist.

The Tahn ships went to general quarters and lifted for space.

Intelligence was quite correct—the only Imperial squadron in that sector of space was being held in reserve. The Tahn were being "attacked" by the four destroyers that had escorted the liners into the Fringe Worlds. Four destroyers and nearly a thousand small, unmanned drones.

The drones were Spoof missiles packed with electronics that gave them the signature in every range except visual of full-size warships.

And for once the Empire was lucky.

Atago brought her ships into battle formation and moved in for the attack.

And the liners roared down toward Cavite City.

They were, of course, immediately seen and reported by Tahn infantrymen, but by the time the reports reached Atago, she was six hours off Cavite. And she had worries far more serious than what she thought were transports reinforcing the Empire's ground forces.

She would not discover what the Imperial attack fleets actually were for another hour.

Seven hours to evacuate a world . . .

The blunt torpedoes that were Sullamora's commandeered liners settled down onto Cavite Base, their bulk crushing the debris under them.

Then Kilgour's evac scheme went into motion. He had organized the civilians into fifty-person groups, each group salted with guardsmen and women that would be part of the new, to-be-formed division. Civilians—Kilgour had dubbed them evaks—brought only what they could carry in small daypaks, which were no more than sandbags equipped with slings. In the last few hours, the civilians had been staged forward to any shelter close to Cavite City's field. The shelters were mostly improvised—and many noncombatants died under the periodic Tahn bombardments.

Sten paced on the bridge of the *Swampscott*. All screens were active, showing the scurry toward the liners and the sky above that might lead them to safety.

Sten felt naked on that bridge—it was one of the two pagodas on the *Swampscott* that stood outside the ship's armor. It felt more like a stage set for a livie than a command center. It stretched two stories tall, with huge screens on all sides. Foss, whom Sten had field-commissioned and put in charge of the ship's C3 section, was more than twenty meters away from him.

Sten watched the swarm and prayed to a god still unknown to him that somehow everyone would board before the Tahn came in. He also found space in his prayers that Alex would be one of those on board as he watched the inexorable tickdown on a chronometer that told him when the *Swampscott*, and the liners, must lift.

And while he was at it, he made another request to the heavens—that Brijit would be among the civilians. He had seen General Mahoney, unconscious in his bubble pakked stretcher, loaded onto a liner.

The timer moved down through final seconds.

The screens showed Cavite Field, bare and empty, gray under drifting smoke clouds, with flashes of fire from incoming Tahn rockets.

Warrant officer Alex Kilgour stood beside him. "Ah hae them, lad. Thae's all 'board't."

Sten touched the com switch on his chest. "All ships. This is the *Swampscott*. Lift!"

Dust boiled across the shattered concrete as the liners took off on Yukawa drive.

"On command . . . main drive . . . three . . . two . . . one . . . Mark!"

And the liners and the four ships remaining of the 23rd Fleet vanished.

Below them, the Tahn final assault began.

Fewer than 2,000 soldiers of the First Guards held the thin perimeter. Their best had, under orders, been evacuated on the liners. They were commanded by Mahoney's chief of staff, who, violating the same orders that Mahoney had planned to break, had remained behind with his soldiers.

The Tahn assaulted in wave attacks.

And were slaughtered.

The First Guards died on Cavite.

But they fulfilled the prophecy that Sten's first training sergeant had made years earlier: "I've fought for the Empire on a hundred different worlds, and I'll fight on a hundred more before some skeek burns me down... But I'll be the most expensive piece of meat he ever butchered."

Three Tahn landing forces had invaded Cavite. One had already been shattered. The other two made the final assault on Cavite City.

They won.

But they also ceased to exist as fighting units.

Brijit van Doorman was *not* among the evacuees.

Supreme triage had been done with the casualties, and those who were dying or, more cruelly, could never be restructured enough to be fit for combat were left behind.

And someone had to stay behind to keep them alive. Dr. Morrison volunteered.

As did Brijit.

The first Tahn shock grenade shattered two orderlies who were posted near the entry to the underground hospital. Then the door exploded inward, and a Tahn combat squad burst into the ward.

Dr. Morrison, her empty hands spread, stood in front of them. "These are wounded people," she said slowly and calmly. "They need help. They are not soldiers."

"Stand aside," ordered the Tahn captain commanding the squad. He lifted his weapon.

"These are not combat soldiers," Morrison started. "There are no resistants or arms—"

The burst from the Tahn officer's gun blew Morrison nearly in half.

Brijit screamed and hurtled at the captain.

He hip-swiveled and fired again.

Three rounds cut Brijit in half.

The officer lowered his weapon and turned to a noncom. "The Imperial whore said there is no one here capable of bearing arms. They are not necessary for us."

The sergeant saluted and raised his flamer.

CHAPTER SEVENTY-FOUR

LADY ATAGO, ALTHOUGH not a believer in ceremony, had positioned things very nicely. She was not able to take the surrender from General Mahoney as planned. That really did not matter. She thought that her livie 'cast to Heath would be equally dramatic.

Atago stood in front of the *Forez*, grounded in the center of Cavite Field. To one side, guards chivvied endless lines of surrendered Imperial soldiers.

She expected the 'cast to be sent directly to the Tahn Council. Instead, her broadcast was intercepted by Lord Fehrle. He stood in formal robes, very small on her monitor.

Lady Atago covered her surprise and reported.

"My congratulations," the image of Fehrle said. "But this is not enough."

"I apologize," she said. "What more could be required?"

"You have won a victory, lady. But the Empire has made much of their warriors on Cavite. Heralding them as martyrs and signposts of the eventual victory, and so forth."

"I am aware of their propaganda 'casts."

"Then I am surprised that you have not already made the appropriate response," Fehrle said. "There must be no iota of victory in this defeat. The forces on Cavite must be shown as totally destroyed."

"They are, Lord."

"They are not," Fehrle corrected. "If one single Imperial soldier returns to the Empire, somehow their information specialists will find a way to turn that into an accomplishment."

"Let them. We still hold the Fringe Worlds."

"Do not dictate policy to me, Lady Atago. Here are your orders. Pursue those ships that evacuated the Imperial survivors. And destroy them. Only if there are no—I repeat, *no*—survivors will the Emperor be properly shamed."

Atago started to speak, then rethought. "Very well. I shall follow your orders."

The monitor screen went blank, and Lady Atago strode toward her battleship. She would follow orders—but soon, she realized, there must come a reckoning with those rulers of the Tahn who were more interested in paper achievements than in real victories.

CHAPTER SEVENTY-FIVE

TWO OF THE Empire's destroyers survived the spoof attack, broke contact, and set a deceptive orbit that rendezvoused them with the escaping liners.

Fact—the fast liners were moving at many multiples of light-speed. But to Sten it felt as if they were in one of his least favorite nightmares, fleeing some unknown monstrosity through waist-deep mud. Another illogical perception he had was that the Tahn ships were coming after them, even though there was no particularly valid military reason for them to pursue the shattered elements under Sten's command.

The first casualty—of sorts—was the underpowered

picket ship. Less than two hours off Cavite, it was already faltering far to the rear.

If there had been room or time for humanity, Sten would have ordered one of his two destroyers to take off the picket ship's crew and blow it up. But he was sadly lacking in either department.

He found himself with the very cold-blooded thought that the picket ship, limping farther and farther to the rear, still might be of use. If the Tahn *were* after him, the rust bucket might provide an early warning.

Cold-blooded—but there were too many corpses from the past few months. All Sten could do was try to keep the living alive.

He put the two modern Imperial destroyers in front of the liners, Y-ed to either side of the three columns of ships. There were more Tahn ships potentially to worry about than the ones that might be coming up on the tail end of the convoy.

Commander Halldor's *Husha* and the other 23rd Fleet destroyer were positioned as rear guards.

The *Swampscott* flew two-thirds back and above the liners. Sten was very grateful that Sullamora had very experienced crews on the liners—at least he didn't have to concern himself with proper station keeping. He had more than enough troubles of his own.

Spaceships in stardrive, being relatively nonstressed, did not creak.

The *Swampscott* creaked.

They also did not feel as if they were about to tear themselves apart.

Every frame on the *Swampscott* shuddered as if a largish giant outside was working out with a sledgehammer.

"And we're only at full power," Tapia growled. She touched the large red lever controlling engine power. It was marked QUARTER, HALF, and FULL SPEED. Then there was a manual safety lock. If that was lifted, the *Swampscott* would, at least in theory, go to WAR EMERGENCY power, guaranteed to strain and destroy its engines if applied for longer than minutes.

Sten, Kilgour, and Tapia were in the *Swampscott*'s main

engine control room. Sten had immediately promoted the
ship's second engineer to chief and assigned Tapia to him.
He semitrusted the man but had privately told Tapia that if
the man broke, she was to relieve him at once.

"And if he gives me lip?"

Sten had looked pointedly at the miniwillygun holstered
on her hip and said nothing.

Warrant Officer Kilgour would run the central weapons
station in the *Swampscott*'s second pagoda. Just below his
station was the cruiser's CIC and second control room. The
rest of the men and women from Sten's tacships were scattered throughout the ship.

Sten had decided to promote Foss to ensign. He had also
told Kilgour that warrant rank or not, the Scot was to assume command of the *Swampscott* if Sten was killed or
disabled. He guessed he had the authority. If not, that was
something to hassle about when and if they reached safety.

For the moment, there didn't seem to be anything for
him to do. The crew was at general quarters—modified.
Half of them were permitted to sleep or eat. The food was
mainly sandwiches and caff brought to the stations. Those
who chose to sleep curled up beside their positions.

Sten turned the bridge over to Foss—the ship was on a
preset plot—while he and Kilgour made the rounds.

The engine room was hot and greasy and smelled. The
late van Doorman probably would have fainted seeing his
carefully polished metalwork smeared, the gleaming white
walls scarred and spattered. But spit-shining was something
else there wasn't time for. Just keeping the *Swampscott*'s
engines running was herculean.

Sten looked around the engine spaces. Tapia and the engineer had everything running as smoothly as possible. He
started toward a companionway.

"Commander," Tapia said, rather awkwardly. "Can I ask
you something?"

"GA."

"Uhh . . ."

Kilgour took the hint and went up the steps to the deck
above. Sten waited.

"You remember—back at the fort—when I said I

wanted a transfer? I was being funny then. Now I'm serious. When we park this clotting rust bucket, I want reassignment."

Sten wondered—was Tapia starting to crack?

"Ensign," he said. "If we get this time bomb back, all of us'll get reassigned. Hard to run a tacdiv when you don't have ships. My turn. Why?"

"I just checked Imperial regs."

"And?"

"And they said you get your ass in a crack if you go to bed with your commanding officer."

"Oh," Sten managed.

Tapia grinned, kissed him, and disappeared down a corridor.

Sten thoughtfully went up the ladder and joined Alex.

"Tch," Alex clucked. "Hold still, lad."

He swabbed Sten's chin with an arm of his coverall. "Th' lads dinnae need t' ken th' old man's been flirtin't wi' th' help."

"Mr. Kilgour. You're being insubordinate."

"Hush, youngster. Or Ah'll buss y' myself."

The com overhead snarled into life.

"Captain to the bridge. Captain to the bridge. We have contact!"

Sten and Alex ran for their battle stations.

Contact was not the correct description.

The skipper of the picket ship had seconds to goggle at the screen, and then the Tahn were on him.

Two destroyers launched at the picket ship without altering course.

The ship's captain snapped the com open.

"*Swampscott . . . Swampscott . . .* this is the *Dean*. Two Tahn—"

And the missiles obliterated the picket ship.

The Tahn fleet knew they were closing on the liners. They spread out into attack formation and moved in.

Commander Rey Halldor may have been a clot, but he knew how and, more importantly, when to die. Without waiting for orders, he sent the *Husha* and its sister ship arcing up and back, toward the oncoming Tahn.

The Tahn were in a crescent formation, screening destroyers in front and to the sides. Just behind were seven heavy cruisers and then the two battleships, the *Forez* and the *Kiso*.

Halldor's second destroyer died at once.

But the *Husha*, incredibly, broke through the Tahn screen.

Halldor ordered all missiles to be launched and the racks to be set on automatic load launch. The *Husha* spat rockets from every tube, rockets that were set on fire-and-forget mode.

The *Husha* spun wildly as it took its first hit near the stern. A Tahn shipkilling missile targeted the *Husha* and homed. It struck the *Husha* amidships, blowing it apart. Probably Halldor and his men were already quite dead before they got their revenge.

Two Tahn destroyers took hits in areas vital enough to send them leaking out of battle. And then three of Halldor's missiles found a heavy cruiser.

For an instant it looked as if the Tahn ship's outer skin was transparent, then it turned flame-red as the cruiser was racked by explosions. And then there was absolutely nothing where the ship had been.

The 23rd Fleet still had teeth in its final moments of life.

Sten thought he could still see the blips where his destroyers had been on the screen, even though the ships had died seconds earlier.

Probably an afterimage, he thought.

Sten had wondered what gave people the guts to throw themselves at death, to give the suicidal orders instead of running. And he also wondered, if that situation ever came up, whether he would have enough *cojones* to do it himself.

But he never formally made the Big Decision. There were too many other orders to blurt out.

"Navigation. Interception orbit."

"Aye, sir. Computed."

"Mark! Engines."

"Engine room, sir."

"Full emergency power. Now! Mr. Foss. Everyone into suits."

"Yessir."

"Weapons . . . clot that. Give me all hands."

Foss turned the com onto the shipwide circuit.

"This is the captain. We're going in. All weapons stations, prepare to revert to individual control."

Foss had Sten's suit in front of him. Sten forced his legs in and dragged the shoulders and headpiece on.

"We are now attacking," he said, choosing his words carefully, "a Tahn battlefleet. There are at least two battleships with the fleet. We are going to kill them." He should have found something noble to end his 'cast with, but his mind refused to come up with an "England Expects," and he snapped the com link off. "Foss. I want the CO of the destroyers."

A screen brightened, showing the bridge of one of the Imperial ships.

"Captain," Sten began without preamble, "the convoy's yours. We're going to try to slow down the bad guys."

"Sir, I request—"

"Negative. You have your orders. Stay with the liners. *Swampscott*, out. Foss! Damage control."

"This is damage control, Skipper," came the drawl. "What do you need?" Sten found a moment to regret not knowing that officer—anybody who could sound that relaxed would be valuable.

"Dump the air."

"It's gone."

The suits would make the men more awkward, but the vacuum would lessen the damage from a potential hit.

"Weapons! Are we in range?"

"A wee bit longer, Commander."

And the *Swampscott* went into its first—and final—battle.

Possibly the Tahn had become cocky. Or, more likely they found it impossible to take seriously the bloated hull that was charging at them.

The *Swampscott* may have been a disaster of space architecture and a ship long overdue for the boneyard—but it was very heavily armed. It had a Bell laser system forward, Goblin launchers fore and aft, secondary laser stations scattered around the ship, and chainguns running the length of those horrible-looking hull bulges. The ship's main armament consisted of long-obsolete Vydal antiship missiles. There were two of them, mounted amidships, between the pagodas that were the command centers.

Kilgour watched the three blips representing Tahn destroyers arc toward him and thumb-activated the Bell assault laser in the ship's nose. The laser was as obsolete as the ship it was mounted on, being not only robot-guided but equipped with verbal responses.

"Enemy ship in range," the toneless synthesized voice said. Kilgour touched the ENGAGE key.

The laser blast ravened the length of the Tahn destroyer, and the weapons system decided that the target was no longer in existence. Without consulting Kilgour, it switched to a second destroyer and opened up.

"Target destroyed . . . second target under attack," the voice said, almost as an afterthought.

The laser ripped most of that second destroyer's power room into fragments.

"Second target injured . . . am correcting aim."

Kilgour slammed the OVERRIDE and NEW TARGET keys. The destroyer was out of battle, and that was enough.

Possibly miffed at being told what to do by a human, the laser switched to stutter mode and lacerated the length of the third destroyer before reporting.

Three down, Alex thought. No more'n a zillion to go.

The *Swampscott* was through the destroyer screen, headed for the heart of the Tahn fleet.

There were three weapons not controlled by Kilgour. They were the huge Kali missiles designed for Sten's tacships. There had been three of them left in the tac division's armory, and Foss and Kilgour had jury-rigged rack mounts for them on the *Swampscott*. Foss had sworn there was no way to run the control circuitry into the weapons control center—it would be easier for him to set up a control helmet/center on the bridge itself.

Sten was fairly sure that Foss was lying, wanting to actually shoot back instead of just being a behind-the-scenes electronics wizard. But he didn't care. Alex would have more than enough hassle trying to make some sense of the elderly and frequently contradictory weapons-control systems already mounted.

Foss had the control helmet plug rigged into his space suit. Sten stared at the central screen and blanched. The monstrous *Kiso* filled the screen, and Sten thought they were about to collide before he realized that Foss had the screen at full magnification.

"Sir," Foss said. "I have a Kali on standby. Target . . target . . . target acquired."

"Launch," Sten ordered, with no expectations.

The Kali wobbled away from the *Swampscott* without the initial guidance the proper launch tube would have provided. Then it straightened, went to full power, and dived toward the *Kiso*.

And the *Swampscott* took its first hit.

The Tahn missile tore through the skin of the bridge went out of control, and then exploded less than fifty meters away from the ship. The blast was close enough to smash the entire bridge.

All that Sten knew was a stunning impact, finding himself hurled through the air to slam against a console and staring straight up at what should have been steel to see—see, without sensors—the Tahn destroyer's nose light as it fired a second missile.

His headphones crackled.

"Stand by." It was Kilgour. "We have an incoming . . target acquired . . . ha-ho. Gotcha."

A Fox missile took out the Tahn rocket. Directly behind it, Kilgour had sent a Goblin. The Goblin scattered fragments of the Tahn ship across a wide area of space.

Sten wove to his feet and looked around the ruins of the bridge. Everyone was dead, down, or hurled out into space.

He recovered and keyed his mike. "This is the captain

Switching command to CIC. Damage control...seal the bridge."

He stumbled toward a hatch, undogged, and went through it.

Outside, in space, the Kali missile circled aimlessly. It had been given its aim point, but the operator had not completed his procedure. The Kali waited for further orders.

The bridge was a still life—"Technocracy, with Corpses" —for a moment, and then a figure moved.

It was Foss.

He looked down at the scrap metal where his legs had been. His suit had already sealed itself, surgically amputating the few bits of ligament and flesh.

Foss felt no pain.

He dragged himself on his hands toward the control panel. It was still semialive. He switched to a still-undamaged tertiary system and became his missile once more.

The Kali surged toward the *Kiso*.

The Tahn antimissile officer had seen the hit on the *Swampscott*, seen the Kali begin its aimless orbiting, and told the *Kiso*'s target acquisition systems to ignore the now-harmless missile.

The Kali came alive! The Tahn officer's hand was moving toward his computer's controls when it hit.

The missile struck the *Kiso* in its drivetubes, ripping apart the AM2 fuel storage and sending the antimatter cascading toward the ship's bow.

The *Kiso* vanished in one hellish, soundless explosion.

Foss had time to see the flash light the inside of the bridge, to watch it turn red, and to realize that the red was his own blood, spraying across his suit's faceplate, before his eyes looked beyond anything and he sagged forward onto his controls.

Before Sten reached the CIC, his new command center, the *Swampscott*, took three more hits.

Sten struggled on, praying there would still be something left to command.

Most unusual, he thought, seeing one of the corridors

twist and warp in front of him. I am hallucinating. But I am not wounded.

He was not hallucinating. One of the Tahn rockets had hit near one of the ship's mainframes, and the *Swampscott* was bent and twisted.

Sten forced his way through the warped steel tube. His mind recorded observations as his ship rocked around him and explosions sent shock waves through the hull:

Here was a casualty clearing station. Shock blast had killed everyone inside it but left them frozen. Here was one of Sten's med officers, his arms still in the access holes of a surgical bubblepak. Behind him were his corpsmen standing ready. And the casualty inside the pak.

All dead.

Here was an antifire-foam-flooded compartment, where the sensors had evidently gone wild and dumped foam on a fire that could not exist. Sten saw three suited forms struggling toward the exit through the foam but had no time to help them.

A temporary damage-control station, where an officer— Sten recognized the black-anodized suit arms that were used to denote command rank—was calmly ordering damage teams into action. Sten wondered if that was the drawling, unruffleable control officer he had been on the com with earlier.

And then he found the hatchway into the CIC, undogged the two hatches, and returned to command of the *Swampscott*.

Coms chattered at him, and specialists tried to keep the chaos in some sort of order:

"Forward Goblin launchers do not respond to inquiry No verbal reports from stations."

"Secondary engine room reports damage now unde control."

"All controls to forward laser station fail to respond."

There wasn't much left of the *Swampscott* to command But still, filling a screen—and not a magnified view thi time—was the bulk of the *Forez*. Lady Atago's flagship.

The battleship was vomiting fire, firing everything— anything—to stop the *Swampscott*.

There was an extremely unauthorized broadcast: "Ah hae y' noo, lass." The chortle came from the weapons station on the deck above. Then Kilgour launched two Vydals, one slaved to the missile under his control, and sent them surely homing into the *Forez*.

Fire fed on oxygen, and flame and explosion mushroomed down the corridors of the *Forez*. The explosion tore a wall chart from a bulkhead and sent it pinwheeling into Admiral Deska. His eviscerated corpse spun back into Lady Atago, smashing her helmet into a control panel.

She would not return to awareness until long after the battle ended. But command switched smoothly to the *Forez*'s own CO. The battle continued.

The next strike was on the *Swampscott*.

It was deadly, crashing through the armor plating into the ship's main engine room before the weapons officer commanding it touched the DET switch.

A hell of sudden fire filled the engine room and then disappeared.

Tapia had been swearing at the engine temperature gauges, praying that they were lying and knowing they were not, when the rocket exploded. A tiny bit of shrapnel cut through a superpressure hydraulic line. Hydraulic fluid razored out at more than 10,000 feet per second.

The fluid cut Tapia in half as neatly as a surgical saw.

The *Swampscott* went dead in space, still holding its original speed and course.

The two ships, the *Forez* and the *Swampscott*, slid toward each other. None of the Tahn warships could chance firing—the odds of a missile hitting the wrong target were too great.

The battleship loomed up toward the *Swampscott*.

And the cruiser's chaingunners found a target.

The chainguns that lined the two hideous midships bulges were useful only against ground troops or close-range in-atmosphere targets. But now, in deep space, the gunners had a target.

They held their firing keys down; their shells yammered toward the *Forez* and tore the battleship's sides open as if they were tinfoil.

Sten stood on his command deck wordlessly. There was nothing left for him to order.

Another explosion rocked the *Swampscott*, and Sten fought to stay on his feet.

A hatch slammed open, and Kilgour dropped down into the CIC. "Tha's nae left f'r me to do ae there," he explained. "Shall we b' boardin't th' clot?" He still sounded unconcerned.

A larger blast shattered around them, and Sten was down, losing consciousness for bare seconds. He recovered groggily and got back to his feet.

Where was his CIC officer?

Oh. There. Lying with a splinter of steel through his faceplate.

Sten numbly saw that there were still two screens alive in the CIC. One showed the fast-vanishing drives of the convoy, the other, the gutted hulk of the *Forez*, still vomiting fire at him.

Where was Alex? He might know what to do.

Sten stumbled over a suit. Kilgour lay sprawled at his feet. Sten bent and touched monitors. All showed zero.

Sten wove toward a still-functioning com panel. His gloved fingers found a switch, and he began broadcasting.

"Y . . . Y . . . Y . . ."

The universal signal for surrender.

And would they never stop? And would they never receive?

The *Forez* ceased fire.

Sten slumped down on the deck and waited for the Tahn boarding party. Maybe they wouldn't board. Maybe they would just stand off and obliterate his ship.

And Sten did not care what they did.

He was very tired of the killing.

<u>STEN</u>

The first book in the million-selling SF adventure series.

Vulcan is a factory planet, centuries old, Company run, ugly as sin, and unfeeling as death. Vulcan breeds just two types of native – complacent or tough. Sten is tough.

When his family are killed in a mysterious accident, Sten rebels, harassing the Company from the metal world's endless mazelike warrens.

He could end up just another burnt-out Delinquent.

But people like Sten never give up.

STEN 2

The Wolf Worlds

The second book in the million-selling SF adventure series.

The Eternal Emperor ruled countless worlds across the galaxy. Vast armies and huge fleets awaited his command. But when he needed a 'little' job done right, he turned to Mantis Team and its small band of militant problem solvers.

Just then the Emperor needed to pacify the Wolf Worlds, the planets of an insignificant cluster that had raised piracy to a low art.

And Mantis Team could use all the men it needed – as long as it needed no more than two.